"When I tried to figure out why I liked the book so much, two things came to mind. One, when it was over I didn't really feel like I had read a book; I felt as if I'd been a part of the story. That's very difficult to achieve. Two, I realized what Edwards' style reminded me of…Several times reading this one I thought to myself, 'This woman could be the next Susan Elizabeth Phillips.' And I don't write that lightly." —ColumbusDispatch.com

"A delight from cover to cover…My favorite aspect is how skillfully Ms. Edwards weaves emotional subjects throughout the novel…*On the Steamy Side* is much more than a sexy romance. It [has] depth and humanity. This series is headed for my keeper shelves."
—*A Romance Review*

"The snappy, fun-loving dialogue and overall camaraderie with this cast of characters makes for great reading."
—*Babbling About Books*

"The plot, the humor, the angst and the romance are superb, and Edwards' writing style is as crisp and clean as a freshly starched toque-blanche. Reader, party of one, your novel is ready." —*Reader to Reader*

"Louisa Edwards continues her 'Recipe For Love' series with her latest book, *On the Steamy Side*. And boy, is it ever steamy! You could fry an egg between these pages of bubbling-hot romance! With the popularity of the Food Network, Louisa Edwards' delicious series will be a huge hit with foodies and romantics alike."
—*Fresh Fiction*

"Steam up your reading with *On the Steamy Side* by mega-talented Louisa Edwards." —SingleTitles.com

"Fast-paced and scintillating…Boiling and searing love scenes aside, the complex relationships and self-discovery shared with the unique backdrop of the cutthroat and competitive culinary arts [world] forces the reader to consume page after page as voraciously as the chefs can dish it up." —*Romance Readers Choice*

"Louisa Edwards' fast-paced, sparkling *On the Steamy Side* has sizzling sex scenes, complicated relationships, and unique settings, with an undercurrent of humor." —*Long and Short Reviews*

"If you need a real feel-good, make your heart sing and your body tingle kind of afternoon this is the perfect recipe for success." —*Coffee Time Romance*

"From start to finish, I devoured and enjoyed every moment of this book. Miranda and Adam worked well together like . . . honey and cayenne pepper . . . a little sweet and a little spicy with an end result to make you say 'Wow.'" —*Cheryl's Book Nook*

"The strength of this novel is substantial . . . The writing, the other characters, the setting, the nuances, and the imagery are marvelous. . . . Food and its various meanings and permutations are a fluid and discernible part of the writing in this book. It includes themes of home, heart, family, and nourishment, what people need to survive, and how the food we eat can communicate more than words can provide." —*Smart Bitches, Trashy Books*

"A deliciously fun read. The plot and eccentric characters are well written, and the kitchen sizzles with hot passion."
—*Romance Reviews Today*

"Sophisticated, romantic, mouth-watering and sizzling hot."
—*The Three Tomatoes Book Reviews*

"*Can't Stand the Heat* is a delightful blend of chemistry, competition, and cooking, and it was just what I was looking for. I loved the fast-paced scenes that make you feel the controlled chaos of a restaurant during dinner hour, as well as the slower-paced scenes such as Adam teaching Miranda how to cook…I'm eagerly awaiting Edwards' next release in the series. Here's hoping it's as good a read as this terrific debut."
—*All About Romance*

"Snappy, exciting, adventurous, and totally unexpected. *Can't Stand the Heat*…is one of the best light-hearted culinary, romantic novels this reviewer has read in a very long time! Grand job, Louisa Edwards."
—*Crystal Reviews*

"Make sure that you have a good lazy day to spend with *Can't Stand the Heat*, and don't start reading this one in the evening, or I guarantee you will be up all night!"
—*The Romance Reader*

"The author blends love and recipes into a fun romp. Fans will enjoy the pizazz and flavor that Louisa Edwards brings to her warm tale."
—*Genre Go Round Reviews*

"A funny, lovable story about two unlikely people falling for each other. The plot, characters, and setting comes together to form a wonderful, light-hearted, culinary romance that is a blast to read…I can't wait for the next 'Recipe for Love' novel!"
—*The Book Lush*

"Delish! Creative debut author Louisa Edwards will have you eating out of her hand as you read her witty, insightful, foodie romance...*Can't Stand the Heat* is filled with steamy passion, realistically described settings, a distinctive plot and characters that beg for their own stories. Watch for more to come from this talented new author."

—SingleTitles.com

"Mmmm...Louisa Edwards' debut effort—*Can't Stand the Heat*—is *yummy*!! The witty repartee between Miranda and Adam, the snappy dialogue between Adam and his staff make this a fun, sizzling, read...And all the food talk in between these covers? Make sure you're not reading while hungry."

—*Drey's Library*

"Louisa Edwards has cooked up a sassy and sexy contemporary romance. With the popularity of the Food Network so high these days, this novel has arrived just in time to delight foodies and readers both. The food descriptions alone in this book are enough to set your mouth watering...I predict a delicious future for this new writer."

—*Review Journal*

"Ms. Louisa Edwards is definitely an author to watch! Her descriptions make you feel like you can almost smell the food Adam's cooking! *Can't Stand the Heat* has what it takes to affect all of your emotions—joy, sorrow, fear, hate, and love."

—*The Romance Readers Connection*

"An exquisitely prepared romance seasoned with scorching hot love scenes, *Can't Stand the Heat* is truly an unforgettable dish. You can't miss this delectable and mouthwatering debut!"

—*New York Times* bestselling author Kresley Cole

St. Martin's Paperbacks Titles by

LOUISA EDWARDS

Can't Stand the Heat

On the Steamy Side

Just One Taste

Just One Taste

LOUISA EDWARDS

St. Martin's Paperbacks

JUST ONE TASTE

Copyright © 2010 by Louisa Edwards.

For information address St. Martin's Press, 175 Fifth Avenue, New York, NY 10010.

EAN: 978-0-312-35647-7

Printed in the United States of America

St. Martin's Paperbacks edition / September 2010

St. Martin's Paperbacks are published by St. Martin's Press, 175 Fifth Avenue, New York, NY 10010.

10 9 8 7 6 5 4 3 2 1

To my sister, Georgia, whose life is more like a romantic novel (*Persuasion* by Jane Austen, to be exact) than anyone I know. Thank you for loving romance as much as I do!

Acknowledgments

Thank you to my fabulous editor, Rose Hilliard, and my lovely agent, Deidre Knight, for keeping me on course with this series. And big thanks to Jeanne Devlin and Katy Hershberger for the best PR any author could hope for! I'm lucky to have all of you on my team.

This book would not have been written without the support and encouragement of the Romance Divas, specifically all my Chat buddies, and my writing gurus and heterosexual lifemates, Roxanne St. Claire and Kristen Painter. I don't know what I'd do without you—probably sit on my couch and watch *Project Runway* all day. Thank you for kicking me into gear and filling my head with ideas for books and making me laugh harder than anyone ever.

Special thanks to my beta readers, Nic Montreuil and Kate Pearce—this book would be a shadow of itself without your input.

Thank you to my mother, Jan, who reads every version from the roughest draft to the final, finished book, and to my father, George, who likes to correct my grammar.

And to my husband, Nick, whose tireless patience with

frozen dinners and recipe testing is rivaled only by his insightful edits on my books. Every time we sit down for a discussion of my latest draft and you tell me what works, what doesn't, and why, I know exactly how lucky I am. Thank you for being a fantastic husband, a perceptive reader, an adventurous eater, and my best friend. I love you.

Prologue

Wes Murphy stared down into the huge stainless steel stockpot and watched a single golden bubble pop to the surface of the soup. Time to add the vegetables.

The chaos of preparations for the evening's dinner service whirled around him, chefs shouting to each other, cackling jokes about what they got up to at the bar after service last night, calling requests for help with one dish or another, but Wes's corner of the kitchen was quiet.

A little apart from the crowd, as always.

Wes didn't care. He was finding it hard to care about much, these days.

Thank God for Market, he mused, sweeping a wooden spoon through the simmering broth. *Cooking might be all I've got left, but at least it's something I can throw myself into.*

A sweet, lightly accented voice floated through his mind.

When you cook, it is chance to draw out from yourself everything you are feeling. Yes? Add it to the food. Stir in a pinch of sadness and a spoonful of fear and what do you think! Something magical happens.

Wes felt one corner of his mouth kick up at the memory of Deirdre Nickoloff's soft, round face. Mrs. N. was the one who taught him to cook, sure, but she'd done more than that. She'd taught Wes about the kind of person he wanted to become.

He scooped up his diced butternut squash. The perfection of the cuts, each piece uniform and pristine, soothed something inside him. And as he added the squash to the broth, already rich with white wine and shredded chicken, Wes closed his eyes and remembered Mrs. N.'s cooking philosophy.

Shit. He hoped his painful regrets didn't make the soup taste bitter.

Half an hour later, Wes was checking under the salamander broiler to make sure the crusty bread he'd spread with tangy herbed butter and parmesan cheese came to a nice golden toast color when a determinedly cheerful voice startled him out of his culinary haze.

"Hey, need any help with plating?"

Wes grinned up at the first guy who'd gone out of his way to be friendly when Wes showed up for this externship from the Academy of Culinary Arts.

Jess Wake smiled back, crisp and neat in his black and green server duds. The way he combed his dark auburn hair back before service made the kid seem older, somehow—or maybe that was the familiar ache of loss in his eyes.

Wes knew that look intimately. He'd surprised it on his own face more than once in the last six months.

"You're a super trouper, man. Thanks." Wes was extra grateful, considering Jess had been treating the kitchen like a quarantined zone ever since Market's sous chef, Frankie Boyd, had dropped him like a bad habit.

They dipped up the bowls of fragrant, steaming soup in silence, neither of them paying much attention to the kitchen hubbub. It was clearing out, anyway—the guys on the line had a sixth sense about when family meal was nearly ready, and they tended to congregate around the bar out in the dining room, like a pack of hungry wolves circling a lame sheep.

When the kitchen was empty, Wes felt some of the tension leave his friend's slim frame.

"You don't need to help me take it out to them," Wes offered, taking pity on the guy. "I got it."

"No, it's fine." Jess had his Brave Little Toaster face on, all straight shoulders and chin up.

Wes shrugged. If Jess wanted to torture himself, it was his prerogative. Not like Wes had a leg to stand on in the Making Healthy Choices department, anyway.

That's probably why they'd fallen into this friendship, Wes reflected as they loaded the bowls onto two trays. They weren't that close in age, and their childhoods couldn't have been more different—but he and Jess were both Love's suckers.

And they were both pretty good at acting like everything was fine. Wes was impressed with the matter-of-fact way the kid hefted one of the trays and carried it out of the kitchen, head held high and a grim smile on his face.

Wes followed him, ready to jump in and defend Jess if the wolves were ravening harder than usual—as a server, Jess was used to the more sedate, polite responses of restaurant guests to the arrival of food; he might not realize that if he was too slow handing off a bowl of soup to one of Market's hungry line cooks, he was liable to draw back a bloody stump instead of a hand.

But by the time Wes joined him in passing around the goods, Jess had already emptied his tray and was turning to head back to the kitchen.

"Not going to stay and eat with us, then?"

Sous chef Frankie Boyd, resident Brit punk badass and Breaker of Young, Innocent Hearts, looked up from his ungainly sprawl against the bar. An unlit cigarette dangled from his lips, bobbing as he thinned his lips.

"Not hungry," Jess replied without looking around, so he didn't see the expression that flashed over Frankie's face. Wes did, though, and it was intimate enough, real enough, to make him look down and away, almost embarrassed to have witnessed such a private moment.

For a minute, the only sounds in the dining room were the bang of the kitchen door behind Jess and the noise of Wes's kitchen comrades sucking down soup. The happy slurping was punctuated by occasional moans of pleasure.

Guess the soup wasn't too bitter after all. Huh.

And as Wes watched the savory steam curl up from the bowls, he thought again of Mrs. N., her plump cheeks flushed pink with the heat of the ancient stovetop in the tiny, functional kitchen of Heartway House.

Those bad feelings, you put them in the pot and the cooking transforms them into nourishment for the body. And the parts that cannot be transformed, those escape into the air as smoke and mist, gone from the body forever.

Gathering up his empty tray, Wes followed his friend out of the dining room.

Jess looked up, surprised, when he swung open the door. "You're not having dinner with the crew?"

Wes balanced the tray on an empty corner of counter. "Lost my appetite."

"Hmm." Jess's blue gaze was entirely too sharp as he surveyed Wes. "I know why I don't want to break bread and shoot the shit with the cooks. What's up with you?"

Wes tensed the way he'd been taught, under his skin, deep down where it wouldn't show. He could lie to Jess, easy as breathing. He could say something partially true—

always the most convincing sort of story—such as how he didn't feel totally accepted by the other cooks, how they were suspicious of externs after what happened with the last wacko culinary student to invade their kitchen. He could even give up a real truth, like the master of misdirection he'd been trained to be, and say he was worried about what would happen once his externship was over and he had to leave Market.

But as Wes stood at his station and stared at the closest friend he'd ever managed to keep, he knew he didn't want to lie to Jess.

Sucking in air heavy with the scents of seared meat and roasting vegetables, Wes said, "I told you before about the woman I left behind at the academy."

"One of your professors." Jess nodded, no judgment showing anywhere on his earnest, young face. "I know you miss her. Hey, at least once the externship is up, you can go back and see her again."

Wes's lips twisted. "Yeah. What I didn't tell you was . . . well. The way I left?" He shook his head, heart thudding hard and achy in his throat. "I can pretty much guarantee she's not going to want me anywhere near her."

"What? Why? I thought you had this hot and heavy thing."

"Hot and heavy" didn't really cover it. "We did. And now she hates me." He laughed, but it hurt, so he stopped. "The worst part is, I can't even blame her because I did it on purpose. I made her hate me. And then I ditched her."

Wes crossed his arms over his chest and waited for Jess's condemnation. After all, what Frankie did to Jess was pretty similar to what Wes had done to Rosemary, now that he thought about it.

Love 'em and leave 'em—easier said than done, he thought wearily. *Who's the Breaker of Young, Innocent Hearts, again?*

But all Jess said was, "I think you'd better start at the beginning. The real story, this time, Wes."

So Wes told him. All of it. And hoped that when he ran out of words, he'd still have a friend.

The worst of it was, Wes knew that if it came right down to it and he had to choose again—between his happiness and protecting Rosemary—he'd make the exact same decision.

Even if it meant hurting both of them in the short run. Because in the long run? She was definitely better off without him.

Sorry, Mrs. N., but there ain't enough soup in the world to transform all the crap inside me into anything good.

Chapter 1

Six months earlier . . .

"I came here instead of Dartmouth specifically to avoid classes like this one. The horror. The humanity! Where did I go wrong?"

Wes shook his head at the plaintive tone. He thought about laughing, but he didn't want to throw fuel on the fire. Once Nathaniel Goodwin started bitching, it took an act of Congress to get him to stop.

True to form, Nate was undeterred by the lack of response. "No, seriously. I'd rather be in a class on serving techniques or whatever, front-of-the-house, waiting-tables type stuff," he said, naming every culinary student's least favorite learning track. "I'd be all over it. I'd be *down*. But no." He shuddered theatrically. "It's *chemistry*. My dad always wanted me to be a doctor. Dude, I could be pre-med right now if I wanted to take a bunch of chemistry classes."

Wes stuck his tongue in his cheek to keep from saying what *his* dad wanted him to be. Also to keep from popping the snot-nosed kid a good one.

Sometimes it royally sucked to be the oldest guy in every classroom. Most of these kids were here at the Academy of

Culinary Arts fresh out of college. Some were even younger. The only school Wes had ever attended regularly was Hard Knocks U, or as his father liked to call it, the School of Experience.

Trust a con man to put a good spin on a life of petty crime and ignorance.

"At least you're not failing," Wes said, wincing at the memory of his last exam score. He didn't know why he couldn't seem to grasp these concepts; it was as if his brain simply refused to see food as a collection of molecules. "Quit whining, princess. You just have to get through it and ace the final in a few weeks. Then you can ditch this Popsicle stand for the bright lights of Atlantic City and your choice externship gig."

"Externship," Nathaniel breathed, in tones normally reserved for spiritual revelation. "God, that's going to rock."

Wes scowled. "I can't believe we're on different rotations. You get to leave in three weeks, you scumbag. I have to wait another six!"

The Academy of Culinary Arts schedule wasn't structured like an ordinary university; students entered on staggered rotations all through the year. Every student completed two full years of study, eighteen months of academics with six months of externship sandwiched in between, but there was a new crop of graduates and a new batch of incoming newbies every three weeks.

"That's right," Nathaniel crowed. "I'll be working in a real restaurant, learning from the best, while you slave away here writing book reports and stuff. Suck it, beeyotch!"

"It's not fair. They ought to schedule it by age—old-timers like me should get first dibs, since young'uns like you are barely mature enough to handle doing your own laundry for the first time."

"Half a year in a top restaurant," Nathaniel mused,

focusing in on the fun part of the conversation with his usual laser precision. "Hot damn, I'm glad I'm gonna be a chef. This beats med school all to hell."

"Come to think of it, the externship's not all that different from a med student's residency, except without the hospital. Unless you slice off a finger or something, which I wouldn't be surprised if you did. Klutz."

"Speaking of which, have you heard back from any of the restaurants you applied to?"

Externship slots at top restaurants were few and therefore were fiercely coveted. The Ivy Leaguers had nothing on culinary school kids when it came to fighting and backstabbing for a chance to scrub floors in the kitchens of the greats. Wes had thrown his hat in the ring for Daniel Boulud, Tom Colicchio, and Devon Sparks.

"Nothing yet." Wes shrugged, tried to act casual. "I'm not worried, something will come through. Maybe not my top choices, but I'd be happy anywhere in New York City, really."

"Dude, you should totally apply in A.C.! Then we could hang after dinner service."

Wes suppressed a wince. Nate was a nice enough kid, but, unlike him, Wes had more on his mind than having a good time and pissing off his old man.

That second part was more in the nature of a perk, as far as Wes was concerned. Mostly, he wanted a real life as a real chef, and he was willing to do whatever it took to get there.

Including Food Chemistry 101. The bane of his existence.

"What's up, bitches?"

Nathaniel's face lit up like he just got parole. "Hey, Sloane's here!"

The lanky brunette rolled her eyes and slid onto the stool next to Nathaniel. She immediately started giving him a hard time, which he grinned at and ate up like she was doing dirty talk or something.

Wes tolerated their schoolyardish brand of flirtation for about half a minute before he was forced to tune it out in self-defense.

"Hey, did either of you ladies hear anything about the new prof?" she was asking.

Wes and Nate exchanged clueless looks. "What happened to Prentiss?"

"Gone," Sloane said. "Some kind of medical emergency or something."

"Wow." Wes blinked. The implications swirled around his head. "Who the hell did they find to replace him on such short notice?"

"Our illustrious president didn't have time to search around much, that's for sure," Sloane said. "God only knows who we're going to end up with this late in the term. I wouldn't be surprised to see Todd the janitor up there talking about carbohydrates and lipids."

"Awesome," said Nate. "Bet Todd won't give us any homework."

Wes hooked his long legs around the bottom rung of his stool and frowned. He was already not doing so great in this class—would a new instructor make his life harder or easier?

Wes wasn't used to getting bad grades at the academy. He worked hard, he excelled, he went above and beyond. He was at the top of his rotation.

Food Chem might change that. If he didn't bring up his grades in this class, he was looking at the number two slot, which could affect whether or not he got one of his top choices for the externship.

It was the subject, he mused. Food Chemistry . . . such a cold, distant way to look at something as vibrant and full of life as the magic that happened in a kitchen.

He shrugged to himself. Didn't seem likely that a new instructor was going to make much of a difference, one way or the other. Wes would just have to work harder.

He leaned his elbows on the high table to watch the rest of the students trickle in, yawning and slouching. Food Chem wasn't held in the lecture hall, with its auditorium seating and cooking demo capabilities, nor was it in one of the class kitchens lined with cooktops and ovens, sinks and racks and counterspace.

It was just a room, with windows along one wall that looked out over the tranquil lawn rolling down from the academy's front doors. Four long metal tables were set up facing an honest-to-God chalkboard. It was like being back in high school.

What Wes could remember of his sporadic public school attendance, anyway. Which wasn't much.

He and Pops hadn't really stayed in one place long enough to formulate what you might call good study habits.

Wes frowned, thinking about his dad. He tried to calculate how long it had been since he'd heard from the old man—at least a year. Which meant it wouldn't be too much longer before he popped up again to try and pull Wes back into the life with a well-planned investment fraud or a watertight piece of identity theft. He sighed. Or maybe just a request for a little ready cash to tide him over until the next big score.

The past few years, their interactions were a lot closer to loan applicant and bank officer than father and son.

It was always feast or famine with Pops and money. The man was damn good at swindling it out of people—but holding onto it? Not so much.

The classroom door opened, jarring Wes from his thoughts, and admitting a young woman Wes didn't recognize. He frowned. Most of the students in his section had been in overlapping rotations together, through the thicks and thins of the grueling culinary arts program, for the past eight months. They'd wrestled with pasta dough together, learned basic hygiene and kitchen safety together, broken down flocks of chicken and fabricated countless fish and brewed up gallons of stock together.

He knew most of their secrets, their histories and their hopes, even if none of them knew Wes's. Gathering potentially useful info like that was an early survival tactic that he'd never quite lost.

But this chick? Was so brand-new she practically squeaked.

Or wait. That was her shoes.

Wes stared at her feet, realizing all at once what was so strange and different about her.

She was out of uniform.

The Academy of Culinary Arts had a strict dress code. The place was famously well run and hyperregulated; there were severe consequences for breaking any of the myriad rules and regulations set forth by the academy's president. Some of the worst penalties came from code-of-dress infractions.

Everyone at the academy wore black pants, a white chef's jacket, and regulation black leather kitchen clogs. Every single person, from the chef instructors to the students on up to President Cornell. No exceptions.

Except, apparently, New Girl.

Who was clad in what looked like regulation geekwear. Baggy khakis that made her appear even shorter than she was, topped with a beige T-shirt featuring . . . Wes's feet slipped off the rung of his stool.

Whoa. Is that a freaking Wookie?

And on her feet, squeaking against the sterile tile floor with a noise like she was wearing Styrofoam panties, were black Converse sneakers.

Wes stared in silence. In fact, the whole classroom went dead quiet, as one by one, the sleepy culinary students registered the stranger in their midst.

New Girl didn't appear to notice, at first. Clutching a stack of notepads and papers to her chest, she shuffled quickly, head down and shoulders hunched, up to the front of the classroom. But instead of taking a seat at one of the student tables, she kept going.

Wes watched, fascinated by this tiny stick figure of a person, all jerky movements and shiny blond hair twisted into two messy braids down her back.

Until she reached the podium next to the chalkboard, where she paused, appeared to take a deep breath in, and turned to face the class.

And Wes got his first good look at her face.

Wide-set blue-gray eyes. Her bottom lip was plumper than the top, giving her a permanent pout. And her nose . . . damn it. Wes had to swallow hard. Her nose was interesting rather than perfect, and it was enough to take her face from merely pretty to knockout striking.

She looked like the beautiful starlet they cast to play the smart girl; the one who transforms by the end into the gorgeous woman she always was, with the help of contact lenses and pants that fit.

And obviously, she was the newest addition to the teaching staff.

Wes stared. Food Chem had just became his favorite class.

"Oh," she said, her wide eyes going even wider at the sight of the class sitting there, silently watching. It was as if she were surprised to see them. "Um. Hello. My name is Dr. Rosemary Wilkins."

She paused, glanced at the chalkboard.

Wes knitted his brows. Surely she wouldn't . . . okay, maybe she would.

Dr. Rosemary Wilkins stepped to the board, grabbed a piece of chalk, and wrote her name in careful, looping script.

Dusting off her hands, she turned back to the class and continued. "I have a bachelor's degree in organic chemistry from Yale, a Ph.D. in physical and analytical chemistry from the University of Virginia, and a Ph.D. in biological chemistry from Bryn Mawr. I'm here at the academy to study food. By which I mean, of course, the chemical processes and interactions between ingredients under controlled conditions. The ACA has unparalleled facilities for the kind of research I'm interested in conducting . . ."

She trailed off, mumbling something down at her notes. Wes was pretty sure he caught the words "wish I were there right now . . ."

Visibly bracing herself, Dr. Hot Stuff's vague gaze found the class again. "At any rate, your previous professor had to leave unexpectedly, so I'm stepping in. To teach you. Somewhat . . . unexpectedly, as I said before." She cleared her throat, eyes darting left and right. "So. What do you want to know?"

Wes looked around the room. He could practically hear the crickets chirping.

A wash of red suffused her cheeks, but she pressed onward. "I mean, here you are. At one of the premier culinary schools in the United States. From that, I infer that you all want to make good food. Don't you want to know the reasons behind what works and what doesn't? Unless . . ." She paused, looking uncertain. "Oh dear. You don't think of cooking as a creative endeavor, as 'art,' do you?"

Wes propped his head on his hand and watched her wring her hands. He couldn't understand why the combination of her nervous speech and jerky gestures was hitting him right in the libido.

As a simple reflex, his brain started cataloguing what he knew about her, sizing her up.

She looked about Wes's age, maybe even a little younger. She certainly wasn't older. Which meant she must've been in her teens when she got that first degree.

Dude. Prodigy alert.

One of the students, Bess, a plump blonde who'd proven multiple times over the course of this class that she was categorically *not* a prodigy, said haltingly, "Are you really a teacher?"

Wes winced. Well, at least she hadn't asked if Wilkins was a real doctor.

"No." Dr. Wilkins looked bewildered at the very idea. "I'm a scientist. I thought I already said . . . at any rate, this may be my first time in front of a class of real live students, but at least you won't be stuck with me for very long, since this rotation is almost over."

Another long silence. Wes watched their new teacher shift her weight from side to side, fingers gripping the podium so tightly they went white at the tips.

Wes studied her. He noted the curve of her pink cheek, the quickness of her breath. She was short, he decided, but perfectly proportioned. Her skin was like the porcelain tableware they used at La Culinaire, the academy's student-staffed restaurant, creamy white and so fine it was almost translucent.

Not that Wes was any kind of expert on school, but even he could tell that little Miss First-Time Teacher was bombing this class in a big, bad way. It was painful to watch her try to untangle her tongue enough to get to the actual sharing of information, and his classmates' deep and abiding silence wasn't helping.

One good question would probably get her going, Wes thought. But when he sat up and raised his hand, he knew deep down that he didn't deserve the grateful look she shot him.

As much as he wanted to tell himself he was heroically stepping in to save her from the humiliation brought on by her absentminded-professor routine, he couldn't.

Because Wes had never been very good at lying to himself. And when he looked into his delectable new teacher's blue eyes, he saw more than a brilliant, beautiful, painfully awkward woman.

He saw someone who held his grade—his future—in the palm of her little hand.

Shit, Wes, what are you doing? Don't be that guy.

He dropped his arm hastily back to his side, but it was too late. She'd already zeroed in on him.

"You have a question?" she asked eagerly.

"Yeah," Wes said, licking his lips. "Sure. What I wanted to know was what you meant by what you said earlier. About not seeing cooking as an art form?"

"Oh!" She looked surprised. "I'm not sure what you mean. Can you elaborate, Mr. . . . ?"

"Murphy," Wes supplied, adrenaline buzzing up his spine. It was weirdly intoxicating to have her full attention. "I was interested because it seems like you don't think there's anything creative about cooking."

"Well, wouldn't you agree that the process you know as cooking is truly little more than the chemical reaction of ingredients to each other, to heat, et cetera?"

"Sure, but there's more to it than that."

She frowned. "What did you say your name was?"

"Murphy. Wes. And I mean, I couldn't tell you the chemical reasons behind it, but cooking is more than boring, set formulas playing out in some predictable pattern."

"Chemistry isn't boring." She bristled, clearly stung. "Only an idiot would dismiss the importance of the fundamental building blocks of our world."

Wes sat up straighter. "Hey, I'm not insulting the field of chemistry! I just meant—there's more than the ingredients in the kitchen. There's the chef, too, and that random human element messes up your clean chemical equations every time."

The annoyance cleared from her expression like storm clouds scudding out over the ocean. "That actually brings up an interesting point . . ."

And she was off and running, spouting statistics about human error in experimentation and the degree to which every experiment was compromised by the simple fact of having been thought up by a human scientist.

After the initial scramble to haul out notebooks and pencils, the only noise from the students was the furious scratch of lead against paper as they struggled to keep up with the volume of information spewing nonstop from Dr. Wilkins.

Wes took notes in the shorthand he'd developed years ago and tried to ignore the eat-shit-and-die glares he was getting from his fellow students. So his question got her onto this topic—it wasn't like sitting there in an embarrassed silence was that much more entertaining.

He did take a break occasionally to crack his knuckles and look up at the front of the classroom where Dr. Rosemary Wilkins paced slowly from one end of the blackboard to the other.

Beside him, Nathaniel was scribbling so hard he snapped his pencil point. "Shit! How many days are left in this term, again?"

Wilkins flipped one loose, golden braid over her shoulder and put her hands on her hips, shaping them into sweet curves beneath the concealing cloth of her cargo pants.

"Not enough, man," Wes said, eyes eating up every motion of her pretty little body. "Not near enough."

Chapter 2

Rosemary sank into the space-age comfort of her ergonomic desk chair. Her bones felt like liquid; she had to stiffen every sinew to keep from sliding straight onto the floor.

Folding forward, she let her head rest on the polished mahogany surface of her cherished desk.

There. That was better.

Instead of contemplating what an intensely awful mess she'd made of her first class, Rosemary smoothed her cheek against the fine-grained wood and thought about the first time she saw this desk, in her grandmother's study.

She'd written her first and second dissertations on that exact desk in her dorm room at UVA, and when she left for Bryn Mawr, she took it with her. The administrations were always so nice and agreeable about allowing her to exchange the particleboard monstrosities that came standard to the dorms for her grandmother's antique George III writing desk.

Well, they all agreed eventually.

A few of the institutions of higher learning she'd attended had initially balked at the inconvenience of moving out and storing the inferior furniture, but Rosemary could be quietly insistent when she wanted something.

Grandmother's desk, with its gently slanted writing surface and multiple cubbyholes and interesting drawers for stashing bits of research and source materials, was actually something Rosemary needed. She did her best thinking at that desk, and given that she was a genius, that was really saying something.

The Academy of Culinary Arts president, Wally Cornell, gave in almost without a fuss. He understood a hard limit when he heard one, and when he'd first approached her about moving her research to the academy's brand-new, state-of-the-art food lab, he'd made it clear that he'd move more than furniture to partner with a scientist of Rosemary's stature.

The premier culinary school in the United States, the ACA turned out scores of highly qualified restaurant professionals year after year. Most of the current darlings of the food world were ACA alums, including luminaries like Devon Sparks.

She couldn't understand why it had taken so long for such an illustrious learning facility to place a heavier emphasis on the chemistry of food. Not only was it fascinating and Rosemary's current research obsession, it was an essential area of study for culinary students. Cooking was nothing more than the ways different ingredients with various properties reacted to one another. How could anyone expect to be certified as a competent professional chef without understanding the processes behind those reactions?

Most people didn't care *how* things worked, in Rosemary's experience. They only wanted to know that they *did* work.

She shook her head, confounded as always by that mentality.

Then she sighed, her circuitous thoughts circling around again to force her to face the unpleasant fact that, genius or not, she hadn't done her beloved subject justice in that classroom today.

The overwhelming silence from the students, their blank, apathetic stares, were like pressure in her ears, like diving underwater until the sheer weight of the ocean above threatened to crush her lungs.

Her mouth had dried, her heartbeat increased, her skin prickling with clammy sweat—unmistakable symptoms of an incipient panic attack.

She'd been ready to squeeze her eyes shut and just wait for it to all be over, and then . . . Wes Murphy.

He of the bright smile, overlong dark hair, and eyes that defied easy color categorization. At first she'd thought they were plain brown, but the longer she looked at him, the more tints registered, everything from mossy green to tawny gold. The word "hazel" didn't really seem adequate. And that scar through his left eyebrow, barely noticeable except when he arched that brow at her in clear and obvious challenge.

That challenge somehow cut through Rosemary's rising anxiety and enabled her to actually start talking about science. She had an uncomfortable feeling that the non-stop lecture format hadn't truly engaged her students' minds, but Rosemary wasn't sure what else to do. Her youth had excused her from teaching duties in graduate school, so she had zero practical experience to draw on.

She rubbed at the smudge her breath made on the polished surface of the desk and fretted about the class.

Especially that Wes Murphy. Rosemary couldn't stop remembering the curl of his lips when he asked her what she meant . . . Rosemary went hot all over just thinking about it.

Which felt very strange. Maybe she was coming down

with something. Oh no, and her medical kit was still packed in one of the boxes she'd asked maintenance to cart over from her previous office in the lab!

It's fine, she told herself. *The lab isn't far. The boxes will be here soon.*

She mourned the loss of her tiny cubicle at the lab. It was more of a converted storage closet, really, which was why President Cornell had made her switch. There was no way she could take student appointments in that cramped little space, he pointed out. Accurate, but still. She missed the privacy, the way the lab was all set up exactly as she preferred, with no surprises anywhere.

She missed the sterile cleanliness.

A squeak at the door nearly stopped her heart. For Buffy's sake, were there mice here? That was all this dirty little room needed.

No, it was only the ancient hinges protesting the weight of the heavy office door. She'd left it slightly ajar, probably in a subconscious effort to provide herself with an escape route should the interior of the office prove overwhelming.

She frowned again. Was the door a little more ajar than it had been a moment ago?

Another squeak had her jumping in her Aeron chair, which was set to maximum recline and reacted to her quick movement by flipping her backward. Rosemary scrambled to right herself, which was hard to manage while simultaneously drawing her knees up to her chin, but no way was she leaving her poor, defenseless legs to dangle over the edge of the chair into rodent territory! They might swarm!

A tense moment of silent struggle with the chair later, however, Rosemary still didn't see any small, furry bodies scurrying toward her. The door was definitely a little more open, though.

Attempting to wrestle herself back from diving straight into the deep abyss of one of her more potent neuroses, Rosemary regulated her breathing and forced her brain to list the possible reasons for the door's movement:

1. **Mice.** Unlikely, as none had appeared, but it had to be considered. Mainly because she wouldn't be able to focus on any other possibilities until she at least put the rodent hypothesis on the list.
2. **A breeze.** It was an old building, liable to be drafty.

Rosemary liked that one. It had definite potential. To test it out, she carefully removed her black denim jacket and sat clutching her knees to her chest. She concentrated, trying to detect any movement of air against her bare arms or through the thin material of her favorite EMPIRE STRIKES BACK T-shirt, but felt nothing. Sighing, she went back to her list.

3. **A serial killer who stalked and murdered geniuses.**

Weirdly, this one freaked her out less than the rodent hypothesis. Possibly because even at her neurotic worst, she understood that a psychopath would be unlikely to be able to ascertain her IQ simply by looking at her.

Even if she did fit the science-prodigy stereotype to a T, from her messy ponytail and tortoiseshell glasses to her *Star Wars*-dominated wardrobe.

There was a fourth possibility—it could be one of her students with a question about the lecture or the homework she'd assigned.

Gulping, Rosemary checked her watch. That last one might actually be the scariest. The door hadn't moved in two minutes and fourteen seconds. Before she could debate whether or not that was sufficient time to allow a relaxation of the feet-off-floor policy, she heard a distinct snuffling noise.

Stiffening, her gaze shot to the door, which flew open and banged against the empty bookshelf behind it, sending up a cloud of dust.

Something rushed into the office, too fast for Rosemary to identify.

The thing was low to the floor, but still far too tall for any mouse that hadn't been irradiated or genetically engineered. It rounded the corner of her desk and screeched to a halt, the blur of brown and white resolving into a small dog, tongue lolling out of a wide, panting mouth.

Rosemary stared at the dog. The dog stared back. Neither blinked.

Until footsteps sounded in the hall. Rosemary lost the staring contest when she glanced at the unobstructed entrance to her office. The dog took the opportunity to scoot into the enclosed foot well of Rosemary's desk.

"What in the name of Joss are you doing?" Rosemary gasped, gripping the edge of her desk and peering underneath. The dog was curled in the dark hidey-hole, its white teeth catching the light as it continued to pant.

"Come out of there. I mean it! I'm allergic to pet dander! And I haven't unpacked my Kleenex or my Claritin yet!"

The dog's brown eyes glittered in the dim underdesk light, almost as if she'd rolled them dismissively.

Rosemary didn't want to panic, she truly didn't.

As the philosopher and statesman Douglas Adams had said, *Don't panic*. Those were excellent words to live by, and she strove for that, she really did. But sometimes, in some situations, panic was unavoidable.

Situations such as, for instance, when a knock on the doorframe drew Rosemary's attention.

"Anybody home? And, um, anyone seen a short white dog come this way?"

Low, caressing tones with a hint of bite, like smooth Irish whiskey, and the shiver that ran down her spine and heated her blood told her exactly who it was.

A moment later, a tousled head of brown hair appeared, followed by a lean-hipped whipcord of a body. He peered inside, an apology in his tawny eyes.

"You!" she exclaimed, establishing her command of the obvious.

"Me," he agreed, mouth quirking into a grin.

Rosemary straightened and walked around her desk, crossing her arms over her chest. "I mean, hello, Mr. Murphy."

"Just Murphy," he said. "Or Wes. And hey, sorry about the canine invasion—we were coming to visit you, but Lucille got away from me."

"Lucille? Is that the animal's name?"

"As in Lucille Ball. Lovable but trouble-prone," Wes said. "I promise you, she earned it. Like Macho Man Randy Savage or The Undertaker. She could go pro with the causing of trouble, isn't that right, snooks?"

That last was said in an affectionate voice to the dog, who'd scrambled out from under the desk to gaze up at Wes in obvious adoration. Rosemary wouldn't have been surprised to see the thing pee in a circle around him.

"I believe you," Rosemary replied, feeling slightly over-warm, hyperaware, and just generally uncomfortable with approximately one-point-eight-two-eight-eight meters of disturbingly attractive man taking up all the air in her office. "So."

"So," he said, scooping Lucille into his arms. The dog heaved a happy sigh and laid her head on his muscled shoulder. "Hi. How'd your first class go?"

Rosemary narrowed her eyes. Was he mocking her? These things could be so difficult to interpret. Cautiously, she said, "You were there. How do you feel it went?" Then, thinking maybe she didn't actually want the answer to that question, she added hastily, "I mean, due to the short notice I was given, I wasn't as well prepared for your class as I would've liked. Next week's will be better."

He actually laughed. "Oh, I hope not, Professor. Sincerely. I had a ball."

Lucille's head shot up at the word "ball," evidently something of a Pavlovian response. When no one appeared to be tossing around a spherical object, however, she put her head back down on Wes's shoulder.

It was awfully . . . cute. Rosemary frowned. Something very odd seemed to be occurring in her midsection. Had she forgotten to eat lunch again?

"Well, Doc, I really just came over to thank you for an interesting lecture and to . . . well, to apologize." He ducked his chin, looking up at her from beneath his lashes. Rosemary swallowed hard.

"No apology necessary," she said. "It's never wrong to ask a question."

"Right, but if I said anything that made you think I don't respect your work, or the course material . . . that's not the case, I promise. And I'm very sorry."

He smiled winningly, and Rosemary found herself smiling back without meaning to, even though there was something a little off about the whole conversation.

Not for the first time, she wished she'd made more of a study of facial expressions and emotional cues. She vaguely sensed an undercurrent to this conversation, but she was helpless to decipher it.

"Are you all settled into your new digs?" Wes asked, changing the subject before Rosemary could decide how to respond to his apology. "I can see you've already made some changes—that's a great desk."

"Thank you!" Rosemary stroked it affectionately. "It was my grandmother's."

Wes dragged his intense gaze from the desk to give her another of those slow, lopsided smiles of his, one lean hand scratching at the dog's head by his ear. "It's gorgeous. Eighteenth century?"

"Um, yes." Rosemary blinked.

He nodded. "Right. So I guess we'll be going. Unless you can think of a reason we ought to stay?"

That smile made Rosemary's empty stomach clench, the muscles in her thighs tensing and releasing in an odd, quick motion that sent shivers down her legs. She retreated behind her desk and sank into her chair.

"No, that's . . . good-bye," she managed to say, though it was faint and reedy, and the gleam in his green-gold gaze let her know he was every bit as aware of her as she was of him. And now her head was whirling, the room too hot all of a sudden, and she could hear her heartbeat in her ears, strangely loud, so loud she almost missed it when he said abruptly, "Shit."

Another extra-loud heartbeat later, and he'd whisked himself into the office and shut the door behind him, pressing his back to the wood. Lucille's legs were stiff against his chest, as if the little dog were pushing away from Wes's chest and attempting to launch her small body to the floor.

Rosemary blinked. And then she heard it—footsteps treading heavily down the hallway.

Chapter 3

"Sorry, Doc," Wes apologized. "I didn't mean to swear. But if it's okay with you, L-dawg and I'll be hanging here for just another second or two."

This was really not his day. First, Dr. Rosemary Wilkins turned out to be the one woman on the planet who didn't gush and coo over Lucille's sweet, furry self, thus rendering his plot to use her as his ace in the hole null and void. He was starting to worry that this whole scheme was about to seriously backfire.

Wilkins froze, eyes wide. Wes raised a brow and shook his head, trying to plead silently without going over the top. It was a little tricky—he had to make it clear that he didn't want to be discovered, while not in any way actually impeding discovery.

Getting in trouble with Cornell was all part of the plan.

"Why not?" she stage-whispered. Her brows creased in adorable confusion.

"Come on, just keep quiet for a second. Please? If they catch me with Lucille, it'll be bad."

Another knock, another startled jolt from Wilkins. Flighty little thing, wasn't she?

"Dr. Wilkins? Are you in?"

Right on schedule. Wally Cornell, president of the Academy of Culinary Arts, stickler for rules, and animal-hater extraordinaire.

Showtime.

"Dr. Wilkins?" Cornell repeated. "Was that you? I hate to be a bother, but I escorted the maintenance fellows over here with your belongings from the lab. Oh yes, thank you, you may put the boxes down. I know they're heavy."

"My things!"

Wilkins elbowed him aside and threw open the door. "Set the boxes over there, please. Finally, hallelujah, at last," she said, hands clasped in gratitude.

Cornell stepped back to let the boxes through, but there weren't that many. The maintenance guys finished up and Cornell stuck his head in to beam at Wilkins ripping into her boxes as if they contained the lost Ark of the Covenant.

Wes gave him a little wave, projecting as much sheepish guilt as possible. The pleased smile on Wally Cornell's round face dimmed as he took in Wes and Lucille.

"What . . . is this?" he asked, in his querulous way.

"Oh, thank the Maker," Wilkins crooned to something in one of her boxes. She was down on her hands and knees scrabbling around, and Wes wanted to thank *her* maker. Somebody sure went to some major trouble perfecting the curve of her pert little ass. If any of the teachers he'd encountered had looked like that from behind, he would've had a better high school attendance record.

She sank back on her heels holding something small and squarish that she then squeezed, spurting a generous glob of clear gel into her palm.

Hand sanitizer, Wes realized. *That's what she was so worked up about?*

Rubbing furiously, Wilkins sighed something that sounded an awful lot like the kind of satisfaction normally reserved for that first deep breath after a mind-melting orgasm. "That's better. Now. What was that, President Cornell?"

The prez looked ready to stomp his little foot. "I said, would you like to explain this?"

He hadn't, but okay. Wes didn't like to quibble when the man was pointing right at Lucille.

Wilkins waved an airy, sterilized hand. "That's one of my students. And a dog."

"A dog!" Cornell was outraged. His whole head, much of it on view due to an unfortunate case of male pattern baldness, turned bright red.

"Domesticated subspecies of the wolf," Wilkins clarified. "Member of the Canidae family, of the order Carnivora. Beyond that, breed classifications are, by and large, unscientific and unreliable. This one, for example, doesn't belong to any breed I'm familiar with."

"A mutt." Cornell's voice went up another octave. "On school grounds. This is outrageous, the rules are very clear. Students are not allowed to have pets on campus!"

This was where it got dicey. If Wilkins was really as unfazed by Lucille's cuteness, and Wes's charm, as she seemed to be, he might be in real trouble.

"She's not a pet," he said. *When all else failed, start talking,* his dad's voice whispered in his ear. *Keep going until you're either out of the jam, or you're tossed in a cell.* "She's a working dog. Like a service dog? Not a seeing-eye dog, I mean. Obviously. Ah . . ."

"Obviously not," Cornell sneered. "As if anyone would bother training a mutt to be a guide dog."

Wes checked to see how Wilkins was taking all this.

She stood up and faced the president, an odd expression on her pretty face. "You keep emphasizing that word, *mutt,* as if you'd find the dog more acceptable if she were a purebred animal. Am I to understand your rules only apply to mixed-breed dogs?"

Cornell sputtered but she didn't give him a chance to respond. "Because that would be extremely illogical. Not only is it prohibitively difficult to determine true breed lines with any degree of accuracy, it's also pointless to exclude mixed-breed animals."

"Why is that?" Wes asked, hope starting to beat in his chest like a drum.

"Ever heard of heterosis? No? It's a genetic phenomenon also known as 'hybrid vigor.'" She paused. "Still nothing. Well, simply put, in deference to you, President Cornell, the mixing of breed bloodlines often results in a healthier animal with a longer natural life span. Purebred animals, on the other hand, are prone to all sorts of illnesses and conditions, even neuroses." Her mouth turned down for a moment, and she muttered something that sounded suspiciously like "I should know."

"I don't see how that's relevant, Dr. Wilkins," Cornell blustered. Evidently, her neat little dig about his intelligence had skimmed right over his bald head. "The point is, this student has broken the rules, and here at the Academy of Culinary Arts, that merits punishment."

"That won't be necessary," Wilkins said. Her strong little chin tilted up, and her blue eyes sparked with something that made her look righteously pissed. "No rules have been broken. I've read your bylaws, you see, and article fourteen-point-one mentions only that students are not allowed to bring or keep a pet on campus."

Wes raised his brows at her, and she gave him a little shrug. "Eidetic memory. I see something, I remember it."

President Dickhead wasn't having any of it. "Exactly so, Dr. Wilkins. The rules are clear."

"They are," she agreed. "Insofar as they pertain to students. Faculty, on the other hand, is another matter."

This was awesome, like having an out-of-body experience where his astral projection was watching a fast-paced tennis match. Wes's attention swung back to Cornell, whose color had upgraded to puce.

"You don't mean to suggest . . ."

"I'm not suggesting anything." She was supremely calm in the face of the prick's mounting fury. "I'm stating a fact. The dog belongs to me."

Wes laughed. He couldn't help it.

This was turning out even better than he'd planned.

Time for phase two . . .

"And as of this morning, I'm a member of the faculty." Rosemary didn't look at Murphy. She couldn't risk it, and anyway, she wanted to keep her eyes on the short man currently fuming in front of them.

The way Wally Cornell shook with impotent rage was really quite satisfying to watch.

She couldn't stand his sort of snobbery, looking down on someone else for circumstances they couldn't control. It was abominable, not to mention illogical.

"You can't expect me to believe you are the owner of this, this, this . . . mongrel. This student already as good as admitted it belonged to him! Give me your name, young man."

"Wes Murphy." He shot Rosemary a look she didn't have time to decode. "And I guess I act kind of proprietary about Lucille, here, because I take care of her for Dr. Wilkins."

The poor president looked befuddled. "Wait. You're a dog-sitter? Not a student?"

"Culinary student, in my second-to-last academic rotation before externship." Wes dashed Cornell's hopes for a satisfactory and face-saving conclusion to this altercation. "Definitely a student. And I wouldn't say I'm a dog-sitter." He paused thoughtfully, long enough to have Rosemary looking at him in alarm. "More of a . . . research assistant."

Wait. What? All hands on deck! Time to make the jump to hyperspace!

This charade had officially gone too far. It was time to eject President Cornell from her office and get the situation under control.

"So kind of you to drop by, President Cornell," Rosemary said, a touch too loudly. "But as you can see, I have a lot to do, unpacking and so forth, so if you don't mind . . ."

"I most certainly do mind," the little man sputtered. "This is the first I'm hearing about a research assistant. If you'd only said you needed one, I could've raised enough funds to include it in the budget, but as it is . . ."

Rosemary tried hard not to look at Wes, who laughed and spread his hands. "Did I say 'research assistant'? I meant . . . well, actually, it's more like Doc Wilkins is assisting me. With my research for my final project."

Cornell squinted until he looked as if he'd gotten a face full of sulfuric acid fumes. "Final projects aren't due until the end of the second year of the program, after the externship."

"I wanted to get a jump on mine," Wes said easily. "Complicated stuff. Going to require lots and lots of chemistry and background knowledge of the type only Professor Wilkins can provide."

Cornell turned his squint on her. "I wasn't aware you were willing to serve as a final project advisor."

"I'm not. Mr. Murphy is an exception." She made her voice as firm as she could. Better nip this in the bud before she found herself advising twenty stressed-out students on their final projects. She had enough stress of her own to deal with. "His project is vitally interesting, from a scientific standpoint. I couldn't resist the chance to help guide and mold his experimental procedures and research."

Cornell, finally ready to accept that he wasn't going to get to expel anyone today, nodded and turned to leave. Behind his back, Wes stuck both his thumbs in the air and looked impressed. Rosemary tried not to be proud of having mastered the art of deceit, but couldn't quite manage it. She'd always been accomplishment-oriented.

At the door, Cornell paused. "I'll look forward to reviewing the results of your study. What's the subject of this fascinating final project, anyway?"

Rosemary's self-congratulatory giddiness fizzed away like carbon dioxide reacting with water to form a dilute solution of carbonic acid in a glass of lager.

She stared at Wes, speechless. Those green-gold eyes blinked back at her, and she actually saw the idea take shape deep within them—they narrowed a fraction, which was accompanied by the slight arch of the scarred eyebrow and a minute curl of his well-shaped upper lip. He looked . . . wicked. And happy about it.

"Aphrodisiacs," Wes said, gaze never wavering from her face. "Together, Dr. Wilkins and I are going to prove which ones are a load of hooey." He grinned, slow and devastating. "And which ones work like a charm."

Chapter 4

The lab was still and quiet, no chemicals bubbling, no machines whirring. The air was heavy with the earthy scents of sweat and sex. Moonlight filtered through the tall, narrow windows, highlighting the smooth, bare limbs splayed upon the central table.

A sigh. A rustle of movement, the sensual slide of skin against skin. The whisper of wet heat was the only warning before a scorching, ravenous mouth descended over a small, taut nipple. More sighs, then a moan, the temperature in the room skyrocketing as the bodies on the table writhed in glorious, messy harmony.

"I've never felt like this before." Between kisses, tongues pushing hard and deep, bodies moving together.

"I know." Sexy purr of a voice, shivers cascading as it moved closer to brush the words against the shell of an ear. "It's the pon farr."

"What?"

His eyes glowed warm and green-gold in the cool moonlight. "The mating cycle of the Vulcans is upon you, but I won't let you experience the lingering death, Dr. Wilkins. If we mate, I can save you."

Rosemary sat up, heedless of her nakedness in her haste to touch her own ears. Yes! They were pointed, like a Vulcan's! It was a dream come true!

Oh. Wait.

With a sigh, Rosemary opened her eyes and blinked sleepily into the darkness, glad there was no one there to witness her skin glowing bright red with embarrassment. Her blush felt hot enough to set off radioactivity alerts.

"Hi," she said to the featureless black of her room. "My name is Dr. Rosemary Wilkins, and I have *Star Trek* sex dreams."

The sad part was, even in a fake confession to an empty room she couldn't bring herself to admit the worst of it.

Memories of dark hair falling into bright hazel eyes, kissing that smile as broad shoulders held a strong body above her—oh no, the pon farr wasn't close to the worst of it.

Because Rosemary knew exactly who her dream "mate" was.

Wes Murphy. The ridiculously sexy, rule-breaking *student* who was now her research assistant.

She groaned, pulled the pillow over her head, and recited chemical formulae until she fell back into a restless sleep.

"Knock knock. Dr. Wilkins?"

Wes shouldered open the door to the chemistry lab, struggling not to drop his heavy armload.

Dr. Rosemary Wilkins crossed her arms over her small, high breasts and gave Wes a look that lowered his core body temperature by at least five degrees.

He couldn't help it, though. The sliver of T-shirt flirting out from beneath her white lab coat made him smile. He squinted; as best he could make out, the shirt appeared to feature the mathematical sign for pi floating on a blue background, surrounded by clouds. It took him a second, but he finally got it.

Heh. Pi in the sky.

"Well, hello there, Dr. Wilkins. Nice day, isn't it?"

"What?"

She blinked at him as if she barely recognized his face. Wes tried not to be offended.

"Remember me? Your research partner? I'm here to start setting up our experiment," he said, putting down the big, rectangular cooler.

The confusion cleared from her pretty blue eyes and she colored up as if he were searing her sweet cheeks with a hot skillet.

"Right! Of course, I'm sorry. I was engrossed in my . . . doesn't matter. Yes. Aphrodisiacs! I've actually done a little preliminary research into the subject."

"Fascinating," Wes murmured, sauntering around the lab table.

Rosemary—he'd decided he liked thinking of her as "Rosemary"—jittered as he got closer. She actually backed off a few steps, only stopping when Wes did. "I want to make something very clear." She held up a finger. "I'm studying the chemical effect of nutritive substances on the human body—I don't have time to get sidetracked into mythical hoo-hah like aphrodisiacs."

"So why did you help me out with Cornell?" Wes thought he knew, but he was very curious to see what she'd say.

"I shouldn't have. It was a lie, and I hate lies."

"For a good cause, though," Wes pointed out.

She shook her head. "It doesn't matter. A lie is a lie is a lie. As a scientist, I'm dedicated to the truth."

"Then why—?"

She pursed her pink lips. "Like many heads of school

administration, President Cornell has let the power of being in charge of his little universe go to his head and turn
him into a petty dictator. Not only that, he's mentally neg-
ligible and has no true interest in knowledge; he recruited
me heavily so he could use my name to raise the academy's profile and secure donations for research. His only
concern is the eventual monetary gain the school stands
to make. I have no respect for him. And I didn't like the
way he spoke about your dog."

Wes blinked. That was way more information than
he'd expected. "Wow. Do you always say exactly what you
mean?"

She knitted her brows, those so-blue eyes going opaque
with confusion. "Why would I ever say something other
than what I mean?"

"To get along. To do well. To fit in."

"Those things are irrelevant. Besides, I have an IQ of a
hundred and eighty. There are relatively few people for
me to 'fit in' with."

Wes's bullshit meter exploded. "No way."

She frowned at him. "I agree, the intelligence quotient
test is flawed and inaccurate, but I assure you, I did score
a one-eighty on it."

"Not that," Wes said. "The other bit. About how you
don't care about fitting in."

No one, but *no one,* was that secure. In Wes's experience, every single interaction was about figuring out
which parts of yourself to hide and which parts to reveal
so as not to get called out and shunted to the outskirts of
the group.

Just like with a good shallot-and-mustard vinaigrette,
blending was imperative. Always.

"Oh!" Her eyes widened like blue saucers. "No, that
part's true, too. It's illogical and impractical to be overly
concerned with the good opinion of others. The only true

measure of success is the attainment of one's personal goals."

She sounded as if she were reciting something she'd been told repeatedly. Starting to get righteously ticked, Wes asked, "Where'd you get that pearl of wisdom? *Star Trek*?"

Wilkins stiffened. "For your information, *Star Trek* presents a highly intelligent, forward-thinking universe of characters and morals—if more people lived their lives according to the precepts set forth by the Federation, the world would be a better place."

Wes held up his hands in surrender. They were getting off-track. "So. You're helping me get one over on Cornell. And meanwhile, you're supposed to be researching how food makes people feel? Sounds to me like aphrodisiacs are right in line with that."

"Yes, but I'm doing real science," she said cuttingly. "Aphrodisiacs are anecdotal nonsense. The FDA ruled on them more than twenty-five years ago, and they found no correlation between sex drive and any over-the-counter remedies, including popular so-called aphrodisiacs like truffles, ginseng, almonds, and so on."

"That's because there've never been any reputable, conclusive tests done," Wes argued. He'd looked into it. *Know enough about your background story to be able to riff on it.* That was one of the best lessons Pops ever taught him.

Rosemary cocked her head, eyes going vague in a way that told Wes she was considering what he'd said. "I suppose that's true."

Sensing that grudging acceptance was the best he could hope for at this point, Wes smiled winningly and said, "Great! Want a snack? I brought oysters."

She narrowed her eyes at him.

Wes held up his hands in surrender. "Kidding! Not

about the oysters, I mean, I did bring them. But they're for the experiment."

"I don't follow."

Wes cocked his head at her chilly, blank stare. "You know. Oysters? Most potent of all aphrodisiacs?"

She arched one brow, eyes flaring with annoyance, and Wes hid a grin. He liked how fiery she got when he ticked her off.

"Of course I've heard that," she said. "I was simply astounded that you would begin with such an incredibly pedestrian example. And such an easily disproven one, as well. Most of the educated world now agrees that oysters are associated with sexual feelings due to their relationship to the coining of the very term 'aphrodisiac' along with the story of Aphrodite rising from the spray of sea foam in an oyster shell. The sea foam, of course, being a metaphor for Zeus's ejaculate."

Wes blinked. "You know a lot of weird stuff."

She shrugged. "I told you. If I read it somewhere, it's in my brain forever. There's no escaping it."

"That actually sounds kind of sucky," he said.

"You have no idea. It's really crowded up here." She rapped her knuckles against the side of her head, making her messy blond topknot wobble. "I've got the moves to the Thriller dance squashed in next to the chemical formula for vinegar."

"Do you ever get confused?"

"No."

Awesome.

"Another theory on the oysters-as-aphrodisiacs myth," she said, "is that their high levels of zinc contributed to overall health during a historical period where zinc deficiency was common. Better health leads to increased sex drive."

"You don't say," Wes replied, starting to unpack the

cooler. He cracked open one jar and inhaled deeply, breathing in the smell of the ocean.

Rosemary drifted closer. "How are you planning to set this up?"

Wes looked up from his preparations, making sure to set his face to "innocent inquiry" beforehand. "Oh! I thought I'd just mess around with oysters and see what different preparations do for me."

She pursed her lips. "That's not terribly scientific."

Wes shrugged. "I'm not really a scientist," he confided as if it were a big secret. "That's what I was hoping to count on you for."

She stared down at the array of dishes Wes had unpacked. "I've never had oysters."

"No way. I love 'em! When I was a kid, I ate fifty-two in a single sitting, at a wedding in Seattle. I was sick as anything afterward, but it never put me off them."

That was one of the best weddings he and Pops ever crashed, Wes remembered. Hundreds of guests who didn't know each other; about half of them didn't know the bride or groom. Easy pickings. Wes didn't remember how much Pops got pawning silver snatched off the gift table; he didn't like to think about that.

But he vividly remembered the food at that wedding: smoked salmon wrapped around creamy, tangy mascarpone dotted with bright green chives; tiny, individual spinach tartlets jazzed up with caramelized shallots; a four-tier wedding cake that actually tasted great; and of course, enough oysters on the half shell to clog a toilet.

She stared at him, eyes round and impenetrable. "Charming. If we might get back to the science?"

"Sure." He really enjoyed the easy, natural way she rocked that white lab coat. Wes was wearing a white jacket, too, but somehow his normal, perfectly tidy chef's whites looked dingy compared to the eye-dazzling purity of her white coat.

In fact, the whole lab was a little squint-inducing. Every surface gleamed; the chrome fixtures at the deep double sink against the back wall were nearly blinding. Not a single instrument was out of place; every beaker, every Bunsen burner, every microscope shone as if it had recently been attacked by rogue bottles of mutant antibacterial spray.

Maybe what he really liked was *her.* A thought that scared the piss out of him, actually, but what could he do? He was starting to remember why things went south between him and Pops—Wes had never really had the stomach for conning, even the relatively victimless crimes where supposedly no one got hurt.

But he was here. He'd already toppled the first domino; he might as well follow and see where he ended up. Who knew? There might be more at stake than his grade.

"As you pointed out, Dr. Wilkins, I don't have much in the way of science yet. What I do have are three different kinds of oysters I sweet-talked out of Chef Roberts; supposedly they each represent a different genus."

She liked that, he could tell. "Of course, because there are three main genera of edible oysters; which are separate, you understand, from the gem oysters, which yield pearls. What do you have here?"

"Sydney rock oysters," Wes said, wiping a few drops of liquid from the rim of the first plate.

"To represent the genus *Saccostrea,* I presume," Rosemary said.

"Just so. These were shipped in from the Wingan Inlet in Eastern Victoria. That's New Zealand, not Canada. I did a quick ceviche with lime and orange segments, slivered ginger, and toasted hot chiles."

Then Wes pointed at a plate full of small, juicy-looking oysters resting on their halved shells. These shells were flat and rounder than the others. "Belon oysters, from Brittany in the north of France," he said.

"Of the genus *Ostera,*" Rosemary put in, as if she couldn't help herself.

"Right," Wes said, amused. "I kept these raw and on the half shell, but I did bring a nice little mignonette to go with. Just minced shallot, olive oil, lemon juice, and cracked black pepper. Then over here"—he indicated the next plate—"we have the most common and popular oyster, the Eastern or Virginia oyster."

"Crassostrea," Rosemary muttered.

Wes bit his lip to keep from cracking up. "They might be common, but they're delicious. All perfect and plump, these are so great fried in a nice cornmeal batter. Or just as God intended, with a good, horseradishy cocktail sauce. Which I also happen to have."

"I see you came prepared. For lunch, if nothing else."

"Thought you might be hungry. And don't worry, I intend to document any interesting results."

She cocked that brow again, like a quizzical bird. "What results do you think you might find, exactly?"

Hopefully, whatever love potion is in these bad boys will convince you it's a good idea to start thinking up ways to get that pristine lab coat all nice and dirty.

But Wes was smart enough to keep that potential end result to himself. "I thought maybe we could test to see whether different preparations of the supposed aphrodisiacs have different effects on the body. I'll develop some different recipes, and we'll pay students to test them out. Won't have to be big bucks; everyone around here's always strapped for cash." He paused. "I'm assuming you don't want to falsify our results for President Cornell, since you hate lying so much. I noticed yesterday that it didn't come all that naturally to you."

She bristled as if he'd insulted her. "I think I acquitted myself perfectly adequately, considering the exigencies of the situation."

"I'm not a hundred percent on what that means, but anyway, I wasn't trying to insult you. Lots of people would consider it a very good thing to be a bad liar."

"Humph. I'm not accustomed to being bad at anything," she groused. "With the possible exception of reading facial expressions and social cues. Other people can be so bafflingly irrational."

She was truly unlike anyone Wes had ever met—and, what with one thing and another, he'd met all kinds. "Very true. So, you wanna try some oysters? See what happens?"

"Nothing will happen beyond a quenching of hunger," she stated, then paused. "Actually, a great many things occur the moment a bite of food makes contact with one's mouth. I could go through the entire process, from taste buds to intestinal tract, but I assume that would be inappropriate and unwelcome."

Fascinated, Wes leaned one elbow on the table and rested his chin in his hand. "I wouldn't worry about being inappropriate, but it's probably not superappetizing."

"That's what I thought." She sighed, then brightened. "Points to me for interpreting the situation correctly, though!"

"Do you really have a point system?"

Rosemary slid him a sideways look. "It's a colloquial turn of phrase indicating pride in an accomplishment."

"Ah," Wes said. He wouldn't have been a bit surprised if she did have a point system, with distinct numbers of points awarded for different levels of personal success.

Social engagements probably didn't rank all that high on her value scale.

"Well?" She was watching him expectantly. "Are you going to eat them or not?"

"What, alone? You're not going to try even one? Come on."

"I'm not in the market for a bout of food poisoning just now, Mr. Murphy."

"I'm going to tell Chef Roberts you said that. He gets a bit touchy when people malign the freshness of his fish."

"Fine! Pushy. I'll begin with the Sydney rock oysters," she declared. "Because the acid in the lime juice will have cured the oyster flesh, rendering the risk of bacterial infection much smaller than with the raw oysters."

"Not much of a risk taker, hmm?" Wes went straight for the Virginias, big and bold and slippery in their smooth shells. He doused his in cocktail sauce and tipped the whole thing straight down his throat like a shot of vodka. It burned going down, just like a shot, but as the bright brine and tomato flavor exploded over the back of his tongue, Wes smacked his lips and started getting another one ready. He could do this all day.

"Risk is only practical in controlled laboratory circumstances," Rosemary said, daintily arranging her Sydney before slurping it down. "Oooh. That's . . . that's really good. But it mostly tastes like the lime segments . . . just saltier and spicier."

"You can't control the outcome of risky behavior," Wes argued. "That's what makes it fun. Makes you feel alive. Come on, try one of these." He nudged the plate of Belons closer to her, along with the little cup of mignonette.

Rosemary waffled for a moment, visibly torn between her fear of bacteria and her inability to allow Wes to have one up on her.

"They're perfectly safe, I promise," Wes coaxed.

"If I get sick, you're driving me to the hospital," she warned.

"You won't," he promised. "Go on. Just one taste."

As if afraid she might change her mind, Rosemary scooped up one of the smooth, circular shells and tilted her head back, popping the whole oyster into her mouth without even bothering with the sauce.

Wes watched the elegant line of her pale throat work as she swallowed, and felt a zing of heat up his spine.

Note to self: the lady can't resist a challenge.

Chapter 5

Rosemary squeezed her eyes shut and let gravity do its work, every muscle braced for the inevitable panic-induced freak-out. Shellfish were dangerous! Everyone knew that. They were hosts to all sorts of bacteria. She hadn't eaten a raw oyster since she first learned what happened to a person's internal organs when they threw up.

But the instant that oyster slid into her mouth, the powerful flavor of the ocean beat her hypochondria into submission. The whole world narrowed to the patch of tongue currently tasting the distillation of sea breezes, salty waves, and sunlight that Wes had forced her to eat. She'd never tried a raw, unadorned oyster before. It was delicate and bold at the same time, a combination of flavors Rosemary was instantly sure she'd remember for the rest of her life.

She might have moaned a little.

"Good?" he asked. She could tell without looking that his smile was back, and smirkier than ever.

He was standing too close, Rosemary thought, the electric awareness of his nearness all over the surface of her skin. Did he have no personal boundaries? She shifted uncomfortably, feeling too warm, the tops of her ears tingling with enough heat to make her want to check that they hadn't suddenly gone pointy.

Don't think about Vulcans, she repeated to herself. It was unnerving to have him here in the lab with her, standing beside the table upon which her incredibly humiliating yet breathtakingly sensual dream took place.

"Yes. It's good," she managed, hearing the odd breathlessness of her own voice but unable to do anything about it.

"These are awesome," he agreed amiably. "So. Are you feeling anything yet?"

Hmm. Had she registered the rise in temperature before or after eating the oysters? Or was that due to the memory of her dream? "Like what?" she hedged.

His eyes twinkled in a way that made Rosemary notice again what an extraordinary mix of colors they were, brown and green all shot through with gold. "Oh, you know. Do you feel like doing the horizontal mambo yet?"

Wes waggled his brows like Groucho Marx, which made her want to smile, but didn't really dispel the spiraling tension that coiled between them. "It would take more than a couple of shellfish, Mr. Murphy."

"Come on, call me Wes. After all, we're research partners now."

He smiled again, dimples winking into existence in his tan, lean cheeks, and Rosemary lost her cool. "Okay, enough. I know what this is. You're flirting with me, aren't you?" Rosemary accused, feeling a hot flush prickle up the back of her neck. "I may not be an expert on social cues, but even I can see where this is heading."

A slow, lopsided grin lit Wes's face as he peered up at her from his slouched stance over the table. "I wondered how long it would take you to catch on. Guess you really are a genius!"

Rosemary sputtered. She'd expected him to deny it! Most people tended to backpedal when confronted with the naked truth about their motivations. Not Wes, apparently, which was just her luck.

"I *am* a genius, thank you so much, and exactly what do you think all this leaning and smiling and, and, all these *oysters* are going to accomplish?"

He quirked a brow. "Beyond the obvious? Just kidding. Sort of. Come on, Doc, lighten up and enjoy the experiment."

She stood there and felt the world skew ever so slightly out of focus. Racking her brain for any possible scenario that might shine the light of reason and rationality on this odd scene, only one thing came to mind.

"You think if you cozy up to me, it will help your grade in Food Chemistry 101," she said, wondering whatever happened to her usual modulated, detached tone of voice. She sounded . . . pissed. Which was odd, because she'd always considered anger to be a highly unproductive emotion more suitable to less evolved beings who enjoyed being ruled by their feelings. Rosemary preferred to avoid the question of emotion altogether. Which maybe explained her anger—Wes Murphy had incited more feelings in the short time she'd known him than Rosemary had suffered in years.

She watched now as he straightened up and backed a step away from the table, cheeks flushed a hectic red, his wide, mobile mouth curving into a frown. "That's not what this is about."

Rosemary regarded him with curiosity. His response dampened some of the heady, swirling ire that filled her chest at the idea of being used. She wondered if he meant what he said.

"Good," she replied after a moment. "Because I'm not planning to evaluate the performance of anyone in your class. It would be ludicrous of me, considering how few weeks I'll have to observe you. No, your entire grade will derive from the final exam, which has already been prepared by my predecessor, and you can rest assured, there will be no fudging or tweaking of test results. I would consider that highly unethical, on par with skewing the outcome of a lab experiment. I'd sooner strip naked and dance the hula in front of the entire class."

That surprised a snort of laughter out of Wes, who'd held himself stiff and distant through her whole response. Rosemary didn't understand why, but for some reason she didn't like to see him that way.

So when he unthawed enough to loll against the table and shoot her an amused glance along with a terse, "Understood," she was glad. And then annoyed at herself for being glad. And that made her head hurt, so she decided to ignore both sentiments and get back to work.

"I'm afraid my allotted time for frivolous inanity is up for today, Mr. Murphy," she said, turning back to her notes. "Please don't make too much noise as you pack your things and leave."

She usually had zero difficulty losing herself in the fascinating research in front of her, but somehow, today she felt hyperaware of the quiet movements behind her—cloth brushing against cloth, the clatter of plates and the cooler scraping against the floor as it was lifted. She unwillingly tracked every movement of the strong, tall body behind her. And when he got to the door and reached for the handle, she held her breath, certain that he wouldn't leave without saying anything.

As usual, she was right.

"I'll be back tomorrow," he said. It sounded like a promise, caressing and full of warmth. "With chocolate truffles. And maybe a Barry White CD."

Rosemary jerked her head up to look at him—even she

got the Barry White reference—but with one last cheeky smile, he was gone and Rosemary was left alone with her notes in a lab that felt inexplicably cold and empty.

Shivering and buttoning up her lab coat, Rosemary paused with her chilly fingers pressing a button halfway through its hole as she realized something.

Frak me. I'm in serious trouble.

Wes slammed his lump of brioche dough onto the kneading board with more force than strictly necessary.

Half a week and four research sessions later, Wes still hadn't quite come to grips with the rush of guilt and shame and just general wrongness that had overtaken him when she called him out about cozying up to her for a grade.

Everything in him wanted to deny it, and of course that was what he did—but not out of simple self-preservation.

He wanted it to be true.

Wes wanted to be the kind of person who would never think about using the attraction sparking between himself and his conveniently young, good-looking teacher. He hated the fact that still, however many hard years on his own without Pops, working the angles was his first impulse.

The look on her face when she accused him . . . Wes didn't want to see that expression again. Ever.

The wet *thwap* of dough against wood almost drowned out the discreet vibration of the cell phone in Wes's pocket.

There were only a few people who had this number; Mrs. N. would only use it if it were an emergency. Pops, on the other hand . . .

Wiping his sticky, floury fingers on the damp side towel he used to keep his station clean, Wes checked the chef instructor's progress around the classroom. Chef

Wolensky was about eight students away, trying to help Nathaniel figure out why his dough looked more like soup than anything else.

Wes ducked to the back of the bakery classroom, behind a couple of speed racks filled with trays of cookies iced with intricate white lace patterns, and flipped open his phone.

"Weston! My boy!"

Wes closed his eyes. "Hi, Pops."

"Why are you whispering? What did I tell you, Weston—never whisper, it makes you look guilty. Project total confidence and no one will question you!"

"I'm in class right now," Wes informed him. "And talking on my cell won't get my brioche to rise, so make it snappy."

Pops clicked his tongue. "So touchy. And so eager to get the old man off the phone. Anything going on that I should know about?"

Wes cursed silently. His dad was still way too good at reading him. "Nothing big," he said, hoping to give just enough to get Pops to quit poking around. "I was thinking about running a short con, but it's not going to work out. So. Back to the straight and narrow for me."

"Oh?" Pops perked up right away. "And what manner of con would tempt my sweet, reformed son to take up his old father's wicked ways once more?"

Wes screwed up his face. He should've known better than to give his dad an opening.

"Nothing, Pops. It was just to get my grades up in this one class, but it's over now."

"Tell me about the mark."

"Let it go, please."

"Oh, come on, boy. Indulge an old man's pride in his son! It's been years since we got to have a good chat about the game."

Despite everything, the guilt and regrets, the knowledge that he was working on living a better way—sometimes, Wes admitted to himself, he actually missed living on the road with Pops. Figuring it couldn't do any harm, since the con was off now, anyway, he said, "Well, there's this new professor, right. In Food Chem, the class I'm sort of flunking? And she's . . ."

He shook his head, stymied for a moment on how best to describe the most fascinating woman he'd ever met.

"A looker, is she?" Pops asked. "I bet she's a blonde. Tell me she's a blonde, Weston."

Wes couldn't help it. He grinned. "She is. And at first I thought she was all vague and dreamy, in that not-all-there kind of way brainy people are sometimes . . ."

"Good quality in a mark," Pops observed.

"Right, only she's really not. She's sharp as hell when she's paying attention."

The way her mind worked boggled him. On the surface, she seemed distant and clinical, but beneath that nerdy exterior, Wes sensed . . . well, a nerd. But a nerd who made his heart jump into high gear whenever she was around.

"Hmm. Is that why you stopped the con?"

Wes rubbed a scrap of dough between his thumb and forefinger, the springy, elastic texture of it odd against his skin. "No. Not really. I just . . . I guess I remembered why I quit doing that stuff."

Pops sighed, but didn't launch into one of his diatribes against Mrs. N. and the folks at Heartway House for corrupting Wes with their law-abidingness, so Wes had to be grateful for that. All Pops said was, "So what's the blonde brain's name?"

"Dr. Rosemary Wilkins."

There was a long pause during which Wes actually

heard his father's breath quicken slightly. "And which class was it?" he asked, all studiedly casual.

"Food Chemistry," Wes said slowly. "Why?"

"Jesus, Mary, and Joseph, boy! Do you know who that is?"

Wes's stomach clenched at the excitement in his father's voice. "No."

"You remember the last con we ever ran together?"

How could he forget? They'd been in Reno. Wes had been playing a child math prodigy while Thomas Murphy was the bumbling dad who'd been conned by a talent scout into giving up their life savings. There'd been several layers of complications to it, all geared toward getting the chosen mark to part with cash, first to help the beleaguered pair, then to front money for the math prodigy kid to count cards at a casino.

It was the con that landed Wes in Heartway House, and he'd been damned lucky not to be shuffled off to juvie. "Yeah. So?"

"Remember the book that gave me the idea? Remember who wrote it?"

"No."

"A Dr. Helen Wilkins. Married to another hotshot scientist, and they had a kid named Rosemary who was supposedly the inspiration for the book. It's got to be the same family. And if they are, Weston—you've landed in the honeypot, my boy, because they are loaded!"

Every alarm bell in Wes's head started clanging simultaneously. "Whoa, slow down there, Pops. There's no guarantee it's the same Wilkins family. I've never seen Rosemary wear anything flashy; I think she even lives in campus housing. So just cool your jets."

There was that insanely expensive antique desk in her office . . . but maybe Wes would just keep that little tidbit to himself.

"The worst of it is, she's wasted on you," Pops nearly wailed. "A prime pigeon like that, just waiting to be plucked, and you won't touch her."

Wes bit his tongue and carefully didn't disagree with his father on that last bit. "Yep, it's too bad, Pops. But she's probably not related to the book woman, anyway."

"Well, what are you planning to do with your ex-mark?" Pops asked. "Cut her loose completely?"

"Oh, shit." Chef Wolensky was approaching Wes's empty station with a frown. "I've gotta go. I'll talk to you soon. Stay safe."

Wes flipped the phone closed without waiting for a response and strode back to his station with purpose, as if he'd had a perfectly legitimate reason for lurking around by the sinks for ten minutes.

He didn't want to examine too closely exactly what his endgame was with Dr. Rosemary Wilkins. The idea of wanting something real was like a new cut from a clean, sharp knife—it seemed okay on the surface of it, but give it a good poke and he was ready to whimper for mercy.

Chapter 6

Wondering if he could get Rosemary to show some of the same softness she'd betrayed that first day in her office, Wes smuggled Lucille across the quad and into the lab for their daily research session. But his lovely lab-coated quarry was nowhere to be seen.

"Where could she be?" Wes asked a clearly uninterested Lucille. He peered around the small, barren lab. Nope, not hiding under a micrometer or something. Lucille jigged up and down in an obvious bid for the walk she'd been promised.

He sighed. "Okay, this is a bust."

Maybe they'd find her in her office. They took off, skirting around the green and keeping a sharp eye out for marauding security officers. And sure enough, as Wes chivied his recalcitrant fuzzball up the creaky stairs to Dr. Wilkins's new digs, he heard her voice, staccato and precise, if muffled, from down the hall.

Yahtzee, he thought with satisfaction. *The doctor is in.*

Old habit had him pausing at her door, just to check if he could hear anything incriminating through the narrow space.

She seemed to be alone in her office, from what he could tell. On a phone call. He could only hear the murmur of her voice, then a pause, then Rosemary again. But what was she saying?

Even while knowing down to the tips of his toes that it was dumb, not to mention an invasion of her privacy, Wes leaned closer and closer until his body was pressed against the doorjamb. His ear was as close to the opening as he could get it without actually humping the door.

And just as Rosemary said, "No, Mother, for the last time. The *Journal of American Science* declined my article. I'm not going to call and harangue them about it," Lucille leaped into action.

Apparently excited by the suddenly raised and familiar voice, she danced a quick circle in place. Then, finding that not enough to relieve her feelings, she darted a circle around Wes.

Who was still holding the leash.

Tangled inextricably, Wes was in no shape to react smoothly when Lucille then decided that a circle in the hall was as nothing compared to the joy of turning a circle actually in the office with the familiar voice, and jerked on her end of the leash with all the force of her small, wriggly body.

Off-kilter, legs bound together at the knee, Wes tottered against the door, which swung wide and dumped him on his ass in front of a shocked Rosemary.

Lucille yipped, mightily pleased with herself.

Rosemary stared in silence for a long moment before saying into her phone, "I'm going to have to call you back."

Wes offered a sheepish smile and a shrug as she slipped the cell into the pocket of her cargo pants. "Well. Fancy seeing you here."

She blinked. "This is my office. I work here."

"I know. It was a joke to cover the awkwardness. But it didn't fly, and I had to explain it, which produced even more awkwardness. I'm not doing so hot here, am I?"

"Maybe you'd do better if you got up off the floor," she suggested.

Struggling with a frantically leaping mixed-breed dog who definitely had a buttload of stubborn, excitable terrier in her makeup, Wes wrestled his way to his knees and said, "I'm trying. Scout's honor. Could you just . . ."

She breathed out something that sounded weirdly like "Oh, for Buffy's sake," and bent to unclip Lucille's leash from her collar.

Wes clambered to his feet with another sheepish grin. "Thanks. I'm starting to feel like a perpetual damsel in distress around you, Doc."

Rosemary gave him a narrow look. "I can only infer that you enjoy it, given how frequently you appear in my presence."

"What can I say? I'm a glutton for punishment. Plus, I like how my insides go all squishy when you swoop in on your white horse and make all the bad stuff go away."

"The association of a white horse with heroics is a throwback to medieval paintings of Saint George fighting the dragon. He's usually depicted on an ivory stallion, which isn't terribly common, unless it's a Lipizzaner."

The way her mind darted around the conversation like a hummingbird gave Wes a dizzy, drunken feeling that he thoroughly enjoyed. "Oh yeah? Lipiwhatsits are white?"

"Lipi*zzaners,* and frequently." She blinked as if suddenly becoming aware that they'd gotten off track. "Did we have an appointment?"

"It's about that time." Wes tapped his nonexistent watch before shoving his hands in his pockets. He was wearing black jeans under his chef jacket today, not quite a uniform violation that would get him in trouble with Cornell, but not exactly the letter of the law, either. He liked skating on that edge.

"The aphrodisiac project." She groaned and slapped her palm against her forehead. Wes didn't think anyone actually did that.

"Bad day?" Wes gave her his most sympathetic face. She jerked upright and squinted at him suspiciously. "The door was open! And sound carries in these old buildings. Couldn't help but overhear."

"Hmph. Well. At any rate, yes. I'm sure someone will be interested in my study on the quantum mechanics of protein chain linking in the digestive tract, but apparently, the *Journal of Science* is not."

"Sorry to hear that."

"It's inconsequential." She waved it away, but the unhappy set of her mouth didn't change. "What I need to focus on now is the question of how to help a room full of bored, disinterested culinary students gain a closer understanding of food chemistry."

"In other words, your lesson plan."

"Isn't that what I said? You're very repetitive. And what is that dog doing?"

Lucille was busily investigating the dusty corners of the office, no doubt finding many intriguing smells along the way.

"Don't mind her, she's conducting her own form of research."

Rosemary smiled, and it warmed something in Wes. He rested a hand on her gorgeous desk.

"Can I make a suggestion?" he asked. "I don't want to give you unsolicited advice, but—"

"Just spill it, Mr. Murphy. What is it you want to say?"

"Well, about your paper—and your class lecture—why don't you try to make it a little more . . ." *Interesting. Lively. Fun.* He searched for the right word. "User-friendly.

Maybe you need to spice the whole thing up, give it some flavor and zest. Sex sells, right? Even to the *Journal of Science*."

She looked disgusted. "You sound like my mother. 'You have to give the editors what they want, Rosemary! Publish or perish, Rosemary!' Ugh."

"Oh, come on. The *Journal of Science* guys might be big-brained nerds like . . . ahem. I mean, they might be scientists, but they're guys, too. Right? Tart up that article, and I'll bet you a million bucks they take it. It's just like our class. I bet the students would soak everything in even better if you made it more interactive."

Rosemary opened her mouth, probably to deliver another scathing indictment of Wes's bonehead ideas, but then she paused. "I wonder," she mused, stroking her fingers across her lips in a thoughtful way. "I hadn't considered taking the kinesthetic approach, but perhaps you're right. Even if modern teaching methodologies have been shown to overemphasize the hands-on style of instruction—still, that could be very useful."

"If nothing else, it would take up a bunch of class time," Wes pointed out.

Her eyes glittered happily, setting off a rapid tattoo in Wes's rib cage. "So it would. Thank you, Mr. Murphy. I'll have to try that methodology."

They didn't manage to work on their aphrodisiac research that afternoon, but Wes left her office feeling as if he'd made a huge breakthrough.

Rosemary never failed to astonish herself. One of the greatest minds of her generation, the youngest woman ever to graduate from Yale with highest honors, future winner of the Nobel Prize—and yet, here she was, holding a beaker and facing down a classroom full of wannabe chefs.

"This hard-boiled egg has been soaking in a solution of white distilled vinegar for the last seventy-two hours. What do you think will happen when we take it out of the beaker?"

Blank looks all around, except for the grin creasing Wes Murphy's handsome face. Unreasonably irritated, Rosemary thrust the beaker at him. "You. Murphy. What will the egg be like?"

"Um. Slimy?"

"Let's find out. Come up here."

Wiping his hands on his thighs, Wes stood and sauntered to the front of the classroom, where he stood facing her. Motionless.

Rosemary shook the beaker, careful not to spill. "Well? Go ahead."

"Do I need gloves or anything?"

"It's only vinegar. Your fingers will be fine."

He looked doubtful, but all he said was, "Good. These fingers are my fortune, Doc." Waggling them, he flashed a grin at the audience of students and stuck his hand in the beaker.

He pulled the egg out and rinsed it at the faucet in the corner, at Rosemary's direction.

"Oh, sick," he said, feeling the once-hard shell sloughing away under the cold running water. "I was definitely right about the slimy."

"Now drop it," Rosemary said.

He slanted her an incredulous look. "Doc, I know you said it's hard-boiled, but it's still gonna make a mess."

"I'm not interested in your hypotheses, Mr. Murphy. Kindly do as I say."

Shrugging, he tossed the egg into the air with an unnecessarily theatrical flourish, saying, "You're the boss."

The egg arced up above their heads and then began its downward trajectory. Wes moved back a pace as if to save his black leather chef clogs from the indignity of being splattered with hard-boiled yolk, but when the egg hit the floor—it bounced.

Everyone gasped. Rosemary calmly swept out a hand and caught the white orb in her palm.

"Anyone know why that happened?"

"The vinegar, obviously," Wes said, his face alight with curiosity. He reached for the egg again, and Rosemary let him take it, telling herself it was for the good of the demonstration, not because she liked the slide of his fingers against hers.

"Yes," she confirmed. "The acid in the vinegar attacks the calcium in the eggshell, dissolving it slowly. Just as slowly, the vinegar penetrates the denser proteins of the egg white, turning them rubbery."

"What would happen if you soaked other stuff in vinegar?" Wes wanted to know. "Man. Bones have a lot of calcium. I bet you could make a chicken drumstick look like it came from a rubber chicken."

"Correct. This is a good demonstration of the importance of vinegar in the kitchen. Edible acids like vinegar, citrus juices, and so on, are extremely useful in terms of breaking other foods down, or they can be used to preserve other foods, as in canning and pickling. In ceviche dishes, acid is used, usually with finfish but sometimes with shellfish . . ." She studiously avoided looking at Wes, but felt her cheeks get hot anyway. "That is, to cook the fish. Without heat. Although really, it's more of a quick pickle. Any questions?"

Several hands shot into the air. Flushed with success, Rosemary was about to call on the first young woman when she felt a brush against her hand. Wes clasped her wrist and rotated her hand so that her palm was up. It immediately itched, sensitive to every current of air that moved across it.

Wes dropped the egg onto her palm and closed her fingers over it lightly. "Thanks for the fun," he said, low, with a swift, secret smile no one else saw. "You really know how to show a guy a good time."

Then he was strolling back to his seat, leaving Rosemary to somehow regulate her heart rate and get through the rest of the class.

Which went surprisingly well, once she remembered how to breathe without smelling his rich, complicated scent of salt and smoke. The other students were abuzz with questions and ideas, ways to relate the demonstration back to their reading, and Rosemary found herself actually enjoying keeping up with them.

The whole time, though, she was acutely conscious of Wes in the front row, the white cuffs of his chef jacket rolled up to reveal sinewy, tanned forearms dusted with black hair. He crossed those arms on the table in front of him and rested his chin on his wrists, a smile warming his eyes to tawny gold, and he didn't say another word for the rest of the period.

He didn't have to. Rosemary knew she'd be replaying his soft voice whispering about fun and good times until she fell asleep that night. And possibly even after that.

Maybe tonight, he'll be a Cylon.

The thought filled her with a strange, elated anticipation.

Yep. Totally frakked.

Chapter 7

The days passed in a blur of designing new hands-on chemical demonstrations for her students and afternoons in the lab where Rosemary faced, for the first time ever, considerable difficulty in keeping her busy mind on her own studies and off her irritating, fascinating research partner.

After the bouncy-egg-ball class, Rosemary had to admit that not all of Wes's ideas should be dismissed out of hand. He'd certainly been correct about what constituted a more interesting, vibrant learning experience.

Perhaps, just perhaps, he was right about her paper, too.

That paper. She'd toiled over her study of protein inhibitors and chain linking for months, meticulously recording data and interpreting her findings. It was a brilliant paper, she knew that. And yet they still didn't want it.

Rosemary didn't deal well with rejection. Discouraged and angry in equal measures, she distracted herself by doing more in-depth research into Wes's proposed project. The subject of aphrodisiacs turned out to be more intriguing than she'd originally thought—not that she'd said as much to Wes.

But on her own, late at night when she was avoiding her bed and the possibility of any disturbing dreams, she read. And thought about the strange moments of connection, attraction, and intimacy she'd felt while sharing a variety of reputed aphrodisiac snacks with Wes.

And she allowed herself to become aware of the possibilities inherent in this new, all but untapped, area of study. What she planned to do with it, she still hadn't decided. But something fresh and exciting, something groundbreaking, waited for her—she was certain of it.

Now if only she'd had the sense to keep her mouth shut.

How did every conversation with her brilliant, analytical, uncompromising mother end up with Rosemary defensive and justifying herself?

"Mother. No. Listen to me. If you would just—"

"What is it, dear? I'm elucidating an opinion on this fantastical new scheme of yours! Are you having a break with reality? Aphrodisiacs are not real science!"

Dr. Helen Wilkins paused for breath, and Rosemary leaped into the breach. "Mother!"

"What?"

Having finally managed to jam a word in edgewise, Rosemary wasn't entirely sure what she wanted to say. Other than "good-bye."

So she said that, and hung up the phone. She didn't need to hear the rest of her mother's treatise on the importance of publishing articles in order to advance career standing, anyway. She'd been hearing it since she was nine—and she'd been able to recite it from memory after the first time.

It wasn't any easier to take, knowing that her mother was a total hypocrite. Dr. Helen Wilkins was a renowned psychologist, but most of her fame came from a string of best-selling self-help books rather than true academic research.

Rosemary laid her cell phone on the lab table. She was still regarding it in disgust when Wes walked in with his customary cheerful, "Knock, knock."

He never did the second line of the joke. That was just one of the many mysteries that made Rosemary want to pick him apart like a newly discovered chemical compound.

Damn her intellectual curiosity! It made her burn to know everything about him: his favorite movie villain, what shampoo he used that made him smell like green apples, how he'd gotten that scar through his eyebrow, how he came to own a scruffy, high-maintenance little dog like Lucille, why he hummed to himself when he worked, what he looked like when he'd just woken up . . .

Rosemary forced herself to stop. She couldn't be thinking about that right now. Not while he was walking over to her, flashing that smile that made the whole room seem filled with his presence, as if he were a much larger, more physically imposing man.

Wes hoisted the familiar cooler onto the lab table one-handed, muscles standing out in stark relief along his lean forearm. He wasn't a bodybuilder type, which Rosemary was glad of. That kind of wide-shouldered, no-neck jock always made her feel uncomfortable, almost embarrassed. As though she were foolishly attempting to carry on a conversation with a gorilla.

And she was no Dian Fossey.

"Whatcha smirking at, Doc?"

Rosemary wiped her expression clean. "Nothing. I wasn't." *Damnation. No more internal babbling!*

"Oh no? I thought maybe you were happy about this." He waved a piece of paper at her, grinning expectantly.

"I have no idea what that is," she snapped, still flustered.

"Huh," he said, squinting at the paper. "That's funny,

because your name is right here on it. Next to my grade on the final exam. I passed!"

"Oh, that," she said, unable to resist joining him in a smile. It was easier to resist joining his silly victory dance—at least until he swung an arm around her waist and whirled her out into the middle of the lab, away from the tables, the room spinning around her until the only steady point of focus was Wes's face, lit up with laughter.

She'd been surprisingly sorry to reach the end of her run as professor of the Food Chemistry 101 class—thanks to Wes's timely intervention, it had turned out to be far more entertaining than she'd thought possible.

And if part of her was intensely happy that the end of the class didn't mean the end of her time with Wes, she intended to keep it to herself.

"Yes, that," he crowed. "I'm an A student, top of the class, teacher's pet! Bet you didn't think I'd pass, did you?"

"Stop spinning me, you nitwit," Rosemary gasped, laughter bubbling up inside her like acetone peroxide powder that had been heated enough to explode. "Of course I knew you'd pass."

"You're a better teacher than Professor Prentiss was, especially after we started getting down and dirty with some actual experiments in class. But still, I got this grade without any extra help from you," he said with a fiercely satisfied emphasis that made her frown. He seemed prouder of her lack of help than he was of the grade itself.

"You know," she said, disentangling herself from the distracting warmth of his arms. "You never did answer my question."

He smiled, and it should have looked free and easy, except Rosemary noted the tiny, spidery lines of tension that appeared at the corners of eyes gone dark green like the inside of a cored-out piece of jade. "What question is that?"

"If you weren't making a nuisance of yourself and sticking to my side like you'd been epoxied there in order to weasel a good grade out of me, then why? Why bother, is what I want to know."

Strangely enough, the tension around his eyes eased. In fact, his whole face softened, just a bit, into a look that Rosemary could only categorize as "sympathetic." She crossed her arms over her chest defensively, suddenly and viscerally understanding how a cat felt when its fur was rubbed the wrong way.

"Come on, Doc. Don't tell me nobody's ever wanted to spend time with you, just for you."

His gently playful delivery deflated some of her need to snap back at him. "I'm not usually treated as a leper, if that's what you're asking. But no. Historically, my company hasn't been highly sought after when it comes to social occasions."

"Not a big party girl in high school, huh?" Wes asked, moving back a few paces as if aware of how raw she felt. He hopped up on the high lab table behind him and regarded her with his head cocked to one side, scarred eyebrow arched inquisitively.

"I was twelve when I graduated from high school. Fourteen when I completed my undergraduate degree. No, I didn't attend many keggers."

"That must have been so weird," he breathed, sounding shell-shocked the way people always did when they began to actually confront the reality of what it meant to be a child prodigy. "Did you have any friends?"

Rosemary squeezed her arms tighter around herself to ward off the stab of loneliness, still sharp even years later. "Not really. My first year at Yale, the only people besides professors who paid any attention to me were the upperclassmen in my advanced Organic Chem course. I was flattered, of course—for about three minutes, until one of them made it clumsily obvious they were only talking to me to see if they could trick the brainy preteen into doing their homework for them."

He made a rough noise and his swinging feet kicked the door of the cabinet below the table with a sound like a gunshot. "No wonder you assumed I was scamming you. Damn. How many times has something like that happened?"

"Enough that I don't really want to talk about it anymore," she said, moving to unpack the cooler he'd brought in, just to give her hands something to do.

"Fair enough. But I still wish you'd tell me those Yale assholes' names so I could go beat the snot out of them. We're not that far from New Haven."

She shot him a look that had him rolling his eyes. "Yes, Doctor Smarty Pants, I know where Yale is. You don't need a college degree to have a working knowledge of where to find them."

"You didn't go to college?" she asked, focusing in on a rare smidgeon of real information about Wes's past. He wasn't evasive, exactly, but she'd go back to her campus housing after spending an afternoon with him and realize that never once had the conversation centered on him.

"Decided to come here instead," he said, moving to help her with the unpacking. She'd paused for a moment, arrested by the opportunity to pin him down.

"But you didn't just graduate from high school," she prodded. "I assumed you'd gone to college before deciding to become a chef."

Wes wasn't looking at her; his attention was focused on the large stainless steel bowl he'd pulled from the cooler. "Nah, I took some time off after school. Bummed around, saw the world. I was never that big on formal education, to be honest." He shot her an utterly unconvincing smile.

"That probably shocks you, huh? But I'm here to tell you, school ain't fun when you ain't smart."

"Stop that," she said, her voice sharper than she meant it to be. "Don't pretend to be stupid, because I won't believe you."

The motions of his hands slowed to a stop; in fact, everything about him stopped. Rosemary would almost swear he stopped breathing.

It felt like an hour, but could only have been seconds before he moved again. When he did, it was only his head, turned toward Rosemary like a clockwork doll. His eyes sought hers, the expression on his face still and blank. And then, with a shock of disbelief, Rosemary realized she could read his emotions as if they were scrolling down her computer screen.

She'd scared him—but part of him liked it, and he wanted to believe what she said. Rosemary glanced down at his hands on the edge of the bowl. He wanted to believe her with an intensity that curled his fingers into white-knuckled fists.

"Come on, Wes," she said softly, echoing his words from earlier. "Don't tell me nobody's ever seen you for who you really are before."

The bowl, chilled from its sojourn in the cooler, seared against his palms like the coils of a superheated electric burner. But Wes couldn't make his fingers unclench until his heart stopped kicking like it wanted to escape from the prison of his rib cage.

Her eyes were so damn blue, and so piercing—but not icy, not cold at all. They made him feel naked, though, like she could laser through his chef whites and his skin and his bones and see all the way to the frantically beating heart of him.

For once in his life, he didn't know how to react.

He came up with: "So. D'you want a strawberry?"

She blinked once, making him afraid she'd push and push and not let him have the easy out he needed, then she pursed her lips and leaned over to peer into the bowl.

"What nice specimens of the genus *Fragaria*."

"Uh. Yeah. Strawberries are my favorite fruit, pretty much."

Wow, sound dumber, Wes.

Evidently, Rosemary agreed this time, because she was giving him her patented scornful look. Wes found himself welcoming the return to normal with relief.

"Strawberries are not a fruit—at least, the part we eat isn't derived from the ovary of the plant, as a true fruit's flesh would be."

"Whoa there, Doc, getting a little hot and heavy for me," Wes said. He was only mostly kidding.

"Oh, shut up and give me a berry," she said, all grumpy and cute. Her shiny blond hair was caught up in a messy knot on top of her head. An actual knot, too, not a bun or whatever; it really looked like she'd twisted her hair into a rope and tied a knot in it, close to her scalp. The end of the hair rope tufted out of the top of the knot, just begging to be tugged.

Wes restrained himself manfully and handed over a big, plump strawberry. "I found a few references to strawberries in a couple of old aphrodisiac cookbooks—not sure if they're really supposed to have any supersexy properties or if they're just pretty and fun to cook with."

"There is something sensual about them," Rosemary said, biting into the berry. Wes's mouth dried up as he watched her pearly teeth cut into the cool, ruby flesh, juice staining her lips deep pink.

"I'll say," he croaked, temperature soaring. "Hey, I brought something else, too. Hold on a sec."

Reaching into the duffel, he rooted around until he'd pulled out all the various pieces of the fondue pot and laid them on the lab table. He assembled the device quickly, suspending the stainless steel pot on its spindly legs over a brand-new can of Sterno. He lit it up to warm the pot, then carefully removed the covered, insulated bowl from the cooler.

He'd made the fondue ahead of time so all he'd have to do in the lab was warm it up. And try not to picture Rosemary naked and painted in swirls of dark chocolate.

She sniffed appreciatively as Wes poured the chocolate liquid into the fondue pot. The scent got stronger, headier, as the mixture heated.

"What's in that?" she asked, leaning down until her face was almost in the bowl.

Wes had to grin. No one could resist chocolate fondue. "It's bittersweet Scharffenberger chocolate, very pure, melted with cream, butter, and a little cognac for depth of flavor."

"Is it ready? I have to taste that. Give me one of those."

She selected a berry as if she'd be docked five bucks for every blemish or irregularity, then dipped it in the pot.

Warm, silky chocolate dripped from the tip of the berry as she lifted it to her mouth, and her tongue darted out to catch the drops, a sigh of happiness high in her throat.

Wes ground down on a moan and shut his eyes to the sight of her biting into the strawberry, chocolate smearing her lower lip, her eyelashes fluttering as she hummed in enjoyment.

Seeking a distraction from the temptation incarnate beside him, Wes reached for a berry just as Rosemary eagerly went back for seconds. Their fingers tangled in the bowl, but instead of flinching as if she'd been burned, as Rosemary sometimes did when he strayed too close, she tightened her grasp on his hand in a compulsive clasp.

Desire was a spark that leaped from her skin to his like a fire popping and crackling into flaming life.

The weeks of careful seduction, playful advance and retreat, peppered with judicious brushes of fingers, hips, flanks as they moved past each other in the quiet, enclosed intimacy of her lab—all of Wes's plans, his good intentions, his knowledge that this was different, she was different—all of it flew out of his head in that instant.

He slid his hand up to circle the fine, thin bones of her wrist and tugged firmly, pulling her slight body in against his larger one. She fit against him like a teaspoon inside a tablespoon, curves angling together in all the right places to lock them into place with a nearly audible click of perfection.

Her strawberry-stained lips parted, wet and irresistible, and Wes had never been all that good at resisting temptation. He ducked his head and swept his hungry tongue across her startled, gasping mouth. Rosemary's wrist trembled in his grasp, the leap of her pulse easily discernible through the fragile skin beneath his fingertips. Wes grinned into the kiss and took it further, tongue stroking fast and deep.

One fluttery kick of a heartbeat later, she was kissing him back.

Wes couldn't contain the gruff, satisfied noise that rumbled in his throat. He didn't even try to stop his free arm from winding around her back and hauling her in even closer so that his thigh—lucky, lucky thigh!—slid between her legs and forced her higher.

She tasted like spring and sunshine, sweetly tart and eager, and he devoured every tiny whimper and muffled gasp. Her hands were in his hair, flexing and pulling, the slight pain a counterpoint that somehow drove the swirling pleasure even higher.

A clatter at the door pierced the fog of lust surrounding

them like a slice from a sharp chef's knife—there was a frozen moment of disbelief, followed by dismay as Rosemary wrenched herself out of his arms and stumbled back in horror, her gaze fixed on something behind him.

With a sense of inevitability, Wes turned to find President Wally Cornell gaping at them in transparent horror, eyes bulging like popovers.

Chapter 8

"What . . . is the meaning of this?" Cornell's voice was strangled and squeaky, like a mouse gasping for its last breath.

No mice, Rosemary thought hysterically. *That's all this situation needs!*

"President Cornell," Wes said smoothly, stepping sideways just enough to block her from her small, irate employer's view. "This isn't what it looks like."

"Oh no?" Cornell asked. "It's not an illicit, inappropriate embrace between a professor and her student? At my academy! This has to be the worst day of my professional life. First the debacle with the Market extern, and now this . . ." He squeezed his eyes shut and scrubbed a palm over his large expanse of forehead.

Visions of her career imploding in scandal warped through Rosemary's neocortex at light speed, but Wes radiated calm. Unless you happened to be standing right behind him and staring at the rigid lines of his shoulders and back, as Rosemary was. She could see he was holding himself too carefully, none of his loose-limbed, easy sprawl evident now—but she couldn't hear it in his voice.

"As a matter of fact," Wes said, his voice firm, "she's not my professor. Final grades for Food Chem 101 are in. I passed, so that's that. Nothing to worry about."

"Nothing to worry about," Cornell moaned. "This academy prides itself not only on its culinary reputation, but on the professionalism with which we imbue our graduates—a professionalism which you, Dr. Wilkins, have clearly violated by getting involved with a student. I dropped by to tell you I'm having lunch tomorrow with one of the academy's wealthiest donors, an influential man who will undoubtedly want a tour of the lab his donations helped pay for. I wanted to make sure the lab was presentable—oh, God. What if he'd walked in on this scene with me?"

Cornell's hysteria was contagious. Rosemary started to hyperventilate. Only a little. But the laboratory air was so thin and cold all of a sudden!

As if he could hear her short, sharp breaths, Wes casually moved back until he was close enough to touch. Ashamed of her weakness but unable to resist the comfort, Rosemary latched onto the back of his shirt with one hand and immediately pulled in a big, cleansing breath that carried his scent: the tang of apples and the salt of warm, healthy male.

Fortified, Rosemary managed to push through the rising tide of neuroses to say around Wes's shoulder, "I apologize. I don't know what to say. This is . . . it shouldn't have happened."

The strong, lean back beneath her clutching fingers stiffened even further. "Don't apologize," Wes said, half turning and forcing her to let go of him. His eyes were bright with frustration and something else, something fierce. "We didn't do anything wrong. This"—he swept a hand between them—"isn't wrong."

Cornell sputtered. "It was made abundantly clear to Dr. Wilkins when she was hired that the academy has a strict policy against faculty dating students. So yes, Mr. Murphy, this little affair is indeed wrong. Think how it would look to the donors!"

Her insides wibbled. The loathsome little man was right. No one would ever believe she hadn't been toying with one of her students, playing favorites and massaging his grades—frak, maybe they'd even think she slipped him the answers to the final exam!

Panicked, she stole a glance at Wes, who was watching her with an expression she couldn't decipher.

Great, of all the times for her to lose her special Wes Expression Decoder Ring. But it wasn't a happy look, she got that much. And when he angled his gaze over to Cornell, the cold roughness of his voice confirmed it.

"Deep breath in, Prez. How do you want to play this? Because you can kick us both out of school, but it sounds to me like you did your damnedest to woo Dr. Wilkins here into moving her research over to your fancy lab." He shot her a wink. "And why not? She's very wooable."

Rosemary jerked as if he'd zapped her with a fully charged ventricular fibrillator.

"Oh, my God. The donors. All the people I talked to about the emerging field of food science and how we'd be leaders, making discoveries, breaking new ground." Cornell rubbed his hands over his shiny, bald head. "What will I tell them all?"

"Why do you have to tell them anything?"

Cornell's hands dropped, along with his jaw. "Are you suggesting I cover this up?"

Wes shrugged. "The way I see it, you have two options. You can blow your new, potentially lucrative research department to pieces by firing your star scientist—or you can walk out of here right now, and none of this ever happened."

Whiplash was most commonly described as an injury

resulting from a sudden wrenching distortion of the spine, as from a car accident, or falling off a bicycle—or from being forced to jump from one all-consumingly horrifying topic to another without any apparent bridge between them. Rosemary's neck actually ached.

"I can't do that . . . if it comes out later that I knew, and looked the other way . . ."

"What's the likelihood of that happening? We're not going to tell. And no one knows you're here, do they? Even if our relationship were to become public, you'd have plausible deniability. You were never here; you saw nothing. You're completely innocent."

"You're right," Cornell gasped, hope breaking over his shiny face. "No one could prove I knew anything about this."

He backed toward the door, still looking shaky, but all Rosemary cared about was that he was leaving.

"Very true," Wes agreed. "You're completely safe, your lucrative research department stays intact, and no one gets fired or suspended. Everybody wins!" He glanced over his shoulder at Rosemary, who found it difficult to keep her smile from taking over her entire face. "Besides," Wes continued, "the doc and I aren't through with our research for my final project yet. Something tells me we're getting close to a breakthrough."

"Yes," she said, surprised and pleased by the even smoothness of her own voice. "We have a few more tests to run, experiments to conduct, before we can be sure of what we're dealing with here. But I, for one, look forward to analyzing the results."

Wes gave the smile back to her, the slow, honest smile that lit up his entire body from within. They stood there, grinning like demented idiots at one another while Cornell threw his hands in the air and said, "I don't want to hear about it! Oh, my God, I need to get out of here."

He rushed out, slamming the lab door behind him hard enough to make the strawberries jump in their stainless steel bowl.

"That was amazing," she told him. "I was there for the whole thing, and I still don't know how you got him to leave."

Wes shrugged. "Pretty simple—I just looked at the situation from his perspective and showed him the shortest, straightest path to getting what he wants: a craploved of happy donors with their wallets open, shelling out the green for your big, pretty brain."

He sauntered over and scooped up a strawberry, his eyes never leaving hers. He tipped his head back and held the stem as he swirled the berry in the chocolate fondue. Rosemary's breath caught in her chest when he bit into the treat.

"So what do you say, Doc?" Wes licked a trickle of juice from his lower lip. "Wanna do a little experimenting with me?"

He could actually see the shiver race over her skin. He tracked her body's reaction to his words—first the tremor that made the fine hairs on her arms stand up, then the tightening of the buds of her nipples, their sweet contour barely visible against the line of her lab coat. Her pupils expanded as if he'd dimmed the lights, and her tongue came out to wet her lush, pink bottom lip, mirroring his own.

It seemed a waste for her to be licking her lips when he could be doing that for her.

Wes pounced. She shrieked a little, startled at his sudden movement and how quickly he was there, surrounding her with his arms and pinning her against the lab table with his body, but it was a happy sound. Almost a laugh, pitched high with nerves and anticipation.

Since the same blend of *are-we-really-gonna?* and *hell-yeah!* was moshing around in Wes's midsection, he didn't pause. Just searched her clear blue eyes for a hot second, then lowered his mouth to close them with a kiss.

The thin, fragile skin of her eyelids trembled under his lips, her lashes tickling him mercilessly. Wes kissed his way down her nose, lavishing extra attention on the bump of cartilage at the bridge that gave her face the edge that made it endlessly fascinating to him.

Her hands wavered in the air beside him like birds unsure of where to perch until Wes finally reached her mouth and pressed his tongue between her lips, searching out the hot, yielding sweetness he'd found there before. Then she clutched at his biceps spasmodically, her fingers digging into muscle and forcing a groan out of him.

He loved the way she responded to him, all unconscious sexiness and unrehearsed pleasure. Wes panted into her mouth and watched her eyelids flutter, the two of them like kids ditching curfew to snatch a few more stolen moments together.

They scrabbled at each other's clothes, gasping and laughing at how stupidly hard it was to deal with buttons and zippers. It was fumbling and awkward and *real,* and nothing had ever felt so good to Wes.

He tugged the lab coat off her shoulders but it tangled around her elbows, making her twist and struggle a little, while Wes stopped, his attention captured by her T-shirt. It was black, covered in brightly colored boxes in a familiar pattern.

"It's the periodic table of elements," Rosemary said, apparently miffed at the silence. She shrugged, wiggling her torso to try and dislodge her trapped arms from the sleeves of her lab coat, a hot red flush rising in her cheeks.

"I can see that," Wes said, a surge of warmth making his throat tight. She was just so damn . . . what? He didn't even know. All he knew was that he had to kiss her again, right that second.

She kept her lips in a tight line for a moment, maybe thinking he wanted to mock her for wearing the dorkiest shirt ever created. Which, to be fair, was what he should've been inclined to do. What should definitely not happen was that the sight of her in that ridiculous shirt made every drop of blood in his body race to his dick, swelling him painfully thick and tight against the zipper of his jeans.

He wondered at exactly what point his life stopped making any kind of sense. But when her mouth softened and she let him in, her eyes sliding closed as she melted against him, her arms still trapped so that she had to trust her weight to him—Wes decided he didn't really care.

So the world was nuts and he'd suddenly discovered a kink for geeks. There were worse things.

Like, for instance, being walked in on twice in one night.

He grasped her shoulders and moved her gently back, grinning when she swayed a little. "Hey, I'm going to go lock the door. Just in case. Okay?"

"Okay," she said.

When he turned back, lights switched off to discourage intruders, the door closed and secured against any further interruptions, his heart stopped for a second.

She was gone.

"Rosemary?" he called, feeling like an idiot. Was there a back exit? Had he spooked her or something, made her run away?

"Here," came her voice from somewhere near the floor.

Wes quickstepped around the lab table to find Rosemary on the other side, her lab coat and his chef jacket spread on the floor and one gorgeous scientist sitting nervously erect on the makeshift blanket.

His heart pounded out a quick, primal rhythm. The relief that she was still there with him, combined with the hesitance and barely veiled apprehension in her face, made him want to lunge and cover her before she had a chance to escape.

But he wasn't an animal. None of the things he'd seen and done in his extremely checkered past had turned him into a mindless thug, and he wouldn't be one now, either.

"Are you sure about this?" he asked, the hoarseness of his voice giving away exactly how hard it was for him to ask that question.

She didn't answer in words, but took a deep breath that lifted her rib cage—which Wes could suddenly see in sharp detail because she was whipping that black dork-shirt over her head.

Once it was off, she didn't seem to know what to do next. She paused, then folded the shirt carefully, all precise edges and perfect alignment, and set it aside.

Wes followed this ritual to avoid focusing on the slender curve of her waist, the delicate lines of her ribs, the translucent quality of her pale skin, the small, round swells of her breasts covered in plain black cotton. If he noticed those things, if he let himself think about them too much, all his high-minded humanity would go up in smoke and he'd fall on her like a starving lion.

She finished folding the shirt and crossed her arms quickly, hunching her shoulders and tucking her hands high. She still hadn't looked at him.

Wes dropped to his knees in front of her. "God,

Rosemary. You look . . ." He'd never regretted his ditching school so much before. Maybe if he'd gotten a better
education, he'd have better words to describe how she
made him feel, sitting there exposed and vulnerable in
the fading afternoon sunlight.

"What?" she asked, her eyes flashing to his. She was
all defiant, ready to snatch that crazy shirt up and put it
back on.

"Like an angel," he said, then immediately felt like a
moron. Could there be a worse, more overused line in the
history of men talking their way into women's pants? But
it was all he could think of, the closest he could come to
expressing how ethereally lovely she was, the line of her
graceful neck caressed by tendrils of the golden hair still
knotted atop her head.

She snorted, obviously as unimpressed with his woo-
ing as he was, but there was a pleased smile flirting with
the corners of her pretty, pink mouth. "Fair's fair," she
hinted, giving him a sidelong look from under her lashes.

Wes inched closer. "What? You want me to get rid of
this?" He plucked at the white sleeveless shirt he wore
under his chef jacket.

She nodded, breath hitching as he scooted forward
until their knees touched. Her eyes were huge avid pools
of outright desire that made Wes glad to take his shirt
off—it was getting hot in that lab.

He grabbed the back of the shirt and pulled it over his
head, tossing it aside immediately.

Her eyes flicked after it, her fingers twitched, and he
knew.

Leaning to grab his discarded shirt, Wes met her startled
gaze and slowly, carefully, folded it into a neat square and
laid it atop hers.

Between one breath and the next, she was on top of

him, her hands in his hair and clutching at his neck and shoulders, her soft mouth voracious on his.

And all Wes could think, before pure, unadulterated lust dragged him under, was: *Hey, which one of us was supposed to be the starving lion, again?*

Chapter 9

Rosemary didn't think she'd ever been quite so aware of her own body before. It was intensely fascinating; she couldn't help cataloguing the physiological changes.

When Wes kissed her, for example, her heart rate sped alarmingly and she could feel herself growing warmer all over. But especially between her legs—that spot, usually nothing more than a monthly annoyance or a place to meticulously wash, throbbed with heat. Every time she shifted, she felt the liquid evidence of her desire and it made her want to be smooth, languid, silky . . . until Wes took off his shirt.

By the power of Grayskull, he was truly a magnificent specimen of the human male anatomy. His pectoral muscles were lean and wiry, yet sharply defined. His abdominal muscles laddered down his torso, dusted with dark hair that arrowed into his black denims. The jeans hung low enough on his narrow waist to expose the hollows on either side of his hips, and Rosemary licked her lips, wanting to . . . His shirt!

His shirt was wadded up on the floor, wrinkled and wrinkling, and . . . she had to get a grip. No one stopped in the middle of sex to harangue a man about the way he cared for his clothing. Did they? Probably not if they wanted to find themselves in a sexual situation with said man again anytime soon.

But while Rosemary was attempting to talk herself down, Wes was cocking his head and looking at her intently. He gave her the barest hint of a smile, understanding turning his eyes bright jungle green, then he reached over and folded that cursed shirt.

And Rosemary lost her composure.

Completely. Utterly. She could actually feel her brain giving up the fight, switching off, and letting her body— for the first time in her entire life—take control.

Heat. Pressure. Friction. A warm mouth, agile tongue stroking hers, fingers gripping her waist tightly enough to cause contusions, and all she could think was: *This. More. Now.*

There was no time to think, and she didn't want to, anyway. It shocked her down to her bones, but all she wanted was to feel this, to live in her body and feel every single thing Wes did to her—and he was doing a lot.

He'd worked open the buttons on her baggy cargo pants and started shimmying them down her hips. She'd fallen behind.

Dipping her fingers into the waistband of his jeans was like passing them through the blue flame of that Sterno burner—dangerous, and hot enough to sear the skin from her fingertips. Exhilarated, Rosemary worked the button loose and pulled down the zipper, gasping when the hard, tumescent length of his penis immediately sprang into her hand.

Yikes! Okay, wow.

"Laundry day?" she managed to ask. Was that breathy squeak really her voice?

"Guh," he said.

She tore her stare from the long, smooth erection filling her hand and peeked up at his face. His head was thrown back, his chest heaving, and the look on his face was more indicative of pain than pleasure.

Rosemary snatched her fingers back, certain she'd misunderstood the technique somehow.

But he whimpered piteously and she realized, no, she couldn't have misunderstood. Because (a) she was a genius, and (b) it just wasn't that complicated.

And sure enough, when she sucked in a breath and put her hand tentatively back on Wes's groin, he gasped, "Yes, please. Do that. God, your hands . . ."

Flush with renewed confidence, Rosemary explored the hot skin pulsing against her palm. Intellectually, she knew what she was feeling—the corpora cavernosa running the length of the organ had become engorged with blood, which she could feel throbbing against her fingers with every rapid beat of Wes's heart. Yet somehow, for once, the clinical version of events didn't seem to encompass the entire experience.

Wes was hard. His penis was erect and ready for intercourse because of *her*.

He made a small noise and she rubbed her hand up and down it soothingly, but Wes didn't seem soothed. He shuddered, hard, and grabbed her wrist to stop her from moving her hand again.

This time, Rosemary waited, wanting more information about Wes's reaction.

"It's too much," he said, opening his eyes to stare at her. His pupils were blown, another symptom of sexual arousal. Rosemary shivered, her heart knocking hard against her chest. "Too much," he repeated. "Christ, your hand. I'm going to . . ."

He didn't say what he was going to do, but Rosemary thought she understood. If she wanted to get all the way to the actual intercourse part of this, she had to keep things moving. Wes clearly was in no shape to do it—he'd frozen them in this strange little tableau, her hand on his erect penis, his hand covering hers, neither of them moving except for the great, panting breaths they heaved in.

Stretching up, she laid her mouth against his and pushed her tongue inside. He growled, the sound reverberating through both of their chests where they were pressed together. Rosemary felt the vibration against the sensitive tips of her breasts, still covered by her bra, which she suddenly wanted off her.

Unable to work the hook left-handed, Rosemary broke the kiss to say, "I need my hand back."

"Are you sure?" Wes asked. There was an urgency in his voice that Rosemary normally associated with dire situations.

The idea that maybe from his perspective the removal of her hand would be considered dire made her heart speed up.

"Because I need both hands to unhook my bra," she told him. "Then you can have it back. My hand, I mean."

He gulped and stared at her glassily.

"Or . . ." She hesitated, then just said it. "Or we could do something else."

"Swear to God, if you suggest an experiment or a pause for more research or something, I might die right here."

"No!" He was going to make her say it. Fine. She had no silly inhibitions about what was essentially a mechanical function. "I meant something more along the lines of coitus."

He blinked. "Oh, my God." He gulped. "That shouldn't be sexy. What is wrong with me?"

It must have been a rhetorical question, because he didn't give her a chance to answer before he released her wrist in favor of folding both strong, lean arms around her back. Before she knew it, the release of her hand was a moot point anyway, because Wes worked some magic on her bra clasp and the offending garment loosened. In fact, at this moment it was only held in place by the pressure of his chest against hers.

Rosemary noticed all of this at a remove, through a haze of heat and rushing blood and firing synapses. His mouth was on hers again, claiming and searching as if the mysteries of the universe were locked behind her teeth. She wasn't one hundred percent certain that they weren't. This kiss was already showing her things she'd never expected. Like the fact that she was desirable. Extremely so, if Wes's labored breathing and intense eyes were anything to go by. Not to mention the fact that she suddenly and irrevocably understood that her body wasn't just a machine intended to shelter the powerhouse of her brain. No, her body had a life of its own, winding around Wes's and rubbing in sharp, jerky, instinctive movements that made both of them gasp.

Wes got the rest of their clothes off, and by this time, Rosemary didn't give a good goddamn where they ended up because she was entirely focused on Wes easing her back to lie against the scratchy material of their jackets, a thin cloth barrier between oversensitive skin and hard lab floor.

His hands swept down her rib cage and back up again, thumbs just grazing the undersides of her breasts. Without meaning to, Rosemary arched her back, pushing herself toward his touch.

"God, you're gorgeous," he said, his voice rough and deeper than she'd ever heard it. "I can't believe how this is between us. Can you? I mean, shit. Why haven't we been doing this for weeks?"

"I don't know," she said. "I can't think. Don't want to think."

"That's a first, I bet. Am I right?" His grin was conspiratorial, mischievous, as if the two of them were in cahoots, sneaking around behind her brain's back.

Rosemary began to entertain serious fears that she was losing it.

"Stop talking and kiss me," she demanded. "Also, quit tickling my ribs and touch me already. I ache."

Fire flashed through Wes's eyes and his fingers closed, with satisfying, electrifying alacrity, around her tingling, swollen breasts.

Rosemary's lungs contracted suddenly, forcing her to suck in air with a noisy gasp. His hands were rough, callused in spots from holding a chef's knife, and felt amazing on her naked skin.

"That's very nice," she breathed, once she reconnected the neural pathways that would allow her to form words. Wes smiled up at her, eyes hot and intent, and then proceeded to steal her cognitive processing function away again by thumbing her nipples in slow, measured circles. The pink buds flushed darker and tightened into knots of near-painful sensitivity, until every flick of his fingers made Rosemary squirm and press herself harder into his hands.

"Oh man," Wes said. "I'm gonna make a meal out of you."

Before she could ask what he meant, he'd dipped his head and put his mouth over her taut, distended nipple. She cried out, awash in sensation, waves of pleasure spiraling out from her breasts to warm her whole body and turn her brain to mush. Wes moved to the other nipple while Rosemary tossed her head, her hair whipping across her face, getting in her mouth and making it hard to breathe.

Or maybe that was Wes, again, because even when his hand reached up to brush the tendrils of hair from her face in a gentle, delicate gesture that felt at odds with the ravenous, insistent pull of his mouth against her breasts, even then—she still couldn't breathe.

And it didn't get any easier as his mobile lips and clever tongue left her chest and wandered down her torso, delving into the shallow bowl of her navel, nipping soft bites into the quivering roundness of her abdomen. When he nuzzled his face into the crease between her left thigh and her hip, Rosemary actually choked and scrabbled at the jackets beneath her, looking for something solid to hold on to in a world gone suddenly bright and sharp-edged with pleasure.

He scraped her soft inner thigh with his beard-roughened cheek, then licked a hot stripe up the gently abraded skin. Rosemary shuddered, her mind gloriously blank until it exploded with light and color the moment he lowered his mouth to her sex. Wes licked her open with slow, smooth passes of his agile tongue, and the sensation blurred and ran together until Rosemary couldn't have parsed out what he was doing to which part of her if she'd been given a labeled diagram of female genitalia.

All she knew was that it felt amazing. *She* felt amazing. She was alive, so alive, shivers racing over her skin, her hands reaching out to grasp his strong shoulders where they propped her thighs apart to give him full access.

Tension pulled her belly tighter than high-tensile wire, and Wes kept pushing her higher and higher until, all at once, it broke over her like an epiphany, like a ground-breaking Nobel-worthy revelation, like the frakking Big Bang—and for the first time in her entire life, Rosemary understood exactly what the huge deal was about sex.

Which, when she took it to the logical conclusion, made her pretty curious about whether it could possibly be better once they got to actual intercourse.

So when Wes knelt up, his hands braced on her

still-quivering, widespread thighs, and said, "Hold that thought, sweetness—I've got a condom in my wallet," Rosemary thought less about the dangers of disease and odds of pregnancy even when using birth control, and more about *yes, please.*

Scrambling for his wallet and the key to the gates of paradise inside, Wes realized he'd lost any hope of playing it cool approximately ten minutes ago.

He glanced over his shoulder at her sprawled form. She looked elegant, somehow, if a little dirty in the best possible way. There was something filthy sexy yet heartbreakingly innocent about the way she relaxed against their white jackets, her fair skin glowing faintly peach and pink, flushed with the aftermath of pleasure.

Wes had to shut his eyes against the image before his hands started to shake and he fumbled the condom. But shit, she was something else. The way she moved under his mouth, all abandoned and unselfconscious. He hadn't expected that. He didn't know what he'd expected, exactly—maybe more commentary, something more clinical and critical. Whatever it was, he hadn't been prepared for the way going down on her felt. It was like licking into an oyster, all liquid brine and satiny smooth against his lips.

Addictive.

And the satisfaction he got out of those amazing sounds she made when he fucked her with his tongue? Unreal. If his cock weren't a bar of solid lust between his legs right now, Wes might be tempted to categorize what they'd already done as the best sex of his life, and call it a night.

His dick thumped a heavy throb of disapproval, and he palmed it casually, the press of his own hand soothing the ache momentarily.

"Got it," he said, turning back to Rosemary with the foil-wrapped pack held up between two fingers.

She blinked up at him and smiled. It was a smile he hadn't seen before, warm and wanting, but it looked good on her. Wes took a moment to savor it, but another pang of desire coiled at the base of his spine and he abruptly needed to be touching, like right fucking now.

"Hey," he said, scooting closer and running his hands up her thighs and over her hips. Because he could. "Did you miss me?"

That got him a raised eyebrow. "You were gone approximately twelve point two seconds, Wes. I coped."

He grinned. "You aren't nearly fucked out enough, Doc, if you can still calculate time to the first decimal place."

She licked her lips in an unconsciously sexy gesture that had Wes grabbing his dick again, this time with the intent of staving off imminent orgasm. "Maybe you should do something about that."

In answer, Wes surged up her body and claimed her mouth. He thrust his tongue in, steady, strong strokes that mimicked what he wanted to be doing with his cock. Rosemary whimpered into the kiss, her body losing some of its lassitude and curling up against him, seeking more pressure, more touch, just more.

Without taking his mouth from hers, Wes fumbled the foil packet open and got the condom out and situated. He had to roll it down quickly to avoid overstimulating himself before he even got near her, but then it was on, and her legs were hooking around his hips and drawing him in, and before Wes knew it, he was gasping out a shocked breath and pressing the first inch of himself inside her.

Rosemary froze, her eyelids fluttering, and her hands clenched hard on his shoulders. Her thighs were rigid against his sides, and Wes gritted his teeth, forcing his body to a standstill. After a moment, though, the tight constriction around the sheathed head of his penis eased. Her thighs loosened and her eyes opened wide to stare up into Wes's face. For once, he was the one who couldn't read what she was thinking, but when her hands urged him closer and she bent her knees behind his ass to press his hips into hers, he at least knew what she wanted.

Careful now, Wes pushed his way in, doing his best to ignore the hot, clinging nirvana of her body in favor of watching the play of emotion across her face. He caught surprise, and heat, and impatience, and then more surprise mixed with pleasure when, about halfway in, he suddenly lost the battle with his body and surged the rest of the way in one swift stroke.

"Oh," she cried, tilting her head back. "Oh, more of that."

Wes agreed wholeheartedly, and his hips were way ahead of both of them, snapping forward and back in sharp thrusts that sent him deep. She gave so sweetly around him, her body in constant, welcoming motion as they surged together. The slick, sweaty slide of their hot, straining bodies pushed the jackets aside until his knees were on the cold laboratory floor. She arched away from the cold at her back and Wes hauled her up to straddle his lap, one hand under her pretty, round ass, working her against him. Dipping his head, he kissed her again, and that second point of intimate contact, the wet, hungry glide of her tongue against his as her internal muscles constricted mercilessly as she shattered for the second time in his arms—it all combined in a rush of pleasure and physical joy so great, Wes shouted as he came.

Chapter 10

Everything in Rosemary's body felt wrung out and limp. She knew, intellectually, that she'd just experienced one of the most explosive internal upheavals the human body was designed to accommodate—but somehow she felt more drained than muscle contractions, increased blood flow, and postorgasmic levels of neurohormones in her brain could account for.

"You okay?" Wes asked, his voice shredded and raw. He was holding her gently now, his face pressed into the side of her neck, and Rosemary wrapped her arms around his head, feeling strangely protective.

"I'm wonderful," she told him. "Everything about that experience surpassed my expectations."

"Seriously? Wow, I was expecting an itemized critique of my performance, or something. A procedural checklist with items ticked off—stimulate clitoris, check. Provide oral pleasure, check. Last longer than a pathetic ten minutes—oh wait. Whoops! Not so much."

"Are you saying it wasn't good?" Rosemary demanded, amazed that there might be some objective measure of sexual intercourse that could give anyone the impression that what she and Wes had just done was less than amazing.

"No! That's not what I'm saying at all." Wes lifted his head to meet her stare. Positioned as they were, with Rosemary wrapped around him like a koala clinging to a tree, his move put their faces less than an inch apart. When he licked his lips, Rosemary could almost taste the echo of their last kiss.

Distracted, she said, "Then what did you mean?"

"Honestly?" He huffed out a laugh. "It was too good. I mean, I felt like a kid, out of control, everything taking me by surprise—I don't know what it was about you, Doc, but you turned me into a fumbling virgin!"

Rosemary felt tension begin to seep back into her limbs. "I wasn't aware that virginity was a contagious condition," she said. "My apologies."

Wes jerked back, eyes wide. "Wait. What? That was your first time?"

She nodded.

He stared. "As in, ever?"

Rosemary dropped her arms from his shoulders, uncomfortable and embarrassed. For the first time tonight, she wished she had a robe or something to cover up her naked body. "It's not actually a disease," she pointed out. "I was being sarcastic. For effect."

"No, I know that," Wes said, clutching at her arms as she attempted to extricate herself. "Hold on, let me—"

Holding on to the bottom of the condom, he pulled out of her carefully, the motion causing an unwelcome aftershock of pleasure. The tender, swollen nerve endings around her entrance burned a bit, but it was nothing compared to the sting of humiliation in her cheeks.

Wes's hands were as gentle as if he were handling volatile chemicals when he laid her back against their ersatz blanket of tangled, discarded jackets before getting up to dispose of the condom in the trash can by the door. Rosemary took the opportunity to shrug on her lab coat as he turned back to her. She held it closed over her breasts and lifted her chin to meet his gaze calmly.

"Fuck," he breathed, his mouth turning down into an unhappy curve. "This is coming out all wrong."

"I think you're being very clear," Rosemary said, the chill from the floor leaching up into her bare thighs and making her shiver.

"I'm not, I promise you," Wes said. He grabbed his jeans from the pile of clothing and pulled them up his lean hips, not bothering to faster them up properly. "I don't even know what I'm saying. I'm just so surprised. Why didn't you tell me beforehand, Doc?"

She shrugged, wanting to get up and put her clothes back on but still embarrassingly uncertain if her legs would hold her. "It didn't seem pertinent."

He shook his head. "Not pertinent? Oh man. It was way pertinent. I would've done things completely differently."

"Well, I wouldn't," Rosemary said, compelled to honesty.

"Your first time shouldn't have been here, on the floor in a lab," Wes said, gesticulating in a wide circle that encompassed her beloved refuge from the world outside. "It should've been in a bed, with the lights low and some kind of fruity music with violins, or something. There should've been champagne and chocolate truffles and . . ."

He broke off, glancing away, flags of color flying high on his cheekbones.

"And what?" Rosemary asked, her curiosity as insatiable as ever.

"And . . . it should've been with somebody wonderful, a great guy who'd take things slow and make it all safe and good."

He looked down, his brown hair falling over his forehead in sweaty, disordered spikes and tufts that made her fingers itch to push it back, and something in the slump of his shoulders gave Rosemary a sudden insight into what might be going on.

She inched closer to him. "I had chocolate-dipped strawberries," she reminded him. "And the security floodlights outside the window gave everything a very nice, muted glow. There was no music, but I'm not a big fan of classical stringed instruments, anyway. I prefer David Bowie."

Ducking her head a bit, she peeked past his hair to catch the glimmer of a half smile quirking up one side of his mouth. "Yeah? Bowie, huh?"

"Yes," she confirmed, scooting nearer until she could put her hand on his cheek and raise his head. Locking her gaze with his, she screwed up her courage to the sticking point and said, "I also prefer my lab to just about any bedroom I've ever occupied. And as for the last part—you described it perfectly."

"What do you mean?" His eyes clouded, the hazel eyes troubled.

"Somebody wonderful," she whispered. "A great guy who'd take things slow and make it all safe and good. That's exactly what I had, Wes. I wouldn't change a single variable. I'd be too terrified that might alter the outcome, and I like where I am right this very second too much to risk it."

Something flashed across his face and Rosemary would've given a year's worth of research to know what he was thinking.

"Me, too," was all he said, and he followed it up with a kiss and an enfolding embrace that banished the chill from Rosemary's bones.

They got dressed in companionable silence; a little

awkward, certainly, but tinged with a giddy sort of anticipation that reminded Rosemary of the feeling she got
when she was on the brink of a breakthrough in an experiment.

He walked her back to her building, a housing facility
for faculty that was more like a row of condos than a dor-
mitory, on the edge of campus. With a quick look around
to ensure the coast was clear of students wandering home
from the next-door recreation center, patrolling security
guards, or marauding academy presidents, Wes pressed
her back against the door of her apartment and delivered
a scorching good-night kiss.

Rosemary kissed him back, her spine melting into the
door. What happened next?

"Do you . . . would you want to come up for a while?"
she asked. *Curses.* Did one never grow out of this terrible,
painful social discomfort? She'd thought herself over it
long ago, but evidently not.

Wes didn't seem to notice. He let his body rub against
hers, his weight keeping her deliciously trapped, and
pulled back just enough to catch her gaze.

"You have no idea how much I'd love to, Doc. But I've
got Lucille; she's been shut up in my dorm all afternoon.
Gotta let my baby out to do her thing. I could come over
after, though. If you want."

The rush of disappointment cleared Rosemary's head.
"No," she decided. "That would be impractical. It's late
now, and we both have work to do tomorrow. There are
some avenues of inquiry I'd like to pursue on the aphrodisiac project."

"Oh ho," he crowed, leaning his hands against the door
on either side of her head, so there was breathing room
between their bodies, but Rosemary still felt surrounded
by him. "So you admit there's something to inquire about,
huh?"

"Maybe," she said repressively. "Perhaps. We won't know until we test my theories."

"Mmm," he hummed, dipping his head to nuzzle into her neck. "I've got a few theories I'd like to test, myself."

"Stop it," she said, in spite of the full-body shudder the touch of his mouth induced. "From now on, the lab will have to be off-limits for . . . for—" She didn't even know what to call what they were doing.

"Shenanigans?" he supplied. "Sexual escapades?"

"Intercourse," she said firmly.

"God." Wes moaned. "Are you trying to torture me?"

"I'm merely attempting to apply the correct label to the situation. Any pain you feel is merely a negative externality."

"You're going to kill me dead," he told her. "Talking like that, then sending me away? Heartless."

"I invited you up," she cried, smacking his chest. "You're the one putting your dog's needs ahead of your libido. Which, I suppose, could be considered admirable."

"Even grumbling is cute on you," he said, landing one last kiss against her temple before stepping back.

Despite the seasonably warm temperatures, Rosemary felt cold the instant his arms dropped away.

"Good night, then," she said, suddenly feeling ridiculously shy. She turned to fit her key to the lock.

" 'Night, Doc. It's been . . . well, like nothing I ever had before. I'll see you tomorrow."

The intensity in his voice had Rosemary's fingers clenching around her house key. She whirled to get a look at his face, to try and figure out what he meant by that cryptic statement, but he was already walking away.

She stood there watching the lean line of his back and shoulders, listening to the crunch of his shoes against the gravel pathway, and felt something unfamiliar trying to take hold in her chest.

It lodged there, just under her breastbone, as she went about her nightly routine. She climbed into bed, her mind filled with images from the evening, along with a healthy dose of satisfaction at not being a virgin any longer. Not that sex with Wes Murphy felt like ticking something off her to-do list, but there was an element of personal accomplishment to it. A milestone passed, an important rite of passage observed.

Better late than never, she supposed. And really, she was glad she'd waited.

Despite the physical exhaustion of her body, and the way her muscles felt well used and pleasantly sore, Rosemary had a difficult time falling asleep. It was that strange feeling in her chest that distracted her and kept her awake; it felt as if someone had attached electrodes beneath her skin, buzzy and almost painful, but shockingly stimulating, too.

As she relived each thrilling moment of mind-blanking pleasure with Wes, everything inside Rosemary lit up like the filaments inside a light bulb. What was this? It felt very similar to the accounts she'd read of the chemical reactions to ingesting mind-altering drugs.

Could this be . . . happiness?

With that troubling yet exhilarating thought, Rosemary finally tumbled into a fitful slumber.

Sometime during the night, however, she must have attained full REM sleep of the deepest, heaviest type, because when she finally blinked awake in the light of the sun streaming in through the slats of her blinds, she wasn't alone.

A small, white-furred canine face was approximately two centimeters from Rosemary's nose.

"Oh!" she gasped, freezing to her sheets.

Seeing that she was awake, Lucille gave a pleased yip

and pushed her cold, wet nose into Rosemary's cheek. Her front paws were planted on Rosemary's chest, two small points of pressure bearing down with what felt like more than Lucille's twelve- to fourteen-pound weight.

"Ew, get off," Rosemary said, struggling for breath. Because of the dog's paws, she told herself, not because the fact that Lucille was in her apartment meant that her devoted owner probably was, too.

"Wes?" she called, her voice tentative. "Did I forget to lock the door last night? Hello?"

The only answer was another snuffling nudge of Lucille's nose, this one followed by a dainty taste of Rosemary's chin.

"Ugh! I am not a chew toy." Sitting up dislodged her bed partner, but Rosemary's attention was all for the bit of paper that crackled under Lucille's scrabbling paws. Rescuing it from potential destruction, Rosemary unfolded it with shaking hands.

> *Hey Doc,*
> *Something came up—an opportunity too good to miss. I've got a shot at my dream job, so I'm off to New York City. Take care of my baby for me, will you? Cornell already thinks she's yours, and I won't have much time for walks in the park once I start my externship. Besides, she likes you.*
> *Yours,*
> *Wes*

Rosemary fell back against her pillows.

Lifting the piece of paper, she read it again, even though the words were already etched into her memory.

He was gone. After last night, after the tentative steps she'd made toward being normal, like other people, letting

someone get close—and it hadn't meant more to him than
a momentary diversion, easily forgotten in the clear light
of reality.

She ranked, once again, a distant second behind someone's career prospects. It should've been a worn, comfort-
ably familiar pain after growing up in a big house staffed
by tutors and nannies, but it wasn't. It was new and horrible, like a vacuum pump attached to her chest, sucking all
the light and energy from her until all that was left were the
hollowed-out, skeletal remains of her rib cage. She probed
the left side of her chest with cold fingers. Was her heart
still in there, at least?

It thudded weakly, sluggish and slow, but there. Good,
then. She'd just . . . get up. And get dressed. And go to the
lab . . . *oh frak, the lab, where we—no! Pull it together,
Wilkins,* she lectured herself, working to control her
breathing.

But the images from the night before, the memory of
Wes above her, against her, inside her—the terrifying,
wonderful intimacy of it all—had her light-headed in moments, air whistling in her lungs.

Two astonishingly heavy paws landed back on her
chest, compressing it further. Lucille's bright black eyes
blinked down at Rosemary, who shuddered and sucked
vainly for air.

Lucille barked once, sharply, then sandpapered her
tongue across Rosemary's cheek.

Rosemary jolted, tugged out of her head and back into
her body. Lucille butted her in the jaw with the top of her
wiry little head, and Rosemary shocked herself by sobbing out loud.

She reached for the dog, who gamely allowed her to
tuck the smaller body against her empty chest and curl in
a ball. The wiggling weight was an unexpected comfort;

even her doggie smell, warm and alive, made Rosemary feel better.

Lucille made a low, rumbling noise, and Rosemary scratched behind her silk ears. "I know. He left you, too. But we don't need him, do we? No. Of course not. I've never needed anyone, and I'm not about to start now. We'll be fine, just you and me."

Lucille whimpered a little.

Rosemary squeezed her eyes shut. She didn't believe it, either.

Chapter 11

Five months later

Every muscle in Wes's body twinged with the kind of bone-deep ache that came from hours of standing hunched over a cutting board in the fiery pit of hell also known as a professional restaurant kitchen.

He eased down on the bar stool next to Jess, moving all slow and careful like an old guy, his joints so used to tension and stress that the sudden relaxation was almost more painful than staying on his feet.

It was just the two of them, for the moment—the rest of the kitchen crew was still clearing down their work stations; the servers were all down in the locker room changing into street clothes.

Wes shot his friend a sideways glance. They hadn't had time to talk after Wes spilled his tale of woe and tragedy—pretty much the second he was done, the line cooks all trooped back in, loud and obnoxious and lively as ever. Jess had pressed a hand to his shoulder with what looked like a sympathetic grimace, and hurried out front to do his impression of Best Waiter Ever.

"So," Wes said.

"Yeah," Jess replied. "One question."

Wes fought to keep his voice even and light. "Shoot."

Jess skewered him with a look. "Why the hell did you leave her?"

And there it was. The question Wes asked himself every day. He answered Jess with the same words he repeated to himself: "I had to. It was the best thing. For her."

That pissed Jess off a little, Wes could tell by the red spots that appeared on his pale cheeks.

"And you get to decide that, do you?" he spat with all the venom of someone who'd recently been dumped "for his own good."

Wes clamped his jaw. "In this case, yeah. Look, we got caught, okay? And I thought I talked our way out of it, but I was wrong. Cornell thought it over, and decided he liked his chances of keeping everything under wraps better if he broke us up. He wanted to keep his star scientist, the one the donors were so excited about, but me? The definition of disposable. And he found the perfect leverage, too."

Gut churning, Wes recalled the scene. He'd just gotten back to his tiny apartment off campus and gotten Lucille settled for the night when there was a knock at the door. Cornell. Calmer, more rational—and therefore, more dangerous. He'd offered Wes a very simple choice.

"He was willing to keep our relationship quiet, and let Rosemary stay at the academy, on one condition. I'd leave to take over the externship at Market, and not contact her again. He made it pretty damn clear that he'd weighed the risks, and without the assurance of it being over between Rosemary and me, he wasn't willing to take the chance of a scandal. Basically, I could stay and let him ruin Rosemary's reputation, or I could make a quiet exit stage left. And, incidentally, walk into the opportunity of a lifetime, working at one of the hottest restaurants in Manhattan." Wes shrugged. "It didn't take a genius to figure that one out."

And man, offering that externship to Wes had been a stroke of brilliance on Cornell's part. It shored up his own plausible deniability—why would he give such a plum position to a student who'd misbehaved? And, incidentally, it made it next to impossible for Wes to ever convince Rosemary that he'd left her for any reason other than to advance his career.

Wes had known, the instant he made his deal with the devil, that he'd never be able to take it back.

Jess frowned. "So you left. Without even talking to her first."

"I couldn't—if I'd explained what was going on, she might've felt obligated to quit, or tell Cornell where to shove it, or something. I couldn't put her in that kind of position. You have to understand how important her research is to her."

"More important than you?" Jess asked quietly.

Wes started to laugh until he caught the solemn look on his friend's face. "Wait, you're serious? Yeah, man, the research is way more important to her than I ever was." He held up a hand and continued over Jess's immediate objections. "And she's right."

Whenever Wes questioned whether or not he'd done the right thing, all he had to do was remember the way Rosemary's whole face brightened when she talked about her experiments, the way she seemed to come alive in the lab. There was no way he could take that away from her.

What could he give her to replace it, after all? One ex-con man, slightly used, maybe a fixer-upper if you squinted? He'd already given her his best friend.

"Hey," he said, remembering. "I left my dog with her, to keep her company. That counts for something, right?" It ought to; he missed that silly little animal like crazy.

Jess threw up his hands. "I'm surrounded by idiot men who think they're no good for anyone!"

Wes found himself grinning. He'd been around Jess Wake long enough to know that when he got melodramatic and flaily like that, it meant he wasn't really mad. They were still buds.

And after all these months of doubts, regrets, and recriminations—through Wes's first, surreal days at Market, the drama of Chef Temple's romance with Jess's sister, and the trauma of working under the slightly schizo celebrity chef Devon Sparks while Chef Temple and Miranda Wake were off on their non-honeymoon—looking back on his decision now, Wes still thought he'd done the right thing by leaving.

No matter how much it hurt.

He probed his rib cage thoughtfully. He couldn't be sure, but maybe the ever-present ache in his chest had lessened slightly, just from having talked about it. Huh.

Slowly, a few of the other chefs and servers trickled into the bar area to collapse onto stools, all moving like Wes had, as if their bones were made of glass.

"Hurts," huffed Quentin, the tallest, quietest dude Wes had ever met. It wasn't a question—Quentin didn't do questions, for some reason no one seemed to know or want to explain to the new guy—but Wes nodded anyway. Light from behind the bar glinted darkly off his bald, sweaty head when Quentin nodded back.

"Feels good, though, too. In a weird way," Wes said.

He looked at the other chefs and front-of-the-house folks slouched in boneless, postbattle sprawls around the bar of their restaurant, Market. None of them looked like they thought he was nuts.

Well, sure. If it didn't feel kind of awesome to be this tired, this played out after a hectic dinner service, they wouldn't keep doing it. But there they all were.

Wes looked around the U-shaped bar between Market's two dining rooms. Usually populated by Market's trendy, smartly attired customers, the bar made a strangely classy, sophisticated background for the sweaty, wild-haired cooks and harried waiters slumped together in exhausted silence.

It had been a brutal service. The kitchen got weeded twice, but their *capitán,* executive chef and owner of the restaurant, Adam Temple, kept them at it until they pulled themselves clear.

Wes had thrown himself into it, head down, focused and intent, even if all he really did was scut work. As the resident culinary student extern, aka escapee from the Academy of Culinary Arts, aka kitchen bitch, Wes got all the shit jobs no one else wanted to tackle.

He didn't even care. It was real work, worthwhile, and besides, the harder he worked, the more it kept his mind off . . . things. Things he had no business thinking about anymore.

"You girls planning to sit here all night, or come down to Chapel for the festivities?"

The low Cockney drawl of sous chef Frankie Boyd had Wes instinctively struggling to sit up straighter in his chair.

Beside him, Jess flinched hard at the sound of his ex's voice, just once, before settling deliberately back into a slouch.

Most nights saw nearly the whole gang of them trooping downtown to their favorite Lower East Side dive bar, but as Wes looked around at the tired faces of the other cooks, he thought maybe Frankie was on his own in the wild afterparty department.

Apparently, Frankie saw the same thing because he said, with an audible sneer, "Fine, then. Adam's off home to his girl, so I'm for Chapel all on my lonely—though maybe not alone for long. Don't wait up, darlings."

Wes shot Jess a look, but the young man's face was set in a stubbornly blank expression.

"Aw, Frankie, don't go," said Violet Porter, sleepy and round-cheeked. As pastry chef, she'd normally have been long gone by this time of night, but Violet was a trouper. When the kitchen got slammed, she stuck around and helped out. "Come play the game with us."

"What game?" Wes asked.

Frankie wandered over to lean negligently against the opposite side of the bar. Wes had been right—he was sneering harder than Billy Idol singing about dancing with himself. "The game, you berk," Frankie said. "The one all chefs play."

Shrugging, Wes glanced at Jess, who reluctantly supplied, "It's called 'Last Meal.' "

"Yeah," Violet put in, her eyes brightening. "If you were on death row, scheduled for the chair or whatever tomorrow—what would you ask for as your last meal on earth?"

"Kind of morbid." Wes wasn't shocked or anything—he didn't shock all that easily, and he already knew chefs were a messed-up bunch, as a rule—but he'd brushed close enough to prison once upon a time that the idea of death row sent a chill straight down his spine.

"That's the point." Billy Perez, the quiet young Latino guy who worked on the fish station, looked up from his intense contemplation of his hands. He had burn scars notched up and down his fingers and arms, like the other cooks around the table.

Wes was starting to accumulate his own collection. He was weirdly proud of it.

"Right," Frankie put in, his eyes on Jess. "There's nothing like the threat of losing everything to focus a man's mind on what really matters."

Jess's head came up at that, anger brightening his blue eyes. "So what's your last meal, Frankie?" he asked, his voice harsher than Wes had ever heard it.

"What, you haven't heard?" Frankie smiled and pushed away from the bar, doing a funny little bow. "I'm never going to grow up, so I'm never going to die. I'm the punk-rock Peter Pan, me."

Over the chorus of groans and catcalls, Frankie said, "Chapel awaits. You girls have fun braiding each other's hair, now."

The other chefs and servers didn't let Frankie's defection keep them from playing. Violet got the ball rolling—her last meal choice was her mom's rhubarb pie. Quentin wanted fried green tomatoes—"Comfort food, man"—the bartender, Christian Colby, picked homemade tagliatelle in Bolognese sauce. Billy Perez chose Chef Temple's duck confit cassoulet with a shrug.

"What? I like the way we make it here."

Wes nudged his friend in the ribs, breaking Jess out of the semiparalysis Frankie always seemed to induce in the young waiter. "What would you have?"

Jess sighed. "I don't know. If we're going with comfort food from childhood, I feel like all I ate growing up was frozen pizza. Kind of lame. What about you?"

Wes was about to toss out some quick response, something easy and facile that would hide who he really was out of sheer force of habit. But glancing up at the group of people around the bar, his coworkers—his friends—Wes felt a powerful blast of belonging, as if he'd finally come home. The sensation was unfamiliar enough that for a long moment, he almost didn't recognize it.

When he did pin it down, finally, he had to swallow back a totally idiotic surge of emotion. But it was unreal to find this here, after so long. And it made him remember exactly how not at home he'd felt back at the academy.

Most of the time there, at least.

Which, of course, brought to mind that thing he wasn't supposed to think about.

Or, more specifically, that person.

Rosemary.

Longing swept over Wes in an unexpected rush, replacing his physical aches and pains with the much more insidious hollowness in his chest. Before he could think twice about the vulnerability of sharing even this much, Wes said, "I'd have strawberries dipped in chocolate."

His voice was cracked and rough enough that everyone at the bar noticed, but Wes refused to duck his head. "And it's a fantasy, right? I can have whatever I want?"

"Sure," Jess said, gentle understanding pulling his mouth up at the corners.

Wes smiled, even though he was pretty sure it was the saddest specimen ever. "Then I want the strawberries served by a gorgeous blonde in a *Star Wars* T-shirt."

Before anyone could question him about that idiosyncratic little detail, Chef Adam Temple and his right-hand man and Market's manager, Grant Holloway, slammed out of the kitchen in the midst of a full-blown Boss Throwdown.

"But we've talked about expanding—maybe this is a sign!" Grant argued, his boyish face red and a little wild.

Adam snorted, curly dark hair sticking up as if he'd been gripping it in frustration. "Sure. A sign that no one on the Upper West Side is into Latin Cajun fusion mumbo jumbo."

"Come on, at least let me find out what the rent is."

"It's the building next door. It's going to be the same as ours."

"You don't know that."

"It's a waste of time."

"Is not."

"Is too!"

A rustle of bills distracted Wes from the epic battle, and he looked over in time to see Violet Porter taking bets on who'd win. The cooks were loyally sticking to Chef Adam's side, but the servers looked pretty confident in their odds.

Only the bartender, Christian, shook his head at getting in on the action. He was watching Adam and Grant arguing with a frown. As if he felt the weight of Christian's gaze, Grant glanced at the bar and stiffened immediately.

"We can finish this discussion later," he said, with as much dignity as possible through a clenched jaw.

"Fine. I'm dead on my feet anyway. Hey, good service tonight, guys," Adam said, turning to the assembled line cooks draped around the bar. "We pulled it out, we fought hard, and every one of you came through for me. I'm a proud papa. Now go home and get some rest, or go blow off steam someplace else."

Christian nodded and started locking down the bar, and the cooks and servers hauled themselves up and started sorting their shit out to leave, amid quite a bit of moaning and complaining.

Wes felt like he'd been beaten all over with a wooden soup ladle. This probably wasn't the best time to corner his boss.

The bitch of it was, though, he didn't think he'd be able to get a wink of sleep unless he got this conversation over with. He steeled himself.

"Hey, Chef? You got a couple minutes?"

Adam paused in the act of shrugging on his coat, his gaze immediately intent on Wes, who tried not to shift or toe the floor like a shy kid or something. "You bet."

"Good luck," Jess whispered out of the corner of his mouth as he grabbed his backpack off the bar. "I'll be up late doing homework tonight; text me later and let me know how it goes."

Wes nodded and waved him off, swallowing down an

unwelcome flock of nervous butterflies. Adam Temple was, quite simply, the coolest boss in the world. He was a kick-ass chef, a great leader in the kitchen, and he'd made Wes feel welcome and accepted right from the start.

Somehow, none of that made it any easier to talk to him about this.

Once the dining rooms had cleared out, Adam flopped onto the barstool next to Wes.

"So. What's up with Grant?" Wes was aware he was stalling, but decided he was fine with it.

"Oh man. I love the guy, and he's got mad skills when it comes to running the front of the house, but when he gets an idea into his head it's like the rest of his brain goes out the window. You know the restaurant next door?"

"That weird Cajun place that's always empty?"

"That's the one." Adam nodded. "Anyway, they shuttered yesterday. Heard it from their meat supplier, who's pissed because they owe him money. Grant wants to look into what it would take to expand Market into the available space."

"Makes sense. I mean, Jess keeps talking about how slammed the bar gets with walk-ins and people waiting for tables."

"We could maybe use some more space," Adam conceded, "but things are tough out there right now. And I just got finished buying out our last investor, which rocks—but doesn't leave us with a ton of extra money lying around."

Wes sat on his hands to keep from fidgeting. "So . . . does that mean you don't have the money to hire another line cook?"

Adam's head whipped around. "Let me guess. You don't want to go back to the academy."

"I can't go back." Wes winced the moment the words were out of his mouth. "Wow. That sounded less melodramatic in my head."

Adam didn't question him, because he was the coolest boss ever. But he also didn't look terribly happy; his face got serious and pinched in a way Wes didn't think he'd ever seen before.

"Look, man. I would love to hire you on—I'm planning on it, in fact—but I've gotta be honest. I was counting on having the extra time while you went back and finished up at the ACA to make a spot for you. You're saving our ass right now, when it comes right down to it, doing the kind of work you're doing for nothing. I feel like a shit half the time, like I'm taking advantage of you, because you're a damned good cook. And God knows, I'm dreading the day you leave—but I can't afford to keep you on full-time right now."

Disappointment was a hard lump in Wes's throat, too big to swallow. *Can't go back, can't face it, can't face her. If I see her again, I'll mess everything up, and she deserves better than that.*

"I've got some savings. What if . . . what if I stayed on for free? For the experience? Like a stage," Wes said, referring to the ancient practice of a young chef apprenticing himself in a successful chef's kitchen.

Adam leaned back in his chair. "I'm not going to lie, that would rock for me. But for you—Wes, man, are you sure you wouldn't rather stage someplace else? In Paris maybe, in some famous kitchen that would look good on your résumé. I could probably help you out with that; I've got some connections. And Devon Sparks, he spoke highly of you after his stint running the kitchen here. That dude knows everyone worth knowing."

The lump in Wes's throat wasn't getting any smaller, but now his head was whirling with possibilities. "That's . . . shit, I don't even know what to say. That's an amazing offer, Chef. I appreciate it more than I can tell you—but if it were up to me, if you didn't mind, I'd stay right where I am."

Until he said it, he wasn't sure that was how he felt. But the moment the words were out of his mouth, a feeling of rightness took over his whole body, and he knew.

"Are you sure?" Adam wanted to know, his eyes keen on Wes's face.

Wes looked up at the ceiling and tried to get his spinning thoughts to settle down. "Hey, I know it would probably be good for my career to stage with some Michelin-starred, cheese-munching Frog, but despite how much I love foie gras, I've never been a huge fan of the French."

Adam smiled but still looked skeptical, so Wes dug deep and gave him a portion of truth. "Maybe Market doesn't have a Michelin star yet, but you guys are building something here. Something amazing, and I want to be part of that. Plus . . ." Wes blew out a breath and got his voice under control before it could wobble. "I'm not ready to move on yet," he said.

And there it was. That was as close as he could get to admitting the whole truth—that working at Market felt like his last link to Rosemary. He'd left her and whatever it was they'd built between them to come here; he'd be damned if he left before wringing every last drop of goodness he could out of that shitty, fucked-up situation.

He couldn't go back to the academy and pretend not to care about her. Cornell would be all over them, and all this heartache would've been for nothing. Chances were, he'd never see her again. The thought sliced through him with a sudden, vicious thrust. And even the wide, welcoming smile on Adam's face and the clasp of his hand as he welcomed Wes aboard couldn't quite mask the pain of it.

But Wes had learned early on that life wasn't fair, and things didn't happen just because you wished for them.

You got nothing but bones to work with? It was up to you to make soup out of them.

Adapt and regroup, boy, Pops used to say. *No point wasting time and energy on what can't be changed.*

Good advice. Of course, Pops would no doubt have pushed Wes to work Adam over for whatever connections and favors he could get out of him, then leave him in the dust without a backward glance.

But Wes didn't have to be like that. He could choose his own way. And if he chose to stay at Market because he liked the people there—because he liked who he was when he was with them—that was fine.

Maybe he'd never see Rosemary again, but that didn't mean he should stop trying to be the kind of man a woman like her deserved.

Chapter 12

One week later, and Wes was finally starting to settle into the knowledge that his time at Market was extended indefinitely. He didn't have to bail on his buddies on the line in the kitchen; he didn't have to leave the life he'd worked hard to scratch out for himself.

And, most importantly, he didn't have to test his own admittedly weak resolve by seeing Dr. Rosemary Wilkins again.

It wasn't permanent, and there was always a sense in the back of his head that maybe, if he messed anything up or didn't deliver, he'd be out on his ass in the cold. But all he could do was make himself as indispensible as possible so that when things picked up, Adam would have no choice but to hire him full-time.

And until then, life was pretty damn good. He'd been promoted up the line to garde-manger, the cold appetizers and salads station; he hung out with Jess Wake and his other friends from the restaurant at their favorite after-hours hangout bar, Chapel; then he stumbled a few short blocks to his tiny one-room studio apartment in a fifth-floor walkup in Chinatown and fell into bed—or futon, as the case might be—just as the sun was rising.

If, nine nights out of ten, his dreams were invaded by a certain petite blond chemist, no one had to know about it.

Wes pounded up the stairs of the Seventy-ninth Street subway station, thankful once again to escape business commuter hell, packed trains hurtling down to the Financial District, each car bulging with office drones choking in ties and suits, hauling around brief-cases and laptops.

He was a salmon swimming upstream, the one lone guy in jeans and a battered leather jacket, with a nylon messenger bag holding his roll of knives against his hip.

It was good to be a chef.

He grinned into the bright blue of the sky, that amazing September sky that reminded him of the bluest eyes he'd ever seen, except he wasn't thinking about that, so he dropped his gaze to the busy city streets instead.

Cabs blared their horns at pedestrians who were stupid enough to be texting while crossing Broadway. Up and down the street, the jingling metallic ring of shop owners raising the chain-link security gates in front of their doors accented the shouts from construction guys working on a site around the corner. The air smelled like roasted honey and burned butter from an enterprising vendor setting up his cart to sell hot candied nuts on the next block.

Wes soaked it all up, letting the life of the city fill in the cracks inside his head and heart until he felt almost human.

He was ready to cook.

Jess Wake was the only one changing in the locker room when Wes got there. They both liked to arrive early; Wes wanted plenty of time to get his prep work done for his own station—lots of vegetables to peel for garde-manger—and still have time to put something tasty together for family meal. Jess had confessed he came in before his shift officially started because he couldn't stay away, the poor sap.

"You beat me," Wes said, stowing his knife roll on top of the bank of lockers while he unfolded a freshly laundered white chef's coat from his bag. Working clean was one of the precepts drilled into ACA students, and it was one Wes had embraced wholeheartedly. He liked to get to the end of a hectic night's service without a single smear or stain on his rolled-up white sleeves.

It didn't happen often, but a man could dream.

"Yeah," Jess said, his mouth going crooked in that way that meant he wasn't sure if he should grin or frown. "I'm a masochist, I guess."

"Is he here yet?" Wes hadn't seen anybody in the kitchen, but he hadn't checked the back alley where a few of the chefs congregated for a smoke before getting down to work.

Jess's shoulders slumped. "I don't even know. I'm too much of a chickenshit to go looking for him, and what good would it do, anyway? We've both made our positions clear. I love him. He knows it. And I know he loves me back." The fierce light faded from Jess's dark blue eyes. "At least, I thought I knew that. Now I'm not so sure."

Wes felt a pang of kinship. Jess was so fucking gone on Market's Brit punk sous chef. He and Frankie Boyd had been an item for a few months, just long enough for Jess to come out to his sister, get superinvested in the relationship, and get dumped. The poor kid had been pining ever since— not that Frankie was doing much better, as far as Wes could tell.

He didn't get their deal at all; they were stupid in love. Nothing was keeping them apart except some dumb idea that they were better off apart. As someone who knew about pining, Wes found himself frequently struggling with the desire to knock both Jess and Frankie on their stubborn asses.

"Pfft, come on, dog. Frankie's head over nuts for you, anybody can see that."

"It doesn't matter," Jess said, shrugging into his work shirt. "We're over. I know that. I just wish I could get my idiotic heart to believe it."

"I know what you mean," Wes said. "Sometimes it's hard to let go, even if holding on is like gripping the handle of a pan straight out of the oven with both hands."

"You're thinking about her, aren't you?" Jess's look was knowing, but he was smiling again, which helped Wes get past the freakiness of talking about this stuff. He didn't think about it that often, but somehow bringing the topic of sex right out there on the table made him remember, oh yeah, Jess is gay.

But he was Wes's buddy, too, so in the end it wasn't that difficult. "Yeah, I still think about her. But it wasn't going to work. There were reasons we couldn't be together, and those reasons still exist, so I finally had to move on. I'm not going back to the ACA, not going to see her again, and it's done. I'm through torturing myself. You might want to think about that, buddy. It's not like this is the only restaurant in New York City. You could get a job someplace else, someplace where you don't see Frankie every damn day and remember how things used to be. Shit or get off the pot, man."

Jess flinched, his already milk-white cheeks going even paler. Wes immediately felt like an asshole, but before he could apologize, the locker room door swung open and in sauntered Frankie Boyd.

The tall sous chef took in his ex standing half dressed with Wes, and scowled ferociously. Jess put his hands on his slim hips and glared right back, the tension between them filling the air with crackling sparks.

Oh yeah, these two were *so* over. Right. Wes rolled his eyes and finished buttoning up his jacket. He grabbed his knives in a rush and made for the door.

"Like I said," Wes tossed over his shoulder, one hand on the doorknob. "I think it's time for you to stop torturing yourself." He whisked out the door, slammed it shut, and shot the lock home. It was a simple double-cylinder dead-bolt lock with a twist knob; all the doors down here were equipped with them. Wes had no idea why, but he did know that it wouldn't be long before another employee showed up needing to change into uniform.

"Hey!" sounded from inside the room, Frankie's Cockney accent muffled through the thick door. "Did you just—fucking hell, he did! He locked us in."

"Wes!" Bang. "Ooooh, I'm going to kill you when I get out of here." Jess didn't sound happy. The ingrate.

"It's for your own good," Wes called. "Don't worry, someone will be along soon to let you out. If I were you, I'd take advantage of this time to hammer some shit out. But then, if I were you, I'd be locked in there with a gorgeous miniature blond science nerd, not a skinny dude with Sid Vicious hair."

"Oi!"

Wes shrugged. To each his own. "In the meantime, work. It. Out."

"Do not leave us in here! Wes!"

Ignoring his friend's cries, Wes pounded up the stairs to the kitchen whistling a happy tune to drown out the banging from the locker room.

He'd done his good deed for the day. Wonder what his reward would be?

Jess leaned his forehead against the locked door, his entire body clenched in horror.

"Wes?" he croaked. "If you can still hear me, I want you to know you're dead to me now. Just FYI."

"Aw, don't take on so, Bit. Hardly the end of the universe, is it?"

"Don't—" Jess ground his molars, tried to hang on to his composure. "Do not call me that, please."

"What? Bit?" Jess squeezed his eyes shut, wished he could close his ears to the telltale *snick* of Frankie's lighter and the faint hint of smirk in his voice. "Why shouldn't I? You're still a bit of all right, same as you were when I first clapped eyes on you all those many moons ago."

Against his will, the memory shimmered into view in the foreground of Jess's mind. His first sight of Frankie, unbelievably tall and shocking, with his sinewy pale Englishman's arms on full view due to the ripped sleeves of his black T-shirt. The dark outline of the tattoo on his bicep—Patti Smith, godmother of punk, though Jess hadn't recognized her at the time.

Now? He could sketch the figure from memory.

Not that he needed to. Jess had never been all that great at drawing, anyway. Photography was his thing, and he'd practiced on Frankie. A lot.

There was a file on his laptop at home full to the brim with portraits of the man behind him, in various poses from full-on raging punk rocker, on stage with his electric bass at Chapel, to sneaky candid shots of Frankie, shirtless and smoking among the pillows cushioning the floor of his attic apartment, affectionately known as "The Garrett."

It was a good thing he almost never managed to print his stuff out unless it was for school, Jess reflected, the metal door cold against his heated skin. Because at the rate he was going, he'd have worn the edges off every single photo with constant handling.

He couldn't fall asleep at night without clicking through his treasure trove of pictures, snatching what echoes of happiness he could from the images of things he could no longer have.

Would no longer allow himself to have.

Bracing himself against the door, Jess turned to face the man who was stuck in his mind and his heart like the hook of a pop song on endless repeat, stubborn and painful and annoying as hell.

The knowledge of how Frankie's mouth would curl into a sneer if he ever knew Jess had just equated him with a Top 40 hit gave him the strength to straighten up and say, in a somewhat level voice, "I know it goes against the grain, Frankie, but if you wouldn't do your best to make this as difficult as possible, I'd appreciate it."

Frankie's black eyes were dark, glittering opaquely in the dim light of the locker room. "Can't think what you mean, Bi—sorry. Was your mate what locked us in here, not me. And he wants us to work it out. Care to take a stab at what he meant by that?"

Jess shivered at the emphasis Frankie placed on the word "stab," the barest hint of tongue curling over his thin upper lip making Jess have to close his eyes again.

God, he was pathetic.

A rush of displaced air stirred the hair at his temples, a sudden warmth along the front of his body, and Jess opened his eyes to see Frankie mere inches away, that steady dark gaze trained on him like a hypnotist charming a snake. The cigarette smoldered, forgotten, between the long index and middle fingers of Frankie's right hand, which he raised to Jess's cheek in a soft caress.

"Want to tell me again how *hard* this is for you?" Frankie's low voice was pure sex as it slipped into Jess's ears like honeyed poison, but it was the tenderness in his touch against Jess's shivering, starved skin that jolted him out of his trance.

Jess got his palms against the tough meat and bone of

Frankie's shoulders, and shoved. "Cut it out. You had your chance—God knows, I would've given you everything. Anything."

The surprise at Jess's move faded from Frankie's face, to be replaced by something darker, a blend of regret and resignation that made Jess's stomach hurt. "That was the problem, yeah? You would've kept giving, and I would've kept taking, forever and ever, amen. And then what? You'd be happy waiting tables every night of the rest of your life, going down the pub to watch me thrash with the band at the weekend, spending your tips on pints? That's not the life for you, Bit."

Jess shook his head hard, so pissed he couldn't be bothered to get on Frankie's case for using the nickname that still had the power to twist Jess's head all around. "Bullshit! That is such a load of self-serving crap, Frankie. I can't believe you're still . . . God, it's like you haven't heard anything I've said the fifty other times we've had this same, pointless, gut-wrenching conversation!"

There it was—the patented Frankie Boyd sneer. "What? You mean, that you could be with me, work here, and still go to school, do your art and photography clubs, make new friends, all of that shite?"

"Yes! It isn't shite, or shit, or whatever, and you know it! I was doing all of that before we broke up, and since then, nothing has changed."

Frankie started patting his pockets agitatedly, looking for his cigarettes, before realizing he had one already lit in his hand. He took three deep drags around the silk filter, the tip glowing red hot in the gloom, an ember as bright as the anger burning in Jess's belly. He wanted to look away, but he couldn't.

Every time. The same damn arguments every time. They couldn't be together because Frankie wanted him to have some mythical "real college experience," grow up and go to classes and become a real boy. As if hanging out with guys his own age would magically make Jess normal, make him fit in, when it never had before.

He had friends at school, sure—kids he ate lunch with and walked to the photo lab with, studied with and joked with around the dorms. But the only place he'd ever truly fit? Was in Frankie's arms.

Frankie, who'd loved him back. Just not enough.

"Of course nothing's changed," Frankie scoffed, his voice roughened with smoke. "You're still here, aren't you? Spending all your free time working at Market, instead of out gallivanting and making mischief like you should be doing."

The pang caught Jess squarely in the chest, making it hard to breathe. "Are you saying you want me to quit?"

Frankie studied the stub of cigarette still pinched between his fingers, then dropped it to the cracked linoleum floor to smolder sullenly. "Once you get away from here, you'll see just how much world there is out there. There's a lot more to life than Market and me, Bit."

Pain like Jess hadn't experienced in weeks welled fresh and bright from the wound Frankie inflicted so casually.

He wants me to go. He wants to stop seeing me every day, anymore, maybe ever. He wants to stop being reminded of what we had, what he threw away.

And what Jess wanted? Mattered as much as it ever did, which was not at all.

Reeling, hurting, Jess lashed out with unerring precision and slashed into Frankie exactly where he knew it would bleed the heaviest.

"Oh, believe me, I know. Just ask Kevin Howard."

Frankie froze, one combat-booted foot raised to stamp out the cigarette. "Who the buggering hell is Kevin Howard?"

Jess shrugged, adrenaline making the movement jerky.

"Guy from my photography club. We went out last weekend, after I got off work."

Frankie's eyes widened, and Jess could practically see him casting his mind back, trying to remember if he'd seen Jess at Chapel, the usual after-work hangout for all the Market staff. "You . . . went out. After work. With some guy."

"He's not just some guy," Jess said deliberately, even though, if he were honest, that was exactly how he'd described Kevin to his sister when she asked about the date. "He's someone I know from school. A photography student, like me. He's taller, though. Dark hair." He laughed, and the sound actually hurt as it pushed out of his throat. "Guess I have a type."

Frankie's foot fell to the floor as if he were a puppet whose strings had been snipped. He dropped to one of the benches in front of the lockers, his face blank.

"Come on," Jess said, sharp and snide. Every word like broken glass in his mouth and he welcomed it, wanted to slash at Frankie and make him bleed. "Don't tell me you're upset. This is what you wanted, right? You cut me loose so I could go out and be normal. Well, normal gay guys go clubbing, it turns out. We dance, we let strangers buy us drinks, and sometimes, we find someone who's looking for the same thing we are—and we fuck."

Frankie flinched as if Jess had actually spat a razor blade at him, and for an instant, Jess almost backed down and told him the truth, that nothing had happened. Because Jess knew himself well enough to know that casual sex in some skeevy club was never going to make him happy.

But then Frankie said, as toneless and calm as if they were discussing the weather, "Right. Sounds like a good time was had by all," and rage exploded in Jess's chest.

Bile pushing up the back of his throat in a stinging rush, Jess said, "Did you hear me? I had sex with him. Kevin.

Are you going to sit there and tell me that's what you wanted?"

Please. Please tell me you know that's a lie. Tell me you never wanted it to come to this.

"Wanted you to be happy, Jess."

For some reason, it was the fact that Frankie used his given name that broke Jess. "Fuck," he sobbed, hating himself, hating both of them. "I can't do this."

Turning back to the door, he pounded the side of his fist against the metal, uncaring of the bruise already purpling on his stupid, fragile skin. "Is anybody out there? Come on, open up! Open—"

The lock clicked over just before the hinges screamed a protest. Grant stood on the other side of the door, confusion and concern giving his handsome, boyish face a quizzical look.

"Are y'all okay in here? Why was the door locked?"

"Ask Wes Murphy," Jess growled, shoving past his immediate supervisor. "If you find him before I kill him, that is."

Chapter 13

The orders came in fast and hard, Chef calling them out in a loud, clear voice from the pass.

It was the height of dinner rush, and the heat of battle was on. Wes was working garde-manger, which meant if a table ordered salads or appetizers, he pretty much set the pace for the entire ticket.

"On order, a four-top, one endive, two dumpling, one tower; one pork, one trout, two lamb, one well, one regular."

He added the new orders to the list in his head, his hands automatically reaching for what he needed to get the plates going. The endive salad was chopped to order, to keep the edges of the crisp white vegetable fresh and clean, so that was last. The dressing was already made up, and sat in a squeeze bottle with the rest of his mise en place ranged around his station at the stainless steel counter.

The tower had to be started first. A nickname for the inventive way they plated Market's house-cured charcuterie and pickled vegetables, the tower took time to build, but once it was done, it was ready to go and could easily wait for the other two dishes to catch up.

The dumpling order was his autumnal chicken soup,

which had graduated from a smash-hit special to a regular menu item yesterday. Wes still got a tingle of pride every time an order came in for it, but on a night like tonight, when they were getting slammed hard and it was up to each cook to knock out as many perfect meals as he could, that tingle got lost in the shuffle pretty quick.

Not that all emotion left the kitchen when the tickets started piling up and they were hit hard—hell no. In fact, when Wes had to push his way down the line to race downstairs to dry storage to grab a new hunk of Earl Grey tea-smoked duck breast because the piece he'd started with wasn't up to snuff, he nearly got hip-checked by a coldly furious Frankie Boyd as he ran by.

Other than one wild, white-lipped look, Frankie hadn't shown much obvious reaction to having been locked in a room with Jess—but the sous chef had been riding Wes all night, pushing him harder and mocking him louder than anyone else.

First Wes's mise wasn't tight enough, the bottles of sauce and infused oils, bowls of chiffonaded parsley, diced chives, and all the other assorted accoutrements that garnished his plates, weren't arranged according to Frankie's suddenly nitpicky standards. Leaving aside the fact that the unwritten commandment of the Market kitchen was Thou Shalt Not Screw With Another Chef's Mise, Frankie was over the top about it. His rant must've lasted a good five minutes until finally Adam stepped in and drew him aside, talking to him in a low, worried tone.

A certain amount of flak was normal and expected; Frankie was never going to be one of Wes's biggest fans. Wes knew and accepted that. But tonight was clearly exceptional.

Shit. Guess they didn't work things out.

Shaking his head at the stubborn pointlessness of it all, Wes grabbed the duck and hauled ass back upstairs, moving as fast as he could. They couldn't afford to fall behind. If they did, if they got weeded and it was all his fault? Wes couldn't even imagine the hell of it. He still felt like he was on shaky ground here, a little—like every day was a chance to prove himself a valuable part of the team, especially knowing Frankie, the boss's best friend and longtime sous chef, didn't like him.

So if Wes was the one who brought the kitchen to a standstill? Yikes. Frankie would probably spontaneously combust.

Which made Wes wonder how Jess was doing. He considered it for all of two seconds before deciding, fuck it, he was already off his station, he might as well take another two seconds to stick his neck out into the dining room and check on his friend.

"Behind," he called, booking up the line of chefs all bending, whirling, slicing, reaching. Wes tossed the duck breast on his cutting board—clean of scraps, he noted absently, President Cornell would be so proud—and ducked around the end of the counter to get a view of the dining room through the open pass-through window.

Chef Adam Temple, expediting meals, tasting dishes, and wiping plates before sending them out on servers' trays, barely spared Wes a glance. He might wonder what his garde-manger man was doing off the line, but until it became an issue, Wes knew Adam would keep his cool. It was kind of awesome working under a chef who didn't blow a gasket over every little thing.

Wes peered out into the atmospherically lit dining room, the golden yellow of the covered lights seeming dim after the bright fluorescence and leaping grill flames of the kitchen.

He scanned for Jess's red hair and finally spotted it near a table in the corner. A deuce, it looked like, although only one person was seated at the table and the second place setting had been cleared away.

Wes squinted, trying to make out his buddy's facial expression—if he still looked murderous, Wes thought maybe he'd skip out on Chapel and head home early tonight to avoid the wrath of Jess—when he was distracted by the very weird sight of the guest's handbag wiggling.

Seriously. The oversized purse, one of those jobbies that looked like it had originally graced some cowboy's saddle on a multimonth cattle drive over the open range, *moved on its own*. He would've thought maybe the woman had kicked it or something, except he could clearly see her shapely, slender legs crossed at the knee, feet well away from the bag, which was positioned beside her chair.

Jess hadn't noticed it. Or at least, he hadn't jumped or anything; he appeared to be reeling off the specials, his back to Wes. He was blocking the rest of the woman, but neither of them seemed agitated.

Another shimmy from the bag on the floor drew Wes's attention once more. He was just about to ask Adam if he'd seen it, too, when the bag gave a huge lurch and a very familiar white, furry head poked out of it—to the accompaniment of gasps from nearby tables.

Wes's entire body turned to stone. Silently willing Jess to move to the side, an inch, just an inch, he waited with frozen breath to see the face of the woman at Jess's table.

And then Jess did move, jumping back about a foot when he caught sight of the dog panting up at him from the handbag, and Wes realized he hadn't really needed his friend to move at all—he'd known who the woman was the instant he saw Lucille.

Dr. Rosemary Wilkins. Here. At Market.

Holy shitballs.

Wes kind of wanted to duck and hide, but that was

ridiculous because she obviously knew he was here. She must've come here specifically to see him, and didn't that just make his blood want to pound right out of his skin?

"Murphy," Adam barked in his ear, making him jump a foot in the air. "Orders are piling up. You tired of tossing salads? Think I should give your job to Matt? He's probably sick of washing dishes, maybe you could switch for a while."

The sarcasm in his boss's usually happy-go-lucky voice got Wes's brain working again. "No, Chef. I'm on it. I just . . . well, are you seeing this?" He gestured out at the dining room where Jess was leaning close to Rosemary, clearly using his body to try and shield the now constantly wriggling bag from the rest of the dining room. He appeared to be trying to politely inform Rosemary that it was against restaurant policy to allow pets other than service animals like seeing-eye dogs—and from the familiar mulish set of her dainty jaw, Jess could see she was having none of it.

And when she raised her voice to reply, he could hear exactly what it was she was having none of.

"Do not try to tell me I can't bring my dog in here," she said, loudly enough to cut through the quiet hum of the other diners' conversations. "I've read countless primary-source accounts describing Manhattan's famously canine-loving populace. You allow dogs everywhere! I've seen it with my own eyes; since I've been in the city, I've encountered a Pomeranian at the Museum of Television and Radio, a Dalmatian at the Met, and a Shih Tzu at the Natural History Museum."

"Those weren't restaurants," Jess pointed out, his voice louder than usual, too. Wes had to grin. Trust Rosemary to be able to fluster the best server in the joint. Of course, he remembered guiltily, he'd sort of softened

Jess up beforehand, so maybe it wasn't fair to award her full points for that.

"I don't care. I've seen *Sex & the City,* I know New Yorkers bring their pets into dining establishments. Just because I'm not, technically, a New Yorker, you want to discriminate against me? Or is it because this isn't a Louis Vuitton handbag? Ms. Bradshaw and the others did mention that, but I didn't imagine it was an essential variable."

"No! Not at all," Jess replied, casting a helpless glare of mute appeal over his shoulder. He caught Wes's eye and something flickered over his face. A moment of pause. Maybe . . . shit. Maybe recognition.

Now Wes really wished he'd ducked. Or at least that he hadn't told Jess quite so much about Rosemary. His friend definitely knew enough to be able to put two and two together.

"What the hell?" Adam asked, sucked into the drama playing out across the restaurant.

"Crazy, right?" Wes said brightly. "Okay, guess I'd better get back to work. We've got orders for three towers, yeah?"

He backed away from the pass, unable to take his eyes off Rosemary until he absolutely had to. It was insane—he absolutely didn't want to face her, and yet he couldn't stop drinking in the sight of her, like a wino who'd been handed a full bottle of Château Lafite Rothschild.

He'd almost made it when Jess's voice rang out clear as crystal goblets ringing together in a toast.

"Let me guess. You're here to speak to Wes Murphy, aren't you?"

Adam whipped around in time to catch Wes's wince. "Hold it right there, asshole. What's this got to do with you?"

"Well . . ."

"And I'm not leaving until I see him," Rosemary replied,

just as loudly. Moses on toast, did they think it was a play and they had to perform for the cheap seats?

Adam's large, square hand descended on the scruff of Wes's neck. "I don't know what the hell is going on, but you're going to go make nice, get the dog lady out of my restaurant before somebody calls the health inspector, and then hustle your skinny Irish ass back onto the line. I'll fill in for you for a few minutes, but make it snappy."

"Yes, Chef," Wes said weakly, feeling the way Lucille looked the few times he'd dared to rebuke her.

Man, he'd missed that silly little dog.

As Jess appeared at the kitchen door wearing an evil smile that promised payback, Wes tried to ignore how much more he'd missed Rosemary. Who he was about to talk to for the first time since he'd kissed her good night all those months ago.

His feet felt like lead, but his blood was racing through his veins as if it were in a hurry to catch a train. He must have looked like yesterday's soup, warmed over, because even Jess's fully justifiable triumph faded a little when Wes reached him.

"Come on, I'll walk you out," Jess said, with almost no trace of glee.

"I don't know if I can do this," he said. God, just seeing her across a crowded restaurant had felt like having the heart yanked right out of him.

"You owe her this," Jess said bluntly. "You left her. She doesn't know why. She's pissed, probably hurt, and God only knows what scenario she's concocted in her head to explain it all."

"I know that," Wes growled back, but then a thought occurred to him. If she was here . . . did that mean she'd left the academy, and all its research opportunities, behind? If she'd already decided that, on her own, maybe he could explain what had happened. Maybe . . .

Wes pressed his lips closed and tried to look calm and in control while his pulse thundered in his ears.

Jess easily shattered any pretense at calm with his whispered parting comment as he deposited Wes in front of Rosemary's table. "Here he is, ma'am, the one and only Wes Murphy." Leaning in, Jess said, "You want my advice? *Work it out.*"

And with that, the little shit was gone, leaving Wes twisting in the wind, staring down into the lovely storm-blue eyes he'd never thought he'd see again.

She stared, silent and implacable in a T-shirt bearing the inexplicable slogan BROWNCOATS, while Lucille went bananas and started trying to claw her way through the leather side of the bag to get to him.

What the hell was he supposed to say? *Quick,* he told himself. *Pretend she's a mark! Go into your patter! Say something, anything!*

"Um. Hi."

Oh yeah. Smooth like butter.

Rosemary resisted the asinine urge to touch her hair, fix her clothing, or run her finger across her teeth to check for lipstick. Just because she'd put on a touch of light neutral beige-pink gloss this morning did not mean she was dressed up. Nor did she need to!

This wasn't a date. It wasn't even a social call. It was purely business.

Lucille, it appeared, had not gotten the memo. She'd managed to deduce that the handbag's zipper was the only thing standing in the way of her joyous reunion with Wes, and was accordingly gnawing on it, growling low in her throat the whole while. It was distracting.

That was the only reason Rosemary hadn't gotten down to the business at hand yet, she told herself. It certainly had nothing to do with the way the sight of Wes Murphy, all one-point-eight-two-eight-eight meters of him, made her temperature skyrocket. Just because his wavy chestnut-brown hair curled around his ears and the nape of his neck, and his eyes were the color of nickel chloride hexahydrate, and his wide, mobile mouth had kissed her mouth and her other parts besides—none of that was any reason to lose focus.

Pulling herself up and ignoring the gyrating handbag at her feet, Rosemary held out her hand for a cool, detached greeting.

Except the moment his long, scarred fingers touched hers, she felt anything but cool and detached.

Frak! She hadn't accounted for the possibility that she might react as uncontrollably as ever to Wes Murphy. All the literature indicated that once the initial lust was sated, the chemical attraction was sure to fade!

Stupid *Sex & the City*. Talk about an unreliable research source. First they were wrong about the acceptable code of conduct for taking pets into public areas, and now this?

She met Wes's changeable green eyes—*fickle as the rest of him, damn it*—and was surprised to see something flicker there that she didn't expect. Was it an answering heat?

He didn't give her a chance to decipher it, kneeling instead to make a fuss over the wildly happy Lucille. The dog was, as usual, quite vocal about her feelings, and Rosemary felt the stares of the other diners like prickles along the back of her flushing neck.

"God, I missed you, baby girl," Wes was crooning as Lucille attempted to fit his entire nose into her mouth. His somewhat long nose was too much for her, so she settled for trying to lick it off his face.

Rosemary ignored the curl of bitterness in her chest that wanted to hear those words, or something similar with perhaps less infantilization, from Wes about herself. "If you're quite done fawning over the animal you abandoned," she said acidly, "I have something important to speak to you about."

From his position on one knee beside her chair, they were almost eye to eye. Wes kept his hands moving soothingly over Lucille's head while the dog shuddered in obvious transports of delight. Rosemary vehemently squashed any memories of those same hands stroking her thighs, her sides, her . . . stop it!

"I know," Wes said, his voice heavy with emotion. "There's some stuff I need to say to you, too. But I have to get back to work, and Lucille really can't be in here. Lots of restaurants will let you have your dog at the table if you sit outside, if there's sidewalk seating. But this ain't Paris, and somebody really will call the health department. Or at least blog about it."

Caught between two burning needs—one, to settle her business with Wes so she could escape his still dangerously attractive presence for good, and two, to get away from the staring, whispering tables full of people around her—Rosemary gritted her teeth and said, "Fine. I'm staying at the Carlyle. There's a bar off the lobby."

"Right, Bemelman's. It's kind of famous." He paused. "That place is pretty swanky."

Rosemary shrugged, annoyed at the digression. "It's where my parents always stay when they're here on lecture tours. What difference does it make?"

"Oh! None. I guess I would've thought they wouldn't allow pets."

"For what I'm paying, they ought to allow me to bring in my own personal menagerie. Anyway, so you'll meet me there when you get off work?"

"Sure, okay. It'll be late, though."

Rosemary waved that away as unimportant, gathered

up her squirming purse and stood. Studying his handsome face intently, she said, "Based on empirical evidence, I really shouldn't trust you out of my sight."

Ouch. But what could he say when it was nothing less than the truth? Maybe he'd had a good reason for walking out on her last time, but that didn't make him an honorable man. Much as he wanted to be, it never seemed to work out well for him. Or anyone around him.

He watched her leave, Lucille panting over her shoulder, and felt a fist squeeze around his heart.

She was right not to trust him. He didn't trust himself.

Even telling her the truth about why he left wouldn't change that.

Chapter 14

Wes did a discreet sniff check on the street outside the Carlyle Hotel. The doorman looked on, smirking a little in his gold-braided uniform.

"Just got off work," Wes felt compelled to explain. He'd stripped off his reeking whites in the locker room, keeping an eye on the door the whole time in case Jess or Frankie decided this was another opportune moment for revenge, but luckily he'd made it back into his normal-guy clothes without incident.

"Sure," said the doorman. "Lemme guess, adult video store?"

Wes looked down at what he was wearing. Soft gray Levi's and the battered leather motorcycle jacket Pops gave him when he turned twenty over an unzipped blue hoodie. Now that he wasn't constrained to the academy's prison-strict dress code, he'd ditched the leather clogs in favor of sneakers, which he was still wearing.

Nothing about that said skeezy to Wes. He shrugged, and the motion shifted his jacket and sweatshirt just enough that he remembered what he had on underneath.

Crap. He was wearing *that* shirt. It was white, although faded a little dingy over the years, and featured a large blue star in the center of his chest with the word PORN in red letters inside it.

Okay, that was a little embarrassing. But jeez, it's not like he knew he was going to be seeing Rosemary today!

He zipped up his hoodie, covering the porn star and arched a brow at the doorman. "It's just a shirt, dude. What, you gonna tell me there's a dress code in the hotel lobby?"

"Hey, if you're okay with it, I'm okay with it," the guy said.

"Then step aside, man. I'm going in!" Wes waited for the doorman to open the door for him with a lavish, unnecessary flourish, then prowled through as if he owned the joint.

He'd learned early on that the key to fitting in was total confidence. Look as if you belong there, and everyone will assume you do. Hell, if he swaggered hard enough, the chick working the reception desk would probably take a surreptitious cell phone photo of him so she could figure out what rock band he was a member of.

Wes strode straight through the lobby to the almost-hidden door into Bemelmans Bar, a gorgeous, golden room filled with old-school heavy leather banquettes, dark wood tables, and a big, shiny baby grand piano. The far wall danced with a whimsical mural, and there, beneath a scene of two stylized rabbits in formal wear picnicking in Central Park, Rosemary sat with her nose stuck in a book.

Her blond hair was loose, for once, shiny and a little mussed, as if she hadn't bothered to brush it in a while. Her white button-down shirt had a round collar and puffy sleeves like a little girl's dress, but she was wearing a black corduroy men's vest over it, and the overall look was enticingly wacky in some way Wes couldn't really define.

She was so . . . herself. From the tips of her unmanicured nails to the top of her smooth, high forehead, Dr. Rosemary Wilkins was just there. Doing her thing. Not giving a shit what anyone else thought, and looking so goddamned adorable sitting there reading, that Wes had a hard time not pouncing on her.

He wanted to unbutton every one of those buttons, slow and steady, revealing inches of creamy skin and the pretty curves that tended to dominate his dreams these days.

Instead, seeing that she had a martini glass in front of her, he went to the bar to get a drink.

When he set his glass of Guinness on the table, she blinked up at him, her wide blue eyes startled.

"Oh! You're here."

"I said I would be," he reminded her. He hated that she was so surprised. Not that he didn't understand why, but still. It sucked.

"Good," she said at the same time as Wes blurted out, "Listen—"

They both stopped, flustered. "Look, why don't you sit down," she said finally. "And then I'll start."

"Ladies first," Wes said, sliding into the chair. The square table was small enough that their knees bumped, sending shocks up his legs.

She shifted in her chair, a slight squirm that heated Wes all the way through. "I don't want to talk about what happened at the academy," she said abruptly, puncturing the cloud of sensual warmth surrounding Wes.

"What?" he said stupidly.

"I mean, I *only* want to talk about what we did in the lab—or wait, not what we did in the lab that last night. Not at all. Let's just retcon that, pretend it never happened. Okay?"

Cold shot through Wes's chest. "No, hold up. Rosemary, I need to tell you—"

"If it's about that last night, I don't want to hear it." She cut him off with a chop of her hand and a firm tone, but it was the way her breath sped up, the pulse in her throat visibly spiking, that shut Wes's mouth.

He clenched his fists on the table and blew out a breath, unbelievably frustrated. This had to be the first time in his life he'd been ready to beg a woman to talk about what it meant that they'd had sex. "Rosemary."

"If you persist in bringing it up, I'll have no compunction about getting up and sticking you with the bill," she warned. "And cocktails here are not cheap."

Forcing his hands to relax, Wes grabbed his beer and took a deep drink. "Fine. We'll play it your way, for now. But it's not because I can't afford to pay for your fifteen-dollar martini."

"Dirty martini, actually," she informed him. "With extra olives, which I already ate."

"Your drink of choice is vodka mixed with olive juice?"

"I don't think so," she said, taking a thoughtful sip. "It's okay, but it's not the one. I'll keep looking. I have a system."

He could only imagine her quest for a favorite cocktail. There were probably taste graphs and preference flow charts involved. Affection for her welled so suddenly and sharply that he had to take another drink to keep from leaning over and kissing the faraway look off her face.

"Anyway, that's not important right now. I wish you'd stop forcing me off topic. I'm trying to talk to you about our project!"

"Project?" Trying to follow a simple conversation with Rosemary was apt to leave a man feeling about as swift as a monkey trying to do calculus.

"Yes!" Impatience was a cute look on her. "You know. The aphrodisiac project."

"Oh right. Well, you know, I officially withdrew from

the ACA a week ago, so I'm not going to need to turn in a final project," Wes said.

"I know, that's why I'm here." She glanced down at her drink, her lowered lashes hiding her expression. "President Cornell mentioned to me that you wouldn't be coming back."

"I'm sorry you had to find out that way," he said. This sucked. Hugely. She said she didn't want to talk about it, but he had to tell her anyway.

She pressed her lips together into a firm line. "I don't want any apologies from you," she said.

"Then why are you here?"

She leaned forward, eyes glittering in the yellow light from the hand-painted lampshade on their table. "I want to continue the project."

"On your own?" He hated the idea of Rosemary checking out aphrodisiacs with some other eager assistant.

"Of course. I always work alone."

"Not always," Wes felt compelled to point out.

"No," she said, pursing her lips. "You're right. And again, that's why I'm here. To get your permission to continue the research on my own. Considering that it was technically your project to begin with, I felt it was only ethical to let you know what I've discovered since you left, and what it could mean."

"Wow, you're really serious about this." Wes felt like a moron for taking so long to see it, but he'd been distracted by their personal shit. And he remembered exactly how dismissive she was of the whole idea to begin with, so her current level of barely restrained enthusiasm was a shocker.

"I never joke when it comes to research," she said. "After you left, I wondered if there might be something to the whole aphrodisiac thing after all—especially the chocolate-covered strawberries." Her cheeks went pink at even a sideways reference to That Night, but she soldiered on, her voice growing stronger and more excited as she explained her discovery.

"I did some in-depth testing with several groups of students as test subjects, and based on those results, I managed to isolate a particular proximate nutrient in the *Fragaria* plant that, when combined with the alkaloids in chocolate, augments the documented physiological effects of those alkaloids on the brain. Serotonin levels rose thirty-two-point-oh-four percent higher when the theobromine and phenethylamine from the chocolate was ingested along with the new protein strain I pulled from the strawberry."

She paused dramatically as if waiting for Wes to leap from his seat and shower her in confetti. The image of a chimp tapping away at a calculator vivid in his mind's eye, Wes said, "Um. That sounds . . . good?"

"Good?" She stared at him. "It's nothing less than a breakthrough! Serotonin is the chemical in the brain that controls feelings of happiness. When it rises swiftly enough, it produces a euphoric state, making the owner of the brain in question more apt to be receptive to sexual advances, and able to enjoy them."

"I get that. So aphrodisiacs can be real, I guess. Isn't that what we were trying to prove? What are you still researching?"

Her eyes shifted to the side. If she knew how to lie, Wes would be watching for other telltale signs right about now—but Rosemary wasn't built like that. A supposition she confirmed with her next, obviously reluctant, sentence.

"If I can distill and combine those nutrients into a single substance, maybe intensify the power of the reaction through dosage, I can create a marketable product to enhance human libido. The applications are endless—and lucrative, as it turns out."

"Hmm, I guess there probably would be some folks out

there willing to pay cash to enhance their sex lives. Especially if it's for something actually based on scientific research rather than, like, powdered rhinoceros horn."

Rosemary leaned both elbows on the table. "I don't have to guess about it; I know. When I told my father about the *Fragaria* breakthrough, he mentioned it to a contact of his at a pharmaceutical company, and now Progressive Mutual wants to fund my continuing research."

Wes started, heart doing the lambada in his chest. If that was true, then President Cornell and his threats had just become truly irrelevant.

He opened his mouth to tell Rosemary the whole truth about why he left the ACA in the dead of night, without a word, whether she was ready to listen or not—but then she went on, saying, "And even though I know there's no such thing as luck, and the world is nothing more than a collection of random events and coincidence, it still feels like amazing good fortune that I happened to be at the academy when I had this breakthrough! Aggravating as it is to have to share the credit, not to mention the ownership of the research with a toad like Wally Cornell, the labs there are second to none in terms of the equipment I needed. I doubt if I could have isolated the *Fragaria* nutrient in any other lab in the country."

His heart stopped. If she needed the academy lab, Cornell still had him boxed in. Wes couldn't tell her the truth yet.

Aware of a sneaking relief that he wouldn't have to listen to Rosemary choose her research over him, Wes's mind raced for a way to keep her from walking out of his life forever. If he could just keep her around long enough, cement his place in her life, then maybe by the time she finished with the aphrodisiac project, he could make her forget the way he'd . . . used her and ditched her. Right.

But she could've just tracked down his phone number,

Wes's pragmatic brain piped up. She didn't have to come all the way down here. The surge of hope that thought induced was almost painful in its intensity.

Maybe he hadn't killed every possibility of a chance at a future with her after all.

The pause had gone on long enough to make Rosemary antsy.

"Look, I didn't come here to try and cut you out of the pharmaceutical deal completely," she said, tapping her fingers on the tabletop. "I'm willing to discuss a percentage. A small one."

Wes smiled, every inch of his body alive with possibilities. "Tell me the truth, Rosie. You missed me. That's why you're here."

The loosening of her jaw hinge, dropping that soft mouth open, told Wes he'd hit home.

Setting her chin at a stubborn angle, Rosemary met him stare for stare. "Let's get back on track. All you have to do is tell me you understand, that you relinquish all rights to the project, which is only fair since, let's face it, you've contributed very little—and then we'll never have to see each other again."

"Or," Wes said, leaning in for the kill. "I could refuse to approve the project going forward without my involvement."

She licked her lips, the color washing from her cheeks until she was approximately the same pale green as her dirty martini. "What are you saying?"

Blood throbbing through his veins, Wes stretched his arm across the table and easily captured her hand. He tugged at it, pulling her closer until he could bring her hand to his mouth. "I'm saying I don't give a shit about the money." He pressed a kiss to the center of her palm, and when her fingers curled reflexively, he set his teeth to the heel of her hand and bit gently.

She was salt and heat and life against his tongue, and the way she gasped fired him up like a wood-burning grill.

This was his chance, and he was taking it.

"But," he continued, never taking his eyes from hers, "I want to stay on the project. I want to help with the research. And I want the chance to prove there's more between you and me than simple chemistry."

Chapter 15

Maybe she should've asked Wes if he wanted his dog back, but since Rosemary wasn't prepared to give Lucille up, it would've been a pointless exercise. Polite, perhaps, but pointless.

He'd abandoned Lucille, and she deserved someone who would love her and take care of her and never leave her just because he got a better offer from someone else.

That settled, Rosemary nodded and marched down to the lobby to get some information.

The concierge didn't bat an eye when Rosemary asked him to recommend a place to leave her dog for the day.

Instead, he clacked away on his computer for a bare moment before offering her a list of doggie day-care facilities within walking distance of the hotel.

Rosemary chose one called Peaceful Paws Day Spa, where Lucille would no doubt be pampered to within an inch of her spoiled little life. Rosemary picked it mostly because they offered a Webcam option so that anytime she wanted, she could log on to their site and pull up a live video of Lucille having her toenails painted or whatever.

When she dropped Lucille off, Rosemary found herself lingering in conversation with the sympathetic-eyed receptionist.

"She doesn't like squeak toys, they freak her out," Rosemary said. "And anything remotely bone-shaped is fair game, as far as she's concerned, so I wouldn't leave any expensive fountain pens lying around unless you're into ink showers. What else?"

"Your baby will be just fine with us," said the receptionist, whose stylishly understated badge announced her name as Aimee. "We'll take wonderful care of her, Ms. Wilkins. I promise."

"It's Dr. Wilkins," Rosemary said automatically. "And she's not my baby. She's a canine companion, and I'm responsible for her welfare." A strange lump rose into her throat, making it hard to speak. "I'm all she's got."

"It's only for a few hours, Dr. Wilkins," Aimee soothed, gently ushering Rosemary toward the door. She'd already given Rosemary the URL for the Webcam feed and lifted an unhappy Lucille up for a good-bye kiss.

Rosemary never would've pictured herself as the kind of person who deliberately put her face within licking distance of an animal's tongue, but she was learning all sorts of things about herself these days.

For instance, that she was not as immune to a certain chef's charms as she'd hoped.

It was slightly disconcerting how quickly Wes had taken the information she'd shared with him and turned all her careful plans inside out. But Rosemary didn't get to be one of the youngest Mensa candidates in history by being slow to adapt.

Once she finally managed to tear herself away from the Peaceful Paws Day Spa's beautifully appointed lobby, she focused her mind on the problem at hand.

Namely, on the puzzling problem of Wes Murphy and his refusal to ever react in any logically predictable way.

He was the one who left, and then sent a letter saying he was never coming back. So what was he up to now, acting as if he wanted to be with her?

That question kept her occupied on the short cab ride through Central Park, under a tall canopy of trees in full autumnal glory. She was still turning it over in her mind when they pulled up at the corner of Columbus and Seventy-seventh, right in front of the green awning with MARKET picked out in gold lettering.

They'd agreed she would meet him at the restaurant, since he had to work, and Rosemary could set up her laptop anywhere.

He'd claimed he'd clear it with the management, but the recognition followed by alarm in the maître d's eyes as he spotted Rosemary told her maybe Wes hadn't gotten around to it yet.

As impeccably blond and clean-cut as a model for one of those wholesome designers who made all-American clothes for frat boys, the maître d' hurried forward, one hand out. "Welcome back," he said, and Rosemary had to give it to him—he didn't sound like he was lying. Maybe it was the Southern accent. During her studies at UVA, she'd learned that the sweet honeyed drawl of the South masked all manner of unpleasantness.

Deciding to put him out of his misery, she hefted her laptop case. "Decided to leave the dog at home today. I presume a MacBook Pro won't alarm anyone, or need to be reported to the health department."

Relief settled over the man's tense features like a veil. "Ah. Of course. Are you dining alone?"

"I . . . well." She wasn't sure what to say, but before she could go into the whole explanation, one of the waiters came hurrying up. It was the same young man who'd waited on her yesterday, she realized. The one who ratted her out to Wes, then gave him that cryptic advice before taking off.

"Grant, it's okay," the young waiter said. "She's here for Wes. He said to stick her at the bar until the lunch rush is over."

The maître d', Grant, pursed his lips in annoyance. But when he looked back to Rosemary, any hint of aggravation was smoothed from his even, regular features. "Of course! Right this way."

"I'll show her, if you want," the waiter offered.

Grant glanced at the bar, then back at the two of them. The door behind Rosemary opened and a group of four laughing people spilled into the entryway. Grant's face cleared, decision made. "Okay, thanks, Jess. Enjoy your lunch!" he said to Rosemary, already moving forward to greet the new party.

The young red-haired waiter, Jess, leaned in confidentially as he led her to the U-shaped bar. "Grant avoids the whole bar area whenever possible; he's a good manager, so we all try to help out with that."

"Why would he want to avoid the bar?"

"He's got some kind of feud going with the bartender, Chris. No one really knows what it's all about, and it's weird because, normally, Grant is the one making peace between the warring tribes, ensuring the waiters don't annoy the chefs too much, and vice versa."

Intrigued, Rosemary asked, "Are you this candid with all your guests? I'd think sharing gossip would be frowned on."

Jess laughed. "You're not just some random guest! In fact, you've been *part* of the gossip around here for long enough that I feel like I know you."

Swinging her heavy laptop case onto an empty stool at the end of the bar, Rosemary put her hands on her hips. "Explain that in further detail, please."

His eyes widened. "Oh, hey! Not in a bad way. And I'm not even talking about the general restaurant gossip that everyone knows, anyhow. But Wes is a friend of mine, and he's been talking about you pretty much since he showed up here. Well," he amended thoughtfully, "I had to squeeze it out of him after I noticed he'd get all morose and broody sometimes, and I wanted to know why, but finally he 'fessed up about this woman he was totally hung up on back at the academy. And after that, you know, common decency and a lot of beers dictated the whole thing."

Rosemary's head whirled, but being a genius had its advantages. Hoisting herself onto the tall barstool, she managed to unravel the stream of chatter with relative ease, and honed in on the important bits of missing information.

"He talked about me?" She needed some clarification on that point. "What did he say?"

Jess leaned on the back of the chair next to hers. "Well, at first he wanted to be cagey and, you know, like a guy about everything. But over time I got pretty much everything out of him, I think."

Propping her head on one hand, Rosemary regarded Jess with fascination. "Has anyone ever tested your cognitive abilities? Your brain appears to function in a unique way."

"Wow," Jess said, a shadow lifting as he laughed, making his navy blue eyes light up. "I think that's the nicest way anyone's ever called me a freak."

"Having an IQ on the high end of the bell curve doesn't make you a freak." Rosemary compressed her lips. She didn't mean to sound so stiff, but come on. What was with all the discrimination against smart people? When did mediocrity become desirable?

"That's right," Jess said. "He told me you're wicked smart."

Of course. That was the first thing everyone thought of when they had to describe her.

"He got you down pretty accurately when he told me what you looked like, too," Jess continued, studying her face with a detached, critical air that made Rosemary feel as if he were studying a portrait of someone he knew, searching for a likeness. "If I didn't know for a fact that Wes's eyes glaze over whenever I talk about photography, I'd think maybe he had an artistic bent, just from the level of detail he achieved in his description. It wasn't hard to recognize you."

"Wes is more verbal than visual," Rosemary agreed, scooching her stool closer to Jess. "Tell me more about what he said I look like."

Jess opened his mouth, then snapped it shut when the bartender, a short man with longish hair who'd escaped Rosemary's attention until now, sauntered over. "Boss man," he said to Jess out of the corner of his mouth. "Incoming. Detonation in five. Four. Three . . ."

The bartender casually moved back to the other end of the bar to top up a wine glass just as Grant descended on Jess in a cloud of tense smiles and snapping eyes. "Jess! I believe table fourteen is ready to order."

Red scorched up Jess's neck and into his cheeks. "Oh! Right, sure, of course. I'll get right on that. Rosemary, it was a pleasure talking to you."

"I hope we'll get a chance to chat later," she said, frustrated. There went a prime source of inside information and insight into Wes's inscrutable actions.

Maybe she could extract some data from Grant— except he was already giving the bartender a parting sneer and hurrying back to his station.

Fine. If she couldn't make any progress on the Wes

Problem, she'd just have to buckle down and get some real work done.

Booting up her laptop, Rosemary settled in at the bar and lost herself in a paper dissecting the relative merits of nutrient absorption through whole foods versus in pill form.

But every time Jess passed on his way to and from the kitchen, turning in orders and toting hot plates out to his tables, he gave her a quick, secret smile that made Rosemary think of Wes, sitting in a bar somewhere after work and unburdening himself of everything he thought and felt about Dr. Rosemary Wilkins.

It certainly wasn't the intricacies of nutrient absorption that kept the corners of her mouth tugging up into a grin.

The third time she caught herself fighting a smile, Rosemary paused in her reading, fingers frozen on the keyboard, suddenly suffused with fear.

She couldn't afford to allow Wes Murphy to elicit any further emotional reactions from her. He wouldn't be the cause of any more smiles, or any more tears—she had to keep him at a safe remove.

The memories of what happened when she let him close were too fresh, too raw. He'd hurt her once. Probability dictated he could and most likely would do it again. What kind of genius would she be if she ignored the burden of evidence and probabilities and let herself care about him again?

Well. She'd be the sort of genius who deserved exactly what she'd no doubt get—a broken heart.

Chapter 16

Most of the guys had already started breaking down their lunch mise and setting up for dinner service when Grant tore into the kitchen like a blond tornado, looking for Adam.

Wes, standing at his spot near the front of the kitchen, away from the hot line, was close enough to hear Grant's voice tremble with excitement as he said, "We've got walk-ins!"

Groans echoed up the line. This was not good news—if these late lunchers ordered multiple courses and lingered over everything, it could seriously put the kitchen behind in terms of getting switched over and ready for dinner. At least the lunch menu was designed for the office crowd, with quick, tasty dishes that didn't take half an hour in the oven to finish.

Still, no one was happy about a couple of extra lunch tickets at three in the afternoon—except Grant. Who was practically bouncing on the soles of his feet like a kid who needed to wee.

The next words out of his mouth explained his agitation. "It's Eva Jansen!"

Market skidded into the big time with a sudden jolt.

There were three kinds of guests who revved any professional kitchen into high gear: restaurant critics, celebrities, and restaurateurs. Especially restaurateurs like Eva Jansen, who was not only restaurant royalty after her father started the biggest culinary competition in the U.S., but who also had a stratospheric rate of success in her own right, and a reputation for spotting big talent early.

As happy as most of the line cooks were at Market, every single one of them would give his left nut for a chance to make Eva Jansen notice him.

When Eva Jansen noticed a chef, that chef got a perfectly appointed restaurant in a prime spot, and all the considerable money and power of her company, Elegant Hospitality Group, behind making a go of it.

Grant lowered his voice, but Wes clearly heard him say, "She's checking out 422."

At Adam's blank look, Grant huffed out an exasperated breath. "Next door! The restaurant space that just opened up."

"Well, well, well, isn't that interesting?" Adam mused, tugging thoughtfully at his ear. "Bet she wouldn't have looked twice at that joint if we weren't doing so well."

"Probably not," Grant said, "but we *are* doing well. Well enough to expand, maybe a more casual extension of Market—more bistro-, brasserie-type food. The Market Bar. Adam, we've talked about this."

Adam's eyes lit up with the possibilities; Wes could see it from where he stood. He could also see the exact moment doubt crept in. "I know, man, but maybe we should take what we've got and stick to what we know we can succeed with for a little while longer."

"You always do this," Grant exploded. "We have this chance *now,* we have the desire, the skill, the drive—opportunities like this don't come along every day. Hell, they don't come along every year! Every five! Maybe the timing isn't perfect, but will it ever be?"

Adam looked torn. "Maybe . . ."

Clearly sensing an opening, Grant pressed his advantage. "I'm not saying we make an offer today, boss. We still need more info. And it so happens we've got a couple of experts in our dining room right now who are probably dropping pearls of wisdom all over the bar. All we need is someone to spy on them!"

Amusement pulled at Adam's mouth. "What about Christian? Bartenders are supposed to be good at listening."

"I don't trust him," Grant argued.

"Why not? I really don't get your issue with Chris. He's a great guy."

Wes watched Grant waffle over how to deal with that one for a second before he decided to put the guy out of his misery. Wes cleared his throat. "Um, I might have an alternative."

Two pairs of surprised eyes turned on him, making Wes fumble his chef knife. "I mean, if you want someone who can repeat Eva Jansen's entire conversation back to you, word for word, my . . . friend can do that."

"What friend?" Adam said in unison with Grant asking, "Who, the dog lady?" All incredulous.

"Yeah, that was actually my dog," Wes admitted. They both goggled at him. "Sort of. Not important," he said hastily. "The key fact here is that my friend sitting at the bar out there, Rosemary, she's got a photographic memory. Anything she sees or hears, she remembers. So you want me to ask her?"

Grant looked at Adam, who nodded, a mischievous grin making him look like a naughty schoolboy.

"Worth a shot. I want to know what Eva 'The Diva' Jansen thinks of her lunch here, anyway," Adam said.

"But be subtle," Grant cautioned as he walked Wes out to the dining room. "It could be considered, you know, tacky to spy on customers. I don't want her to figure out what we're doing."

"Not a problem," Wes assured him. He'd caught sight of Rosemary at the opposite end of the bar from a very put-together woman in a sleek suit and a younger guy wearing black-rimmed glasses that reminded Wes of Elvis Costello, and nodding at everything the woman said.

He studied the body language for an instant, the way the man inclined his head toward the woman, the way she looked right at him as he responded, and decided the young guy was probably an executive assistant of some kind, subordinate but valued.

If Wes were running a con, he'd be cursing his luck right about now that the assistant wasn't female and susceptible-looking.

"Hey, gimme your shirt," he said, starting to unbutton his white chef coat.

"What? No!"

Wes rolled his eyes as Grant clutched at the collar of his forest-green organic cotton button-down like a timid nun. "We need to swap. How else can I be subtle about hovering around the bar?"

Grant didn't look happy, but he did start unbuttoning his shirt.

A few slightly awkward, clumsy moments later, Wes was putting on his best waiter face and ambling out to the bar. Luckily, Jess was already there to take the Jansen party's order.

This allowed Wes to sail past the ordering couple as if he didn't even see them, his gaze trained on Rosemary's bright blond head bent over her open laptop. The remains of her lunch sat forgotten on the bar—she'd had the charcuterie plate. The knowledge that everything she'd eaten had been prepared, sliced, and arranged into a tower by his own two hands tingled through him in a satisfying rush.

Taking immediate advantage of the built-in reason for his presence at the bar when there was already a waiter clearly handling orders, Wes leaned past Rosemary's shoulder and grabbed the plate, nearly bobbling the silverware. He collected everything into one hand with only a small clatter and a muffled curse.

Rosemary looked up, her brow furrowed at the interruption. The furrow smoothed out when her eyebrows shot up to her hairline as she took in his outfit.

"Are we playing dress-up?" she asked. "And me without my Uhura costume."

One part of Wes's brain registered relief that she hadn't spoken loudly enough to garner the attention of their target at the other end of the bar, but most of his (admittedly easily distracted) brain was taken up with imagining Rosemary in the low-cut, skintight flight suit of the Starship *Enterprise*'s hottest crewmember.

"Please tell me you actually have an Uhura costume."

She arched a brow at him. "Maybe. If you can tell me you actually know who that is, you might just stand a chance of seeing it, one day."

Wes fought not to shuffle his feet. This was maybe a little revealing about how much he'd missed her. "I may have rented the original *Star Trek* series on DVD recently. But only because the new movie rocked!"

"It did, didn't it?" Rosemary said, leaning forward eagerly. "The way they reimagined the series using an alternate-universe storyline was completely brilliant. And, of course, they ensured the die-hard-fan vote by putting Leonard Nimoy in a pivotal role."

Behind him, Eva Jansen let out a light, tinkling laugh. Wes resisted the urge to turn around and look at her. "As much as I'd love to stand here and dissect the differences between the *Star Trek* reboot and the original series, I actually did have a purpose in coming out here. See the woman over my left shoulder?"

Rosemary cocked her head to see around him. "The one with the improbably perfect coloring and the poison-apple-red lipstick?"

"That's the one. Her name is Eva Jansen. She's a restaurateur, and my boss really wants to know what she's talking about with her assistant. Think you can eavesdrop a little and give us a report later?"

Those eyebrows went up again; they were getting a real workout. "You want me to be your spy in a game of restaurant espionage? Will I need a code name?"

"It's nothing morally reprehensible or anything," Wes hastened to reassure her. "Just curiosity."

"I think your code name should be Tiberius," she said decisively. "I'll be Uhura."

"Tiberius? As in James Tiberius Kirk?" Wes blinked, then grinned. "Oh my God, this is your version of flirting. How do you say 'I fancy you' in Klingon?"

She opened her mouth to answer, then narrowed her eyes. "You don't really want to know, do you? That was a joke."

"Just a little one," Wes admitted. "So does this mean you'll do it, Uhura?"

"Fine, but you'll owe me. And I'm not deciding right now exactly what you owe me—that will be specified at a later date of my choosing."

The look she flashed him was so arch, so full of mischievous amusement, it took Wes's breath. "I'd be glad to do whatever you decide you want," he said around the hoarseness in his throat. "As long as it doesn't involve giving up on the aphrodisiac project and/or never seeing you again."

Her face stilled. "Actually, I hadn't thought of that."
She paused, her fingers picking at the copper linen napkin in her lap. "I wouldn't ask that," she said finally. "If
you're inclined to help with the project, I won't turn you
down. Sometimes a second eye is the best resource you
can have."

Wes, who vividly remembered being told Rosemary
always worked alone, simply nodded. Hope was a living
thing breathing gently to life inside him—he wouldn't
choke it out by pushing too hard on it and forcing it to be
more than it was.

Of all the many, varied, and embarrassing things he
wanted to say in response, he managed to pare it down to,
"I think we make a pretty great team."

Her smile was slow, hesitant, and just about the most
beautiful thing he'd ever seen. "That we do, Tiberius."

Rosemary watched him go, absently admiring the tight
roundness of his posterior in those black jeans. Most of
her concentration was already on the conversation a few
feet away.

Jess finished taking their order—endive salad with
roasted beets for the woman, charcuterie plate for the man;
Rosemary approved, she'd heartily enjoyed her country-
style pâté and duck salami—and went to deliver it to the
kitchen.

Using her peripheral vision, Rosemary could see the
woman fairly well. A gleaming bob of mink-brown hair
slashed across the pale skin of her high forehead and
cheekbones, and her frost-blue eyes snapped with intelligence.

The man with the stylishly heavy glasses had his back to
Rosemary, but when he twisted on his stool to retrieve a
BlackBerry from the pocket of the jacket hanging over its
back, she saw that he was younger than his companion.

"I like the look of this place," the young man said.

"Nice," Eva Jansen agreed. A wing of shiny, dark hair swung against her cheek as she looked around. "Good integration of design and space into the theme of the place—the moss-green walls, the earth-toned banquettes. And see the wall sconces? I love that copper, the twining leaves. Subtle and stylized, but it gives you a sense of warmth and character. And preps you for a meal that's all about the food and where it came from." She took a sip of sparkling water. "It's all in the details, Andrew."

"Right, Chef Temple's into the locavore movement," the young man, Andrew, said after consulting whatever notes he kept on his PDA.

"Reviews have been stellar, weekend dinner reservations are impossible to come by, and my sources tell me it's turning a profit." Rosemary caught the avaricious gleam in Eva's blue eyes as she leaned toward her assistant. "What's important about that, from our perspective, is how Market has raised the bar for fine dining in this neighborhood. Until recently, unless you wanted a great diner or a nice Sunday brunch, the Upper West Side was a culinary wasteland. Which means what?"

"Um. Untapped potential, ripe for new businesses, less competition?"

She toasted him with her water glass. "Exactamundo, bingo, and you got it, my young protégé. And Market's success proves that there's a—brace yourself—*market* for this caliber of restaurant in this area."

"But is 422 the space for it?"

Rosemary closed her laptop and opened the book on quantum mechanics she'd brought with her. The conversation was about to get good, and she didn't want to miss anything while she pretended to type to keep up her cover. It was easier to turn pages without reading them.

As Eva Jansen and her assistant discussed the pros and

cons of the space next door, Rosemary took careful note of everything they said. But there was part of her that was busily working on what exactly she ought to ask Wes for in return for this fascinating information.

She smiled to herself—just a tiny curve of the lips; anything more would be suspicious, since not that many people found quantum mechanics to be a barrel of laughs—and shook the ice cubes in her empty glass at the bartender.

Tiberius wasn't going to know what hit him.

Chapter 17

"The assistant got out his PDA and Eva dictated some notes about 422 Columbus. Good natural light in the kitchen, she gave bonus points for that, and said someone with a brain designed those work stations. Plenty of space and ventilation, troughs built in for running water. The dining room is, apparently, another story. And then their meals came, which they seemed to enjoy very much," Rosemary reported brightly. "Eva commented on the tenderness of the lettuce leaves and how it contrasted with the satisfying crunch of the bitter endive. Andrew called the duck salami 'sublime' and made her taste it; she agreed."

"Dude," Chef Temple said, rocking back on his heels and sending Wes a pleased glance. "You nailed it."

Rosemary watched the play of joy and relief across Wes's expressive face. She could read him pretty well, she realized. The thought gave her a pang. She wasn't sure she was ready to forgive him, but it seemed as if she might not have any choice. He was just so . . . magnetic.

Tearing her gaze away, she looked curiously around the kitchen. It was her first time in a professional restaurant kitchen, and it was interesting. There was an air of energy and purpose emanating from the many cooks moving past each other in the tight space between the ovens along the wall and the stainless steel countertops in the center.

They were all so focused and intense, their eyes trained on their work, their hands moving swiftly and efficiently as they wielded their sharp knives and tongs, their spoons and side towels. It reminded her of some of the labs she'd worked in as a grad student—each person in his or her own world, but working in tandem toward the same goal.

Then, it was the pursuit of knowledge, now it was dinner. On some level, Rosemary knew she would once have scorned the latter as trivial and superfluous when compared with the former.

But as she watched the activity swirling around her, and saw the way Wes stood taller, his shoulders straighter, when his cooking was praised—she thought maybe there was something to be said for a pursuit that led to a pleasure as concrete as the joy people got from good food in a warm, convivial atmosphere.

"Yes, yes, kudos all around on the food," Grant interjected. "What else did she say about the place next door?"

Rosemary took a deep breath and began to recite. "Andrew said, 422 Columbus appears to have many of the qualities you look for in a space. Eva agreed, noting that its proximity to Market could be a plus or a minus, and only time would tell, but that Market had raised the culinary profile of the neighborhood in general. She likened it to a luxury beach cottage going up on a street in the Hamptons, forcing the price of real estate up."

"Told you," Adam crowed, thwacking Grant on the shoulder.

"What else?" Grant asked, ignoring his friend.

She filled them in on the dining room, the fact that Eva thought it would need to be gutted, but that the kitchen only needed to be refitted with new appliances in order to serve a full restaurant and the assistant's responses about the other spaces on their list of potential Upper West Side acquisitions, along with the details Andrew had read from his notes on each of those properties.

When she'd finished her recital, all three men were blinking at her.

"What?" Did she have smoked duck stuck in her teeth?

"That was amazing," Wes said. "I know you told me about the memory thing, and I believed you, but. Damn."

"Thank you," Grant said, taking her hand. "That was exactly the kind of information we were looking for."

Adam shook his head, but smiled easily at Rosemary. "Yeah, thanks. Not sure what we'll do with all that good info, if anything, but it was sure interesting to hear. And we definitely owe you one. Come out with us to Chapel after dinner service tonight, I'll buy you a drink or three."

Grant was still holding her hand lightly when Adam started to speak, but when the executive chef shrugged off the question of how they might use her data, Grant's fingers tightened on hers until she winced. He dropped her hand at once with an apologetic grimace.

Flexing her fingers lightly, Rosemary said, "Oh, that's quite all right, Chef. Wes has already promised me a favor in return for my help, and I'll absolutely be collecting."

"Yeah, I got you covered, Chef." Wes laughed. He hadn't stopped working the whole time Rosemary was talking—his hands flew across his cutting board, knife flashing as he cut a green apple into perfectly uniform matchsticks. "My ass will probably be black and blue for a week after she gets through with me."

"Whoa, man. So long as you show up for work on time, I don't care what you do with your personal life," Adam said.

"Corporal punishment is not on the agenda." Rosemary's cheeks were burning, but she refused to give in to

Wes's teasing. At least she recognized it as gentle rib-
bing now.

Adam and Grant thanked her again before hurrying off
to get ready for dinner service, Grant frowning at Adam
the whole way.

A passing chef said, "Behind, hot," as he charged past,
nearly braining her with a large rectangular baking sheet
piled with steaming bones.

"Heads up," Wes said, coming to her rescue and whisk-
ing her out of the way of oncoming traffic before she was
showered with hot food.

Clearly, the kitchen was ramping up into high gear for
dinner. "I guess I should leave you to it," she said, reluctant to go. They hadn't really accomplished anything on
her project yet. "I thought we'd have time to talk about the
aphrodisiac study, though."

"Yeah, sorry about that." He ducked his head guiltily. "I
thought I'd have a breather between lunch and dinner. Then
this Eva Jansen thing came up, and . . . crap. But hey!" He
brightened. "Tomorrow's my day off, so we'll have plenty
of time to work things out."

Rosemary looked away. She was no fool—pretty far
from it, in fact. She could read between the lines here.
Something else came up, namely, something to do with
his job at Market, and Wes immediately gave it priority.

Disappointment dragged at her chest. She wasn't even
sure if she was disappointed in him for behaving true to
form, or in herself for failing to anticipate it.

But her own pitiful imaginings and expectations weren't
the point. It was fruitless to get upset over something Wes
couldn't change. He cared more about his job than he did
about her. End of story. And no amount of mysterious
strawberry protein or serotonin surge was going to make
him put her first.

Ignoring the persistent small voice in her head that

said maybe she just wasn't good enough, interesting enough, lovable enough to be anyone's top priority, Rosemary dredged up a smile and said, "I look forward to tomorrow, then."

The smile must have been less than convincing because Wes's eyes narrowed, his bright grin fading. "What's wrong?"

"Nothing," she said firmly. *Nothing except that I've suddenly developed a learning disability when it comes to you, and no matter how many times you make it clear that I don't matter to you in the slightest, I keep hoping you'll magically wake up one day and realize you can't live without me.* "I'm just annoyed about the delay in moving forward. I got started on some of the groundwork today, and I was hoping to fill you in, but I guess I'll do that tomorrow."

"Okay," he said, still searching her face. She made it as blank as two and a half years as the youngest, nerdiest undergrad at Yale had taught her.

"Really," Wes insisted. "I'm sorry about this. I'll meet you at your hotel then, around ten? I swear I'll make it up to you."

"Sure," she said, suddenly desperate to be elsewhere. "Fine, see you then."

Before he could ask the question she could see forming on his face, Rosemary hitched her laptop bag higher on her shoulder and whirled, all but racing from the kitchen. There was a strange, hot prickling behind her eyes and an itch in her throat that forced her to swallow over and over, trying to push it down.

As she stepped out into the crisp September air, Rosemary thought, not for the first time, that she'd happily trade a few IQ points for a little extra in the emotional intelligence department.

Maybe then she'd be smart enough to avoid feeling like this. Or at least, she'd be better able to deal with it.

Although, really, she ought to be an expert at coping with second-place status. After all, growing up the child of a constantly touring best-selling author and a sought-after academic lecturer was perfect training for accustoming oneself to making do with whatever scraps of affection were carelessly tossed one's way.

What would it take, she wondered a little despairingly, to condition herself to stop looking for more?

She thrust her hand out for a cab, flagging one down almost immediately. Clambering into the back, she gave the address for Peaceful Paws Doggie Day Spa and perched uncomfortably on the cracked vinyl seat, which was no doubt crawling with the germs of the many passengers before her. The cab smelled like sauerkraut and shoes. She cracked a window and tried to breathe as shallowly as possible.

Focusing on the way Lucille's whole body would wag when she caught sight of Rosemary after even five minutes apart, she searched through her bag for antibacterial wipes and tried to be grateful to have even one creature in her life who offered unstinting and unconditional affection—while also remembering that Lucille was only hers because Wes Murphy was a faithless, selfish deserter.

Maybe instead of researching chemicals to help humans achieve momentary closeness, she ought to be looking into what it was in the canine brain that prompted unswerving devotion, so she could duplicate it in handy pill form.

Wes frowned after Rosemary, his knifework slowing to a halt. "What the hell was that about?" he wondered under his breath.

Unluckily for him, Frankie happened to be reaching for one of the stockpots stored on the shelving above Wes's station, so he was close enough to hear. The sous chef snorted and said something that sounded like, "You berk."

Knowing he shouldn't start anything up and actually being mature enough not to do it were two very different things, Wes found. "What was that?"

Frankie hoisted the heavy pot down, his wiry muscles standing out in sharp relief under the ripped sleeves of his black CBGB T-shirt. Wes was definitely digging on not having to conform to the ACA uniform standard, but Frankie took it to a whole other level, almost never bothering with a chef's jacket. He had a long butcher's apron on today, already smeared with blood from the rib eyes he'd been portioning.

Giving Wes his patented lip curl, Frankie said, "I called you a berk. Which you are, if you can't comprehend why your bird might be ticked off."

Wes scowled and concentrated on making his knife cuts absolutely perfect, each baton of carrot exactly the same length as the others. "Look, I don't speak Brit punk, so if you want me to understand you when you mock me, you'll have to translate."

"A berk is . . . well. Fuck me. You know, I'm not sure exactly what it means, but come on, mate. You see what 'm getting at. You're a shite, a loser, a pathetic knob, a hopeless, helpless, dickless moron. Better?"

Wes's shoulders wanted to hunch, so he straightened them instead. "Tell me how you really feel, Chef."

Frankie leaned on the edge of the stockpot and regarded Wes with obvious dislike. "You truly don't get why your girl was upset, do you?"

Rosemary's face in the instant before she ran away flashed in front of his mind's eye, pale and a little pinched around the mouth. Wes's stomach dropped, but he shot

Frankie a skeptical look. "No offense or anything, but I'm not about to take relationship advice from you."

Frankie's face darkened at the jab, and he sneered. "No, 'course not. Why would Wonder Wes want advice, even when he's clearly cocking things up with the woman of his dreams?"

Wes couldn't help his start of surprise, the knife slipping sideways and catching the tip of his finger. "Fuck," he muttered, dropping the blade and putting pressure on the welling cut. Slices on the hand tended to bleed like whoa, and this one was no exception.

"Yeah, Jess let slip in the middle of an argument about your infatuation with one of your ACA professors," Frankie said, stretching up to be able to slide a hand into the pocket of his skintight jeans. Wes stared, incredulously sure the dude was about to pull out his ubiquitous pack of Dunhills and light up in the middle of the kitchen, but instead, Frankie produced a Band-Aid.

Tossing the bandage to Wes, he went on, voice dropping to a low, insinuating whisper. "She's a looker, too. Can see why you're interested. Not to mention the lure of the forbidden. Strict teacher, naughty student—loads of wank material there."

"Shut the fuck up," Wes ground out as he wrapped the bandage around his bleeding finger and picked the knife back up. It stung like a bitch, but he welcomed the pain. It focused him on the job at hand rather than the appealing fantasy of smashing his fist into Frankie's smug, sneering mouth.

"What, you're going to tell me it's not like that?" Frankie said. "Because that's not how it looked from the outside, mate."

"I'm not your mate," Wes pointed out. "You've made that crystal clear. So why are you talking to me, man? Just leave it alone."

Instead of the instant smirk and snappy comeback he was expecting, Wes was surprised to see Frankie glance to the side, a solemn twist to the mouth that Wes was more accustomed to seeing in a sneer.

"I may not like you," Frankie said slowly, as if he were forcing the words out with great difficulty. "But Jess does. And, leaving aside that mad stunt you pulled locking us in the changing room, you've been a good friend to him. So maybe I don't hate you with the fiery heat of a thousand suns anymore."

Wes felt like he ought to run out to the back alley and make sure the sky was still up where it belonged, not in pieces all over the pavement.

"Well, shit," he said stupidly. "Thanks. I'm game for a little friendly advice, if you are."

"Let's not get ahead of ourselves. I wouldn't bank on me being friendly," Frankie told him, sounding grouchy. "I'm still, more likely than not, going to need to phrase any advice in such a way as to make it clear that you're an idiot."

Wes suppressed a smile. "I'd be hugely disappointed, and a little frightened, if you didn't. Fire away."

Turning to heave the stockpot onto an open burner at his own station, Frankie reached back above Wes's head for a long wooden spoon, which he then pointed at Wes. "You made that girl sit around all morning, dancing attendance on your whims, just waiting for you to deign to glance her way. And when you do, what is it you say? Is it 'Oh my, how lovely you look today!' or 'Light of my life, how you complete me!'? No. It's 'Do me this favor, there's a good girl. Thanks ever so, now naff off and let me get back to this here man's work.'"

Frankie affected a strange, flatly nasal accent for Wes's lines, which Wes eventually realized was meant to sound American. Even the urge to laugh at Frankie's ridiculous

John Wayne parody faded, though, under the crushing realization that the guy was actually right.

"Damn it." Wes groaned, dropping his knife and putting his head in his hands. "I'm such a shit."

Frankie clapped him on the back hard enough to nearly buckle Wes's knees. "Finally, we agree on something!"

"The first woman who matters to me, and I'm a complete disaster. I keep messing things up with her—it's as if the more I want it to work, the more it all falls apart."

Frankie went back to his station and started heaping chunks of butternut squash into the stockpot for tonight's soup special. "Don't be a ponce. From what I saw, all is not lost—the girl fancies you. God knows why. So what are you going to do about it?"

Wes grabbed his knife back up and attacked his carrots. "You're right," he said, mind racing ahead to the next day. "There's got to be something I can do to let her know how I feel. Or wait. I'm thinking about it the wrong way. It's not about how I feel. It's about showing her how much she matters."

This was it. Fate had pushed Rosemary back into Wes's life, and he was taking his shot. Maybe he couldn't convince her he'd been attempting to do the noble thing by leaving her for his job at Market—it didn't sound believable, even in Wes's head. But, with a little effort, he might be able to get her to see that he'd changed. Maybe they could just leave the past where it belonged.

"Now you're getting somewhere, mate," Frankie crowed. "There, you see? Knew you couldn't be as dumb as you look."

"I'm smart enough to do whatever it takes to keep Rosemary, now that I've got a second chance with her," Wes said, an idea forming.

It would mean a long night of very little sleep after a full day's work, but if it made Rosemary smile in that

shocked, delighted way of hers, it would be so completely
worth it.

And if it worked, he was going to owe Frankie Boyd.
Big time. The biggest. *Luckily,* Wes mused as a group of
servers, Jess Wake among them, clattered up the stairs
from the locker rooms, dressed and ready to set the dining
room for dinner service, *I know exactly how to repay him.*

Chapter 18

Rosemary dressed for her day of work with Wes as if she were putting on a suit of armor rather than a pair of brown corduroys and her favorite tan sweater with the suede elbow patches.

She'd stolen the sweater from her father's open suitcase years ago, while he was unpacking after getting home from one of his lecture tours. It had been quite a while since it actually smelled like her father's signature sandalwood and pine cologne, but even without the scent, the sense memory of sitting on her parents' bed, so happy to be with her dad again, lingered in the fabric as if imprinted on the wool.

Pulling that sweater over her head and feeling the static electricity lift every stray hair until she must look like Drew Barrymore on the *Firestarter* posters—it was like girding her loins for battle.

Well. Not technically. That would be more like putting on her underwear, since the term "girding one's loins" came from the Roman era, when soldiers would pull up and secure their lower garments in order to increase maneuverability during the heat of battle.

"And now I'm babbling nervously inside my own head,"

she said to Lucille, who cocked her ears curiously from her position ensconced like a queen between the pillows mounded on the hotel bed.

"At least I've gotten used to talking to an animal who won't speak back to me. Well, not in my vernacular. You respond in other ways, though, don't you?"

Lucille's fuzzy white tail thumped twice against the bedding.

Rosemary would never have believed how much company one small, mostly silent dog could be.

"Come on, Lucille," she said, jingling the new, pink leash with the rhinestone studs. There was a boutique attached to the Peaceful Paws Doggie Day Spa that carried, of course, the most ludicrously overpriced, overdesigned dog accessories—and to anyone who believed dogs were merely dumb animals, Rosemary would submit the evidence of Lucille's purposeful and deliberate panting after this silly sparkly princess leash. Lucille had her new mistress wrapped around her little paw, and she clearly knew it. One blink of those liquid black eyes, and Rosemary whipped out her credit card.

Stretching indolently, Lucille stood and did a full-body shake before ambling to the foot of the bed and allowing Rosemary to clip the leash to her collar. Which was old and worn, Rosemary noticed with a frown. She'd have to see what else the boutique had today, she decided as they left their room and headed for the elevators, Lucille prancing happily at her side as if she'd been born to lushly carpeted halls and Art Deco décor.

The elevator doors swished closed behind them, enclosing them in a jewel box that descended toward the lobby in a swift, silent rush. Rosemary checked her watch. Nine o'clock. That should give her plenty of time, she thought as the doors opened.

Lucille's head jerked up the instant they set foot in the

lobby. With a tremendous tug that nearly pulled the leash from Rosemary's hand, the tiny dog leaped and cavorted at the very end of her tether, tongue lolling and toes clacking brightly on the marble floor.

"Lucille!" Rosemary tightened her grip on the leash.

"There's my girls." The smooth, velvety voice came from the seating area beside the concierge desk and sent a shiver down the back of her neck.

Wait, I'm not ready! My loins are so not girded for this!

That was all the internal panic she had time for before Wes Murphy was right there in front her, in all his leather-jacketed, windswept hotness, kneeling down to let Lucille lick, sniff, rub against, and generally debase herself shamefully all over his hands.

"Whaddya smell, L-dawg? Huh? Hey, what a pretty leash for my pretty girl!"

Seeing the two of them together gave Rosemary a pang. She felt absurdly like a third wheel.

"If you'd like to get a room, so you can carry out this reunion in private, the reservation desk is right over there," she said.

The tart tone brought Wes's head up, his ridiculously beautiful hair flopping onto his forehead and tangling in his long eyelashes. There were dark smudges under his eyes, as if he hadn't slept well. He blinked, and Rosemary had to close her hand into a fist to keep from reaching out and smoothing back the chestnut locks.

"I missed her," he explained, standing up. "Almost as much as I missed you."

Rosemary froze, feeling cornered. It was exactly what she'd wanted to hear that first day she saw Wes again at the restaurant, but now that he was saying it, she had no idea how to feel about it, much less how to respond.

Five minutes, she mused despairingly. That's all it

took for him to start chipping away at the foundation of the barriers she'd hastily erected around her heart.

Pathetic.

He was still gazing at her with those green-gold cat eyes, waiting for her response. Flustered, Rosemary lifted her chin and said, "You're early. I was just about to drop Lucille off at doggie day care before meeting you."

"Aw, she doesn't need day care. Let's take her with us! I thought we could go to the park, it's such a gorgeous day."

"Oh. Well, I guess that would be all right." It was as if he delighted in throwing her off balance, she sulked as he went to grab an old leather knapsack from the couch he'd been sitting on.

Rosemary compensated for the derailment of her careful plans by being extra terse on the walk to the park. Not that it was a long hike—one block west, a quick Fifth Avenue crossing, and Wes led them to an entrance in the low stone wall surrounding the park.

Dancing and pulling on the pink leash, Lucille was clearly in heaven. Her two favorite humans, the bracing cool of early fall weather, and the myriad fascinating smells associated with Central Park—all of it combined to put her into transports of ecstasy, as evidenced by the high carriage of her fluffy tail and the perk of her pointed, white-tufted ears.

Crossing into Central Park from the frenetic bustle and noise of Fifth Avenue was like entering another world. They set off down the curved pathway, the sounds of the city fading behind them almost at once. Against her will, Rosemary found herself enchanted by the lush, deliberately cultivated wilderness of the park.

As if echoing her thoughts, Wes said, "God, I love the park on a day like this. All these paths winding around through the trees changing color, over bridges and through tunnels—the city is such a grid, and the park is nothing like that. It's wild."

"Frederick Law Olmsted won a competition for the best design," she told him. "The city chose his naturalistic vision of the park over a more formal approach because it made the best use of the varied terrain. They planted more than half a million trees, shrubs, and vines to get it to look like this."

Wes grinned at her, sticking his hands in his jacket pockets. "Have I mentioned today how much I love that big brain of yours? Come on, tell me some more stuff about the park."

She pressed her lips together to stop the flood of information that wanted to pour out. "Are you mocking me?" she demanded. "I can't tell, but I'd prefer it if you didn't."

His grin faded. "No, I'm really not," he said, his voice gentling as though he were trying to soothe a skittish lab rat. "I honestly like talking to you and learning new stuff. You make me curious about the world outside the kitchen, which is something I haven't thought much about the last few years. Too focused on where I wanted to get to, I guess. But when I'm with you, it's like everything opens up, and I can see more possibilities than what's right in front of me."

Rosemary had to concentrate to keep putting one foot in front of the other. "That's . . . a very nice thing to say. I'm not sure how I'm supposed to respond."

Wes's lips twitched, but he treated it as a real question. "Well, I guess you could go traditional and just say 'thanks.' Or you could be all tit for tat and tell me something you like about me."

"That's assuming there *is* something I like about you." The words popped out before she could censor them, and Rosemary bit her lip, feeling exposed, as if she'd just revealed exactly how much Wes had hurt her.

He didn't seem to notice, though. He cocked his head to one side, looking thoughtful, and said, "True enough. So maybe a better tit for tat would be you telling me something true about yourself. Come on, one true thing."

Rosemary thought about what Wes had told her. "I've always been curious," she finally said after a long pause. "Sometimes to my detriment. But people are so incomprehensible, and the world is so mysterious—the only thing that makes sense to me is to try and unlock the secrets of how things really work. Since I know I'll never understand how people work and why they do the things they do."

"Why do you think that is?" Wes asked, taking her hand to turn her down an offshoot path to the right.

"Well, people are largely irrational and illogical, ruled by their emotional responses rather than their intellect—oh. You mean why can't I relate to that, don't you?"

He shrugged, keeping hold of her hand. Rosemary let him, even though it made her stomach jump around nervously. She immediately began to worry about sweaty palms. "You keep telling me you're a genius," he pointed out. "And I believe you! But it seems to me like people aren't that complicated—the fact that we're ruled by our desires and instincts actually makes us easier to figure out."

"Not for me," Rosemary said. "And the reasons for that . . . well, who knows. One of my mother's psychologist cronies would probably tell you it has something to do with not being held frequently enough as an infant—that lack of early attachment to a parental figure stunted my ability to connect with others as an adult." It was her turn to shrug. "Perhaps there's some truth to that. I certainly don't remember being hugged often as a child. My earliest memory of my mother is being given an IQ test when I was four. I was already reading and writing, and I remember being aware that the test was very important to her, and that I had to do well."

"And you did," he guessed softly.

She didn't like the gleam in his eye; it looked like pity. "Of course," she confirmed stiffly. "My mother was pleased, so I was, too. The results of that test got me my first private tutor, and gave my mother the idea for her second book, the one that became a best-seller. *Prodigy: How to Gift Your Child.*"

A hitch in Wes's step, and Rosemary's hand popped out of his. Yep, clammy. She took the opportunity to give her palm a surreptitious scrub over the thin wale of her corduroys.

"I've heard of that book," Wes said. "So, that was your mom?"

"Sure was," Rosemary said, watching Lucille take advantage of the pause in forward momentum to investigate the roots of a deciduous shrub.

"And she wrote it about you. Because of you."

"And took me with her on her book tour. I became something of an expert on hotels that year."

"It's nice that she wanted to give you credit," Wes said.

"At lectures, interviews, bookstores—everyone who came to hear her speak wanted to see me."

"Well, sure, you were kind of the star of the book, right?"

"My mother was the star, Wes. She trotted me out in front of those crowds—rooms full of people staring and whispering and breathing and coughing—ugh." Rosemary shuddered. "I think at first she hoped I'd dazzle them all with my big brain, as you call it, but I couldn't. All I could ever do was stand there. And in the end, she preferred that. I was nothing more than a prop." Suddenly antsy, she pulled a protesting Lucille away from the bush and marched off down the path.

Walking swiftly, Rosemary wasn't sure if she was trying

to outrun the memories beating at her like a heavy down-pour, or the man whose questions had brought them up—but in any case, it was only about ten-point-two seconds before Wes caught up with her.

"Hey, wait up! Shit, Rosie, I'm sorry."

"I don't want your pity," she said over the rush of blood in her ears. She never talked about the past; it was over and done with, what good did it do to rehash it?

"It's not pity," he argued. "I'm pissed. And I wish I'd been there to make you laugh, make you feel better."

When he slipped his fingers around hers again, Rosemary sighed. She had to admit, if only to herself, that the wordless comfort of his touch made the rain in her head slow to a drizzle.

"I didn't have anyone back then." Rosemary frowned, hating the way that sounded. "I mean, I had tutors and a nanny who traveled with us. I was fine. I had a very privi-leged childhood; I was given opportunities most people can only dream about. I visited all fifty states before the age of six."

"And you hated it," Wes said, his hand tightening for a moment. "You were right the first time; you didn't have anyone back then, not really. But you have me now, and I swear, you're going to enjoy today." He grinned at her, a reckless, happy sparkle in his eyes. "I've got a couple of props, but you're not one of them. Promise."

Wes squeezed her hand again, and his heart leaped into his throat when she gave him a small, reluctant smile and squeezed back.

Okay. Progress.

He couldn't believe he'd spaced like that, stopped read-ing her facial expressions and body language, and gotten her onto this clearly painful subject. Talk about breaking the mood.

But he'd just been so thrown by the sudden revelation that Pops was right. *Prodigy* was about her. The book Pops had used as inspiration for their final scam was written by Rosemary's mother. And oh, hey. Yeah. They were filthy rich, too.

It was too freaky weird for words, and the blow knocked him sideways for a good thirty seconds—until Rosemary's agitation started to register.

Hell, maybe it was a good thing. He hated to see her upset, but he knew more about her than he did five minutes ago.

And now, more than ever, he hoped his plan today would work the way he wanted it to.

Their winding path finally curved around and emerged from the trees so they could see the lake.

"It's man-made," Rosemary said. The return to imparting random facts seemed to settle her. "There are more than thirty bridges and arches in the park."

"Well, we don't need to find one," Wes said, steering her left and down toward the bank of the lake. "Because we're going to cop a squat right here."

They walked up a small hillock and down into a dip ten feet or so from the edge of the lake, where the water lapped quietly against the rocks, grass, and roots growing down from the shore. Nestled in a curve of the lake was a tiny gazebo, painted white and peeling, with a slat bench built out along the sides.

"I first found this place when I was a kid," he revealed, pulling her down the hill and into the quiet, enclosed structure. "It was the perfect hideout for a nine-year-old, tucked away, off the beaten track—in all the times I've come back here over the years, I've only encountered someone else in this gazebo maybe twice. It's one of the best-kept secrets of Central Park."

"Not so secret, if you're sharing it with me," Rosemary

pointed out, her interested gaze taking in every detail of the old building.

"Well." Wes shrugged. "You're special." He said it as matter-of-factly as he could, but he meant it with everything that was in him. He meant it so much, he was actually afraid that if he tried to sound sincere, he'd overplay it and come off as sarcastic, which was the last thing he wanted.

This whole day was about making sure Rosemary understood exactly how special she was to him. It was about earning a second chance.

First order of business? Lunch.

Chapter 19

While Rosemary admired the lake spilled at their feet and sparkling in the crisp September sunshine, Wes set the scene. He looped Lucille's leash around a nail protruding from the frame of the gazebo, then excavated two thick blankets from his knapsack, one tartan plaid wool and one heather gray fleece, and spread them over the dusty wooden floor.

"I thought we were going to work, not have a picnic," Rosemary said.

"Can't we do both? Food first—my dad always said, you can't think on an empty stomach."

She looked highly suspicious, but sat down anyway. Picnics were irresistible to most people, Wes had found.

Taking care not to look too pleased, Wes unpacked the rest of the provisions he'd spent so many hours gathering together.

There were paper plates, plastic utensils, and good linen napkins borrowed from the restaurant, along with a miniature cutting board and several small, individual enameled cast-iron pots, their lids secured with kitchen twine.

He unwrapped half a loaf of the light, crusty baguette

Market's pastry chef, Violet, was justly famous for, and arranged it on the cutting board along with a round of triple-cream goat cheese from a Hudson Valley cheese-maker.

Rosemary shivered and wrapped both arms around her waist. "It's a little chilly here, out of the sun," she said.

Why, God? Why do you test me this way? Wes thought. Ignoring the perfect opportunity to skip straight to the seduction was a true feat of will, but he managed it.

"Maybe this will warm you up." Settling himself on the blanket a careful, respectful distance away from her, Wes lifted out the sealed, unlabeled glass bottle, relieved to feel the slip-slide of cold condensation on his fingers, and a pair of wine glasses.

"What kind of wine is that?" she asked.

"It's not wine; not exactly," Wes said, pulling out the plastic cork. "I thought I'd give you another cocktail to try, see if maybe this one is your drink."

The liquid he poured into the glasses was a clear, dark gold, like apple juice—but the smell that wafted up from the bottle was more dark, sensual nightclub than bright, happy kindergarten.

Rosemary sniffed. "I smell . . . nutmeg? And, frak me, a lot of alcohol."

"Good nose," Wes said, impressed. "Yeah, freshly grated nutmeg, plus a whole lot of booze, goes into this punch. Lemon juice to tart it up, sugar for sweetness, white wine and brandy to layer the flavor—it's a classic."

"I haven't made it to punches yet on my list of potential cocktails," Rosemary said, accepting her glass. She took a tiny, ladylike sip, sucked in air through her nose, then went back for a longer gulp.

"That's truly exquisite," she said, releasing Wes from the pleasurable tension that held him frozen in place while she tasted the first of his offerings. Cracking his neck to one side, he pulled the long sleeves of his henley shirt down over his hands and grabbed one of the cast-iron pots. Setting it in front of Rosemary, he reached into his back pocket for his pocketknife.

Wes cut the twine and lifted the little, round lid away, allowing a curl of steam to escape from the pot.

Rosemary inhaled and closed her eyes, then moaned. She actually *moaned*. It was a noise he remembered—had remembered frequently, on purpose, almost every night since, eyes closed, breathing hard, hand doing what came naturally—from their one time together. Wes's groin tightened in an atavistic rush at the unabashedly sensual sound.

"What is that?" she breathed, staring down into the pot.

"Technically, it's called baeckeoffe," Wes said, carefully pronouncing the Alsatian word. Beck-eh-off. Heh. "But basically, it's the most warming, satisfying, delicious little hotpot full of goodness you can imagine."

She poked at it with her fork, releasing even more steam. "Ye gods. It smells amazing."

"I should fucking well hope so," he muttered, thinking of the hours he'd put into preparing it.

Digging in, she got the forkful halfway to her mouth before pausing. "Oh. Is there anything in here I should know about? I mean, anything potentially hazardous? It doesn't smell fishy at all, so I assume no shellfish. Or blowfish, but why would there be blowfish. The odds are against it, right? Maybe you should just list the ingredients."

Quietly adoring her, Wes rattled off what he'd put into the baeckeoffe. "Thinly sliced fingerling potatoes, parsnips, and leeks layered with diced carrot, julienned fennel, and chunks of pork marinated in white vermouth and juniper berries. The whole thing gets doused in Riesling, topped with slices of fresh tomato, and then baked. For hours."

"That sounds complicated and time-consuming," she commented, allowing the fork to complete its journey to her mouth. She chewed for a second, and her eyes lit up. "And also, yum!"

"Good?" he couldn't help asking, even though her opinion was obvious from the speed with which she dove back in for another bite.

"Mm-hmm," she hummed, forking up another piece of perfectly tender pork. At least, it looked tender from where Wes was sitting, and he realized he didn't need to rely on her review to tell him if it had turned out okay—he could taste his own.

Which reminded him. Excavating a jar of whole-grain mustard from the depths of the knapsack, he tossed it to her. "Hey, try it with this."

"Interesting," she pronounced after she'd smeared her next bit of pork and roasted vegetables with the mustard. "It makes the other flavors taste brighter and more vibrant. I can taste the juniper and the floral sweetness of the wine even more clearly. I wonder what chemical it is in the mustard that acts as a flavor enhancer?"

Wes shrugged, enjoying his first bite. "No idea. All I know is, it tastes great. We should check it out, see if we can discover the perfect ratio of mustard to baeckeoffe."

"I postulate that trial and error is the best way to proceed with that particular experiment," Rosemary said, reaching for the French bread. She broke off a hunk—Wes enjoyed the loud, satisfying crunch—and dunked it in the juices pooled around the meat and vegetables in her pot.

"Now you're talking," Wes said, ripping into the bread. "I've never been more truly convinced of your genius."

She smiled around a mouth full of food he'd stayed up late last night preparing, and Wes felt warmth well up in his chest. He loved watching her eat; he couldn't imagine anything sexier.

Well. Maybe if she were eating naked.

Wes's cock had an immediate, and very strong, reaction to that charming mental image. *Down, boy,* he thought. *Your time will come, but it ain't here yet.*

To distract himself, Wes said, "I can't believe you haven't already regaled me with the tradition behind baeckeoffe."

"I don't know it, or I'm sure I would have."

Wes clutched at his chest as if he were having heart palpitations. "What! You mean to tell me there's something you don't know, that I do know? This is a red-letter day!"

She pouted, her full lower lip poking out just enough to make him want to nibble at it. "I know where the phrase 'red-letter day' comes from," she offered. "Do I get points for that?"

"Sure, I can be magnanimous in victory." He took another bite, pretended not to notice her staring at him expectantly.

"Well?" she finally said, with great emphasis.

"Well what?"

"Tell me! The baeckeoffe tradition. You can't tease me with new information and then not share. Unless you want to be cruel."

"That's not what I want at all." Their eyes clashed, the moment suddenly serious and more intense than either of them probably intended, but it couldn't be helped. There was too much unresolved between them for casual, comfy conversation.

Still, to prove he wasn't interested in cruelty, Wes told her the story. " 'Baeckeoffe' translates loosely to 'baker's oven.' On Sundays, the women of the tiny villages of Alsace would prepare this stew, layering all the ingredients carefully together, and then drop it off at the local bakery while they went to church. When they came back a few hours later, the meat and vegetables would be roasted to falling-apart perfection. So you see, it's not that complicated a dish. I just stick it in the oven and let it do its thing."

"That's a lovely story," she said, but she was frowning. "When did you say you baked this, again?"

"I didn't. Last night," he said easily.

"After you worked all day?"

He shrugged.

"And how long did it take?"

"Ah, not that long," he hedged. He wasn't looking for a pity party here.

"You just said it takes several hours in the oven, and that's after you did all the slicing and dicing of the vegetables!" She sounded so accusing, Wes had to laugh.

"Yeah, but I'm superfly when it comes to prep," he said, buffing his nails on his shirt. "Fastest knife this side of the Atlantic."

"No wonder you look tired," she said, her lovely mouth turned down. She was clearly determined to fret about this.

Wes grabbed her hand and held on. "Look. I wanted to do this for you. I got a couple hours of sleep in, so don't sweat it—I'm fine. Okay?"

"I'm not accustomed to this feeling," she said. The lower lip was back. She was going to kill him with that thing, if she wasn't careful. This time, though, it was accompanied by such a bewildered expression, Wes managed to keep his thoughts relatively clean and pure.

"What feeling is that, sweets?" He kept it gentle and quiet, rubbing circles over the back of her hand with the side of his thumb.

"This . . . this . . . this—" She waved her free hand in an unsteady arc, like she was trying to grab the rest of her thought right out of the air. Unable to choose one target for her confusion, her attention darted from the two of them, to the picnic, the lake, and back again.

"You're not used to somebody doing something nice for you, just because they want to," Wes guessed.

She smiled tightly. It looked painful. "In my experience, most acts of kindness are followed by requests for money, time, and/or help."

It hurt him, deep down in a part of himself he liked to pretend no longer existed, that she'd be so kerfuffled by one relatively simple act of caring. And yet, selfishly, he was almost fiercely glad to be the first one to show her what it felt like.

Not to mention the fact that he did have an ulterior motive.

Which he probably ought to be getting along with before this conversation got deeper than the lake behind them.

Emotions were tricky things, Rosemary discovered as she struggled to stuff hers back in their carefully labeled lockbox.

For instance, she imagined many women would have been miffed at the way Wes smoothed the moment over by tidying away their lunch things and busily setting out clean spoons and refilling her punch—but Rosemary was relieved. She didn't want to dissect her feelings and lay them bare. Wes somehow divined that, and she thought it perfectly gallant of him to ignore the prevalent psychobabble about communication and openness being healthy, and allow her to pull herself together with a little dignity.

Rosemary focused on the distraction of wondering what he'd pull out of the knapsack—which was starting to assume magical proportions, like something out of Harry Potter. Could anything other than wizard-space account for the sheer number of items he'd managed to jam into one not-very-large knapsack?

The mystery was solved when Wes produced two small earthenware crocks, glazed a pretty robin's-egg blue, and said, "Pots de crème! Which is basically a fancypants culinary-school way of saying custard."

Rosemary accepted her pot eagerly, and removed the tiny, fragile lid to see a velvety, burnt-orange substance with sparkling amethyst jewels of some kind of sugared flower sprinkled over the top. She glanced up at him, lifting her brows.

"In this case, pumpkin custard with candied violets," he elaborated. Which explained the color.

At this point, not only was Rosemary beyond ready to have a reason not to be talking anymore, she was well conditioned to accept any food whatsoever from Wes's hand.

Positive reinforcement was incredibly motivating, as it turned out.

Dipping her spoon into the pleasingly thick custard, Rosemary brought it to her mouth and slipped it between her lips, fully prepared for something delicious.

Or so she thought—because nothing in her prior experience or existence could have prepared her for the sheer pleasure of this spoonful.

"Oh," she quavered, mouth blissfully full. "Oh, oh."

The lush, earthy sweetness of pumpkin ravished her taste buds, while the crystallized blossoms dotted around the surface of the custard sparkled on her tongue in tiny points of herbaceous fragrance. The homey comfort of autumnal squash and the heady scent of the violets swirled together in a sensual dance that had Rosemary closing her eyes in ecstasy.

She plunged her spoon back in—why was the mouth of the little pot so narrow and hard to navigate?—and was soon in heaven again.

"Good?" Wes asked again, just as he had with the baeckeoffe, and this time it was all Rosemary could do not to call him a moron for even posing the question.

"Are you joking? I want to be facedown in this stuff. I want to swim laps in it. I want . . ." She broke off to spoon up some more.

"I'm glad you're enjoying it," he said, his voice light and bright with amusement. Rosemary was so blissed out, she couldn't even find the wherewithal to take him to task for laughing at her.

"'Enjoying it' is an entirely inadequate phrase to describe this experience." She tipped her head back and basked. "God. I love my lab, but moments like these make me so happy to be done with that part of the experiment. I think I could stay in New York forever."

Wes made a low, rough sound and Rosemary sat up, blinking.

Frak. What did I just say? Panic surged up her chest and closed her throat. Suddenly, the custard didn't want to slip down quite so easily.

Chapter 20

Wes could barely breathe through the wild surge of joy. "Rosie," he said, trying to keep his voice calm and careful instead of shouting like a madman, the way he wanted to. "Do you mean it? You don't have to go back to the academy?"

A scorching hot blush flooded her cheeks, and she wouldn't look him in the eye, but Wes barely noticed because she was nodding. Hesitantly, yeah, but still—and then she said, "I got what I needed from that facility, yes. Which isn't to say I'd never go back; after all, my things are all there, except for Lucille. Not that she's a thing. And not that I'm really thinking about moving here! That would be absurd. Obviously."

"I didn't want to write that note. Cornell made me," Wes blurted, grabbing her hand.

She jerked away, her fingers tightening on the custard pot until they went white. "You were just going to leave without a word?"

"No! That's not what I meant," he said, alarmed. "It came out wrong. I'm just . . . damn, I'm nervous. What I wanted to say was that it wasn't my idea to leave you at all. If it had been up to me, I would've been back the next day, me and Lucille, ready to pick up where we left off."

Rosemary shook her head as if trying to rearrange the thoughts inside it. Moving with exaggerated care, she set the pot and her spoon down on the blanket. "It *was* up to you, Wes. And you made your choice. You chose your career." She looked at him, her eyes the lifeless blue of a frozen pond, and delivered the killing blow. "I wasn't even surprised. It was hardly the first time I was passed over in favor of the chance to leapfrog up the ladder of success."

"It wasn't like that," Wes said, his throat aching. "I swear to you. It was Cornell."

She blinked. "What?"

"President Cornell," Wes said. Even speaking the name aloud made him want to hit something. "He came and found me later that night."

Wes remembered the shock of it—the suddenness of going from the pure joy and thrill of being the first man to ever get to see Dr. Rosemary Wilkins without her clothes on, to the smug, oily insinuations of Wally Cornell.

"He said . . ." Wes paused to study his hands. "Well, some ugly things."

"About what?"

About Wes, mostly—*You really think someone with her pedigree and background, her opportunities and ambition, is going to be satisfied with a piece of rough trade like you for longer than a night?*—and Wes tried not to think about how much he feared the kernel of truth buried in Cornell's smacktalk.

"Doesn't matter," he said. "The main thrust of his conversation was a threat—he swore he'd ruin your reputation if I didn't leave quietly."

Rosemary gasped, her skin draining of all color.

Lucille, who'd been napping contentedly in a patch of sunlight, jumped to her feet and strained at the leash to climb into her mistress's lap.

Her hands came up instinctively to hold the small, wiggly body to her. "And you believed him."

Wes looked out over the lake, watched a cool breeze kick up tiny wavelets and make a flock of ducks take wing. "I didn't think you'd want to risk it. I mean, brass tacks here. You were gonna choose our fledgling whatever over the research you'd been working on for months? No way."

"It should've been my decision to make!" Her voice was raw with some emotion Wes wasn't sure he wanted to name.

He clenched his jaw and forced himself to meet her defiant gaze. "Honestly? I didn't want to know what you'd choose. Maybe it was weak of me, cowardly—I'll cop to that. But I didn't want to put either of us through that conversation."

"So you took the easy road, and left."

Wes laughed, and the sharp bark of it had Lucille's head popping up from the safe circle of Rosemary's arms, ears cocked and alert. "You think leaving was easy? I swear, Rosie, leaving you was the hardest fucking thing I've ever done—and I've pulled some crazy stunts in my time."

Rosemary hunched over Lucille's little body. "Why didn't you tell me this before?" she demanded.

"Because I thought you still needed the lab privileges for your research," Wes said, scooting closer. Close enough to touch, but he didn't, because her body language screamed *Back off or I might shatter into a thousand pieces.* "You were so stoked about it; I didn't want to risk messing that up for you."

"This changes everything. I don't know what I'm supposed to feel now. I didn't want to talk about that night; I wanted to forget about it and move on." She sighed, and he couldn't resist. He lifted a hand to her hair, smoothing a flyaway strand of gold bent on escaping from her braid. He braced himself for her flinch—but it didn't come. Instead, she turned into the touch.

Only slightly, a miniscule amount, as if she breathed in and the breath brought her closer to his hand, but it was enough to make Wes's heart slam out of control. It was enough to give him the courage to say, "Maybe you want to forget that night, but I never will. I couldn't."

She stilled, and her body seemed to loosen, the tension uncoiling slowly and draining away. Her bright blond head tilted until she could catch his gaze, and she said, "I couldn't forget it, either. I couldn't forget you."

Wes clamped his jaw shut on a shout of triumph, but the victory burned in his chest like a lit fuse. "That's why you came to New York to find me."

He loved the delicate rose flush that suffused her cheeks. "Well, it certainly wasn't for your research skills," she said, sniffling.

Wes grinned and tried to pretend his eyes weren't blurring on him, the tears he refused to acknowledge burning behind his eyelids. "What are you talking about? I'll have you know, I meticulously researched every single ingredient that went into this picnic."

Evidently having had her fill of cuddling, Lucille squirmed until Rosemary opened her arms. Four white paws hit the gazebo floor, followed by a cold, black nose as Lucille immediately began foraging for crumbs.

"Oh, really?" Rosemary said. She leaned back on her hands, her body opening like a flower, everything about her lightening up as the atmosphere between them cleared.

She was so beautiful, all relaxed and disheveled, that thin T-shirt straining across her small, firm breasts—the fire in Wes's chest flared and spread.

"What, precisely, were you looking for when you designed this meal?" God, she was practically purring.

Drawn to her like butter melting toward the hottest spot in the pan, Wes knelt up and shuffled around the blankets until he was right there, next to her, above her, sharing the same air with their quickening breaths. "I checked to make sure not a single ingredient has ever been classified, by myth, legend, old wives, or science, as an aphrodisiac."

"And why did you care about that?" A slick pink tongue darted out to wet her plump bottom lip, leaving it shiny and tempting as all hell.

Wes nearly groaned. "Because," he panted, sliding one hand around her back and lowering her gently down to the blanket, "when I kiss you, I don't want there to be any confusion about why you kiss me back."

Her lips parted and that was it. He had to taste them. Framing her stubborn jaw with his right hand, he felt the fluttering of her pulse against his fingertips as he lowered his mouth to hers and plundered it.

She was stiff for an instant, then yielded to him all at once, her body lining itself up with his, limbs flowing seamlessly together. Her mouth yielded, too, softening and opening to allow Wes's ravenous tongue to plunge in, stroke her sharp teeth, her sensitive gums. He ate at her mouth as if he were devouring a ripe peach with all the goodness of the late summer sunshine and cool early rain.

When his tongue tangled with hers, she made a high, inquisitive sound and arched into him like a cat begging to be rubbed. Wes complied, stroking his hand from her jaw, down the line of her neck and feathering across the fragile wings of her collarbones.

His cock throbbed heavily in his jeans. Wes spared a moment to fervently wish he'd had the foresight or optimism to wear sweats or cargo pants, something loose, but then all thought was gone, obliterated by the simple press of her breast in his loosely cupped palm.

Wes honestly didn't know if he'd moved to touch her, or

if she'd arched again and thrust herself against his hand, but it didn't matter. All that mattered was the warm, soft weight of her, the beat of her heart beneath, and the litany of gorgeous little cries that spilled from her mouth when he moved his thumb just. Like. That.

Tearing her mouth away, Rosemary gasped in a breath. "Public," she squeaked. "Us. Out here. We're. Public!"

Her color was high, her eyes bright china blue with desire, and his kisses had swollen her lips to sex-kitten proportions. Wes looked at her bottom lip, always a bit pouty but currently bee-stung enough to shut down his higher brain function, and shook his head sharply.

Plan. He was the man with the plan.

"Right," he said, breathing hard and throttling the need to take that sweet mouth again. "Here, sit up."

It took every ounce of strength to lift himself away from her and back up enough to give her room to move, but once she wasn't sprawled out in front of him like some decadent banquet, it got easier. Marginally.

Lucille whined, her tail thumping the floorboards, and Wes checked to make sure her leash was still secured. Seeing that they weren't about to resume their walk, she gave them a disgruntled look, yawned, and circled in place two or three times before settling back down.

Peeling the fleecy top blanket away from the clinging wool of the tartan, Wes lifted the corner and held his arms out in open invitation.

Rosemary hesitated, some of the hectic blush fading from her cheeks as she glanced around nervously.

Their little oasis in the middle of Central Park was still barren of any life other than the blasé birds and squirrels, and they were used to witnessing all manner of human exploits.

"Come on," he coaxed. "Weren't you saying you were cold before?"

That got her. She snorted and arched a brow at him as she shuffled closer and ducked under the corner of the blanket. "My core body temperature is approaching dangerous fever levels. Feeling cold is no longer an issue of concern."

Wes scooted in behind her, reveling in the waves of heat that were indeed pouring from her slim, fidgeting body. He bracketed her with his legs and arms, giving her his chest to lean back against, and tucked the gray fleece over them.

"Think of me as your trusty old recliner," he said. "Comfy and cozy."

Her slender back pressed against his chest, her curvy hips snugged into the vee of his spread thighs—this was pretty much Wes's idea of heaven.

"A reclining chair makes me think of falling asleep in front of the television," she said, wriggling to get comfortable. "I don't feel particularly sleepy right now."

In the process of settling down, she managed to both elbow him in the side and grind her pert little bottom into his cramped, iron-hard erection. Wes dropped his head to her shoulder, biting down on a groan, caught between the stab of pain in his ribs and the excruciating pleasure-pain radiating up from his groin.

"What's wrong?" she asked, her innocent voice shooting through Wes's fog of desire like lightning through a storm cloud. It focused him, brought him back to himself and this amazing moment, and he turned his head to press his lips to the side of her neck.

Her T-shirt was tissue soft under his cheek, but not as soft as the silky skin of her neck. She smelled clean, as if she only used soap without any of those cloying perfumes or oils to mask the underlying sweetness of her own skin. Wes nuzzled closer, wrapping his arms around her ribs and feeling her heart knocking against his forearm in tandem with the pulse pounding under his kiss.

That same sense of awareness spiked through him again, clearing his mind of everything but the bone-deep knowledge that he was holding something precious in his arms—something unique and irreplaceable, and he had to hang on to it for dear life, because a guy like him? Well, it was incredible enough that he'd been given a second chance.

There wouldn't be a third.

Wanting to thank her for the amazing gift of her body leaning so trustingly against his, Wes nipped the muscle where her neck met her shoulder, just to make her jump, then soothed the spot with his tongue.

She shivered and sighed, and a pit of hunger opened up in his belly. Not for food, but for more of those noises.

Sliding his hand down her taut belly, he found the button fly of her corduroys and attacked it, keeping his mouth busy tasting every inch of throat he could reach. Finally, he got her pants open and loosened enough to plunge his hand between her thighs.

His fingers slipped along the hot, damp fabric of her panties—they felt like plain cotton, ever so slightly rough against his fingertips, and they made him long for the perfect smoothness of the sensitive skin beneath.

"Oooh, Wes," she said, her head falling back. He looked up from her throat to find her eyes open and staring sightlessly at the ceiling of the gazebo, the blue as blank and dazed as the empty autumn sky.

He watched her, drinking in every shift in expression, every hitch of breath, as he carefully, gently, worked his hand inside her underwear and got his fingers on the wet, throbbing core of her.

She shuddered in his arms, hips squirming in ways that made his trapped cock weep. Wes bit down on her shoulder once more and explored the softest, hottest part of her with his hand.

Lucky fucking hand. His cock twitched with jealousy.

Simmer down, he told himself silently. *We're not having full-on sex in the middle of Central Park. That would be nuts. Besides, there's no way Rosemary would be down with that.*

Right?

May the Force be with us—we're so about to have sex in the middle of Central Park!

Rosemary couldn't process it. She really couldn't. Everything was happening so quickly—every minute seemed to bring a new revelation, something shocking that she had to deal with. First she'd found out that Wes had left the academy, not because he'd gotten what he wanted and was through with her, but because he was protecting her. Which was borderline insulting, if she looked at it from a certain angle, but was also sort of touching if viewed from the opposite side. She supposed forgiveness was in order. But forgiveness seemed to go hand in hand with an irresistible desire to jump Wes's bones. Someone should do a study of the make-up sex phenomenon, she thought dizzily. There really was something to it.

After all, here they were in public. Outdoors! And all she wanted was for Wes to pull her down and put his penis inside her and thrust until they both climaxed.

This entire situation was so out of character as to make her wonder if she'd contracted some strange disease that killed inhibition and caused personality shifts.

But the memories of their first night together were fresh enough in her mind that she knew the fever in her blood wasn't caused by illness—it was all Wes.

And this time, he'd made sure she couldn't blame it on any chemistry other than the indefinable attraction between the two of them.

The heel of his hand rubbed exactly where she wanted it most, while his long, dexterous fingers delved between her labia and circled the nerve-rich entrance to her body. He dipped inside, stretching and stroking her, and Rosemary's mind went blessedly blank, the white noise of intense sensation drowning out her chaotic thoughts and fears.

Her hips pulsed, searching for more friction, and Wes gave it to her. The strong motion of his hand pressed against her pubic bone, pushing her body tighter to his, and Rosemary gasped. She could feel his erection, long and thick, solid in the small of her back. He nudged his groin into her, a little helpless movement that scraped the rough, straining fly of his jeans over the knot of nerves clustered above her buttocks.

Snared between his need at her back and his hand stoking her own desires, Rosemary writhed hard enough to lift the blanket. A breeze snuck under, causing refreshing patches of cool air to waft against her heated skin.

Wes's arms and legs merely tightened around her, holding her in place and giving her body something to thrash against, and somehow that extra bit of restraint freed her completely. She moaned and pushed with abandon, letting his clever hand twist the knot of her desire tighter and tighter until pleasure broke over her in a vibrating torrent.

She subsided against him, languid, her interior muscles still clenching spasmodically around his now-gentle invading fingers.

"Mmm," she hummed, floating on a sea of endorphins. "That was nice. I believe I shall forgive you for running away and lying to me."

He dropped his forehead to her shoulder. "Don't joke about that."

"I'm not joking." Rosemary managed to lift one hand

to pet at his head. "I forgive you. And not just because the sex was so nice."

Wes shuddered out a breath and pressed a kiss to the side of her neck. "Nice, huh? Well, I'm out of practice. Next time we'll shoot for 'awesome.'"

Next time. He wanted there to be a next time. Rosemary allowed that to be the first thought to coalesce in her still buzzing brain. She mulled it for a moment, and found that it pleased her.

Almost as much as the iron-hard evidence of his desire for her jammed against her back.

Putting one hand behind her back, she wormed her way between their bodies to cup his erection, making him suck in a harsh breath.

"You don't have to," he said roughly. "This was just for you, this whole day."

"I know," she said, and she did. For once, she understood exactly where someone else was coming from. He'd hurt her, and he knew it. He thought a day of indulgence where he catered to her whims, worked hard, made himself vulnerable and denied himself pleasure, would cancel it out.

But if she understood anything about emotions, it was that they didn't work on such smooth transactional lines.

"You want to make me happy," she said, twisting around in his lap to get a look at his face.

"I really do," he said, his changeable eyes a pure, steady golden brown like ancient bronze coins. "You gonna let me?"

Curling around him like a cat, Rosemary pulled her rubbery legs over his to straddle his hips. "I am. And you know what would make me happy? An experiment."

He sucked in another breath and the muscles of his stomach went hard as rock when she followed her words with a slow caress down his torso.

"What kind of experiment?" he gulped when she reached her destination, curving her palm and measuring the length of his erect penis.

"The kind where I try something I've never tried before," she said, her focus entirely on dealing with his zipper, although the strip of bare muscled abdomen revealed by his twisted pullover kept attempting to distract her.

"Like what?" His whole body went rigid as she eased the zipper down. He was wearing boxer briefs, and his erection was so high and tight that the head of it poked out of the top band of elastic, red and flushed.

Rosemary licked her lips.

Instead of answering in words, which were escaping her at the moment, Rosemary scooted down, ducking completely under the blanket, and sucked the exposed head of his penis into her mouth.

Chapter 21

The inside of Rosemary's mouth was everything Wes had ever wanted. Tight. Wet. Hot—with the added bonus of spine-tingling suspense every time he felt the edge of her teeth.

But she never scraped too hard—just enough to sensitize his already aching skin. Her curious tongue explored the rim and the insanely sensitive spot under the head, then licked back up to poke into the slit at the tip.

That made her pause, and he wished like hell he could see the look on her face as she tasted him for the first time, but all he could do was stare down at the lump she made under the gray fleece blanket and pray that she didn't need a break for some antibacterial mouthwash or something.

Apparently, the slick evidence of exactly how much she turned him on was acceptable to her, because after a brief moment, she made a purring, humming noise and sucked him down again.

Wes fell back against the gazebo railing and reached under the blanket to pull his underwear down. He needed more of her mouth, on more of his cock, but he was determined to let her go at her own pace.

Which seemed to be best classified as "glacial." Except glaciers were cold, weren't they, and nothing about the slow, fiery glide of her tongue over the throbbing veins and tight skin of his hungry dick was cold.

In fact, Wes could feel sweat breaking out at his hairline, the backs of his knees. He could smell sex in the air and it made him want to thrust into her mouth, cram as much cock in as he could.

Fisting the wool blanket at his sides, he forced himself to sit still and endure the searing torture of her inexperienced, enthusiastic, experimental blow job.

He wanted it to go on forever. Unfortunately, he didn't have that kind of control.

In an embarrassingly short span of minutes, she had him panting and twisting his hips, every lollipop lick and affectionate nuzzle sending him closer and closer to totally losing it.

She ran her hands up his thighs and nudged the backs of her fingers into his balls, still trapped in his boxers, and that was it. He shook from head to toe and gasped out a warning before shooting hard.

The first pulse startled a *meep* out of her, but she didn't pull away. He felt her kitten tongue licking him through it, gentling him down as the clenching tension eased, a low hum buzzing against his skin and telling him she was okay.

"Sorry," he gasped when he had control of his vocal chords again. "I should've given you more time to move."

The blanket flipped back and she emerged with a triumphant smile and staticky hair clinging to her damp, red cheeks. "I didn't want to move," she informed him. "I wanted to swallow. All the literature is very clear on that point."

Shit. Was it awful to laugh? He hoped not, because it felt good, almost as much of a release as the mind-shattering orgasm.

"I'm funny now?" she said, clearly miffed. She sat up, tugging her wrinkled shirt back into place and pushing her hair out of her eyes. "Why am I funny?"

"You're not funny," he told her, wrapping his arms around her shoulders and hauling her back into his lap for a kiss. "You're amazing, is what you are."

Her mouth tasted like sweet wine, pumpkin pie, and *him*—Wes licked deep and sucked on her tongue, a primal part of him responding to the flavor with a surge of possessiveness unlike anything he'd ever experienced.

She matched him kiss for kiss, leaning hard against him and silently demanding more—claiming him every bit as much as he was laying claim to her.

I can't lose this again.

The thought beat at Wes's brain like a stand mixer whipping egg whites into meringue.

No matter what it takes, I'm holding on to her this time.

Those words echoed in his head, taking on almost a voice-of-prophecy, James Earl Jones basso overtone, when he tramped up the stairs to his Chinatown apartment after dropping Rosemary back at her hotel, only to find his door unlocked.

Most people in big, bad New York City would probably assume burglary. Wes pushed the door open, yelling, "Pops? You here?"

Which was kind of dumb, he realized as soon as he was all the way inside, because he only had one room. Where was his dad going to be, hiding in the closet?

No. Thomas Murphy jumped up from the futon, dropping the book he'd been reading, and strode to the door to envelop Wes in a strong embrace that smelled of cough drops and cigarettes.

Wes closed his eyes against the complicated mess of emotions his father inspired, and just let himself be hugged.

Pops was good at hugging; he didn't lean in and clap his son on the back in that brainless macho man way—he just hugged. Like the sensitive, emotional Irishman he was.

"How are you, Pops?" Wes's voice was muffled against the fine nap of his dad's soft jacket.

"Dandy and delightful, my Weston, absolutely dandy and delightful."

The heartiness of his voice made Wes take a step back to get a better view of his father's expression.

"Right," he said. "Which is why you haven't shaved in three days."

Thom Murphy was nothing if not fanatical about his personal appearance. "They say a woman's face is her fortune, but it's true for con men, too," he used to tell Wes. "If you look like a bum, you'll get treated like a bum. Look like a king? Well. You know the rest."

Pops rubbed his bristly chin. "I may have come into a spot of trouble, but nothing I can't handle. Think no more about it. How's yourself, Wes? Still cooking? Did you graduate from that school yet?"

Classic Thomas Murphy. Wes sighed. He wouldn't get anything else out of his dad until the man was ready to say more. The fact that he was being so cagey gave Wes a bad feeling about how this visit was going to go down. He was suddenly and fiercely glad he hadn't lost his mind and invited Rosemary to spend the night with him. Not that he'd ever want to bring her up to his shitty little rathole, but for a moment, he'd been tempted. Just for the sheer hedonistic pleasure of falling into well-deserved sleep with the most gorgeous scientist in the world wrapped in his arms.

But now? Faced with Thom Murphy's sharp, bright charm and shifty smile, Wes could only be glad Rosemary was way uptown, snuggled into her luxurious bed at the Carlyle Hotel.

If Pops ever found out his hunch had been correct, and she was richer than chocolate cake? He would eat her for breakfast.

"I ditched out on the academy," he told his dad. "Got a job in a great restaurant instead."

"Nice." Pops approved. Of course he did; he was a big believer in the School of Hard Knocks. "So when're you going to make me something to eat? A man could starve waiting around in his hotshot chef son's apartment. When was the last time you bought groceries, Weston?"

"I know," Wes said. "Sometimes I think I might choke on the irony, but this is what it means to be a cook—I'm not home enough to keep food in my apartment. I eat most of my meals at the restaurant." He dropped his messenger bag on the floor and pushed his sleeves up. "I could probably throw something together, though, if you're really hungry . . ."

"Ah no," Pops said, pacing over to the one grimy window and flicking two fingers between the slats of the Venetian blinds to peer out. "Truth be told, I probably couldn't eat more than a bite. My gut is that tight, Wes."

The tentative, doomed hope that Thomas Murphy might actually have come to visit his only son just because he missed him died a quick, inevitable death. "What's going on?" he asked dutifully. He knew the script.

Ignoring the fact that Wes hadn't really sold the line, Pops shook his head, still handsomely full of stylishly cut silver hair shot through with threads of black. "I wouldn't want to drag you into it. You've a new life here, a good future." Here Pops paused for a slow visual scan of Wes's bare-bones apartment, his meager possessions. "No," Pops said, shaking his head sadly. "I'm sure you'd never be interested in a lovely little investment scheme I've got wind of."

Wes crossed his arms over his chest. "Are you losing your touch, or are you just not trying very hard?"

Pops dropped the act, his shoulders slumping. Mouth twisted in a wry smile, he said, "I apologize, son. I shouldn't have insulted you by trying to play you—it was clumsily done, and unworthy of family."

Not our fucked-up little family, Wes thought, but he kept it to himself. There was no point dragging this out with any extra drama. It had been a long damn day, and all he wanted at this point was to fall into bed and sleep for twelve hours straight.

"So how much do you need?" he said, cutting to the chase.

If Pops was surprised by how quickly Wes brought their familiar little dance to a close, he hid it well. "Two hundred dollars should keep me in tea and biscuits through the end of the month," he said smoothly. "There's a lad. My good boy. Didn't I always say you were a model son?"

If it meant Pops would skip town and go far away from Rosemary, it'd be cheap at twice the price.

"Well," Wes said, tugging his wallet from his back pocket. "There was that time you wanted me to pretend to *be* a child model so you could 'discover' other new modeling talent at the mall. For a fee, obviously."

"Obviously. The only one I remember is Sheila, but I think she sticks in my mind because she was the one who finally called the cops on us." His father's eyes took on a faraway gleam. "Good times."

Wes counted out five wrinkled twenties. "I've only got a hundred on me," he lied, palming the rest of his money and slipping it into his front pocket while Pops was still reminiscing over his ill-fated liaison with Sheila.

"Ah, that's excellent, Wes," Pops said, reaching for the cash. It disappeared instantly, Thomas Murphy's quick fingers plucking it and making it vanish before Wes's very eyes. Wes almost grinned; he'd learned from the best.

Which was how he knew to hold out on his dad—if he

gave Pops exactly the amount he asked for, on top of giving in so quickly on the "loan" in the first place, his father would definitely know something was up.

And a curious Thom Murphy was a troublesome Thom Murphy.

"Listen, I need to get to bed, Pops. I haven't slept more than four hours in the last twenty-four, and I'm on again tomorrow. You want to crash here tonight?"

"Ah no," Pops said, already inching toward the door. "I've got something lined up for the night. Some old friends to see, you know how it is. It's been too long since I hit New York City."

Wes nodded in understanding. "The kind of old friends who run an illegal poker game out of the back of some club, right? Well, go with God."

"Not going to wish me good luck?" Pops winked, and Wes felt his mouth twist into a reluctant smile. His dad didn't believe in luck.

"Nah," he said. "Luck is nothing but taking advantage of opportunities when they come your way. And nobody on earth is better at that than you, Pops."

"Right you are, my Weston," Thom said, slapping his son on the shoulder. "I taught you well, didn't I?"

Wes had a sudden flash of the nights after a run of the bad luck Pops didn't believe in, nights they'd spent huddled over garbage-can fires in alleys behind bars or hiding in the cramped bathrooms of railway trains to avoid the conductor looking for tickets they didn't have as they moved from one city full of marks they'd fleeced, and on to the next.

He looked at his father, the thin, wiry body crackling with energy and fire, his watery brown eyes darting between Wes and the door as if he were planning to make a break for it any second—the man never could bear to stay in one place for too long. Thomas Murphy wanted to be out, doing, seeing, being, playing, conning—he'd never stop, because he couldn't. Wes knew the truth of that the way he knew he himself could never be happy in his father's life. No matter how many times Pops showed up, hoping to pull him back in.

A cocktail of affection and nostalgia welled up in Wes's chest, spiced with sadness and cut with a generous shot of wary caution.

"Be careful out there," he said, avoiding his dad's question. Thomas Murphy had, indeed, taught his son well—but the lessons Wes had learned, about himself, his limits, and the kind of life he wanted for himself, weren't exactly the lessons Pops had meant to instill.

Pops looked down as he shrugged into his slate-gray cashmere sport coat, pulling at his shirt cuffs until they peeked out from the coat sleeves. "Phooey," he said, flashing his trademark grin and heading for the door. "Careful is for fools and weaklings. Be bold, my Weston! Come on, give your old man a hug good-bye."

Strong, skinny arms around his back, a breath of menthol and tobacco in his lungs. Wes squeezed his dad once, hard, and stepped back shaking his head.

He smiled at his father's dramatic flourish as he knotted the light black scarf around his neck, the twinkle in his whiskey-colored eyes just before he slipped out of the apartment and down the stairs, leaving the room feeling extra empty. Thomas Murphy lived so big, he tended to suck all the air out of any room he occupied—after even a mere half hour in his presence, Wes felt his absence like a void.

Wes collapsed on the futon, trying to summon the energy to toe off his shoes and skin out of his jeans. When he finally managed to flop onto his back and get his stubborn button fly undone, he hooked his thumbs in his pockets to pull the denims down and discovered yet another absence.

The money he'd palmed and hidden in his front pocket was gone. A hundred and twenty bucks.

"Shit." But Wes had to laugh. That fucking hug good-bye. He should've known.

Well, it was vintage Pops, that was for sure. He could only hope the fact that his father got one over on him would be enough for the guy, and this would be the last he'd see of him. At least until things were a little more stable with Rosemary.

He didn't fool himself that if they stayed together, he'd be able to hide her from his father indefinitely. Obviously, that was a fantasy.

Or maybe a goal—something to shoot for.

In any case, it was good that he'd managed to put Pops off. And yet, as Wes dropped into sleep, he was aware of a slight, niggling fear that he hadn't seen the last of his father.

Chapter 22

It had already been a bitch of a night—and the restaurant wasn't even open yet.

First Jess went into the Market locker room—after wedging the door open with an aluminum folding chair; he'd learned his lesson—only to discover he'd run out of clean dark green button-downs, and had forgotten to take a load to the wash-and-fold down the block. He found a shirt from a few days ago that wasn't too badly wrinkled or obviously stained, only a minor coffee spot on one cuff, but still. Gross.

He went upstairs, checked the schedule to see what section he was working—automatically checking to see if Frankie was on tonight, which of course he was, but force of habit kept Jess aware of every move the stubborn, gorgeous, maddening asshole made—and groaned when he realized Grant had stuck him with section C.

Section C was Grant's clean, orderly, front-of-the-house code for the chef's table.

Serious foodies, restaurant regulars looking to impress out-of-towners, small groups celebrating special events—those were the kinds of people who booked the chef's table, a six-top set in the actual kitchen in full view of the hustle and bustle of the line cooks, where a diner could observe the preparation of every course from soup to nuts, and get the "authentic kitchen experience."

Part of said experience involved being served, not by waiters—the trained professionals who knew which side to clear from and what silverware to provide for every course, oh no, that would be way too easy—but by the chefs themselves. Jess's job, as table captain, was to explain each course and make sure the cooks didn't flub the service too terribly as they rushed to keep food flowing from their stations to the slammed main dining room. Jess would be smack-dab in the middle of the kitchen, all night.

Okay, off to the side in a corner, but still.

Jess might have whimpered a little. Grant patted his shoulder sympathetically, saying, "I'm sorry, kiddo."

Jess shook his head. "Don't apologize. I know, I've got more hours in than anyone else who's on tonight. Don't worry. I can handle it."

He checked the reservation book to see if it was one of the regulars he knew by name. Party of six, under Drew Gallagher.

"This name doesn't ring any bells," he said. "You know who they are? If they're celebrating something in particular?"

Furrowed brow betraying his annoyance, Grant said, "No, the reservationist didn't ask. Which she now knows better than to forget again, but that won't help us tonight."

"We'll play it by ear." Jess rolled his neck, shrugged his shoulders up and down a couple times like a prize-fighter, trying unsuccessfully to release the tension. "We'll be fine."

Of course he'd be fine, and the additional tips from the added service charge plus whatever the satisfied guests slipped him at the end of the night were extremely welcome.

But this would be the first night in a while that he and Frankie would be face-to-face. Ever since that awful day in the locker room, when Frankie wouldn't quit needling him and Jess had told that ugly lie about sleeping around, they'd done a decent job of mutual avoidance.

It helped that Grant had scheduled Jess for the private side dining room all weekend, which limited his contact with the kitchen—with private parties, they used runners to ferry the food and dishes back and forth, while a seasoned campaigner like Jess oversaw the whole operation.

Sort of a similar setup to the chef's table, actually, except a single chef's table party could last hours, what with all the special courses and tastings—and tonight Jess knew he wouldn't be overseeing back servers and runners, he'd be directing the line cooks.

Including Frankie.

Who gave Jess one searing glance when he entered the kitchen a few minutes after Grant opened the doors to their first diners, then immediately turned his back and hunched over his beloved grill. The red and orange glow of heat as Frankie stoked the flames cast his thin, angular face in demonic planes, his coal-black hair licking up around his head in a nimbus of horns and spikes. It would make an awesome photograph.

Jess wanted him so badly, he could hardly breathe through the longing.

"Everything look okay?" The voice came from the pass, jerking Jess out of his masochistic Frankie-watching fugue state.

He turned to Adam, who regarded him with his hands on his hips, head cocked to the side in that inquisitive way he had, sympathy turning his brown eyes soft. Jess dredged up a smile. "Yeah, the table looks great. The reservation is for five-thirty—the party should be here soon."

The words were barely out of his mouth before a shell-shocked–looking Grant pushed open the kitchen door and ushered in a gaggle of six talking, laughing guests.

One of whom was Eva Jansen.

Darkly elegant in a navy blue sheath dress, New York's highest-powered restaurateur handed Jess her wrap and waited for him to pull out her chair as if she didn't even notice that the entire kitchen had ground to a complete halt.

But as he helped her into the best seat at the table as if she were a queen mounting her throne, Jess caught the gleam of pure feminine satisfaction in her large, almond-shaped eyes. This was a woman who always knew the effect she was having on the people around her. And clearly, she got one hell of a kick out of the intent stares from the Market crew.

Jess glanced around the kitchen as he helped the rest of the party get settled. Billy, the fish cook, and Quentin, the saucier, were exchanging wide-eyed looks, while Violet, the pastry chef, actually left the pastry board at the back of the kitchen and came up to get a better view. Only Frankie seemed unaffected, a glowering monolith towering over the grill.

Even Wes kept sneaking peaks, Jess noticed, from his new spot on the line. He'd been moved up to sauté a few nights ago, to his great pride and joy, but apparently the novel thrill of running one of the busiest stations on the line paled in comparison to the drama playing out at the chef's table.

Everyone looked to Chef, to see how he'd play it, but Adam was cool as a lick of ice cream on a hot day as he went into his standard welcome speech. Jess was proud of him, especially since he knew the guy hated public speaking of any stripe.

Wishing them all a pleasant meal, Adam hurried back up to the hot plate and started calling out orders, which pushed the chefs back into gear.

Jess swung around, pasted on his best and brightest smile, and started his own spiel describing the two tasting menus, both seasonally based, one around butternut squash, with the squash featuring in various, creative ways in each course, and the other around beets. Jess also explained how they asked that the whole table agree on which one to order, to ensure smooth, perfect service.

His first indication that there might be trouble, right here in River City, came after the chefs jumped off their stations and huddled up to get his instructions on how to deliver the first course.

Eva had politely left the decision up to the group, which led to an amusing spate of wary debate and cautious backtracking as her entourage scrambled to figure out what she wanted. At least, Jess was pretty sure Eva was amused by it, if the tiny curl of her perfectly lined and glossed upper lip was any indication.

Finally her assistant, whom Jess recognized as her companion from the other day, made the call for the butternut squash menu. Everyone kept referring to him as Andrew, which was the name Jess remembered, although he assumed the young guy was the Drew from the reservations book.

Pretty tricksy of Ms. Jansen and Co., if what she wanted was to stage an ambush.

And as the chefs circled the table, ready to lay down the first course, Wes's updated chicken and dumpling soup, on Jess's mark, it became clear that "tricksy" was a serious understatement.

Satan's Bride was more like it.

Or possibly Satan's Mistress, because the frankly assessing once-overs Ms. Jansen gave each of the male chefs were anything but blushing and bridal.

She gave silent, hulking Quentin an appreciative glance, and short, wiry Billy got more of a grin than a leer, but Frankie had to bend over to place his portion of soup in front of the guest opposite Eva, and the way she perked up at the sight of him made Jess's blood flare white-hot with insane jealousy.

Frankie, who Jess remembered with a sudden pang was actually bi, not gay, winked at her.

Jess had to take a step back from the table to stop himself from dumping that bowl of steaming hot soup right in her lap.

Or over Frankie's head. Right at that moment Jess wasn't particular about who received the third-degree burns. So long as someone suffered a horribly disfiguring accident, he wasn't going to be picky.

From his position by the pass, Adam caught his eye and shook his head once. That was enough to halt the scalding torrent of aggression racing through Jess's veins, but as he glanced back at the table where Eva Jansen was watching Wes now, with a speculative expression on her beautiful, predatory face, Jess sighed.

It was going to be a long night.

"Find out what she's doing here," Jess hissed, shoving Wes toward the bar.

If ever the Market crew deserved a night at Chapel, their favorite dive after-hours bar, it was tonight.

Wes, however, was having a hard time getting his chill on what with the way Jess was not-so-quietly freaking over the fact that Frankie had invited Eva Jansen to go to Chapel with them after closing.

Oh well, he needed another beer, anyway.

Bellying up to the bar next to Adam and Grant, Wes slid a casual glance over to where Frankie's dark head was bent close to Eva Jansen's elegant coiffure.

"What's that all about?" he asked.

"Oh, come on." Adam rolled his eyes and took a sip of his beer. "You know he only did it to piss off Jess."

Adam tilted his beer bottle, pointing out the sneaky slide of Frankie's gaze to the young man in question. "This whole thing with the two of them is getting stupid. I mean, it's been stupid, but now it's approaching fatally moronic. Maybe I should sic Miranda on him—she's meeting us here." Even the mention of Miranda's name made Adam light up from the inside like someone just flipped his switch.

Grant huffed. "Adam. You are missing the point. Why was Eva Jansen even there again tonight? With her assistant and a bunch of other industry types—I'm pretty sure one of the men with her was Rufus Rigby, the restaurant designer."

A subtle tension entered Adam's frame; if he hadn't shrugged his shoulders in a rough, jerky movement, Wes might not have caught it.

"Let it be, man. Do we have to talk about this now?" Adam sighed.

Wes tapped his fingers on the bar in a rapid tattoo and wished like hell his beer would show up. When these two got going, they sounded like an old married couple.

Before he could make a graceful getaway, a smooth, husky female voice broke in. "If you want to know why I came back to Market for dinner, it's because I was very impressed with the food when I had lunch there a week ago."

They all swiveled toward her. Eva Jansen raised one perfectly shaped eyebrow and said, "But if you want to know what I was doing back in the neighborhood in the first place, just ask."

"Oh, I'm pretty sure I know what you were doing on the Upper West Side," Grant said.

Adam groaned, dropping his head to the bar with a thunk. "Aw, man. Just let it go."

Frankie tore his attention from his ex for long enough to say, "Yeah, mate, what's the problem? If Eva here wants to start up a slap-bang operation next door to Market, I don't see why she shouldn't. Better foot traffic to the neighborhood means more punters for all of us. Plenty to go around."

Even knowing he'd get slapped down, Wes couldn't keep his mouth shut. "But if we have a chance to take all the customers for Market, why wouldn't we go for it?"

Into the silence that followed Wes's contribution came a clear, amused voice.

"Hmm. What did I miss at dinner service tonight? Grant's drinking bourbon, Frankie's bristling like a hedgehog, there's suddenly another woman in the middle of this testosterone fiesta, and the love of my life looks . . ." A redhead, Jess's sister and Adam's one true love, put her slim hand on Adam's stubbled cheek and turned his face up to hers for a kiss. "Mmm. Looks better now."

"I *am* better now," Adam breathed, tugging her down for another quick smooch.

"And I'm Eva Jansen," the restaurateur said, holding out a manicured hand with an interested smile. "You must be Miranda Wake. I've heard so much about you."

"Who hasn't?" Miranda gave a self-deprecating laugh, squinching her eyes shut in a wry cringe to acknowledge the extremely public nature of her relationship with Adam. When they first got together, months before, Miranda had been researching Market for a tell-all exposé about the dirty secrets of a professional kitchen. She fell in love with the chef and decided to cancel the book, but part of it leaked anyway, setting off a whole chain of events that culminated in her offering a heartfelt and exceedingly humiliating apology on Devon Sparks's hit Cooking Channel show.

Things had calmed down since then, according to Jess. At least for Adam and Miranda. Their biggest disagreement lately was over whether or not to get married—Adam was all for it, Miranda was staunchly opposed to any institution that wasn't available to her brother, Jess, as well.

"What you missed," Grant said loudly, gesticulating with his bottle of Jack. "What you just walked in on, Miranda, was yet another session of me nagging your heel-dragging man about the empty restaurant space next door. This time, with bonus high-powered restaurateurs sniffing around the place! Yay!"

"Mother of God," Adam said, squirming on his barstool. "You are wiz-asted, man."

But Eva Jansen looked impressed. Her eyes sharpened on Grant's face like multifaceted sapphires, all cutting edges and sparkling color. "I heard you were the brains of the Market operation," she said silkily. "I didn't realize you were the guts, too."

"Hey," Adam protested. "I resemble that remark."

Grant shot him a look and Wes stifled a laugh. There were appropriate times to reference the Marx brothers, but this probably wasn't one of them.

"What do you mean?" Wes asked Eva, hoping to move things along.

She tilted her head back and drained the last of the cocktail Christian had created for her, an update of a Tom Collins with gin, lemon juice, and a dark-red cherry liqueur. "I mean, everyone in this bar can see the advantages in Market snapping up the space next door for a sister restaurant, but the sous chef is too busy tying himself in knots over the wait staff to bother with it, and the chef owner seems both too worried to overextend himself, and too stubborn to ask for help."

Eva slid from her barstool in the ensuing shocked silence, a feline smile on her scarlet lips. "The restaurant manager and this handsome line cook appear to be the only ones ready to snap at this golden opportunity. With the possible exception of Miss Tell All." She cocked her head at Miranda. "I haven't spent enough time with you to assess your backbone. If you have one, think about injecting some spine into these two."

"Oi," Frankie protested, finally tearing his stare from Jess sitting alone at his table, and tuning in to the conversation.

"Yeah, I think I second that 'oi,'" Adam said, brows lowering. "Where the hell do you get off, lady?"

"Right about here," she said, shrugging her light wrap around her slim shoulders.

A seething morass of tension had descended over their corner of the bar, but Wes felt frozen. It was beyond disconcerting to have an outsider assess their situation so directly and brutally. What on earth did she hope to gain by it?

He should've kept his damn mouth shut. This was none of his business; he was basically just the hired help.

Eva looked around the little group she'd just tossed a bomb into, and settled her gaze on Wes. She handed him a sleek red card on her way out. "Here's my info," she said. "Call me if you get your shit together and decide you want to make a move on 422. It's a good property, and I'm definitely interested—but I'd rather work with Market than compete with you. After all, I live on the Upper West Side. Why deprive my neighborhood of its best restaurant by putting it out of business in its first year? Frankie, darling, walk me out."

Looking more than a little dazed, Frankie offered her his arm and escorted her outside. Miranda watched them go, an indecipherable look on her pretty face, then leaned up to murmur to Adam, "I think I'll go make sure Frankie's not in over his head." And then she was gone, too, leaving Wes at the bar with Grant and Adam.

"Holy crap," Wes said stupidly, staring down at the card in his hand. "What the hell just happened?"

"What happened," Grant said, swaying drunkenly, "is that, once again, it's all on me. Everyone else wants to play a round of wait-and-see, and if I don't do something, we'll never get anywhere. I'm going to have to do it again."

"You're not making a lot of sense, man," Adam said.

Grant screwed up his face and took a defiant slug of bourbon. "I make plenty of sense. I do nothing but make sense. And no one listens! Just like when we were all working for Devon Sparks and you wanted to start Market and I said you should, but you wanted to . . ." He hiccupped. "To wait."

The bartender, Christian, materialized in front of Wes. Finally, his beer! He was starting to think he might really need it.

"Hey, Grant," Christian said quietly. "What's up?"

"You!" Grant rounded on him. "Another shot of bourbon."

The bartender squinted. "You've had a lot to drink, huh? Maybe it's time to slow down, drink some water. Stop talking about stuff you might regret saying later."

Adam and Wes exchanged a clueless glance while Grant shook his head vigorously.

"Shut up," he slurred at Christian. "You think you know everything, just because I told you my secret. What I did. But the joke's on you, pal."

"What are you talking about?" Adam asked, a grim note in his voice.

Grant started to laugh, this rough, tight sound that made Wes uncomfortable. "I'm talking about the fact that I lied to you, Adam. When I told you that rumor, that Devon was promoting that other guy to head chef over you, that was a lie. I said it so you'd finally be willing to quit that awful place and take a chance on our own restaurant."

Whoa. Wes did his best to disappear while sneaking a glance at Adam out of the corner of his eye. The guy was clearly shell-shocked, staring down at his friend, Grant, who'd slumped over the bar and looked ready to pass out.

Adam lifted his eyes to the man behind the bar. "You knew about this?"

Christian nodded. "He got drunk one night a while back, spilled his guts. I told him you'd understand, he should tell you the truth. I hope I was right."

Adam blinked a couple of times, his face blank, before bending to try and peel Grant off the bar.

Wes moved to help, but Adam waved him away. "I've got this," he said in a flat monotone. "Go on, go have fun. Chris, we're going out the back way. Will you tell Miranda I'll meet her at home?"

The bartender nodded and Wes stood back, watching his two bosses stagger to their feet. "If it helps," he offered, "I won't say anything about this. To anyone."

Adam glanced over his shoulder, and something around his eyes softened. "Thanks, man. I owe you."

"After everything you've done for me?" Wes shook his head. "You really, really don't."

Chapter 23

Wes sank down into the seat next to Jess, grateful the guy was sitting with his back to the bar.

"What took you so long?" Jess asked.

Wes shrugged. "Some drama with the restaurateur lady. Hey, you've got trouble, my friend. Your sister showed up and cornered Frankie outside for a confab."

"Oh no." Jess's lips went white and bloodless, his eyes wide. He was the textbook definition of panic.

"Oh yes," Wes confirmed.

Jess started out of his seat, clearly intending to break up whatever private chat his sister and his ex—the guy she'd hated almost from the start, and had done her best to separate Jess from—were about to have.

"Shit, I'm sorry. I have to . . ." Jess gestured helplessly.

Wes's pocket vibrated, his phone alerting him he had a text message, and he pulled the thing out, his heart pumping madly, the crazy situation with Grant and Adam forgotten.

Important bits of his psyche seemed to be wired to that phone whenever he and Rosemary weren't in the same room together. If there was a chance she might be calling

or messaging him, he was tuned in to every shrill chirp or
beep from that damn phone.

> Dn 4 day—hpthsis tsting wll. Where r u?

He grinned, parsing out the text-speak on his tiny, illu-
minated screen. His first impulse was to just call her up
and tell her how glad he was that the hypothesis was testing well, and that she was done with work for the day. But
he knew Rosemary preferred texting. She liked the time it
gave her to compose her replies, to consider her options—if
he called, she'd be all jittery. Which, to be fair, was one of
his favorite Rosemary modes, and he didn't always resist
the impulse to fluster her.

Tonight, however, he was feeling merciful. Using his
thumbs, Wes typed out:

> @Chapel. Corner of Bond & Bowery. Meet me?

He hit send and laid the phone on the table, attempting
to stop the excited, nervous bounce in his leg. He and
Rosemary had seen each other every day since that miraculous afternoon in the park, sometimes just for a few
minutes to grab a cup of coffee, sometimes for a few hours
to grab a little something else.

Every time they came together, it was hotter, sweeter,
more personally devastating than the time before. If they
kept going like this, Wes wasn't entirely sure he'd survive it. He was, however, completely certain he'd die
happy.

"No worries," Wes told Jess as his phone chirped at
him. He snatched it up and waved it jauntily.

"C u soon" was Rosemary's entire message, and he
couldn't help lighting up.

"Looks like I'm going to have company of my own before too much longer," Wes said.

"Great." Jess looked relieved. He was a good kid—Wes could never quite help thinking of his friend that way, even though they weren't that far apart in age. There was an innocence about Jess, though, an inherent optimism that Wes hadn't felt in himself in a long time.

Plus, Jess was just plain nice. He never liked to leave Wes sitting by himself—which, if Wes were into pop psychology, he'd probably want to read a lot into, about how Jess's parents died when he was a kid, leaving him alone with his older sister, the two of them against the world.

Whatever. Wes refused to believe a person's past necessarily dictated his future. "Call me later, fill me in on the fireworks."

"Will do." Jess laughed, but it was tense. Wes watched the kid hurry away, dodging the seething mass of humanity in the empty space between tables that served as a dance floor. He worried about Jess sometimes, the way he wore his heart right out there in the open where the whole world could take potshots at it.

He was still thinking about that as he watched Jess finally make it to the bar door Frankie and Miranda had left by. The young man pushed the heavy door open and went to step through, nearly crashing into a slight, older guy who was coming in. Jess, well-brought-up little dude that he was, took an apologetic step back and held the door open to let the older man through.

Wes's vision blurred and narrowed to the bar's newest occupant—it was his father.

Fuck.

Thomas Murphy shook his leonine head, spraying water droplets in a gentle arc over a group of Lower East Side punks with pierced septums and crazily colored hair.

His father bowed, ridiculously charming and old-fashioned, and said something to them. And instead of responding with shouts of outrage, they smiled at Thom and greeted him like a long-lost brother.

They'd buy him a drink, Wes knew, and send him on his way with good wishes and promises of lifelong friendship. It was one of his father's superpowers—everyone he met instantly became his best bud.

Wes pounded back the rest of his beer and slammed the bottle on the table. He had to head his dad off before Rosemary got here.

Static filled his head, panic speeding his heartbeat at the thought of the demons of his past meeting up with the woman he hoped would be his future.

Before he could even stand up, though, he felt a presence behind him and jerked around to see his father standing at the back of his chair with a pleased expression on his handsome, lined face.

"My Weston! Fancy meeting you here."

"Come off it, Pops," Wes growled. "You knew damn well I'd be here."

"Can't con a con man." Thom chuckled, toasting his son with the glass in his hand. It was amber-colored liquid, and Wes knew that since he'd gotten someone else to spring for it, his dad would be drinking a good small-batch Irish whiskey. If he were on the make, it would be clear and fizzy, something that looked like a gin and tonic but was actually straight tonic with lime. When Thom was working, he liked to pretend he was drinking something stronger than he actually was. The fact that he had a real drink in his hand made Wes relax his shoulders slightly.

Until it occurred to him that his father certainly knew what signal that would send to his only son and ex-partner in crime. The choice of Bushmill's might be a perfectly calculated decision intended to knock Wes off his guard.

There was no way to know. Wes's head ached, reminding him why he'd left his father's world.

"No, don't," he hissed as his father rounded the table and pulled out the chair Jess had vacated. "You're not staying."

"No?" Pops was all surprise, tinged with a little hurt. "But you're all alone here."

Not for long, Wes almost said, but he gritted his teeth on it, knowing that would give him away.

"I'm not staying," he said instead, standing up. Maybe he could head Rosemary off at the door, get both of them back uptown to the soft, dark haven of her hotel room.

"Ah, but you can sit here long enough to finish your drink." For the first time, Wes noticed the glass in his father's other hand.

He groaned. "You got those punks to front you for two Bushmill's?"

"That Noelle is lovely, isn't she? In a rough-and-tumble sort of way." His father's sharp blue eyes glittered with appreciation as he glanced over at the exuberantly dancing orange-haired punk goddess. Noelle was the lead singer of Frankie's band, Dreck, as well as a part-time bartender at Chapel. She had a cute, Kewpie-doll face that she offset with traffic-cone-orange dreadlocks, ripped jeans, and camo wife-beaters.

"Gross, Pops," Wes said. "She's, like, twenty years too young for you."

"Fuck that. You're only as old as you feel, boy." Blithely ignoring Wes's obvious annoyance, Thom plunked himself down and slid the second glass of Irish whiskey across the table.

Wes resisted the urge to turn and glance at the door. He tried to calculate how much time he had before Rosemary walked in.

She was uptown, at least fifty blocks away. Even if she got a cab right away, and if by some miracle she encountered zero traffic, she was still looking at half an hour in transit. Minimum. She could maybe cut that down by taking the subway, but as convenient and practical as it was, Wes knew she'd never be able to force herself onto the 6 train. Underground petri dishes on rails, she'd shuddered once, clearly envisioning herself stumbling out of the subway car infested with every virus, bacterial infection, and parasite known to man.

There wasn't enough hand sanitizer in the world.

Rolling his shoulders, Wes fought to relax. He eyed the Bushmill's. Maybe that would help.

"So, how's the restaurant racket?"

Wes took a sip of the Irish whiskey, sweeter and smokier than its Scottish cousins. "Subtle, Pops. If you want to know how flush I am, just ask. Are you out of money already? The poker players in the city must be better than you remembered."

Thom sat back in his chair, the picture of insouciance. Unless you happened to look at his sharp eyes, like the tawny gold gaze of a hawk zeroing in on a fieldmouse.

"My sweet motherless boy, who I raised on my own from a pup, and he's in a blazing rush to get rid of me," he lamented. "I noticed it the other night, too. Practically pushed me out the door of your apartment—you couldn't even be bothered to give me a bit of a challenge when you hid your extra cash!"

Shit. Wes fought not to shift expressions, but he couldn't help the slight, involuntary widening of his eyes. Somehow, Thomas Murphy always managed to surprise him.

"Come on, Pops," he said, uneasily aware of how completely the opposite of convincing that was. "I'm always glad to see you when you blow through town."

"Usually, you are. That's what has me so perplexed," Thom said, never taking his predatory gaze off his son's face. "Makes a man wonder."

Which was exactly what Wes had hoped to avoid.

Quick! Deflect!

"Maybe I'd be happier to see you if you didn't steal from me," Wes growled, fisting his drink and leaning forward aggressively. "It's tiring to know I need to nail anything easily fenced or pawned to the floor unless I want to lose it."

"Psht." Thom waved that away as if Wes's words were gnats buzzing too close to his face. "Way of the world, Wes, just as you were taught. No, that's not it. You're hiding something from me, something you want to keep all to yourself a lot more than you wanted that extra fifty bucks the other night."

Wes snorted to hide his growing unease. "A hundred, but who's counting, right?"

"What you were counting on was that I'd strip your pockets and leave quietly, go along on my merry way and never the wiser that my son was into something big. Something too good to share with his old man, who raised him—"

"From a pup, a poor motherless boy, yeah, Pops, I know. I've heard the patter—it stopped tugging at my heartstrings when I was about six." Wes stood, his chair scraping loudly against the wooden floorboards. "And I'm not into anything. I'm out of the life for good, I told you that when I got out of Heartway House."

Thom shook his head sadly. "That place ruined you. If I'd known where you were . . ."

Wes felt the old, toxic bitterness trying to turn his guts inside out like a lemon on a reamer. "You'd have done exactly nothing, because we both pulled the job that landed me in there, and they wanted you more than me. If you'd come within fifteen miles of me, they would've grabbed you. They knew you were the mastermind behind that scam, not some fifteen-year-old kid," he said, working hard to keep his voice low and even. "Besides, Heartway House did not ruin me. It was the making of me."

"You were never the same after," Thom said, something dark shadowing his eyes as he lowered them to the glass of amber liquid in his hand. "They took your courage, your hunger—that fire in your belly to be the best, to get one over, to make your bones."

Something creaked loudly, and Wes realized he was gripping the back of his chair hard enough to warp the wood. He shook his head. "No, Pops. They didn't take that stuff from me, they just helped me redirect it. I don't have to lie and manipulate anyone anymore, I just have to do a good job on the line, hold up my end, and send out great food."

Tapping the rim of his glass, Pops squinted through the smoky air of the bar. "I believed that for a while, but now . . . You've got something going on the side, my Weston, do not try to deny it. What did I say when I came in? You can't con a con man."

Wes had never really understood those scenes in movies or soap operas where someone got so pissed off, they threw a wine glass into the fireplace or against a wall or something. It always seemed so obvious, like you'd be stupidly telegraphing your most vulnerable emotions to the whole world.

At this particular moment, though, he thought he could relate. The ugly brew of frustration, dread, nervousness, and anger as his father expertly boxed him into this corner made Wes want to shatter his glass, throw his chair, and upend the table for good measure.

"Fine," he gritted out. "I'll tell you, but then you have to promise to leave it alone. Do you swear?"

Thomas Murphy gave him a look that made his son sigh. "Right. I know, I wouldn't buy it, even if you did swear. But seriously, Pops—this isn't a con, it's my life."

His father blinked up at him, his eyes fathomless and dark with the nameless pain that lurked under Thom's easy charm. "All of life is one long con. Never forget that, and I'll know I've taught you enough to get by in this world."

Wes stared down at him, caught as he always was by the painful claws of affection his father dug into his heart. "Pops. I don't want to fight."

"Who's fighting? We're just talking. And as long as you're up, what do you say to getting us another round?" Darkness slid away, masked by his father's broad, bright smile, and Wes suppressed the urge to shake the man until he dropped the act. But it was useless—no matter how close he sometimes got, Wes knew his dad. The guy had structured his entire life so as to never have to confront his real emotions and problems.

Will the real Thomas Murphy please stand up?

Never gonna happen.

Wes tried to shrug it off. "Sure, you want another Bushmill's?" At Thom's nod, Wes turned and gave Christian the high sign for two more glasses of whiskey. Pops nudged Wes's seat back from the table with his foot, a wordless invitation to sit back down and continue the conversation like civilized men.

"It's not a con," Wes said bluntly, ignoring his own instinct to dance around the issue. "It's Rosemary. And there will be no conning, not from either of us, or I swear to God, I'll cut you off for good."

Chapter 24

After letting the silver fox he'd nearly bowled over into the bar, Jess was more cautious in pushing open the door and peering out.

Where the heck had Frankie and Miranda gone?

Miranda had made huge strides in the supportive-sister department since Jess first came out to her. She hadn't reacted well to the announcement that her baby brother was in love with a guy she considered too experienced, too wild, too . . . everything.

Which, to be fair, Frankie really was. All of that. It blew Jess's mind when Frankie returned his deepening crush. How could someone like Frankie want to be with an inexperienced kid like Jess? And yet, Frankie did. And at first, Miranda was not pleased. To say the least.

She'd gone to excruciating lengths to break them up, in fact—until the night when a disgruntled former employee had returned to Market, coked up and trigger-happy, waving a gun in everyone's face and eventually firing off a shot that could've killed Jess.

Would have, if Frankie hadn't stepped in front of the bullet, shielding Jess and taking it in the shoulder in one of the hands-down worst, scariest moments of Jess's life.

The cops showed up, and the EMTs, and Frankie turned out to be okay after a trip to the ER, but those few short, interminable seconds where he was on the ground, his blood oozing thick and dark and terrifying under his limp body—Jess still had nightmares about it.

More often now that he was alone in his bed at night and had no one to chase the bad dreams away with soft, sleepy kisses.

After Frankie took a bullet for Jess, Miranda lightened up about him. Mainly, though, she'd seemed to finally be willing to try to see her little brother as an adult, capable of making his own decisions.

Shivering in the crisp night air, Jess cupped his hands over his mouth and wished he'd been smart enough to grab his peacoat in his mad rush to keep his bossy, opinionated older sister from talking to his brash, impossible ex-boyfriend.

Although, Jess realized as the sound of quiet voices filtered through the ambient city music of car horns, trucks, people hailing cabs—maybe they weren't fighting. Huh. That would be weird.

He followed the snatches of low conversation around the corner of the old church for which the bar was named, and found his quarry sitting on a cracked cement wall bordering a patch of sparse, dry grass.

"I'm just worried, that's all," Miranda was saying. "It's been a while since you broke up, and it seems like it's still as painful as it ever was."

Frankie grimaced around his cigarette, his eyes deep black pools. "It will get better. It fucking has to, right?"

Geez. Jess's heart squeezed with humiliation. He hadn't thought he was that obvious about how much he was still hurting, every day that he wasn't with Frankie.

He couldn't believe they were sitting there so casually, talking about his innermost feelings.

Hey, maybe it's a good thing, he thought. Even in his head, he almost winced at the sharp bite of sarcasm, but he couldn't help himself.

Maybe between the two of them, the two people who think they always know what's best for me, they can arrange my whole pitiful life for me, and all I'll have to do is show up and live it.

A hard kernel of resentment lodged in his chest, Jess ducked back behind the set of Dumpsters before they could see him. He wanted to know what else they were saying behind his back.

Well, he did and he didn't. If it turned into a poor-pathetic-Jess-we-must-protect-him conversation, he might have to yark in one of those handy Dumpsters.

And Jess wasn't a hundred percent on what he'd do if Miranda started berating Frankie for breaking her baby brother's heart, but it wouldn't be pretty.

So he was a little surprised when he peeked around his big blue metal shield to see his sister sliding her arm around Frankie's hunched shoulders. He looked thin and lanky, the long-sleeved thermal shirt under his olive-green I-AM-NOT-JOHNNY-RAMONE tee clearly not enough to keep him from shivering in the whippy breeze ruffling his black hair like the ruff on an angry dog.

Frankie was surprised at Miranda's sneak-attack embrace, too, if the way his eyebrows shot toward his hairline was any indication.

Miranda, however, was not one to back down. She visibly hugged him tighter and said, "I mean it, Frankie. You haven't been yourself in weeks."

Wait. They weren't talking about how pathetic Jess was?

They were talking about . . . Frankie?

A mind-bending fact that was confirmed when the man in question threw his head back and exhaled a plume of smoke to the sky. "I'm always myself, Miranda. Never more than now."

"When you're being a coward, on every level?" Miranda said, her voice hard.

Jess blinked. He knew his sister didn't pull her punches, but damn. He was struck by the ridiculous impulse to defend Frankie, even though he essentially kinda sorta agreed with Miranda's brutal assessment.

As he'd told Frankie before walking out, Jess knew Frankie was afraid.

Frankie didn't appear to want to cop to it any more now than he had that awful day. He made that wriggle with his shoulders that Jess knew meant he wanted to throw Miranda's arm off and pace, but was too polite to tell his best friend's girl to go fuck herself.

"Think I took the coward's way, do you?"

"I know you did. You even tried to make Jess think it was because you were bored with him."

Jess winced. He never should've told Miranda about that—but she'd caught him at a low moment, brooding on what Frankie had said to him, and he'd let it slip out.

Frankie, apparently stung by the realization that Jess had confided such intimate details to his sister, finally did shake free of Miranda and stand up. "He didn't believe it, anyway. I couldn't make that drivel sound true. Not when it was the furthest thing from."

In spite of himself, Jess warmed at the confirmation that Frankie hadn't dumped him on his ass because he got tired of having a college kid tagging along after him. He'd denied the possibility at the time, but months of second-guessing had allowed doubts to creep in like insidious shadows casting everything he thought he knew into darkness.

Miranda huffed out a breath. "Men. I love how you all think you're so mysterious and enigmatic, when really, anyone who ever saw you with Jess knew instantly how you felt about him. How you felt about each other, really—and yes, I know it took me a while to warm up to you, but Frankie." Her eyes softened as she stared up at the tall, thin Brit smoking like a chimney and doing his damnedest not to make eye contact. "I know you loved him."

The past tense—*loved*—went through Jess like an arrow. Crap, when was this going to stop hurting?

While Jess was still catching his breath at the sharp stab of pain, Frankie mumbled something in response. Something that made Miranda's face crumple in what looked like sadness mixed with bewilderment.

"That's what I'm talking about!" she cried. "I just don't understand you. First with Jess, and now even with that new restaurant space Grant keeps bringing up—it's like you're so afraid of making a mistake, you're paralyzed into doing nothing."

Jess had to stifle the urge to shriek a question about what, exactly, Frankie had just said. It was insanely difficult.

Drawing hard to suck the last bit of tobacco and carcinogens from his cigarette, Frankie scowled. "Pardon me for being an arsehole, but you know fuck-all about it."

"I know how your friendship with Adam and Grant is supposed to work," Miranda said stoutly. "I've been around long enough to see you three in action, and I know for a fact, Adam is supposed to be the cautious one. Grant pushes for change, he brings up new ideas—and Adam resists, for a while. His cue to act usually comes from you, Frankie."

"Bloody hell," Frankie complained. "I wouldn't have let you follow me out here if I knew you'd come over all Freudian and headshrinky. Leave a bloke a few illusions about being complicated and hard to figure, won't you? There's a luv."

But Miranda was relentless. "You're supposed to be the filter—you rein Grant in on his wilder schemes, and you reinforce the good ideas so Adam knows which way to fall."

"You act like we lead Adam around by his nose," Frankie said, dropping his cigarette and grinding it to dust with his boot heel.

"Not at all," Miranda denied. "But you know how he is. When he's in the kitchen, he's in charge—no self-doubt, no questioning, no hesitation. But when it comes to the business side of things? He needs a little nudge every now and then. That's where his two best friends come in. Except this time, you aren't coming in. For whatever reason, Grant is holding open the door, and you're hovering in the doorway, blocking Adam and keeping everybody at a standstill."

"And you can't think of any other reason why poor Adam might be having a crisis of confidence, hmm?" Frankie sneered, already fumbling through his pockets for his crumpled pack of Dunhills.

"Oh no. You're not making this about me," Miranda said, her eyes widening.

"Why not?" Frankie insisted. "Who's closer to Adam than his darling not-wife? If anyone could reinforce his clarity, luv, it's you." He pulled out a cigarette, stuck it between his lips, and spoke around it in a vicious mumble, his eyes trained on Miranda's defiant face. "Or maybe that would be easier to accomplish if you, oh, I dunno, actually agreed to marry the bloke instead of keeping him dangling after you like a fish on a hook."

Jess watched his sister's face take on that familiar, stubborn cast he recognized so viscerally from his childhood.

"I'm not getting married until my little brother has the same rights." As always, his heart warmed in his chest at the lengths Miranda was willing to go to prove that it was still the two of them, shoulder to shoulder against the world.

The fact that she would delay her own happiness as a statement about equal marriage rights never failed to move Jess—but he was never sure if the tears he felt threatening behind his eyelids were from pride in his sister's support, or sadness for the fact that she felt she had to do things this way.

"No zealot like a convert, eh?" Frankie smirked, his lip curling in that infuriating way that filled Jess with equal parts annoyance and frustrated desire.

She stood, shoving her hands in her jacket pockets. "I may not have reacted to Jess's coming out the way I wish I had. God knows, I regret it every day. But I love my brother. At the end of the day, all I've ever wanted is for him to be happy." She regarded Frankie with the ghost of the honest dislike she'd taken to him from the first, turning her mouth into a thin line. "And for whatever reason, scared, idiotic, overgrown little boy that you are, you make him happy."

"And you hate that," he said, still pushing and needling, hard enough that Jess felt scraped raw. God. *Just shut up,* he wanted to say. *Why do you have to bait everyone all the time?*

But Miranda was more than equal to it. "It's not about how I feel about you," she said. "It took me long enough to figure that out, but I did finally internalize that lesson. None of the men in my life seem to be able to do without you—not Jess, and not Adam, either. So quit playing around at life, man up, and be there for them when they need you."

Her soft, inflexible tone seemed to hit Frankie like a

sack full of rocks. He stood there, panting audibly as if trying to breathe through the pain. He was silent long enough
that Jess started to wonder if he was hoping Miranda would
give up, stop staring at him and waiting for a response, and
just go inside.

But at length, after a bit of pacing and a few skyward
glances, as if he hoped he'd find the answer to all of life's
problems written in the light-polluted sky over Manhattan, Frankie spoke.

"You really think I ought to make him listen to Grant
about expanding Market?"

Miranda's face softened. As Jess knew from experience, she was way easier to deal with when she knew
you agreed with her. Or when she thought you were
about to.

"What I really think," she said, placing a hand on one
of the tense forearms Frankie had crossed over his lean
chest, "is that it would be a shame to miss out on this opportunity because you're too busy being afraid of what it
would mean to really consider it."

Jess could actually hear Frankie swallow. "Yeah, all
right," he said, his hoarse voice sending an involuntary,
unwelcome, extremely pleasant thrill down Jess's spine. He
wondered if he was fooling himself to be hoping maybe
Frankie was agreeing to think about more than the new
restaurant space. "I can do that. Consider it, I mean."

Miranda stepped back, a satisfied gleam in her eyes.
"That's all I'm saying. Think it through. Weigh in with a
real opinion, one not based on your own issues right now—
which, by the way, I think you should resolve. In case I
never made it clear before, I like you, Frankie. I liked you
for Jess, once I understood how much you cared about
him."

She made a face, the one that meant she was simultaneously amused and frustrated with herself. "And I know it doesn't matter now; you didn't break up when I thought you should, so why would you get back together just on my say-so? But for the record, I've never seen him as happy as he was with you. You were good for him. And I think he was good for you, too."

Wow. Jess blinked, something that had been coiled tight in his chest for months letting go in a rush of unexpected emotion.

In the back of Jess's mind, buried under the more obvious aches and raw places from the breakup, had been the niggling thought that Miranda was probably secretly glad that he and Frankie weren't together anymore.

He'd hardly noticed how much the idea of that bothered him until it was suddenly gone, shattered to smithereens by Miranda's honest, frank appraisal of their relationship.

Holy jeebus. Even Miranda thinks we're meant to be together. So why the fuck is it so hard for Frankie to get it through his stubborn head?

Frankie shook that stubborn head, a helpless denial that made Jess's throat hurt. His sister's shoulders slumped, the closest she ever came to admitting defeat, and she glanced away, knotting her light scarf more tightly around her neck. "Fine. I can't make you. You'll think about what I said, though, right?"

Jess couldn't hear Frankie's response, but he didn't need to. He'd been treated to multiple renditions of Frankie's patented better-for-everyone-if-we're-not-together speech.

As he hurried back to Chapel, praying he wouldn't get caught eavesdropping after all this, Jess had a hard time keeping the encroaching feeling of hopelessness from taking over his whole body.

Sure, things looked bleak when even the indomitable Miranda Wake couldn't make a dent in Frankie's ironclad resolve. But that didn't mean Frankie would never see reason.

Did it?

Even using the walking directions provided by the GPS in her phone, Rosemary still had to double back twice before she actually found Chapel.

Somehow, even with the name, she hadn't expected to find a bar in the basement of an abandoned church. Or, wait—she squinted at the sign on the corner of the gray stone building. It wasn't abandoned, it had been repurposed into a theater of the absurd, dedicated to exploring experimental music, short-form theater, and performance art.

As Spock would say: fascinating.

Movement to her right drew her attention from the sign, and she noticed a pair of people moving toward a heavy wooden door at the bottom of a small flight of steps. She recognized one of them as Frankie Boyd, the tall, angular sous chef from Market. The woman at his side didn't immediately ring any bells, although there was something familiar about her red hair, petite build, and the even, regular features usually classified as beautiful by modern society.

"Excuse me," Rosemary called. "Is that the entrance to Chapel?"

"Well," drawled Frankie, swinging around to face her. "If it isn't Wes's pretty little genius. How goes it, Professor?"

Rosemary paused, taken aback. "Oh! Well, fine, I suppose. I'm supposed to meet Wes. Did you happen to see him inside?"

"He was at the bar, last I checked," said the redhead. "Hi, I'm Miranda Wake. Jess is my brother."

"Of course," Rosemary said, her brain slotting the answer to the mystery of this strange woman's familiarity into place, with some relief. "There's a strong facial resemblance between you—clearly, your family contains several strong, dominant genetic strains."

"Er. Thank you?" Miranda shook her head, laughing a little. "And Adam thinks I use big words! He's going to love you. Come on inside and meet everyone."

As she followed Miranda and Frankie into the bar, Rosemary mused on the way popular culture seemed to enjoy portraying New York City as this cold, unfriendly place where people interacted mainly through one-night stands and muggings. That hadn't been Rosemary's experience at all.

Everyone was friendly! Even these two, to whom she was a virtual stranger in spite of her relationship with Wes, were quick to offer guidance and chatter about the restaurant and its various constituents.

Miranda was the chef/owner's girlfriend, Rosemary discovered as their motley trio trooped into a low-ceilinged room thick with the scents of tobacco, smoke, and warm bodies. The air throbbed with the sound of many voices, all shouting to be heard over the thrum of rough, angry rebellion rock from the speakers.

"Come on." Miranda beckoned, heading for a knot of men standing at the far end of the bar. After a minute pause, scanning the interior of the bar like an air force pilot searching the clouds for dangers, Frankie jammed his hands in his pockets and sloped off after her.

Rosemary started to follow, but stopped after only a few steps, her entire attention arrested by the fascinating scene unfolded before her.

She gazed around with intense interest. She'd never been anywhere quite like this. It reminded her a bit of the frenzy she'd encountered at the science fiction conventions she'd attended—lots of people from all different walks of life, dressed in improbable costumes and gathered together to form a new community of like-minded individuals. Klingons side by side with Cylons, stormtroopers chatting up stake-wielding blondes.

Somehow, this Lower East Side bar, on a random weekend night, attained Comicon levels of insanity.

Only here, it was a beat cop, still in uniform, although she had to assume he was off duty, leaning against the bar next to an exhausted-looking woman in pink scrubs. The pair was flanked by chefs Rosemary recognized from her brief visits to the Market kitchen, their hair sweaty and wild, their eyes manic. There were artistic-looking types all in black, with strange piercings and makeup, sitting in groups, and at a table in the farthest corner of the dark, smoky bar, there were two men who appeared to be arguing.

Rosemary found her gaze drawn to them like iron filings to a magnet, but it took her a moment to realize it was because one of the hard-faced, gesticulating men was Wes.

Chapter 25

Rosemary stared across the room at her angry . . . what? Lover? She never knew what to call him. Anyway, her Wes. He made a chopping gesture with his right hand, as if he were cutting off a line of discourse, and stood up fast enough to knock his chair over.

The other man stood up, too, his back to Rosemary. He was of average height with a slender build, broad, slightly stooped shoulders, and a full head of silvery gray hair. He appeared to say something expansive, one arm sweeping out in a broad arc, and whatever he said made Wes shake his head in evident disgust.

When he raised his head, his gaze caught on Rosemary's, and she got a surprise—instead of pleasure or happiness, the microexpression she saw flash over his face before he schooled his features was fear.

Huh. Rosemary frowned, reviewing what she'd seen. Eyebrows pulled up and together, a muscle low in his jaw ticcing—yes. According to her new book on reading emotions in facial expressions, upon seeing her, Wes exhibited a classic involuntary fear response.

Hypothesis: Wes is afraid at the sight of me.

Conclusion? Either he is actually scared of me, personally, or it's the fact that I've appeared here, at this particular moment, that prompted the fear.

When he immediately started toward her rather than shying away, Rosemary narrowed her eyes. That appeared to negate the possibility that something intrinsic to her had frightened Wes. Therefore, it most likely had to do with the man Wes had been fighting with.

The man Wes was currently hustling toward the door, whispering low and fierce into the small, older man's ear as they went.

They reached the door, Rosemary never taking her eyes from them, and something passed between their hands in a move almost too fast to track. It was so quick, she couldn't even tell which man had given and which had received.

Wes encouraged the unknown man out of the bar with an insistent hand on his shoulder, nearly manhandling him through the door, but before he went, the older man slid out of Wes's grasp as if his fine wool jacket were oiled.

He turned, his handsome, weathered face alight with mischief, and winked.

Rosemary blinked, and when she opened her eyes, the old man was gone. And Wes was coming her way, his purposeful strides cutting through the shifting masses of people like a shark through flickering schools of fish.

"Hi," he said when he reached her. "Been here long?"

"Long enough to witness your intense conversation with the strange man you just hustled out of here."

She caught the tightening at the corners of his mouth before he managed to summon a credible smile. "Who, that old guy? He's nobody. Just someone I used to know. Hey, you want a drink? Chris makes awesome cocktails. I swear, if you tell him what liquor you like he can practically read your mind. He'll make you the perfect drink for whatever your mood is, guaranteed. I think he can read your aura or something."

He bounced on his heels, pointed at the bar, and Rosemary licked her lips. She was kind of thirsty. But maybe she shouldn't allow herself to be so easily distracted.

"I'm working my way through gin cocktails," she told the bartender, who appeared to be the same long-haired hippy guy from Market. "Surprise me."

"This little lady knows how to order a drink from a master mixologist," the bartender crowed, already filling a martini glass with ice and reaching for a silver cocktail shaker.

"Make it two, thanks," Wes said, then turned to Rosemary. "I think you just made Christian's night."

"Yeah," the bartender, Christian, put in. "Most people who come in here, all they want is beer or whiskey. No more Bushmill's for you, huh, kid?"

It sounded like a perfectly innocuous comment, from the content to the mild expression on the bartender's face as he said it, but because Rosemary was standing pressed so close to him by the crowd in the bar, she felt the tremor that stiffened Wes's body against hers for a single, very noticeable, second.

What in the name of Spock is going on?

Christian slid their drinks across the bar and spun away to fill another order, leaving Rosemary and Wes to puzzle out the contents of their glasses on their own.

Wes leaned in to speak directly into her ear. "Come on, let's go sit down."

She followed him, squeezing through the crush of hard-partying bar patrons, to a table that seemed to be situated some distance from the sound system. At least it was a quiet corner where Rosemary could finally draw a deep breath without fearing she'd either asphyxiate from the

miasma of cigarette smoke hanging in the air, or hyperventilate from the closeness of way too many people.

Wes studied her face as they sat down. "You don't like
crowds, do you?"

"Not so much," she admitted, taking a sip of her drink.
It was still cold, slivers of icy condensation freezing on
top of the very faintly green liquid.

The flavor was smooth, mellow, with a refreshing hint of
something herbal and clean—cucumber and mint, maybe?
And a tartness on the back of her tongue that reminded her
of summer. Lime juice.

"Unreal, right?" Wes said, raising his eyebrows over
the rim of his own glass. "You'd think a dive like this
would serve mixed drinks like screwdrivers and vodka
tonics, but Christian's an artist. They were lucky to get
him to fill in at Market."

Rosemary took another sip, then another, and another,
while she tried to think of something to say. "Is this small
talk? Are we doing small talk? Because I don't excel at
that."

The corners of Wes's mouth twitched. Amusement,
Rosemary thought. Which was an improvement on the
tense pinch he'd sported there ever since she came in.

"We can talk about whatever you want," he said. "Was
there anything else you wanted to tell me about what you
discovered today?"

"It wasn't really new discoveries so much as confirmation that we're on the right track," she said, enthusiasm mixing with the gin in a heady whirl that made the room dance
before her eyes, just a little. A quick jig. Jiggle. She laughed.

"Enjoying that drink, aren't you?" His eyes twinkled
at her across the table. Rosemary sighed and propped her
head on her hand. He was so unbelievably attractive. Like
Spike, Han, Helo, and Kirk all wrapped up in one.

"It's good," she sighed. Inebriation was a strange thing, she reflected, watching the way his face creased so nicely when he smiled. "I feel very . . . slow. And open. The sensation is not unlike what happens when we have intercourse."

He bobbled his drink, spilling a few drops on the table. "Shit." He laughed. "Warn a guy before you come out with something like that."

"And not only intercourse." Rosemary really thought she might be onto something, a correlative effect. "I felt it that day in the park, too, when actual coitus did not take place."

He leaned closer, his whole face alight with fascination. She wondered if it was her or the topic that had him so worked up. Men could be so distressingly focused on physical gratification.

"You felt the same in the park," he said, his low voice scratching pleasurably across her nerves, "because we were making love. The same as that night in your lab, and what we do in your hotel room. And there's more to love-making, to sex, than simply inserting Tab A in Slot B."

She shivered, every hair on her body lifting as if in a chilly breeze. Except she didn't feel cold at all, she felt overly warm, in that way she'd come to associate with being near Wes.

"Some enlightened folks," Wes continued, inching one hand across the small, round table to trail his fingertips across her bare wrist, "might even consider this, what we're doing right now, lovemaking."

"But this is public," Rosemary protested, trying to feel scandalized and not quite managing it. "More public than the park, I mean, because there are actual people all around. People like your boss's girlfriend, whom I met earlier. So it would be weird if they were watching us m-making love."

Why did she stumble on that phrase? It was in common

parlance, a familiar vernacular emblem for the biological process of two humans mating. She knew that. So why was she afraid to say it?

The way Wes was looking at her, she knew he'd noticed it, too. Feeling her cheeks superheat, Rosemary cast around for something to say to take the focus of the conversation off her and her ridiculous hang-ups.

"Why were you fighting with that man, earlier?"

Well. That did it. Rosemary watched as the tension that had mostly disappeared snapped back into Wes's frame, from his shoulders and neck to the corded muscles of his forearms lying on the table. His fingers clenched, briefly, into fists, and his lips tightened. Only for an instant, then he was back to looking relaxed and lazy in his chair. But Rosemary knew what she saw.

Something about the older stranger made Wes nervous and angry.

But when he spoke, his tone was easy and free of any emotion she could detect. "We weren't fighting—it was a minor disagreement about money. As in, he owes me some, and I thought maybe since he offered me a glass of Christian's best Irish whiskey, he could pay me back. That's all. I didn't want to talk about it before because it's kind of embarrassing; I feel like a fool for lending money to someone who'd stiff me like that."

Rosemary thought it over, as best she could through the haze of alcohol. It made sense. The weird impression of shame she'd gotten from Wes, as well as his odd reaction when the bartender mentioned the whiskey he'd been drinking earlier.

His eyes on her face were clear and steady, the pupils wide to drink in the meager ambient light, the irises slender bands of dark green flecked with gold.

Everything about him proclaimed he was telling the truth. So why did she feel so uneasy?

And since when are you an expert on social cues and facial expressions? she asked herself. *You've been wrong—dead wrong—on things like this before. Just let it go.*

"Did he pay you back?" she asked finally, not sure what else to say.

Wes looked down and away, his mouth tightening again. "Not this time. But I'm sure I'll be seeing him again soon."

She nodded and finished her drink. Silence stretched between them for long moments, pulling like taffy, longer and longer but never quite breaking.

Finally, Wes looked up from the condensation rings he'd been drawing on the surface of the table. His eyes were shadowed, expression hidden by the downward sweep of his lashes against his cheeks. "What's your best memory from your childhood?"

It was important not to fidget. No finger drumming, no toe tapping, and especially no licking his lips or tugging at his ear. Those were all easy tells, obvious even to civilians.

Wes knew how to do this, he was just out of practice.

But somehow, faced with Rosemary's scary-smart, analytical eyes, the intent, listening posture of her, he found himself wanting to squirm and spill his guts like a two-bit street hustler caught running his first shell game.

Or maybe it was the fact that she clearly knew something was up. She was about the furthest thing from clueless that Wes could imagine. It was rotten, awful luck that had her walking in on him arguing with Pops.

He thought he'd allayed most of her nameless suspicions about it; he'd laced the vague lie with enough specific truth to be convincing. At any rate, she'd stopped pushing.

But Wes couldn't bring himself to let it go completely.

He knew the signs of a guilty conscience, had lived with them for a long time. He needed to keep Pops away from her, to keep her safe from his father's completely unreliable, totally unconvincing promise not to run a scam on her—a promise made in exchange for a hefty price, of course.

Even with all of that, there was a part of Wes that wanted to tell her everything.

The truth. About Pops, about the Heartway House, about Wes and where he came from.

It was that part of him, the idiotic blabbermouth part, that prompted the question about her childhood. Straight from his hind brain to his tongue, no filter in between. Jesus.

She was blinking at him now, pretty and intense, her soft blond hair falling in a wave over her left shoulder. "My best childhood memory? You sound like a talk show host."

"Really? I never watched a lot of TV. Is that the kind of thing they ask questions about? I thought it was all 'What made you sleep with your wife's mother's best friend's brother?' type stuff."

That got her to laugh. "No, whatever else you can say about my mother, she never dragged me in front of Jerry Springer."

"What else would you say about her? Your mother, I mean." Wes was back in control of his mouth now, deflecting attention back onto Rosemary and away from the scuffle with Pops. He'd rather find out more about her, anyway, than sit here stewing about the utterly immoral and incorrigible man who'd raised him.

Although from the way she buttoned up whenever her mother was mentioned, maybe the Wilkins family wasn't any less of a clusterfuck than the Murphys.

"I'm not sure what you're asking," she hedged. "You

already know she's a best-selling author. My father is an award-winning biologist, spends most of his time on the lecture circuit."

"And that's all you know about them? Come on," Wes pressed, not even sure what he was digging for. Except that even after the hours they'd spent together, in bed and out of it, there was an inner core of her that he knew he still hadn't touched.

What could he say? He was greedy. It was bred into the Murphy men.

She shrugged and drained her glass. "I'd order another one, but I'm still not sure what it was. Which is a shame, because it's definitely a contender for my favorite drink."

"I'm glad you liked it," Wes said, trying not to feel like she was blowing him off.

After a moment of not-completely-comfortable silence, she blurted, "I'll tell you one of mine if you tell me one of yours."

"Wait, what?"

Rosemary flushed so prettily, it made him want to keep her embarrassed and off kilter permanently. "A childhood memory," she clarified. "A good one."

He sat back in his chair, hoping the movement would mask his sudden, full-body clench.

Stupid guilty conscience. This was what it had been angling for all along.

"Yeah, sure," he said, then grinned. "You first."

"Okay," she said slowly, her eyes taking on a faraway look as if she had to scan the deepest recesses of her brain for a single good memory. Wes frowned.

"I think I already told you, my parents spent a lot of time traveling when I was younger. Still do, actually, but back then I went with them a lot of the time. We'd be gone for months at a stretch, together if they could manage to sync up their tour schedules, and just me and Mom if they couldn't. Even when we were all together in a hotel suite, though, it felt . . ." She appeared to struggle for a word that wouldn't sound as bad as Wes knew it had been.

"Lonely," he supplied, knowing he was right.

Rosemary shook her head, obviously wanting to deny it, but all she said was, "I suppose it was fairly isolating. My tutor or a nanny accompanied us on most trips, so that was some company for me. Where was I going with this?"

"Toward one of your happiest childhood memories," Wes said, heart aching. "Not sure how you get there from here, but I'm all ears."

The perplexed frown smoothed from her brow. "Oh, of course. A happy memory. It seems like I should probably say the time I structured my own experiment to test the level of acidity in the new brand of apple juice our housekeeper started buying when I was six, or when my father realized I was reading the back of his newspaper from my high chair at the breakfast table when I was three—but the first thing that comes to mind when you ask about my childhood is this one, random day when I was about nine."

She smiled, a pleased, secret little smile, and Wes felt his spine melt.

"I'm not even sure what city we were in," she went on. "But I know it was on a coast, because my mother's publisher had arranged for us to go sailing. I think there was supposed to be a reporter with it, a segment recorded for some show while we were sailing, but I don't remember that happening. I think the reporter called in sick, but the publisher let us take the boat out anyway. And my father's lecture got canceled, so he came with us. All three of us were there on the boat, on blue, blue water that stretched forever out to the horizon, and the sun was shining. We saw dolphins, and seagulls, and my parents laughed a lot. It was just . . ." She looked down at the table, but Wes still caught it when her smile went wistful. "That was a very good day. And I felt lucky, because I knew my father wouldn't have been with us if he hadn't had a cancelation, which was very rare, and my mother would've been totally involved with the interview if the reporter had been there—but everything came together, for once. And we had a good day."

Her voice trailed off, and it took everything Wes had not to clear the table in a single hurdle and sweep her into his arms for a good cuddle. In fact . . .

"Hey," he said, standing up and holding out his hand. "Do you want to dance?"

She looked at him, eyes wide at the sudden shift. "I don't know how."

"Not one of the things you're an expert on, huh? Don't worry, we won't be crunking or whatever. Over here in our little corner? No one's going to mind if we just put our arms around each other and sway."

Mouth twisting into a shy smile, she stood, too. "I can do that."

Relief scoured through Wes's insides the moment she stepped into the circle of his body. He needed to get his hands on her, the warmth of her against him, sheltered in the curve of his body—anything to ease the persistent, throbbing ache of sadness in his gut for the solitary, overlooked girl she used to be.

"Hey," she said into his shoulder, her breath hot through the thin material of his T-shirt. "Don't think this gets you off the hook, buddy. Quid pro quo—I showed you mine, now you show me yours."

"Later," he said, unable to even imagine what he could tell her that wouldn't be a lie, but also wouldn't minimize the exquisite, delicate pain of her memory. Wes actually remembered his childhood fondly, for the most part. It had its ups and downs, and looking back, he knew there were incidents that would raise the hair and blood pressure of any competent social worker, but he'd loved his dad unconditionally. Every day with Pops was an adventure.

But he couldn't tell her about that.

"Later, I will. I promise," he forestalled her when she raised her head, a protest clear on her face.

He pulled her farther into the shadows, bent his head to hers, and kissed her. She came alive under his mouth, lips parting on a sigh, her whole body lifting into him as if she were levitating.

You're not alone anymore, he tried to tell her with every slide of his tongue against hers, every clasp of his hands around her narrow, slender back.

Even if Wes was nowhere near good enough for her, at least he knew what she was worth. At least he understood how precious she was, how unique and perfect in all her many weirdnesses and eccentricities.

Maybe he wasn't perfect, or anything like it, and he sure as hell wasn't a genius—but at least he knew that much.

He thought about his father's demands, and what he'd have to do to meet them, and hardened his resolve. It was all worth it. Anything was worth it, to keep the woman in his arms safe.

Chapter 26

Over the next few days, Rosemary did her best to ignore the last, persistent niggling doubts about what she'd seen at Chapel.

She wanted to believe Wes's easy explanation; she'd remind herself that she'd misread the situation before, and she really couldn't trust herself not to be overreacting to something completely innocent.

And yet . . . and yet. She couldn't help feeling that things changed after that night.

Rosemary knew she wasn't the most perceptive or sensitive to emotional shifts—generally, it took a seismic quake on par with plate tectonics to alert her to someone's altered emotional state, including her own.

None of which made it easier to ignore the fact that after that night at the seedy, Lower East Side bar, Wes began to pull away from her.

It was subtle at first. A lot of working late at the restaurant, promises to come over to her hotel later that ended with him stealing into bed with her sometime after she'd finally given up and gone to sleep. He began to look worn and drawn, his boyishly handsome face creased with lines of exhaustion.

She tried to ask him about it, but he put her off with excuses about work and how much the job at Market meant to him. In the few minutes they had together, if she happened to wake up when he came in, he talked about his dreams for the future, a restaurant of his own, and she read the truth of that goal in the way his head would lift and his eyes would shine in the filtered blue light from beyond her drapes.

They made love in the dark, his body hard and demanding against her sleep-softened muscles. He came to her desperate and aching, and within seconds, he'd have her aching, too, her confused body caught between somnolence and arousal. When they slept, after, he curled around her and held her so tightly her ribs nearly creaked with the strain, but she never complained.

In the mornings, he'd get up early and play with Lucille, brew coffee in the little hotel pot, and bitch about the lack of a kitchen. Without fail, he asked her about the aphrodisiac research and how things were going. He'd nod and smile, and kiss her good-bye, and that was it.

Rosemary did not like it.

What she hated most was that she couldn't put her finger on exactly what was bothering her. And in the absence of a concrete enemy, her hyperactive brain did what it did best—it began to come up with different scenarios to explain the inconsistency.

Or, as she imagined Wes might put it, she spun into a paranoid freak-out.

The fact that she was aware that her increasingly upsetting conjectures were mostly coming straight out of her own fears and insecurities did nothing to calm her nerves.

Currently winning the pool was her very real and quite justified, she thought, assumption that Wes had pulled away because of something about what she'd shared with him that night regarding her family situation.

Somehow, it was easier to believe he was tired of dealing with someone as emotionally stunted and underdeveloped as Rosemary than it was to consider, for the nine hundredth time, exactly who that sprightly, gray-haired man had been. Not to mention why they were really fighting, or why the dapper stranger winked at her before he left.

After the third day in a row of getting a text from Wes saying service had run long and it would be a while before he made it across town, so she shouldn't wait up, Rosemary closed her laptop with a click and got her jacket.

Lucille, ever alert to the possibility of walkies, popped up off the damask sofa in the sitting area of the suite like a spring-loaded toy.

"No," Rosemary told her. "I already got in trouble once for bringing you to the restaurant. Forget it."

The wagging of Lucille's entire body slowed but didn't stop. The bright canine grin of anticipation was replaced by Lucille's patented Puppy Dog Eyes of Death, and Rosemary felt herself go all gooey.

It was sort of disgusting, but she couldn't seem to control herself. She checked her watch: eleven o'clock. The last customers should be leaving the restaurant by now, surely.

"Okay, we'll go in the back way. Remember Wes showed us the alley behind the restaurant? Yes. I said 'Wes.' If you could stop wriggling so I can put your leash on, I'd be very pleased. I'm serious. Lucille! Okay."

Finally they were ready to go. Rosemary looked down at her best friend, trotting happily along by her right ankle, and smiled. It felt good to get out of her head and back into the world, taking action and making things happen.

"If Wes can't come to us," she said to Lucille, "then we'll just have to go to him. And drag him home kicking and screaming if we have to."

Hopefully it wouldn't come to that.

"Move your skinny arse. Think you own this alley?"

Wes straightened from his slump against the wall as the low, drawling Cockney voice jolted him out of his stupor. He'd ducked out the back kitchen door for a breath of cool air after the inferno of dinner service, but even one minute alone was enough to get him thinking about the fucked-up mess he was currently trying to claw his way out of, courtesy of dear old dad.

He didn't need Frankie riding his ass, too.

Stuffing his fists in his pockets, he gritted his teeth and said, "It's all yours. I just came out to clear my head."

Wes headed for the door, but Frankie caught him by the arm with a quick grimace. "Look, mate. You don't have to go. I was being a prat. You earned a second or two of breathing in air that doesn't smell of sweat, grilled meat, and sizzling oil. You look like pounded crap." He held out his battered pack of Dunhills, eyebrows raised.

Waving away the proffered cigarette, Wes resumed his lean against the brick wall—cautiously, this time. He never knew what to expect with Frankie; the guy hated his guts because he was friends with Jess. Which was more than a little fucked, in Wes's opinion, but no one asked him.

And it sucked extra, because for all Frankie's totally nonacademy-approved insubordination and occasional dickheadedness, he was an amazing chef. Wes had spent hours when he first got to Market just watching the guy's moves at the giant wood-fired grill, of which Frankie was the undisputed king.

But whatever. Frankie was never going to accept Wes, much less respect him. He'd stopped expecting Frankie to get the hell over himself a long time ago.

What Wes didn't expect was for Frankie to prop himself against the opposite wall, one booted heel kicked up against the bricks, look at him from under those hooded eyes and say, "You made your bones tonight, Wes."

"What?" Wes blinked stupidly. The smoke from those obnoxiously expensive cigarettes had to be affecting his hearing.

Frankie's thin lips tightened around his cigarette. "You heard me. I said you were a stud on the line tonight. We could've been weeded right from the start, with that table of ten coming in early, and adding two punters to make an even dozen. And from the minute you showed up tonight, arse dragging and looking like you ain't slept in weeks, I was sure you'd let the side down. But you rocked it out."

There was a very real possibility that Wes might keel over and die. He knew he'd done well during service, held it together when the tickets started spinning out of control and a lot of guys would've crumbled—but he hadn't thought anyone else noticed. Although if anyone would, it'd be Frankie; partly because the guy loved to go all Big Bad Sous Chef and ream Wes a new one for any mistakes, and partly because his beloved grill station was right next to sauté, where Wes had been banging out order after order.

"Holy shitballs," he said stupidly, insane pride making his chest expand like a hot air balloon. "Did you seriously call me a stud?"

"Don't get excited. You're not my type." Frankie smirked.

His black eyes flashed gratitude for lightening the heavy atmosphere in the alleyway.

"Nah, I know," Wes replied, relaxing back into his slouch and enjoying the way the rush of endorphins from Frankie's out-of-the-blue praise made his feet and back quit throbbing with pain for a few seconds. "You don't like 'em tall, dark, and handsome—you prefer short, ginger, and adorkable."

And then he froze. Fuck. He absolutely, positively, under no circumstances should've mentioned Jess! The first time ever that Frankie had something nice to say to Wes, and he brought up the guy's ex? Talk about ruining a perfect moment. "The endorphins," Wes yelped. "They made me say it! Shit, dude, I'm sorry."

He squeezed one eye shut, waiting for the explosion, but all that happened was a long exhale of smoke from Frankie's nostrils, like a man-eating dragon too tired from battling knights and hoarding treasure to bother breathing actual fire.

"Nah, s'awright," Frankie muttered. The guy didn't actually blush and duck his head like a bashful schoolboy, but Wes could tell it was a close call. "Guess there ain't too much use pretending I don't have it bad for Jess, right? Everyone knows. Including him."

"Yeah," Wes agreed, cocking his head. "So what's the problem, again?"

Frankie examined the end of the cigarette he held in the first three fingers of his left hand, then pointed it at Wes. The smoldering cherry winked at him. "The problem is sussing out what the hell to do about it."

Sometimes Wes wondered how he came to be in a position to give out relationship advice to a couple of dudes in love with each other. And as weird as it maybe was, the gay thing was not the part that messed with Wes's head. It was the idea of anyone thinking he knew what he was talking about when it came to matters of the heart.

"Look, man," Wes said, aware that he was taking his life in his hands. "I'm still not seeing the bad here. I mean, what's to suss? You're nuts about him, and he's sure as shit all cuckoo for Cocoa Puffs about you. Quit messing around and close the deal."

"I'm not messing him about," Frankie protested. "That's exactly what I'm trying to avoid."

Wes was willing to bet Jess would disagree. Attempting to be tactful, for once, he said, "What's stopping you from making him happy? I'm sure as shit not in love with the kid, we're just pals. But even I'd like to see him ditch the sourpuss every now and then, maybe smile a little. You know you can make it happen, and I know you want to. So what's holding you back?"

Frankie flinched as if Wes had backhanded him with a wet soup ladle, then scowled. "No need to act like Jess's been pining away without me. I know he's been . . . dating."

The misery in Frankie's voice made Wes want to give the guy a hug. Or maybe a punch in the face, because seriously. He bought that shit?

"If anything, he's been screwing," Wes said bluntly. This time, the flinch was more of a full-on wince. The guy actually curled over slightly, as if to shield himself from a body blow. "I wouldn't call it dating. And I don't think there's been a lot of that—our boy has a highly developed sense of right and wrong, and he knows damn well it'd be wrong to get involved with anyone when he's still hung up on you."

"Fucking hell," Frankie breathed. "Don't mince words, do you? I think I see why Jess likes you. He hates when people try to manage him."

"Which is exactly what you're doing," Wes had to point out.

"Bloody buggering fuck," Frankie yelled, knocking his head back into the wall with a fierce, shocking slam. "I know it," he whispered. "Fuck me, I'm doing that to him. It'd be no wonder if he hated my bleeding guts."

"But he doesn't." Wes was watching his companion closely, and he saw the lightning strike of incomprehension and bewilderment that turned angry punk-rock Frankie into a scared little boy for a full second.

"That's it," Wes realized, feeling a chill of recognition. "Jess loves you—and you have no idea why."

Frankie stiffened all over, like an affronted flamingo; Wes was half afraid the guy'd end up toppling over, what with the way he still had one foot casually propped on the wall behind him.

But Wes knew he was onto something, and he was still riding those superfly endorphins from Frankie calling him a line stud, so he wasn't about to back down. "Don't even try to deny it, man. Believe me, I recognize the signs."

Subsiding into a slumped sulk, Frankie cast him a disgruntled look over the end of his cigarette. "Sod off."

"No," Wes said, flooded with the heady power of being one hundred percent right. "You followed me out here, you didn't let me go back inside when I tried to give you some space—dude, from you, that's as good as a cry for help. So you're gonna stand there and let me help you and Jess, because I am sick to freaking death of watching you two dance around each other like a pair of demented pigeons."

What was with all the bird imagery? Wes shook it off. Not important.

"Look at you," Frankie said with a ghost of his usual sneer. "One good service and you think you're cock of the walk."

"I've had lots of good services," Wes said firmly. "And you know it. Besides, the only one acting like a cock here is you."

That startled a laugh out of the Brit. "Fine! I surrender. I'm at your mercy, O wise one. Fill me up with your psychobabble insights, Dr. Wes."

Refusing to be baited, Wes began ticking things off on his fingers. "One. You think you're making things better for Jess by cutting him loose, but you're wrong. He's fucking despondent, man."

Frankie didn't like that, Wes could tell. He held up his second finger firmly. "Two! You were surprised, just for an instant, when I told you what anybody with a pair of working eyes could see, which is that Jess loves you. I'm reasonably sure he's already spilled the beans about that one, actually, so why the surprise? Unless . . . Three. You think you're not good enough for him."

Resounding silence filled the alley. Frankie's spine was tense where it pressed against the brick, as if he were braced for a kick in the nuts. Wes steeled himself to continue. This next part was where it got rough.

Feeling his way, he said, "I don't know what your deal is. Not pretending to be psychic, man, or your best friend, or some shit like that. I don't know why you feel this way, but I know that look. That oh-my-sweet-Jesus-fuck expression in your eyes that says you're in way over your head and you don't know how the hell to get yourself back up to solid ground."

Frankie still refused to look at him, his black gaze trained solidly on the toes of his own combat boots, but his whole attitude suggested that he was listening with every fiber of his being.

So Wes went for it. Gulping in a breath, he said, "I know that look, because I see it in the mirror every day."

That got Frankie to glance up, surprise and pain written on his angular features. "Yeah?" he said hoarsely.

"Yeah." Wes shrugged. Casual was the last thing he felt, but pride—his besetting sin, according to Pops—

wouldn't let him shuffle his feet or look away. He faced Frankie dead on, head high, and said, "I know I'm way out of my league with Rosemary. Part of that's her—she's unbelievable, I mean, there's not many guys in her league, and most of them are, like, eighty-year-old Nobel laureates. But most of it is me. I put myself square out of her league by lying to her. And it eats at me every day, but there's shit I haven't told her. In our case, it's shit that would break us. I don't know if that's what's up with you and Jess, but I'm going to give you some advice I'm too much of a pussy to follow myself."

A drop of water landed on Wes's forehead, then another on the top of his nose. He looked up at the sliver of sky visible between the buildings. It was starting to rain. He pushed away from the wall and walked up to the kitchen door, aware of Frankie's intent gaze tracking every movement. When his hand was on the door handle, he said, "Tell him, man. Grow a pair and tell Jess whatever you've got going on, because living a lie with the person you love? It sucks ass."

He turned to head back inside, but Frankie's belligerent voice stopped him. "Oi! You gonna tell your bird the truth, then?"

Wes looked over his shoulder into Frankie's challenging stare. The rain was falling faster now, starting to plaster his shock of hair in coal-black tendrils across his pale cheeks.

"I'm smarter than you," Wes said. "I never really thought about it before, but this is how I know—I didn't let the lies pull us apart in the first place."

Frankie snarled through the rain, and Wes shook his head. "Dude. You wanna prove me wrong? Do what I can't. Tell Jess the truth. Whatever it is, it can't be worse than the hell you're both going through now."

He left Frankie there in the pouring rain, holding a wet

cigarette and staring holes in his back, and wondered if he'd crossed a line.

No time to worry about it now.

He pounded down the back stairs and grabbed his gear from the locker room. He had to get to his second shift.

Chapter 27

Rosemary stumbled into a diner at Eightieth and Broadway, soaking wet, and clutching a shivering white mess of dog in her arms.

The tiny, wizened hostess raised both improbably red eyebrows to her hennaed hairline and said, "You wanna sit at the counter, or you want a booth?"

"Booth, please," Rosemary gasped out, feeling Lucille's legs kick against her chest. She was squeezing the poor dog too tightly, she knew that, but she couldn't seem to get herself to unclench until she settled into the dubious comfort of the orange cracked vinyl booth seat.

Without even asking, the waitress, whose nametag read HILDY, brought over a pot of coffee, and flipped and filled the mug in front of Rosemary in one efficient motion.

"Thank you," Rosemary said automatically. She reached for the steaming mug on autopilot, which let Lucille loose. The little dog scrambled onto the seat, gave Rosemary a reproachful look, then pointedly turned away to stare out the large plate-glass window by their booth.

"Is it okay to have a dog in here?" Rosemary asked belatedly.

"We usually ask people to keep 'em in their carriers or purses," Hildy said in a gruff Brooklyn accent. "But I guess she don't look like she wants to make trouble."

"Thank you," Rosemary repeated, this time with heartfelt gratitude. She wasn't sure her legs would hold her for another block of walking around like a zombie in the rain.

Hildy's wrinkled face crumpled up into a smile that made her look like a cheerful hobbit. "You're fine, hon. If the manager gives you any lip, you tell him I said it was okay."

"Okay." Rosemary winced at the faintness of her own voice, but Hildy gave her a brisk, motherly pat on the shoulder and started making the rounds with her coffeepot.

Rosemary wrapped her chilly fingers around the hot ceramic mug, welcoming the burn. It shocked her out of her torpor, zapped her brain out of its current feedback loop of denial and betrayal.

Wes was lying to her. About something big, something huge, if the way he had to work to firm his voice when he talked about it was any kind of clue.

Somehow, despite the fact that she knew—she had *known*—for a week that something was off, she was still completely blindsided now. Rosemary shifted in the seat, wincing at the squawk of protesting fake leather, and breathed through her mouth until the persistent threat of humiliating tears abated.

She would not sit in an all-night diner and sob. She just wouldn't.

Beside her on the bench seat, Lucille scrabbled around looking for crumbs in the cracks. When that got boring, she shifted her attention back to the window, watching the people go by.

In an instant, she was up on her back legs, front legs propped on the ledge running below the window, black nose pressed to the glass. When she went into the full-body wag, Rosemary started to worry about the manager noticing them. She didn't want to get Hildy in trouble. Even though something told her Hildy probably ran this place like a small, aproned dictator, Rosemary attempted to shush Lucille's frantic wriggling.

Lucille, however, would not be hushed. High-pitched whimpers started up, short, staccato bursts of sound that made Rosemary flinch. What was wrong with her dog?

She tried to pull Lucille away from the window, and looked up and through the glass just in time to catch sight of Wes's retreating back in the sea of passing people. He was wearing a black leather jacket, shoulders hunched against the wind and rain, but Rosemary would recognize him anywhere.

Where was he going? Another lie, she realized, because he wasn't hailing a cab over to the east side where her hotel was, he was crossing Broadway now, aiming for the downtown subway.

There was a sense of disorientation commonly described as vertigo, although it would be more accurately classified as height vertigo (or acrophobia) when it felt like this—as if she were standing at the edge of a steep precipice, rock shearing away beneath her into vast nothingness, and wind buffeting her from all sides as if pushing her to jump.

Suddenly filled with renewed energy—anger made decent fuel, it turned—Rosemary leaped out of her seat, pulling Lucille up with her. She tossed a twenty on the table and rushed out of the diner, darted through the busy Broadway traffic, and followed Wes down into the dark maw of the subway.

He refused to tell her the truth? So what. Rosemary

was an expert at discovering the truth about how the world worked. She didn't need him to tell her; she'd find out on her own.

Keeping her chin tucked and Lucille wrapped up in her jacket, Rosemary managed to negotiate a Metro pass out of the bored, nearly incomprehensible attendant in his little bulletproof cubicle. It was a bit of a struggle to work out how to jam the card into the turnstile, but she could see Wes waiting for the train about twelve meters away, so she forced herself to slow down and focus, and the thing slid through the groove and let her through.

She purposely turned away from Wes, walking a short distance down the platform to wait. More and more people trickled down the stairs and onto the platform, filling the space between them until she felt more confident inching her way back toward him. She needed to get in the same car as Wes, or she'd never be able to tell where he got off.

Stolidly ignoring the layers of grit and grime just freaking *everywhere* down here, not to mention the odd scamper of a rat across the tracks, Rosemary swallowed her rising gorge and sidled closer.

The train pulled up with a rush of foul-smelling air and a screech of metal. The doors opened, and Rosemary held her breath, allowing herself to be swept up in the tide of people moving forward.

Do not hyperventilate do not hyperventilate do not hyperventilate . . . oh, frak, I'm hyperventilating!

Unavoidable, because there was no way she could force herself to take deep breaths of the close, recycled carbon dioxide emitted by the people crammed into this metallic tube of death, all coughing and hacking and spitting and wiping their excretions on the doors and seats and the poles in the middle of the car, leaving nothing to brace herself against.

Focus, she told herself. *Now is not the time to worry about phantom bacteria. WWBD, Rosemary? What would Buffy do?*

If she ignored the fact that she wasn't a fictional vampire slayer, and even if she were, her superpowers probably wouldn't help her if she contracted ebola, Rosemary could manage a calm inhalation or two. It got better at the next stop, when enough people got off to allow her to sit down, wedged into the back corner of the car, as far from Wes as she could manage.

There he was, the man she'd allowed into her hotel suite, her lab, her heart—leaning against one of the poles running down the middle of the car, as nonchalantly as if he hadn't a care in the world.

Rosemary narrowed her eyes on his leather-jacketed back, and vowed not to let him out of her sight until she discovered exactly what he was up to.

He changed trains once, at Times Square, which was a hoot and a half. Rosemary managed to keep up with him while keeping him from spotting her. It helped that the general New York City rule was to keep one's head down and make zero eye contact.

When they finally emerged from the stinking depths of hell into the cool, relatively clean air of Delancey Street, Rosemary nearly staggered with relief. She felt as if she'd been through the wars, destroyed the Death Star, slayed a nest of vampires . . . but it wasn't over yet.

She squinted around. The area looked vaguely familiar, and as Wes took off, walking briskly toward a gray stone building on the next corner, Rosemary figured it out.

That bar. Chapel. He'd lied about having to work . . . to come out and drink with his friends?

Even after hearing his betrayal from his own lips, Rosemary still had a hard time believing it. Maybe she was hopelessly naïve, or maybe she didn't want to think something so simple and trite could be worth this much emotional upheaval.

Either way, she obviously had to find out more.

Lucille squirmed, whining to be put down. Knowing the little dog had probably reached her limit of being carried around like a fuzzy handbag, Rosemary debated for a split second before setting Lucille on the damp sidewalk.

Picking up a paw daintily, as if shocked and appalled at the condition of the concrete she had to walk on, Lucille huffed out a breath and charged off after Wes suddenly enough to nearly tear the leash from Rosemary's hand.

Rosemary tightened her grip and tried to keep up. Lucille towed her along until they were inside Chapel, then she put her face to the ground and started snuffling around for Wes's scent.

"Good luck," Rosemary muttered, wrinkling her nose. Even her weak human senses detected a maelstrom of scent markers hanging in the Chapel air, everything from cannabis to cologne.

Her heart pounded loud enough to drown out the beat of music from the speakers. The place was less crowded than the first time she went there; presumably as an after-hours bar, it filled up late.

She surveyed the room intently, looking for Wes's bomber jacket and chestnut hair darkened by rain, and finally spotted him ducking behind the bar.

He reached up for a slim bottle of clear liquor, saying something over his shoulder with that easy smile Rosemary loved so much.

She frowned. Was he working at Chapel now? He never said anything about that.

Starting forward, tugging Lucille, who'd been distracted by a cache of empty peanut shells under a table, along in her wake, Rosemary headed for Wes, determined to get some answers.

But every question flew out of her head when a new customer stepped up to the bar and spoke to Wes.

It was the gray-haired man!

Shrinking back, Rosemary watched their interchange, her mind racing, picking up and discarding different approaches, different possible explanations.

Time, that fundamental quantity so basic it could be used to measure and define other elements, began to play impossible tricks on her, slowing and blipping like a roll of film that had skipped its loop.

She blinked, and the world came into focus.

The real world, not the fantasy world she'd been living in for weeks—and when Lucille finally picked Wes's voice out of the crowd and charged off to find him, Rosemary went with her.

The older man was gone by now. Where? She neither knew nor cared. He was inconsequential, a mere symptom of the diseased mind standing in front of her with an expression of shock and dismay dawning over his handsome face.

"Rosemary! What are you doing here?"

Having no patience with chitchat, Rosemary waved that away. She couldn't seem to take her eyes off Wes, the way his shoulders stretched the material of his soft gray shirt, the way his too-long hair curled over the collar. The way his cheekbones still shone with the remnants of rainwater, and his lush mouth—the mouth she'd felt over every inch of her body—retained a hint of the anger and resignation she'd seen in him when he spoke to the well-dressed stranger.

In a flash of unfamiliar, entirely unwelcome awareness, she became conscious of how she must look. Her clothes stuck to her, damp and clammy; her braids were heavy, wet ropes against her back.

Shoving the pitiful-waif image out of her head, Rosemary drew herself up to her full height.

"Who is that man? The truth this time, Wes." She felt her mouth tremble, and firmed it ruthlessly. "I don't want any more of your lies."

Watching the tentative light die out of his eyes was like watching an experiment she'd worked for hours to meticulously set up suddenly explode right in her face.

But Rosemary forced her knees steady and stared him down.

It's always better to know than to wonder, she reminded herself. *Even when knowing the truth hurts like a stake through the heart.*

Wes felt his insides go liquid with fear, as if he'd swallowed a shot of vodka laced with pure poison—it burned all the way down, and that was only the beginning.

"Who?" he tried, but he already knew it wouldn't fly. Everything was crashing to the ground; all he could do now was try to save the pieces.

"You know exactly who I mean," she hissed, stepping right up to the bar.

Wes glanced around for Christian, who had his eye on them already. He gave the universal head jerk for "take five" and went back to filling drink orders.

Ducking back under the bar partition, Wes came around to Rosemary and reached for her arm.

She flinched away from his touch.

Wes sucked in air and tried to still his galloping heart. *Relax. The first hit always hurts the worst,* he tried to tell himself.

Only he didn't really believe that. The worst was yet to come.

A yip near his feet made him look down to see Lucille dancing on her hind legs and begging for attention. "Hey, someone's glad to see me," he said, crouching to ruffle her fur.

Rosemary jerked on the leash hard enough to yank Lucille off her feet. The dog yelped, and Wes frowned up at Rosemary, but she didn't appear to even realize what she'd done. Her hands were clenched into tight fists and she was up on the balls of her feet, her whole body poised for a fight.

Yeah. No doubt about it. He'd been made.

But she still didn't know who Pops was, he reminded himself. That could buy him some wiggle room, right?

"I told you," he said, keeping his voice light and reasonable, as if they weren't about to have a knockdown drag-out in the middle of Chapel. "That guy's a nobody. Just an old scam artist I lent some money to a while back, and now he won't pony up."

She shook her head mechanically. "No. No, I don't believe that, because if he owes you money, why does he keep showing up here and talking to you? No, you have something he wants. And I bet I know exactly what it is."

Wes stood and faced her, his mind a blur of pure panic. She couldn't know, there was no way she could know— and he saw in her eyes that she'd recognized the emotion all over his face.

Resignation warred with betrayal for control of Rosemary's expression, and Wes felt like his chest might explode. "Fuck," he cursed harshly. "You picked a hell of a time to get good at reading me."

"Oh, I had help," she said, her voice shaking with rage. "I already knew you were lying."

"How?"

"I heard it straight from you."

He took in her appearance again, wet, lank hair and

chilled, pale skin. Her clothes were soaked through. The rain. Oh God.

"You were in that alley when I talked to Frankie, weren't you?" He couldn't believe this was happening.

She nodded, her chin moving up and down like a spasm.

"Jesus, that was an hour ago—you must be freezing! Let me . . ."

Pulling away from his concerned hands, Rosemary all but snarled, "I don't need your help. I don't need anything from you except the truth."

Helpless, Wes dropped his hands back to his sides, aching to wrap her up in something soft and warm and away from this mess he'd created. "I'm sorry, Rosie. I never meant to hurt you."

"Shut up," she cried. Heads turned, even at Chapel, and Wes pulled her with him, protesting all the way, to the door beside the bar. Once they were safely in the back hallway that led down to the storage cellar, and away from prying eyes, she seemed to lose whatever steel had been keeping her upright.

"Don't be nice," she choked out. "I know it's a lie, you can stop pretending to like me now."

"I was never pretending about that," Wes said, her words flicking over the raw wound of his guilt. "I—you're important to me." He couldn't say it, couldn't tell her he loved her for the first time like this, in a storm of tears and anger, when he knew she wouldn't believe him.

"Oh, I'm sure." She tried to sneer but couldn't really carry it off with the way her mouth kept trembling. "Important to your wallet, maybe. How much did he promise you?"

Wes put his hands on his hips, utterly confused. "What are you talking about?"

"Quit playing innocent," she said, her blue eyes flashing

fire and brimstone. "That man, the one you were arguing with. He's from a pharmaceutical company, isn't he? You're planning to steal my research and sell it to the highest bidder!"

Chapter 28

When did he lose his mind? Was it the moment he agreed to his father's ridiculous demands, just to keep Pops away from Rosemary? Or should he go further back, maybe to the first moment he saw Dr. Rosemary Wilkins in that classroom back at the academy.

Wes shook his head like a spaniel shaking off water droplets. "Are you serious?"

"That's an evasion, not a denial," Rosemary said, something behind her eyes shattering. "Oh God. I can't believe I trusted you. I can't believe I thought, even for a second, that someone like you might look at me and see more than an opportunity."

Maybe the whole world had gone insane. This was like living in the Land of Backwards, where up was down and left was right and gorgeous, smart, successful women cried over losers like him. Wes felt sick. "Rosemary, sweets. Don't talk like that. It's not true, I never, ever thought of you like that."

Except he had, hadn't he? Right at the beginning? Guilt threatened to choke him as he stared at the pain tightening her sensual lips into a tight grimace and making her lungs work like a bellows, pushing air in and out past her desire to keep it together in front of him.

All he wanted was to hold her and tell her to let go—but oh, the irony. If he reached for her, the only one screaming "Let go!" would be her.

Even now, he could stop this. All he had to do was tell her the truth. Tell her who Pops was, what he wanted. Tell her about his childhood, and what had landed him at Heartway House. "Rosemary, listen—"

"Stop right there." Visibly getting a grip on her runaway emotions, Rosemary gritted out, "Please spare me another one of your lies. You know, the irony of this situation hasn't escaped me. Here I spend my whole life searching for scientific truth, and then I fall for someone who wouldn't recognize the truth if it bit him in the gluteus maximus. Come on, Lucille."

But the dog wouldn't budge.

Breath coming in harsh, humiliated gasps, Rosemary tugged on the leash. Wes felt his heart splinter right down the middle, spilling acid and pain out into his rib cage.

Lucille plopped her furry white butt on the hallway floor and looked up at Wes, then back at Rosemary. She was clearly torn between the two humans who'd cared for her, cuddled her, fed her, played with her.

"Go on," he whispered to her, making a little shooing gesture. "It's okay, L-dawg. Go with Rosemary."

Rosemary stopped pulling on the leash, her hand going slack at her side. She looked up at Wes, and the deep, real grief on her face stole his breath. "It figures," she gasped. "The first real friend I ever have, my whole life, and even she doesn't want to be with me."

"No, come on," Wes said, his voice breaking. "She's just confused. Go on, pretty girl. Rosemary needs you."

That ripped a choked sob out of Rosemary's throat. She dropped the leash on the ground and backed away. "No I don't. I don't need her, I don't need anyone."

Every word, every tear, every time he stared into those swimming blue eyes, Wes shuddered with paralyzing fear and self-hatred. He could barely manage to hold out his hand to Rosemary—this beautiful woman he wasn't good enough to touch or even look at—but he had to try. "Wait, don't—"

"Leave me alone," she shouted, the words sharp with misery. "I don't want to hear anything else. You're a liar. I never should've had anything to do with you."

Wes dropped his hand. What else could he say? She was right. And even if he swore never to lie to her again, it was only a matter of time before Pops had his hands all over her big, fat bank account.

"I'm sorry." He forced the words through lips gone numb and bloodless with pain.

She blinked away the tears, wiping at her damp face with the back of her hand, and laughed. The harsh, dry sound scoured out Wes's heart like a handful of rock salt in a cast-iron skillet.

Backing away from them slowly, Rosemary said, "I went through my whole life without ever feeling much of anything—and I was just fine with that. Then you had to come along and make me notice how much I was missing." She shook her head. "I could hate you for that alone."

Wes glanced down at himself, dazedly wondering when the bruises would start to show. He'd never felt so battered, not after the worst street fight or barroom brawl. But he said nothing. Just stood there and took it, because he deserved it, and he knew it.

She shook her head, contempt twisting her mouth off center. "Some genius I turned out to be. I let myself get played by an uneducated thief with nothing but cheap charm and a mangy m-mutt dog to his name."

Her voice shook, but she kept her head up defiantly. In a distant, surreal way, Wes was proud of her.

In the more immediate reality, of course, he felt each word like the rough edge of a serrated knife, but pride—his old standby—was enough to keep him on his feet when all he wanted was to go to his knees and beg her to forgive him.

There was no point. She'd made her decision.

And when she turned and walked through the hall door, through the bar, and out into the rain, Wes knew he'd never see her again.

It was hard to imagine being hit by a bus could feel worse than this. Wes counted the seconds until the start of dinner service as he loaded up a tray with the accompaniments for the family meal he'd stayed up all night preparing.

During service was the only time he felt alive—the rush of adrenaline and urgency might be a poor substitute for a true will to live, but they were all he had, so he clung to them.

Rosemary had only been gone—what? Two days? And Wes was already falling apart, as if she'd been the glue that held his life together. Moronic, but there it was.

He couldn't eat. Couldn't sleep. Didn't want to think.

All he could do was cook, so he did that.

Pushing the dining room door open with his hip, Wes was surprised to see Adam, Grant, and Frankie all gathered by the bar. The big shocker wasn't that they were alone out there—Wes was pretty far ahead of schedule on getting family meal ready; even the perpetually starving line cooks hadn't made a mad dash for the dining room yet—but that the three powers behind Market had their heads together, talking animatedly.

It had been a tense few days around here, from what Wes could tell in the midst of his own problems.

But evidently Adam had forgiven Grant's lie, and everything was hunky-dory again.

Wes started setting out bowls of chopped fresh cilantro, lemongrass, ginger, and mint, and tried not to be envious.

"Just imagine," Grant was saying. "The Market Bar. Or the Bar at Market! A more casual, no-reservations, walk-in kind of place."

"We could even do a prix-fixe," Adam replied. "Like a sidewalk bistro in Paris—no menu, just a chalkboard with a three-course meal, different every day, based on what looks good at the Greenmarket."

"Like an even more focused, distilled version of what Market stands for," Grant added eagerly.

"But look, guys, we still don't have the staff to run two kitchens. I can't be two places at once, and unless Frankie's willing to run his own kitchen for the first time . . ."

"Maybe I would be, if I had the right wing man."

The unnatural stillness from Grant and Adam made even Wes stop what he was doing and glance up.

"You've turned me down every time I've tried to promote you to chef de cuisine—" Adam said, waving his hands helplessly.

"What wing man?" Grant demanded.

Across the bar, Frankie's gaze flicked to Wes. "Time for family meal, I think. What did you make for us this time, Wes?"

"Vietnamese sandwiches called banh mi," he replied tersely. "Excuse me, I've gotta get the rest of the stuff."

Numb, confused, and exhausted, Wes could barely muster the energy to think about what he'd just overheard. He concentrated on pulling together the rest of the build-your-own sandwich makings. The short, crusty loaves of

French baguette, the bowls of pâté, spiced ground pork, and the platter of sliced terrine of pork and veal all went onto his tray.

After a bad moment where he almost dropped the heavy tray, he managed to heft it onto his shoulder and get it out to the bar where the rest of the line cooks were finally assembling.

"Holy hell," Adam said. "You made all this from scratch? Even the terrine?"

"Pork terrine is an essential part of the sandwich," Wes said, aware that he sounded like a stubborn idiot but too tired to do anything about it.

Adam and Frankie exhanged a glance that Grant could easily read as serious worry. "Something going on with you, mate?" Frankie asked. For Frankie, who approached most problems as if they were best solved with a wrecking ball, that was bordering on pussyfooting.

"Nothing I can't handle," Wes said, setting the tray on the bar. "Dig in, before the pig gets cold."

It would take more than worry for a fellow chef to keep the line cooks from falling on the food the instant it appeared. They were already cracking open the crusty loaves of bread and slathering the halves with the cold, lightly pink terrine, a cinnamon-inflected chicken liver pâté, and spoonfuls of fragrant ground pork. Fingers dipped into the prep bowls, layering fresh herbs, quick-pickled cucumbers and carrots, and other condiments onto the sandwiches.

Even though the blend of hot spice, sour pickled vegetables, salty pork, and sweet ginger made him want to sing, dance, laugh, and wolf down about four more of the banh mi sandwiches, Wes could only pick at his.

"Something is definitely off," Frankie announced.

Wes flinched, then forced himself still. "Don't put so much Sriracha on it next time," he said mildly.

"Not with the banh mi—that's bloody miraculous, that is, and you know it. I meant with you. What's the matter? You get your girl up the duff or something?"

Somebody gasped, probably Grant, and Wes stiffened while Frankie continued. "Gonna have a little baby Einstein of your very own?"

"Shut your damn mouth," Wes ground out.

Triumph flashed across Frankie's face. "Why? Sawing close to the bone, am I?"

"Frankie," Adam said, a warning clear in his voice, but Wes was already out of his seat and standing, everything that had happened in the past week crashing over his head in an avalanche of bad choices, stupid pride, and bitter regret.

"No," Wes said. "It's over, she's moved on. Left town two days ago. I don't want to talk about it."

He *really* didn't want to talk about it—talking led to feeling, which would probably lead to humiliating things like breaking down and sobbing in front of the two chefs he respected most in the world.

As if Wes didn't already have enough shit to deal with.

But Frankie, as usual, did the opposite of what Wes was hoping for.

He talked about it.

Only, also as per usual, he didn't do it quite the way Wes expected. There was no mocking or gloating or smirking—there was only the sincere, deep understanding buried in Frankie's eyes, and the steadying grasp of his hand on Wes's shoulder.

"I'm sorry, mate. I am. I wish you'd said something sooner."

"Wow," Adam said, wiping his fingers on a napkin. "For serious, man. You didn't have to deal with this all alone."

"I didn't?" Wes felt like an idiot, but he just wasn't getting it. He looked back and forth between Adam and

Frankie, then gazed around at the nodding heads and sympathetic grimaces of the crew standing at the bar.

"No way, dude," said Violet Porter, the words muffled around her mouthful of banh mi. "We got your back."

Just when Wes was starting to feel like shuffling his feet under all the empathetic stares, the cooks went back to eating and laughing with each other, as if everything were normal. Which left Wes standing there, trying to process what had just happened.

It honestly never occurred to him.

Maybe because the number one rule of his family was essentially the same as the number one rule of Fight Club: Don't talk about it. Or maybe just because he was a guy, surrounded mainly by other guys, and it would've felt weird.

Except, the way each and every person cuffed him on the shoulder or made an appreciative comment about the family meal as they finished up and headed back to the trenches made Wes feel like maybe he'd lucked into a new family. One that didn't prize secrecy and the ability to tell a convincing lie above all else.

One that might stick by him when the chips were down, instead of bailing at the first sign of trouble.

Finally, everyone had filed back into the kitchen except Wes, Frankie, and Adam. Grant and Christian were restocking the bar from the wine cellar downstairs, and Adam and Frankie had their heads together in an apparently very serious conversation, so Wes tried to be as quiet as possible clearing up the mess from dinner.

Still off balance from being dragged kicking and screaming back into the land of the living, Wes actually jumped about a foot in the air when Frankie appeared next to him.

"Been meaning to thank you for the other day. For what you said about me and Jess—you made a lot of sense, and I've been trying to think what to do ever since."

"Oh! Well, if I helped at all, I'm glad."

"You did," Frankie assured him. "And I think I've got a plan now, for maybe the first time in me life, but better late than never, innit? Anyway, I meant what I said before, as well. About you being one of us now. And we take care of our own."

And then, just when Wes thought he'd been astonished to the point where nothing else could ever throw him for a loop, Frankie threw an arm over his shoulder for a rough hug. He cast a glare at Adam and said, "Don't cock this up!" then took off for the kitchen.

Swaying in shock, Wes said, "Did that just happen?"

"You're in trouble now," Adam said, laughing. "Once you're in with Frankie, you can never get out again. He's gotta be the most loyal son of a bitch I've ever met. I think that's why he's so hard on new people—he has to make sure they're going to stick around before he gets in too deep."

Bemused, Wes shook his head. This day was taking on some definite dreamlike qualities. He almost wanted to pinch himself to make sure he was awake, but he'd never really understood that. It's not like he couldn't pinch himself in a dream.

Adam put his head to one side, regarding Wes with those sharp brown eyes that seemed to pierce right through to the heart of him. "So," Adam said, elaborately casual. "Are you planning to stick around, or what?"

Wes thought of Rosemary, back in her lab at the Academy of Culinary Arts. Shit. She might as well be on the moon.

"Yeah, I'm in." After the kind of friends he'd found here, the crazy adoptive family he had a shot at? It would take a stick of dynamite to pry him loose. Except . . .

"Assuming, you know, I can make my rent," he had to add, since there'd been a recent drain on his finances that made that whole deal even dicier.

Satisfaction gleamed in Adam's broad smile. "I don't want to get your hopes up, but I think we might have a solution for that. Let me tell you what we're thinking . . ."

As Adam outlined a possible long-term future for Wes with the crew at Market, Wes had to struggle to take it all in.

He was being offered a chance at everything he'd ever wanted—a life, a real honest-to-God life that he could make something of, with people he respected who respected him right back, and maybe even liked him a little. It was heady, overwhelming, amazing—and he still felt as though he'd never laugh again.

Wes listened to Adam, nodded in all the right places, and silently cursed that evil bitch, Karma, who'd come up with the perfect punishment for his many sins.

It seemed he was doomed to always want what he could never have.

Chapter 29

An essential part of the process of getting over an ex you still had to work with, Jess had found, was living your night off to the fullest.

Not that his forays into Manhattan's club scene had done much beyond showing him that a fake ID and an even faker smile got you in anywhere, and yes, in fact, what he'd had with Frankie had been one-of-a-kind, not easily replaceable with a casual trick he picked up at a bar.

Oh, and also that even considering sex with anyone other than Frankie made him feel like a low-down cheating man-ho.

Which probably explained why Jess was spending his precious night off in the photography lab at NYU, working on a chiaroscuro project that wasn't due for another month.

He was such a freaking loser.

When his phone beeped, he tried to fool himself that maybe one of the guys from his dorm was texting to invite him to an awesome party. Blowing out a breath, Jess rifled through his messenger bag for the phone, fully aware that it was probably his sister checking up on him.

He hadn't called her or talked to her much since overhearing her conversation with Frankie; he didn't know what to say or how to feel about it. So he was using the patented Frankie Boyd method of dealing: avoidance.

Real mature, Jess. And also, could you stop thinking about Frankie for thirty seconds?

Sighing, he thumbed his phone on and froze at the message that appeared on the screen.

Meet me @ 422 Columbus. Smthg 2 show you

It was from Frankie.

Jess's legs shook; he had to catch himself against the pan of chemical developer. It occurred to him to wish he could play it cool, but as he raced around the photo lab packing up his things, he knew there was no chance he wasn't going over there.

To hell with being cool and mature. If Frankie wanted to see him, even just to mess with his head—*or his body,* a hopeful voice in the back of his mind put in—Jess was there.

He missed the dickhead way too much.

The subway ride uptown felt endless. When the conductor's voice crackled in over the intercom to announce the train was making all express stops up to Seventy-second Street, Jess nearly cheered.

Finally, he was there. He gazed up at the awning of the building next to Market. 422 Columbus Avenue.

Trying to ignore the rampaging butterflies currently forming a mosh pit in his stomach, Jess tried the door. It was open.

"Hello?" he called. "Is anybody here? Frankie?"

"Back here, Bit." The voice came from another room at the rear of the empty space. Jess wanted to believe it was the creepiness of the deserted restaurant that sent chills down his back, but he wasn't that good at lying to himself.

That damn nickname got him every time.

He wrapped his arms around himself, glad he'd remembered his jacket, and picked his careful way through the dusty space, still littered with detritus from its failed incarnation as a Cajun hot spot.

No big surprise, Frankie was in the mostly stripped kitchen, setting up a table in the empty slot that looked like it used to house a prep station.

"I got your text," Jess said, and immediately closed his eyes in mortification. Of course he got the text. How the hell else would he have known to show up here?

"I'm glad," was all Frankie said, and there was satisfaction in his tone, but there was something about his manner—Jess narrowed his eyes. He'd thought he knew every one of Frankie's many moods, but this was a new one.

Frankie looked . . . at peace. In a high-strung, nervously tense way. He stood in front of the table, hipshot and casual in low-slung black pants that clung to his narrow hips, his checkered Vans planted firmly on the floor. His shirt was black, too, his favorite Ramones shirt with the punk band's seal over the chest. That shirt had been washed and worn to near translucence; Jess happened to know it was softer than silk and had a hole under the left arm, but Frankie would never give it up.

"I want 'em to bury me in this shirt," Frankie would cackle as they mock wrestled over it, rolling through the pillows lining their nest up in the Garrett. "I'm no quitter."

He hung on to things, Frankie did—he didn't like to give up.

Jess, apparently, was his big exception to that rule.

Swallowing down the pain he wasn't sure he'd ever really learn to live with, Jess said, "So are we allowed to be in here, or did you call me over to keep lookout for the cops?"

"Nah, we're all right," Frankie replied. "If the filth show up, we'll tell 'em we got the key from the Realtor."

"And will that be anything approximating the truth?"

"You worry too much, Bit." Frankie's smile was lazy and slow, but something deep moved behind his heavy-lidded black eyes.

Jess felt his heart stutter. Covering, he stuck his hands in his pockets, raised his shoulders, and said, "So if I'm not your lookout, what am I doing here?"

"I asked you to come so I could tell you some things I should've been man enough to own a long time ago." Frankie paused, rubbing his palms down the front of his pants in the only nervous gesture Jess had ever seen him make that didn't involve a cigarette. "Now, as to why you're here—that's another question, one only you can answer. Half expected you'd ignore me, Bit."

Jess snorted. "That's one thing I've pretty much never been able to do."

From the first time he saw Frankie, across a crowded kitchen—while Jess was in the middle of a job interview, no less—every second thought that passed through Jess's brain involved the guy. "Obsession" wasn't a superflattering word, but Jess thought it fit better than "ginormous crush." And after a while, when Frankie seemed to like him back, neither one was quite right.

The way Jess felt about Frankie—he didn't just crush on him or obsess over him. He felt connected to him, as tuned in to Frankie's wild emotions as he was to his own. And when that connection was severed, it was like being cut off from everything good in his life. Like when Frankie backed away, he took all the fun and joy and excitement with him, and left Jess with nothing but pain, doubt, and bits of broken glass disguised as memories.

"I'm glad," Frankie said again, his voice deeper, rougher. Jess felt himself swaying forward, but Frankie cleared his throat and stepped aside, breaking the spell.

When he shifted, Jess could see the table, which was covered with a dark purple and red paisley shawl he recognized from Frankie's apartment. When they first got together it was late spring, and there were still some cool nights.

Back then, Frankie never used to let Jess stay over at his place all night. It bothered Jess at the time, although Frankie always explained it away as being to protect Jess from having his sister find out about their relationship— and by extension, Jess's gayness—before Jess was ready. He'd always thought there was more to it than that, but he hadn't wanted to push.

See what happens when you don't push? You wind up standing still, never getting where you want to go.

Frankie fussed with a corner of the shawl, twitching it straight, and Jess remembered the wonder and discovery of those early nights, curled together in a welter of pillows, pulling that very shawl around them to ward off the chill.

He remembered how it always felt as if they didn't have enough time, as if every moment was gone too fast, like images captured on film, the fleeting reality behind them over and done with, lost forever.

And how true that turned out to be.

His throat closed like a fist, and he stumbled backward. "I can't do this," he said. "I have to go. Sorry."

Frankie stopped him with a word. "Wait."

Actually, it was the naked need in his voice that made Jess pause, look over his shoulder.

The man who, by his mere existence, had forced Jess to come to terms with who he was and what he wanted, stood there reaching out to him. And the look on his face was one Jess had never seen there before.

Like everything about Frankie, it was complicated—a fierce blend of need, terror, regret, and even . . . maybe . . . love?

"I know I don't deserve it," Frankie said, his voice wrecked. "But please. Give me a chance."

Jess crossed his arms over his chest, fingers digging into muscle. Biting his lip until he tasted blood, he muttered, "Yeah, fine. But make it quick, okay?"

Jealousy flared in Frankie's gaze, hot and darkly satisfying. "Why, you have a hot date tonight?"

"None of your business!"

Frankie's mouth curled into a snarl, and Jess braced himself wearily for another fight, but in the next instant, the snarl relaxed into a rueful curve. "Sorry, Bit. Jess. Fuck me, I'm bollocksing this up. I've no right to throw a wobbly about you seeing other blokes. And if you want to leave, I won't stop you. God knows, this conversation falls under the too-little-too-late heading—and now I come to think of it, the whole thing is likely more for me than you. Unburdening my soul, so to speak." He shook his head. "You're well out of it. No reason on earth why you should have to be weighed down with my crap now."

Frankie attempted his usual cocky smile, but it looked wrong on his face. Jess's defensive anger died a swift, certain death.

Taking a tentative step toward the table, Jess tilted his chin at the tray sitting on top of the shawl. On it were a couple of flickering candles, two glasses, and one of the white plastic carafes the Market line cooks filled with water and passed around during dinner service.

"What's in the pitcher?"

Frankie shot him a quick, uncertain smile. "Ah, it's sangria. Want some?"

Jess shivered. On Frankie's birthday, Jess had planned a whole afternoon based on the Lou Reed song "Perfect

Day"—they went to the Central Park Zoo and drank sangria on a blanket in the park, basking in the summer sunshine. When it got dark, they went home to the Garret. And Frankie'd looked right into his eyes and quoted the song, telling him it had been a perfect day—and he was glad he'd spent it with Jess.

He couldn't help wondering what it meant that Frankie made sangria tonight. Was it his punk poetry way of saying good-bye?

Jess pulled his mouth into a smile. "Sure. I'll have a little."

The sangria was a gorgeous dark red as Frankie poured it out, bits of fruit and slices of orange and lemon floating to the top. Jess's fingers brushed Frankie's when he handed over the glass, and he had to glance away to hide the shock that went through him.

Sweet spiced wine coated his tongue with the taste of summer, the memory of one perfect day. Jess sipped and swallowed, eyes closed, lost for a second.

"You remember my birthday, don't you?" Frankie said suddenly.

Jess started. "Of course. It wasn't that long ago."

It only felt like a million years.

Frankie shook his head. "I couldn't believe it when you pulled out that blanket and the thermos after the zoo. You know, I didn't get it until then—didn't make the connection to the song until I saw the sangria."

Jess took another gulp, hiding behind his glass. "It was dorky, I know."

"No," Frankie said, the intensity of his response freezing Jess in place. "No. It was one of the most amazing days of my life. Best birthday I ever had."

Lowering his glass slowly, Jess was at a loss for words. "Really? That's kind of . . . I don't know, sad. All we did was go to the park, see the penguins. Lie around on a blanket."

Frankie gave him a look that suggested they were speaking different languages. "You gave me one of my favorite songs, brought to life. You knew me that well, planned it all out, made it so . . ." He shook his head. "It was perfect. You don't even know. That song . . ."

"Yeah," Jess said, fighting the cascade of emotion this conversation was pouring over his head. "I like it, too."

"But I don't think you quite realized, at the time, how on the nose it was. You still don't get it—but that line Lou sings, about how the person he's with makes him forget himself and think he's someone else. Someone good."

Frankie looked down, studying the fruit in his glass as if it were tea leaves and might reveal some hidden facet of his future. It hurt Jess's chest.

Jess finally knew what to say, though. "You *are* good. I hate it when you talk like that."

Frankie's mouth twisted as though he didn't know whether to laugh or cry. "That's just the thing, Bit. You know me so well, in some ways, better than anyone ever. In other ways, you don't know me at all. Because I never let you. I'm not a good man. I've done . . . Christ. Things I wish I could forget."

"I don't care what you did." Jess knew he sounded impossibly young and stupidly stubborn, but he couldn't help it. "Whatever happened in the past, before we met—it's over now. It doesn't define you."

"God, I'd love to believe that." Frankie spared a smile for the thought, but it didn't stick. "The truth is, we're all defined by our actions. The choices we make have consequences, and you can't erase them by being sorry, or feeling worthless, or . . ." His throat clenched visibly as he swallowed hard, fear moving through his eyes. "Or by explaining that you didn't mean it, because you were an addict, and it was the drugs made you do those awful things."

The world ground to a halt like the carousel in Central Park, revolving in a slow circle that made Jess dizzy. He felt the past rewriting itself, everything he thought he knew about Frankie, about their relationship, taking on new shades of meaning.

"You . . . what?"

Frankie pulled himself up, squaring his shoulders in a way that told Jess he wanted nothing more than to slouch, hide, run.

But he didn't.

"You heard right. I was a druggie, got meself kicked out of school and all. My dad and mum washed their hands of me, and who could blame them, so I picked up and crossed the Atlantic, like many disappointing young English sons before me."

"How old were you?" Jess had a zillion questions, but caution held them back. He didn't want to spook Frankie out of this rare, truth-telling mode.

"Younger than you," Frankie said, mouth quirking. It was a shadow of his usual cocky smirk. "Sixteen."

"God," Jess said, appalled. Four years ago, when Jess was sixteen, he was living with his sister in upstate New York, going to high school and waiting tables for pocket money. He couldn't imagine being on his own at that age.

"I got lucky." Frankie shrugged. "A few months after I hit New York, I met Adam. His parents sort of adopted me, took me in. Got me cleaned up." He smiled, a remembering kind of smile. "I owe them, owe him—I was a right mess. Nobody else would've stuck it out."

I would've, Jess wanted to cry, but he bit it back. How did he know? Maybe if he'd met Frankie back then, he wouldn't have known how to help him.

Well, for one thing, when Frankie was on his own in the big bad city at sixteen, Jess was a kid who'd just lost his parents. So, probably he wouldn't have been a huge help.

But Jess wasn't a kid anymore.

"And you've stayed clean since then, haven't you?" he said, already sure of the answer.

Jess had noticed, of course, the way Frankie glossed right over those first few months before Adam's family found him, but he decided to let that go. For now.

He wished he could be sure it was because he didn't want to overload Frankie, who was already opening up further than he ever had before—and not because Jess was too much of a chickenshit to want to know what kinds of things might have befallen a scared junkie teen on the streets of New York.

Frankie shrugged and hitched one hip up on the table. His posture didn't exactly scream pride in his accomplishment. "Yeah, mostly. Ain't easy, and for a while . . . Christ, for a long fucking while, it was like a balancing act. Every day, on a tightrope over a pit of vipers, trying to keep myself from taking the dive. Convince myself it weren't worth it." He shook his head, brows low and heavy over his shadowed eyes.

"But it got better, right?" Jess was aware he sounded like a scared child, hoping desperately for a happy ending, but geez. Every time he blinked his eyes now he pictured Frankie as a gangly teenager, all rebellion and dyed hair and ripped clothes—well, really, like a slightly shorter version of the man right in front of him. But the idea of either version of that man alone and desperate, terrified, wrenched Jess's guts into knots.

"Yeah, like I said. The Temples helped me, and when Adam started talking nonstop about food and cooking and whatnot, I thought, why the hell not? We've worked in four of the same restaurants together, counting Market."

A thin shaft of light broke through the swirling mess of emotion Jess was flailing around in. He felt like if he could just break the surface, he'd push his head up into fresh, clean air, and a new understanding would be waiting for him.

"Whenever Adam moved jobs, you followed him."

"Dynamic duo," Frankie said, and there was the pride, tilting his angular chin up. "Then later, there was Grant, too. We make a good team."

"Because you trust each other," Jess said slowly. "You balance each other."

Balance. That was the key to everything, wasn't it?

"Adam helped you find your balance," Jess said, his mind racing. "His friendship, and working under him—it gives you the boundaries you need to feel safe. To forget about the past and stop worrying that you'll slip, fall back into that pit." He licked his lips, his mouth suddenly dry. His eyes burned, he hadn't blinked in forever, but he didn't want to take his gaze off Frankie for even a second. "And anything that threatens that balance, like taking on more responsibility, or leaving Market . . ."

Frankie raised both hands and fisted them in his crazy shock of hair, making it stand straight up. He looked at Jess from under his sooty lashes, breathed out slow.

"It's bloody terrifying, Bit."

Jess swallowed, the click of his throat loud in the deserted restaurant. "That includes me, doesn't it."

Dropping his hands to his sides, Frankie stared at Jess, his beautiful, sculpted face completely open, for once. "Bloody hell, Jess. Especially you."

There was a weird noise in Jess's ears, like somebody'd kicked a dog. Jess took such a quick step back, he stumbled and spilled sangria all over his hand. He'd forgotten he was even holding it. Numb, he stared uncomprehendingly at the dark red liquid running down his arm. It looked like blood.

There was that noise again, that funny little whimper, and with a shock of horror, Jess realized it came from him. "Sorry," he gasped. "I didn't mean to . . ."

"Here, it's all right," Frankie said, lifting the tray and whipping the shawl out from under it. He came right up to Jess and started dabbing at the wetness on his hand, but Jess clenched his fingers in the material and took another step back, dragging the shawl with him.

"No," he said, staring down at the cheerful, old-fashioned pattern draped over his wrist. "I mean, I'm sorry for . . ." His voice died out. "Well, for everything else."

"What do you mean?" Frankie's brows drew together.

Jess tried to smile. "It's funny. You know, I always thought if I could just get you to open up, if I could only understand what was holding you back, keeping you from being happy with me, I could fix it. Pretty cocky, huh?"

"Bit—"

No wonder Frankie had fought so hard to keep his life from changing. When every change felt as if it might be the end of his world? Well, Jess didn't have to make things worse. Maybe he couldn't fix it, but he could do that, at least.

"It's okay," Jess said, trying again with the smile thing. Any minute now, he was going to get one right. "I get it. And don't worry. There are a million restaurants in this city; I'm sure I can get another job waiting tables."

Frankie's eyes went dead as coals gone cold after a fire. "You're leaving Market," he said dully.

"Isn't that what you want?" Jess cried, hanging on to control by the slimmest thread. "You said . . . when I'm around, I knock you off balance, make you afraid you're going to fall back into the pit."

"I didn't tell you all that shite to make you go away," Frankie said, starting to pace.

This must be what a yo-yo felt like. "Then why?"

Mouth firming as if he'd made a decision, Frankie strode across the distance that separated them and grabbed Jess by the shoulders. Jess stared up, trying not to yell or cry or any of the other ridiculous things he was afraid he might do, and then they both froze at a loud clatter from the dining room.

Chapter 30

"What the hell was that?" Jess said, clutching at the Ramones T-shirt. Not that he was pissing himself with fear, exactly, but this restaurant was supposed to be abandoned, and it was the middle of the night. "Oh, crap, do you think it really is the cops?"

"Stay here," Frankie said, manhandling Jess around behind him.

Fuck that. Jess followed him to the kitchen door, which was actually more of a big, gaping hole because they'd taken the door off its hinges when they were moving stuff out.

For a moment, the outer room looked like unrelieved pitch-black after the warm glow of candlelight in the kitchen, but when Jess's eyes adjusted, he made out a figure standing next to the front door. The figure was joined by another, and another.

Triple crap.

"Oi," Frankie shouted into the silence, scaring a year off Jess's life. "Who's there?"

"Frankie? That you?"

It was Adam. The man who made Frankie feel safe.

Jess tried not to scowl—obviously, it was better that the intruder was Adam, not a policeman or a criminal, but still.

Straining his eyes as the figures came closer, Jess picked out the bright red fall of his sister's hair, and . . . was that Wes? Great. It was a party.

"Whoops," Adam said, catching Miranda when she stumbled against an overturned chair. "Shoulda brought a flashlight."

"Tell me again why this can't wait until tomorrow?" Miranda huffed. She looked up and Jess saw her eyes widen. "Jess! Did Adam ask you to meet us here?" Her gaze shifted to Frankie, though, and Jess was pretty sure he saw her wink.

He thought seriously about strangling her, but there were too many witnesses, at least one of whom could and would break his arm, so he clenched his jaw and said, "Nope. Just having a chat with Frankie."

"Oh, I hope we're not intruding," Miranda exclaimed, even as Adam grabbed her hand and tugged her forward impatiently, Wes trailing along behind as if he barely registered his surroundings.

"Not at all," Jess said. He glanced at Frankie, who was watching him with shuttered eyes. The moment was gone, cracked like a mirror dropped on the floor, and Jess could only curse his bad luck. And run off to lick his wounds. "I need to be going, anyhow."

Frankie squeezed his eyes shut, but when he opened them, all Jess saw was acceptance. "Thanks for coming, Bit. It was good to see you."

"Don't leave on our account," Adam said, coming up beside them and throwing one arm around Frankie's neck. "I assume we're all here for the same thing."

Adam wanted to tell Miranda . . . and Wes . . . about Frankie's past as a drug-addicted runaway?

The chef beamed at Jess, keeping his much taller best friend in an affectionate stranglehold. "Did he show you?"

Jess blinked. That was actually what Frankie's text said—he had something to show Jess. He'd assumed that meant the sangria, but maybe not.

"We hadn't quite got to that bit," Frankie said quietly, ducking out of Adam's rough one-armed hug and walking away, over to the table.

Jess stood there like a lump, hovering half in and half out, while the other three brushed past him and into the kitchen. The sight of Frankie's whipcord-lean back gave him a pang, and kicked his brain back into gear.

"Why did you ask me to come here tonight?" he said, watching Frankie.

Miranda, sensitive as always to Jess's feelings, stopped beside him and pulled him to her side. The wordless comfort of her embrace bolstered Jess's courage, and he sent her a grateful look.

Adam spread his arms and smiled widely. "To show you his new domain," he crowed. "S'why I brought Wes over—wanted him to see what he'll be in charge of when Frankie's got the day off."

With a sudden disorienting jerk, Jess was back on that carousel in the park, only this time it was spinning faster and faster, his head whirling, hope like a twister spiraling up his chest and into his throat.

"You're leaving Market?"

Frankie shrugged. "Not really. Just going next door, like. Hardly a life-changing move."

Except it was, and they both knew it.

Five long strides brought Jess back to Frankie's side. "Look at me," he said, tuning everyone else out. "You brought me here to tell me you're going to be the head chef at the second Market restaurant?"

"Yeah." Frankie kept his eyes on Jess's face, apparently

fascinated by whatever he saw there. Jess couldn't even imagine what he must look like right now—the freakiest mishmash of emotions were all swirling in his chest, but the strongest one seemed to be joy.

He was smiling so big it made his cheeks ache, but they had to see this through all the way. "Any particular reason you wanted me to know that?"

Slowly, carefully, as if he were touching fine china, Frankie lifted his hands to Jess's shoulders. They were a heavy, comforting weight, anchoring Jess to the earth when he felt like he might actually float away.

Breaking their staring contest for only a moment to glance over at Miranda and Wes, who were standing by the doorway, Frankie rasped, "I wanted you to know that I'm done playing at being the punk-rock Peter Pan. I'm ready to grow up."

He stroked the sides of Jess's neck with his thumbs, making Jess shiver, and that open, naked expression stole back over the sharp planes of Frankie's face as he looked down at Jess. "I wanted you to know that I don't need my whole life to stay the same anymore, so long as my one constant is you. I love you, Jess Wake."

And then Jess was crying, and he didn't care who saw, and no one could see anyway because he was stretching up on his toes and kissing the life out of Frankie Boyd, the man he loved. Who loved him back.

Wes had never been that into watching. Most con men were voyeurs, he'd always thought—at least a little. You had to have a fascination with watching people if you wanted to pick up their tells, figure out what made them tick so you could break them down and get inside their heads.

If he'd ever needed proof that he wasn't cut out for that kind of work? This was it.

He'd averted his eyes from Frankie and Jess way before

they locked lips—and it really wasn't the guy-on-guy thing. Just the way they looked at each other was so intimate, so private, it had Wes squirming and feeling like the worst kind of Peeping Tom.

His eyes had landed on Miranda at first, but she was no help because her hands were clasped under her chin, and tears were dripping down her pretty face, making her beatific smile all damp and trembly, and Wes had had enough of watching women cry to last him a lifetime.

He shifted his uncomfortable gaze to Adam, but the big, bad chef looked like a proud papa, watching his best friend finally pull his shit together, and really—the whole situation was, like, tailor-made to point out what a fucking interloper Wes was.

What the hell was he doing here with these people? The minute they woke up and realized he'd been here the whole time, all awkward and unwanted, they were gonna be pissed.

Deciding the better part of valor was probably getting the hell out of Dodge, Wes started inching toward the door.

"Where do you think you're going?" Frankie said.

Wes glanced back. The sous chef—well, soon-to-be executive chef—appeared to have surfaced from the kiss of the ages, which was just as well. Maybe it made him a horrible person—big news flash there—but Wes wasn't sure he could bear to watch another couple so obviously happy and in love right now.

Not that they looked any less in love when they weren't sucking face, he noticed. Frankie had both arms around the much shorter Jess, the younger man's back to his chest, and Jess was leaning into the circle of his arms as if there were no place on earth he'd rather be. Despite the difference in their heights, they looked like two puzzle pieces who'd just slotted into place.

"Hey," Wes said, going for light and easy and ignoring the knot in his throat. "I was promised a tour of our new digs, not a show. Didn't figure you'd want me around when the curtain came down."

"Why not?" Frankie said. "You helped make it happen."

"What do you mean?" Jess asked.

"Your mate, Wes there, was one of several people to give yours truly a good talking-to in the last few days."

"Oh really?" Jess gave Wes a look that made him squirm.

"Too right. Bloody hell, was like a revolving door—everyone wanted a shot at telling me what a prize idiot I was being."

"It's true," Wes said, pasting on a grin. "I did enjoy calling him an idiot."

"Oh me, too!" Miranda said, raising her hand like a kid in class.

Adam crossed his arms over his broad chest, looking disgruntled. "Damn it, I missed out on the fun. Why didn't you tell me we were having a Bash Sense into Frankie Party? I would've made T-shirts."

Jess laughed, but Frankie was watching Wes. His big grin wasn't fooling Frankie, he had a feeling, and Frankie confirmed it a second later by saying, "Seriously, mate. Thanks for what you said. It . . . made a difference."

Jess turned in his arms, casting a curious look up at Frankie. "What did he say?"

Frankie made a thoughtful clicking noise with his tongue. "Essentially, it boiled down to trust. I needed to trust you—and give you reason to trust me—by telling you the truth. And let the chips fall where they may."

"Hmm," Jess hummed. "Lucky for you, I fell right in your lap."

Frankie grinned wickedly and leaned down to whisper his response in Jess's ear, but Wes was no longer paying any attention.

Hearing his own advice echoed back to him, and seeing the glow shining off those two without the dark cloud of lies and evasions hovering over them—it was like a kick to the head, rearranging everything inside as if someone had upended a drawer and shaken all the contents out onto the floor.

"I have to go," Wes said. "And I don't know when, or if, I'll be back."

Four pairs of eyes looked at him with varying degrees of curiosity and disbelief, but Wes held firm.

He'd never been so sure of anything in his life.

Chapter 31

Most people seemed to find science, chemistry especially, to be cold and hard. Rosemary didn't understand that. How did they not see the serene beauty, the soothing rightness, of a world where logic ruled supreme, where there were correct answers to difficult questions and all you had to do was test until you found them?

She'd all but moved into her lab when she first got back to the Academy of Culinary Arts campus. There was a lumpy, overstuffed sofa in the corner, which she occasionally napped on; she'd bribed one of the culinary students she knew from her class into dropping off food once a day.

Sustenance, shelter, and a place to lay her head—what else did she need? Besides her research, of course.

She was lucky, she told herself firmly, as she extracted a tiny portion of pulpy red strawberry matter to examine under a microscope, lucky that her mind was so stimulated and full, her work so challenging and all-encompassing that it left no room for anything else.

Certainly no thoughts of anyone she might have met in that class, or had intercourse with in this very lab. Nope. Nuh-uh. Not ever again.

Humming a snatch of "Suffragette City" to herself, Rosemary bent over the lab table and set her eye to the scope's lens, fiddling the focus knob with her right hand.

Warm satisfaction suffused her as the molecules came into sharp relief. This confirmed it.

She was a genius.

"Woot!" she shouted, pumping her fist in the air. Her *woot* echoed strangely in the empty lab, which she tried to ignore so she could hold on to the euphoria of being proved totally and incontrovertibly right.

A knock on the door punctured her jubilation like a pin in a balloon. She frowned down at her watch. It was too early for Sloane to be stopping by with whatever leftovers she'd cobbled together from her daily stint at the academy's on-campus restaurant.

Shrugging, Rosemary stripped off her latex gloves, wrinkling her nose at the harsh, antiseptic smell of the powdery residue left on her hands, and went to open the door.

There, in the hall, were three of the things there was no room for in Rosemary's brain—Wes Murphy, faithless lying liar who lied to her, looking just as unconscionably handsome as ever, his tall, athletic frame nearly filling the doorway.

He was holding Lucille, the best friend who'd turned her back when Rosemary needed her the most. And . . . Rosemary blinked. Okay, that had to be a result of the fumes, or something.

But when she opened her eyes, there he still was. Standing behind and a little to the left of Wes was the dapper gray-haired gentleman, Wes's contact from the pharmaceutical company.

Her head swiveled back to Wes, this new betrayal cutting like a scalpel through the scar tissue she'd painstakingly grown around her heart. She wanted to gasp "How

could you!" like some swoony, melodramatic soap character, but her hand moved faster than her brain, for once,
and swung hard on the door, attempting to slam it shut in
their faces.

Wes, damn him, blocked the door with his arm.

"Rosemary," he said. That was all, but it stopped her.
She hated herself for noticing that he looked thinner, as if
he hadn't been eating, and that there were gray, smudgy
circles under his eyes.

And the expression in those dull golden-brown eyes—
she shuddered, battling a wave of recognition. He looked
exactly the way she felt first thing in the morning, before
she had a chance to wall the bad things back up in their
secret hiding place in her head.

She didn't want to see that. She didn't care if he was
hurting, damn it! She sucked at empathy, and it was a loser's game, anyway. What good could possibly come from
opening herself up to someone else's emotions? It was bad
enough having to deal with emotions of her own.

"Get out," she said, wrestling halfheartedly with the
door. She knew she couldn't wrench it out of Wes's grip, but
she tried. "I mean it, I don't want you here, and I certainly
don't want him"—she jerked her head at the older man—
"coming into my lab and snooping around my research!"

"I'm not from a pharmaceutical company," the man
said, his calm, amused smile making Rosemary feel like
a red-faced idiot for tussling with Wes over the door.

She let go and stepped back, breathing hard. Physical
struggle was the refuge of an underdeveloped mind, anyway.

"Like I'm going to believe you," she said.

"It's true," Wes insisted, taking immediate advantage
and pushing the door wider. "Come on, please let us in. I
swear I'll tell you everything."

He and Lucille were giving her matching Big Eyes

expressions, but luckily Rosemary had replaced her blood with ice water in the last few days, so she no longer got melty at the sight.

"I've sworn off fiction," she told him. "Science journals only for me, from now on." She frowned. "Not counting Jim Butcher, obviously. But the Dresden Files transcend petty mortal issues of truth and lie."

Wes leaned on the doorframe and huffed out a laugh, then looked shocked at himself. "God, I missed you."

Rosemary stiffened. That poked dangerously close to a tender, raw wound. Unacceptable.

Retreating quickly, she said, "Come in or get out, but whatever you do, do it quickly. I'm on a strict schedule and I don't have time for nonsense."

Another laugh, rustier than Wes's but still somehow familiar, sounded behind her as she hurried to throw the cashmere blanket from the couch over her lab table. She wasn't taking any chances.

"I like your girl," the older man said. "She's got more spunk than I expected."

"She's smarter than ten of you put together, so watch out, Pops."

Rosemary turned away from her safely hidden lab table and narrowed her eyes on the two men.

"Pops," she repeated. "Do you mean that as a collo-quial term used to signify an elderly man? Or—"

"Hey," the man in question protested, honest affront clear on his face. "Watch who you're calling elderly."

"Shut up, Pops," Wes interjected fiercely. To Rosemary he said, "Yes. That's what I wanted to tell you. I just didn't . . . well, I didn't have the guts before. But Rosie, meet Thomas Murphy. My father."

Rosemary sucked in a breath. He couldn't have surprised her more if he'd introduced her to Thomas Murphy, a fully lifelike T-1000 Terminator.

"Charmed to meet you," Thomas Murphy said, instantly donning a bright, sparkling smile that reminded Rosemary so strongly of Wes, it made her dizzy. Like the effect of blurred double vision, she thought, shaking her head quickly to dispel it.

"I've heard a lot about you," Wes's father continued.

Scrambling around for the pieces of brain that had just exploded all over the floor, Rosemary said, "Well, I've heard next to nothing about you. So I'm sure neither of you would object if I wanted to do a quick DNA test, to confirm your blood relationship?"

She didn't really think she needed the test—now that she knew to look for it, there were certain obvious familial similarities between the two men. The clean-cut shape of their mouths, the high cheekbones and strong jaw, the changeable color of their eyes. Although Thomas Murphy's hazel eyes were more on the twinkling green side today, while Wes's were darker, the green leaching away to tawny brown.

Wes winced, tightening his arms on Lucille enough that she squeaked in protest, but Thomas laughed, a big, hearty, booming laugh for such a smallish man, and clapped his son on the back. "Oh, my Weston. This one is a definite keeper."

"Your logic is faulty," Rosemary said with frozen composure. She could not afford to lose her cool. "Your son doesn't have me, therefore he cannot keep me."

Lucille squeaked again, louder this time, and Wes bent over to set her on the ground, ducking his head so Rosemary couldn't see his face. Thomas, however, was quick to pounce on her choice of words.

"Ah! So you do believe that he's my son."

Rosemary sniffed, her eyes on Wes's crouched form as he unhooked Lucille's leash and ruffled her silky ears. "I suppose. Although I'm not sure what, if anything, that should mean to me now. It's not as if this lie erases the one I thought he'd told—a lie is a lie is a lie."

Thomas shook out his arms, straightening his cuffs where they peeked out from his jacket. "What a simplistic worldview you people of science have. In my world— the world Wes grew up in—there are as many shades of gray as there are stars in the sky."

"Enough with the bullshit, Pops," Wes growled, standing up and leveling a glare at his father. "Shades of gray, my ass. The only color you care about is dollar-bill green. And she doesn't want to hear about that."

Thomas blinked, the picture of innocent surprise. "No? And here I thought we traveled all this way through the wilds of upstate New York to tell her exactly that."

Wes flushed, setting his grim mouth in a mutinous line. Rosemary's neck was starting to hurt from following their verbal sparring match as if it were a game of table tennis.

A cool, wet nose snuffled at her ankles, and she moved without thinking, retreating behind her lab table and hitching herself up onto one of the tall stools.

"Did you have to bring her?" she asked tightly.

"Ah well." Wes tried to smile, but she stared him down. "I was going to take her over to Frankie and Jess's place and let them watch her, but she gave me the Look. You know the one I mean? Where she's all astonished at your stupidity in not realizing what she wants and giving it to her immediately. I caved."

Ignoring the fact that she undoubtedly would've caved, too, Rosemary pushed forward.

"Why are you here?" She drummed her fingers on the tabletop. They needed to get to the point and then get out. Every minute they lingered was another crack in the foundation cementing her memories and emotions away.

Wes rocked back and forth on his heels, clearly debating what to say. Rosemary watched the struggle play out on his face with detached interest. She'd given up her study of human facial cues—that same issue she had with the empathy thing, why bother?—but he wasn't even trying to mask what he was feeling.

An unwelcome chill lifted the hairs at the back of her neck and all down her arms. For Buffy's sake, what else could Wes have to tell her that would make him project so much guilt and anguish?

"My dad's right," he finally said, his voice hitching with a hesitance she'd never associated with him before. "I came up here to tell you the truth. About my past—but also about the present. The reason I kept it from you when my dad blew into town and you saw us arguing that night; it's all bound up together. Shit, I don't know where to start."

"Start with me," Thomas suggested, preening a little. "That's always a good place."

Shooting his father an exasperated look, Wes peeled off his coat, cracked his neck a couple of times like a wrestler getting ready for a match, and blew out a breath. He stared at the ground for a moment, suddenly seeming to shrink into a lost little boy, his entire body clenched against the cruel pain inflicted by a harsh adult world.

Rosemary hooked her ankles around the rungs of the stool and dug her fingers into the rim of the seat under her until the metal threatened to cut her skin. She would not go to him. She would not be moved. At all.

"Okay," Wes said, looking up and meeting her gaze. "Here goes."

This truth-telling thing sucked. No wonder his dad never did it.

There was something especially soul-killing about it when he was ninety-nine percent sure Rosemary wasn't going to forgive him.

A lie is a lie is a lie.

Wes swallowed hard, trying to work around the aching swell of emotion that had tightened his throat ever since she said those words.

He hated to agree with his father, on any level, but yeah—things were very black-and-white for Rosemary. He should've remembered that, he should've expected it. That Thomas Murphy wasn't, in fact, a pharmaceutical rep out to pilfer her precious research did not mitigate the fact that Wes had certainly lied about his identity.

And about so many other things. If you counted lies of omission, which he was pretty certain she did.

It was hopeless. Why was he doing this again?

He opened his mouth to tell her he'd changed his mind, he'd quit bugging her, and wish her a happy life—but the minute he met her direct stare, those blue eyes of hers so deeply banked with pain and disillusionment, he couldn't do it.

She deserved the truth. She deserved the chance to make her own choice based on that truth.

He was through deciding for her. He'd done a totally shittastic job of it so far, anyway.

Deciding to get the torture over with, Wes led with, "My father is a con artist."

Rosemary's gaze flew to Pops, who sketched a quick, graceful bow as if acknowledging the highest of compliments.

Deep, bracing breath . . . "And he raised me to be one, too."

Shock widened her eyes and she teetered dangerously. Wes was afraid for an instant she was about to fall off her perch, but she steadied herself before he could take the opportunity to rush to her side and touch her one last time.

Damn it.

"You asked me once how I got interested in cooking, and I danced around the question," he went on, forcing himself to stand tall under her laser stare.

She nodded. "I remember."

"Well, when I was a kid, Pops and I got caught running a con on a lady who . . . well, it doesn't really matter what con we were pulling."

"I don't even remember that woman's name," Pops said, laughing as if they were going through the family photo album and reminiscing about birthday parties or something.

"I bet you don't," Wes said, the old, familiar bitterness sour as a bite of green apple in the back of his throat. "I know you remember how it ended, though. With you in the wind, leaving me to take the fall."

Turning his back on his father, he fastened his gaze on Rosemary as if she were the one stable point in the universe. Which was kind of what it felt like, sometimes, but Wes didn't want to think about that.

She made a hurt little noise, quickly muffled, but it was enough to kindle a weak flame of hope in Wes's chest. Maybe she wasn't as ready to write him off as he'd feared.

Pressing onward, he said, "I was still a minor, thank Christ, and clearly not the mastermind behind the scam, so instead of jail or a detention center, they stuck me in a halfway house for juvenile offenders. Heartway House."

"And what happened to you there?" Rosemary asked, a thread of fear making her voice thin and reedy. That little flame of hope flared brighter—she was devouring every word as if it were oxygen.

"Nothing bad," he hastened to assure her. He didn't like that look in her eyes, that scared, skittish look as if she were bracing herself for a horror story. "In fact, they were great to me. The couple who ran the house, they kept us boys busy from sunup to sundown, but it wasn't like chores. Or classes in school, which always bored me. I mean, we did stuff around the house, yeah, but the way they did it . . . They took us through hands-on stuff, in areas where we could learn a craft or a skill that would give us a chance at a different kind of future. My favorite part of the day was kitchen prep. I hadn't been in the house a month before I was in charge of all the meals."

He remembered those first days in the kitchen, standing next to Deirdre Nickoloff at the stove, watching her stir and baste and simmer and taste, confident and capable, her kind eyes hinting at a wealth of knowledge she was happy to share with a skinny, sullen kid who didn't even know his mother's name.

"Those Nickoloff people," Pops groused. "Ruined my boy, they did."

Rage rushed through Wes like wind down a subway tunnel. "Stop it," he growled, making Rosemary jump. But he couldn't stop, the words welling up like an oil slick, black and foul and oddly cleansing. "I'm sick of hearing that, sick of you talking about them—you don't know anything. Deirdre Nickoloff gave me a life. She listened to me, she cared about what mattered to me—and she for goddamn sure didn't figure out what mattered to me just so she could hose me for thousands of dollars."

Crap. That was not how he'd intended to spill all that. Rosemary gasped and slid off the stool, her face white with shock.

"You blackmailed your own son?" Rosemary cried.

Thomas Murphy clucked his tongue reprovingly. "I did no such thing. When I expressed my desire to meet the young lady my son is so wild about, Weston here generously offered to finance a little trip I've been wanting to take to Florida. How could I say no?"

"I paid him five thousand dollars to get him to leave,"

Wes said. "And that was after I talked him down from his original asking price of ten grand."

Rosemary shook her head in dazed disbelief. "That's why you pulled away," she murmured. "You were working, like you said—but at Chapel, serving drinks, after a full shift at Market."

Wes nodded, feeling exhausted just thinking about it.

Rosemary turned on Pops, her eyes snapping blue fire. "How could you?" she demanded.

"Oh, piffle," Thom said. "I wouldn't have tried to break you up or hurt your relationship in any way—but if Wes was offering to send me off for a little fun in the sun with deep-pocketed retirees and lonely widows, I wouldn't be much of a con man if I didn't take it, now would I?"

And there it was. The real, underlying truth, unvarnished and ugly and squatting there in the middle of the room like some horrible squatting thing—all this pain, everything Wes went through to get the money to pay his father off so he wouldn't tell Rosemary who he was or make her vulnerable to his schemes—all of it could have been so easily avoided if Wes had only told her the truth about himself in the beginning.

Wes watched Rosemary think it through, and he saw the exact moment she realized it, too.

The tiny, sputtering flame of hope flickered and went out.

Chapter 32

"And I believe that's my cue to skedaddle," Thomas Murphy said, rubbing his hands together cheerily. "Fort Lauderdale awaits!"

Rosemary barely heard him over the roaring of blood in her ears.

The lengths Wes had gone to, the hours of backbreaking work, the stress of dealing with his clearly unresolved father issues on his own—letting her believe the absolute worst of him. He'd borne all of that merely to avoid sharing his past with Rosemary.

It was an extraordinary feeling, to know that she was simultaneously important enough to him that he would endure so much to keep her, and yet so disregarded by him that he would lose her rather than tell the simple truth. A truth Rosemary found objectionable, certainly, but didn't blame Wes for in the least.

Children were at the mercy of their parents; she understood that better than most.

"Yeah, go," Wes said, never taking his eyes off Rosemary's face. He looked tired, defeated, but a trace of anger lingered around his mouth when he said to his father, "You've done enough here, I think."

"I'm off, then," Wes's father said, pulling on a pair of cognac leather gloves as he strolled to the door. "It was lovely to meet you, my dear. And now that I've been paid in full, I'll just be on my way. Ta very much, my Weston, and don't worry! You've seen the last of me. I won't be interfering in your life again."

The quiet *snick* of the closing door echoed like a gunshot between them.

"Don't believe him," Wes said, smiling faintly. "Once a con man, always a con man."

"I suppose that means I shouldn't believe you, either," Rosemary pointed out, unable to refrain from following the line of logic to its reasonable conclusion.

He sighed, shrugged his hands into his pockets. "Probably not," he agreed.

Silence stretched between them for a long moment, broken only by the clack of Lucille's claws over the hardwood floor as she prowled around the lab, presumably on the trail of spilled crumbs.

Rosemary felt adrift, as if the anchor that tethered her to her safe world of questions, answers, and rationality had been ripped away.

"What did he mean by 'paid in full'?" she asked suddenly.

A spark of animation returned to Wes's resigned face. "Oh! That was amazing, actually. When I finally decided I had to tell you everything, I was kind of in the middle of something where, well, I had to tell the guys at Market what was going down."

Rosemary tried very hard not to care that some New York chef knew about Wes's past before she did. "Chef Temple, you mean?"

"Yeah, Adam and Frankie. They'd just offered me a

job, you see—they're planning to expand Market into the space next door. Frankie's taking over that kitchen, and he picked me as his sous chef, his right-hand man."

A wealth of pride shone from Wes's eyes and pulled his shoulders straight, but then he looked away and down, his mouth curving into an unhappy line, and Rosemary got an awful feeling.

"What's wrong?" she asked.

He started, eyes wide. "What? Nothing! I mean, when I told them I had to go, and I explained why—they actually took up a collection and pulled together the rest of the money Pops wanted, so I could pay him off. It was the only way I could get him to come up here with me." He sounded stunned, as if he still couldn't believe his friends had done that for him.

Momentarily distracted, Rosemary frowned. "Wait, why did you think it was so important that he come along?"

Wes scrubbed a hand through his hair, the curve of his mouth turning rueful. "You're gonna laugh, but I actually anticipated that crack about the DNA test. Only I thought you might really insist on it, so I figured, might as well bring the proof with me."

Rosemary couldn't remember ever feeling less like laughing in her entire life. Wes didn't look too happy, either, his mouth flattening out again almost at once. "I also wanted you to see what kind of man my father really is. Because he already suspects you have money, and when he finds out how much, he'll try every trick in the book to get his hands on it."

"As if I'd let him."

He shrugged. "I've seen him swindle people who were—well, not as smart as you but still pretty smart and discerning. Not the type of people you'd expect to lose their savings to a petty thief like him. Heck, I know exactly what my father is, and even I fell for one of his schemes."

"I'm confident in my ability to protect my assets," Rosemary said coolly.

"You know," Wes said, rubbing a hand over his face, "I think I believe you. God knows, Pops has never come up against anyone like you. Really, I should've had more faith in you from the beginning."

"When you left, did they hold that job for you?" Rosemary asked suddenly, not at all sure she wanted the answer.

He shrugged, but his eyes went shifty again, and Rosemary knew she was right. He'd left everything he'd worked toward at Market behind, not knowing what her reaction was going to be.

It was overwhelming. Rosemary felt as if she'd been in a space shuttle simulator for days, her body spun around and around and around, pinned and battered by g-forces far beyond the capability of mortal woman to endure for any length of time.

I can't do this, she thought desperately, panic stealing her breath. *I am not equipped to handle this.*

Wes lifted his head, a genuine smile trembling on his lips. "Listen," he said, then had to stop and clear his throat. "I came to tell you the truth, so here's the rest of it. I love you. I want to be with you, more than I want anything else in the world. All the dreams I've been living on for years—well, I care about them. But next to you? God, it's like trying to compare chocolate to bread."

"What?" Rosemary shook her head, wondering if her ears were shorting out along with her brain and heart.

"Chocolate and bread," Wes explained. "You know, chocolate is great—delicious, naughty . . . and an aphrodisiac, right? Who doesn't love chocolate. But you can't eat tons of it without getting sick. It's not that great for you. It's not the staff of life. Bread is . . . it's basic. A primal need. Essential." His voice cracked a little, and he looked down, red scorching his cheeks. "That's what you are, to me."

Circuit overload. Everything inside Rosemary went into lockdown. She couldn't breathe, swallow, blink . . . there was too much going on for her brain to process even normal involuntary impulses, and she couldn't move, and she'd never been more terrified in her entire life.

She stood there, silent and still, and watched the light of passion die away in his beautiful golden eyes.

It was too much. Way, way too much, and when Wes closed his eyes briefly, and nodded his head once as if agreeing with some decision she wasn't even aware of making, Rosemary still couldn't force her body to move.

"Right," he said. "Well, I wanted you to be able to choose for yourself, knowing everything. And I guess . . . you just did."

Choose? she wanted to shriek. *I choose nothing. I don't even know what's happening!*

She followed him helplessly with her gaze as he searched the room for Lucille, eventually finding her behind the trash can by the sink, and carried her back over to Rosemary.

Twisting his mouth into a smile that didn't reach his eyes, Wes held the terrier up. "She missed you a lot," he said. "I think you should keep her. She'd be happier up here in the mountains than in the city with me, anyway."

Breathing too quickly and shallowly, Rosemary reached out her arms automatically to receive the warm bundle of happy dog.

She looked down at Lucille, cuddled into her shoulder and snuffling at her neck, her weight deeply and undeniably comforting against Rosemary's chest, and when she looked back up, Wes was already slipping out the door.

Frak. He's gone.

She stared at the door leading out of her lab, that haven

of reason and science, where emotions were things to be analyzed and tested for external root causes. She knew everything about this world—had known it, almost instinctively, ever since she could remember. It had been her best escape and her surest sanctuary from her overbearing, demanding parents. In here, no one cared how she dressed, what TV shows she watched or thought were moronic, or that she didn't know how to make friends.

In here, she was safe.

Lucille barked, sharp and loud, right in Rosemary's ear, startling her so badly she almost dropped the furball on the floor, but it lifted the weird paralysis.

"What?" Rosemary said. "You have something you want to add?"

Lucille planted her paws on Rosemary's chest and reared back. She blinked once, growled low in her throat, and then there it was. The Look.

The one that said she was appalled at how stupid Rosemary was for not figuring out what to do, and doing it.

Rosemary's breath caught. "Oh no. I'm not falling for that."

She set Lucille on the floor. Lucille immediately trotted over to the door and scratched at it, glancing back to level the Look directly at Rosemary. Who wrung her hands and tried to marshal her thoughts.

"Okay, I know. He said he loves me. And he left that job to come up here."

Lucille cocked her head, black eyes bright and curious on Rosemary's face.

"Oh God," she said, her mind finally breaking the sound barrier and racing ahead, fast enough to shoot up into the sky, faster than the speed of light. "What he said about making a choice—he chose me. On one hand he had the job of his dreams, a sure thing, and on the other he had

me—a total variable, no idea how I'd react to the other elements in this situation—and he chose me anyway."

She looked down at Lucille. "He really loves me."

Lucille responded by standing on her hind legs and
using both front paws to try and dig her way through
the closed door.

"But what should I do?" Rosemary cried, emotion
threatening to engulf her again.

Lucille barked again, cutting the tsunami of fear and
self-doubt off before it could get Rosemary in a Vulcan
nerve pinch.

"You're right," she gasped. "I have to go after him."

Tearing the door open, Rosemary ran out of the lab
and down the hall. She rammed through the building's
doors and dashed out into the quad, a blast of frigid air
hitting her in the face.

It had snowed at some point while she'd been buried in
the lab; she remembered Sloane remarking on it, laughing while shaking snowflakes off the paper bag holding
Rosemary's dinner.

And it was snowing again now, the sky a steely gray
bleeding out to swirls of white falling silently to the icy
ground. The quad was deserted, all the culinary students
in lectures or in the test kitchens, and Rosemary turned in
a frantic circle, searching for movement, life, anything to
indicate Wes.

There. A solitary figure fifty meters away, trudging
toward the parking lot, hands in pockets, shoulders bowed
against the chill wind.

Rosemary cupped her fingers around her mouth and
shouted, but that same wind grabbed her voice and scat-
tered it. Wes didn't turn around.

She started to run. Cold air drove through her thin lab
coat like needles against her skin, and when she heaved

in a breath, it was like swallowing a jagged ice cube down into her lungs, but she kept going.

By the time she was close enough to make him hear her, she had no more breath to shout, so she stumbled the last few steps in harsh, gasping silence, until he was there, an arm's length away, closer, her hand on his back, fingers too numb to register the roughness of his jacket.

Wes felt her, though, and wheeled around just in time to catch her as she flung herself into his arms.

She didn't know she was crying until he said, "Rosie, no, no, no," and wiped her frozen cheeks with his big, warm hands.

"I love you, too," she choked, frantic to get the words out, to be sure he heard them and believed them and didn't leave.

"Yeah?" he said, and a smile broke over his face, splitting his cheeks wide, and everything inside Rosemary that had jammed up when he told her he loved her jerked loose again, a torrent of joy and adoration and the kind of trust she never thought she'd have in another human being.

"Yes," she told him as he unzipped his jacket and folded the open edges around her back, enclosing her in a cocoon of shocking heat. She burrowed in, winding her arms around his lean, hard waist, and propped her chin against the rigid bone of his sternum. "You're my essential thing. So you really can't go anywhere, at least not without me."

He stared down at her as if he'd never seen anything so miraculous, and Rosemary knew it was true; it was a miracle that they were together, locked in this embrace, their hearts pounding against each other in perfect time.

She was a woman of science; she'd never believed in miracles. But this moment defied all logic, all rationality, every known constant of her life.

Maybe, just maybe, she thought as he bent his head and

singed her cold lips with his hot, devouring mouth, *there's more to chemistry than science.*

"Yip! Yipyipyipyip!"

They broke apart, laughing and maybe crying a little, too, and Rosemary looked down to see Lucille attempting to climb up Wes's leg, her short body contorting with the effort.

Wes scooped her up and wedged her between their torsos, where she huddled happily, and said, "Why do we have this dog again?"

"Because she's smarter than both of us," Rosemary said. "Lucille is a true example of the merits of cross-breeding."

Wes waggled his eyebrows. "It works for dogs, you think it'll work for humans, too?"

"I don't see why not."

"A con artist and a genius," he said thoughtfully, wrapping her even more tightly in his coat. "Wonder what our kids will be like?"

"Kids!" Rosemary froze, staring up at him. She knew panic must be written all over her face, in the rigidity of her body against his, but Wes just laughed.

"One thing at a time, I think. Come on, honey, breathe."

She lifted her face. "Remind me how?"

Wes's eyes flashed pure gold for an instant before he took her lips in a slow, tender kiss that left every corner of her mouth feeling claimed.

Oh yes, she thought hazily. *This chemistry thing needs to be explored. In depth. Lots of tests.*

It would be an extensive study—preferably one that would take the rest of their lives.

Just One Taste Recipes

CHOCOLATE FONDUE

6 ounces of the best bittersweet chocolate you can find
½ cup heavy whipping cream
1 tablespoon butter
2 tablespoons cognac
Strawberries, long stems still attached

If you have a fondue pot, simply combine the first four ingredients and stir them together over the heat source. If not, it's still simple—the only trick is to not burn the chocolate as you melt it.

The most foolproof way I've found is to boil water in a large saucepan. Put the chocolate in a heatproof bowl small enough to fit inside the saucepan. Take the saucepan off the heat, then submerge the heatproof bowl partially in the water, stirring to melt the chocolate. Once the chocolate is liquid, stir in the rest of the ingredients and serve immediately with the strawberries.

WES'S BAECKEOFFE

3 leeks, white and light green parts thinly sliced
1 cup chopped carrots
1 cup chopped parsnips
3 tablespoons minced parsley
1 clove garlic, minced
1½ lbs. pork shoulder, trimmed and cut into ½-inch
cubes
1¾ cups gin
1 cup dry vermouth
1 lb. yellow potatoes, thinly sliced
1 large tomato, sliced
olive oil
salt and pepper

In a large bowl, combine the leeks, carrots, parsnips, parsley, garlic, pork, gin, and vermouth. Cover with plastic wrap and let marinate at least two hours, or overnight in the refrigerator.

Preheat oven to 350 degrees and remove marinade from the fridge; allow to come to room temperature while you slice the potatoes. Since this is a rustic dish, I don't usually bother to peel the potatoes, but you can if you prefer a more elegant presentation.

Lightly oil a 3.5-quart covered casserole, then layer half the potato slices on the bottom of the pot. They can overlap slightly. Season with salt and pepper, then, using a slotted spoon, remove the meat and vegetables from the bowl, reserving the marinade. Layer them over the potatoes, and season with salt and pepper. Cover the meat and vegetables with the rest of the potato slices, and give those a sprinkle of salt and pepper, too. Place the tomato slices over top in a single layer.

Pour the reserved marinade over the whole thing, salt and pepper one more time, then cover and bake for two hours. If possible, use a pot with a hole in the lid to allow steam to escape. If you don't have a casserole like that, just set the lid slightly off center before you put the dish in the oven.

Serve with crusty bread, your favorite mustard (the spicier the better!), and a simple green salad with vinaigrette. Perfect on a cool, autumn day!

FRANKIE'S "PERFECT DAY" SANGRIA

    1 bottle fruity red wine like pinot noir, Beaujolais,
    or rioja
    1 cup freshly squeezed orange juice
    ½ cup lime juice
    ¼ cup honey
    2 ounces brandy
    1 ounce cointreau
    1 cup ginger beer
    ½ orange, thinly sliced
    ½ Granny Smith apple, chopped
    1 lime, thinly sliced
    1 stick cinnamon, broken in half

Combine all ingredients in a pitcher or punch bowl and refrigerate until ready to drink. Serve over ice. Enjoy on a hot day, lying on a blanket in Central Park with the one you love!